ENTWINED WITHIN THE DARKNESS

Book One of Within the Darkness Trilogy

Charley Black

Charley Black

This novel is entirely a work of fiction. The names, characters, and incidents portrayed in it are the work of the author's imagination. Any resemblance to actual persons, living or dead, events or localities is entirely coincidental.

Revised Second edition

ISBN: 979-8-9868877-0-8

Digital ISBN:979-8-9868877-1-5

Cover art by MiblArt

To my husband

For *FINALLY* pushing me to finish after all these years

CONTENTS

CHAPTER ONE

Patience

"I *will kill him. You are mine. Forever."*

Patience jolted awake with a gasp, her breaths coming in shallow pants as the words echoed through her mind. Her heart hammered against her ribs, and her palms were slick with sweat. She lay there for several moments, taking in her surroundings to make sure she was still safe in her own room.

When she finally moved, it was like she had no control over her body; she threw off her sheets and stumbled into the bathroom. Her fingers trembled as she flicked on the light, expecting to see silver eyes in the mirror's reflection—signifying that this nightmare was not just that. But they always faded back to their familiar golden brown hue.

She turned on the faucet, splashing cool water onto her face and neck. The shock brought some relief from the foggy dread that followed every nightmare. This was especially bad; it was the third time this week, and they were becoming increasingly frequent.

Taking a deep breath, she grabbed a plush towel from the rack and dabbed her face dry. Glancing at the clock on her nightstand, it was 4:45 a.m. *Another early morning.*

Stumbling back into the room, she pulled the damp sheets away from the mattress. As she crumpled them into a ball, she could feel the wetness beneath her fingers that had seeped through again. Biting her lip, she tried to recall what had happened in the nightmare. But all she could remember were flashes of images that quickly dissolved like smoke.

The only thing she ever remembered was his red eyes. Laughing at her in the darkness, they stared into her soul, taking everything away from her. They'd been haunting her for years now. Every day, she prayed to the Goddess to reveal her dreams and nightmares, to show her where she belonged. Instead, they stayed locked away inside her—all connected but never revealed.

She trudged down the hallway, holding a stack of rumpled sheets, and stuffed them into the washer, carefully avoiding the pile of wet clothes from the night before.

Stepping out onto her balcony, she inhaled deeply as the cool morning air filled her lungs. She settled into her favorite lounge chair, tucking the comfy blanket around her body. As the sky lightened from deep navy blue to pale pink and orange, she closed her eyes and listened to the stillness of the slowly waking city.

A shiver ran up Patience's spine as she watched the sunrise, and an unfamiliar energy filled the air. Her hair stood on end, and goosebumps rose on her arms. She had a feeling that something different was about to happen, but whether it was good or bad, only time would tell.

The sun was well into the sky when her best friend and roommate joined her.

"Another nightmare?" Michael asked, handing her a cup of coffee before he sat in the chair next to her.

"Yep. Soaked through to my mattress." Her voice was soft with apprehension. His hazel-blue eyes were wide with sympathy, his short brown hair neatly combed back off his forehead. No matter how often he shaved, the five o'clock shadow he always had gave him a ruggedly handsome appearance.

She cradled her mug and inhaled the steam, grateful for the caffeine jolt. "Technically speaking, the herbs did work. They put me right to sleep, but they didn't stop the nightmare."

"Silas was right," Michael said with a sigh.

"Yep."

He rubbed his face, looking defeated. "How many has it been this month?"

"That's three this week and ten total."

"It's getting worse." Michael leaned back in his chair. "Do you remember anything at least?"

"Nope. Just the same red eyes. And the fear and dread." She hated talking about those damn red eyes. The more she talked about them, the more she believed she gave them power.

Her fingers squeezed the mug as she stared into its dark abyss. "I'm sorry," he said, his hand resting on hers.

"Nothing to be sorry about. Not your fault." She sipped the bitter coffee, grateful for his friendship and support. She wasn't sure she would have made it this far without him.

"I know it sucks every time you try something and it fails," he said after a moment of silence.

Tears prickled the corners of her eyes, and she blinked them away. "Each time I try, I feel like I am one step closer to unlocking them."

He nodded, and they sat silently for a while longer, both lost in thought.

Fifty years, and still she had no answers. It had been so long since students at Kilborn Academy found her passed out on the steps of the magical school. No one knew how she had gotten there or how old she had been. She resembled a young woman, but witches aged much slower than humans. According to Michael, she looked the same as she did when they found her.

The Mastria told her it was a dark and stormy night—so cliché, but it was the worst storm they had ever seen. She didn't remember any of it.

A week later, she awoke screaming in agonizing pain, though she had no visible wounds. Red eyes. The same nightmare. The same words every time: *"I will kill him. You are mine. Forever."* The only difference now was she didn't wake up screaming anymore.

Every night, she closed her eyes with aching hopes that the nightmares wouldn't return. She dreaded them yet desperately clung to every fading image, hoping to unlock her trapped past. The fear of what these dreams held was unbearable, but there was a tiny spark of hope that they contained the answers to who she really was.

"What do you want to do now?" Michael asked. "We can always try hypnosis again."

"No. You know what happened last time."

Months ago, their friend Silas suggested hypnosis—which ended disastrously. The hypnotist spoke incoherently, announcing only two words: necklace and sword. She had no choice but to erase the event from his memory to spare him an asylum stay.

"I'd rather not go through that again. It's not worth accidentally killing someone. Plus, mind-erasing is draining. Can we just forget it for now?" she pleaded.

"Yeah, if that's what you want to do. I'm all for it." Michael sat back in his lounge chair, and they both took in the early morning air.

They sat, sipping their coffee and listening to the city wake. These were the moments she loved—simple moments with no thoughts of nightmares or memory loss. A small piece of divine bliss.

"Do you feel it, Michael?" She glanced up into the sky, searching for some kind of sign. "There's something unusual in the air today."

Michael shrugged and glanced back at her. His eyes were confused. "Feels like any other day to me."

She took a deep breath and grinned, excitement radiating through her entire body. "How about we make it special, then? How about we go out tonight?" This new energy meant something. Maybe it was time they switched things up and did something a little out of the ordinary.

"Like out, out? I thought we were heading to Lester's to look at his book about Irza, the God of Iranti."

"Yeah, like dancing and drinking. You know what normal people do. That can wait. We need this more than chasing after another clue." She had been pushing herself too hard recently. Maybe it was time to have some real fun.

"If you are sure, then. Let's go out," he said with a smile.

Today was going to be different.

"It is not like it's every day when Ms. Harrington wants to go out. Let me grab my phone so we can see what's hot," he said, then ran excitedly through the door.

It had been a while since she'd had a good time. Unlocking her memories had become such a priority as her dreams became more intense and frequent. She'd forgotten about fun. She needed to let loose a little to take her mind off her memories.

Michael came back and plopped down in his chair beside her, peering over her shoulder at her phone's glowing screen.

"You find anything good?" he asked.

"No. Everything here looks blah," Patience mumbled, scrolling with one finger.

"Hey!" He shouted suddenly and pointed at the screen. "Check this out—Moarte. Looks interesting."

The opening page beckoned them as it slowly enticed them down a rabbit hole with flashy, vibrant colors until a black screen appeared. Green eyes opened on the screen, and then the darkness fell away, revealing the full body of a small fairy. She was beautiful and playful.

She crooked her finger before she took off, racing through tunnels and hallways. Then she disappeared through black double doors. The words emerged: "Do you dare enter?"

Michael looked at her, excited. She nodded.

He clicked. The doors burst open. Music and lights bombarded them, and then the fairy popped up with a drink in her hand and laughter in her eyes. Text appeared on the screen. "Come play with me." Then, the site's home page popped up.

Dark, fun, and intense. Everything that would easily attract a human.

"Sorry to disappoint you," Patience said, "but it's a vampire club."

"What? How do you know?"

"Search through the site, and you'll find their emblem. I think they have opened a new feeding ground."

His face fell in disappointment as he discovered the hidden emblem of the vampire—the Black Ankh, a cross shape with a teardrop-shaped loop at the top. "Oh, damn. But it looked so good."

"That's because they enchanted the website with a whisper of soul's charm. It lures humans, and since you could be a potential half, you feel compelled to go."

His mouth gaped open. "I felt nothing."

She smiled. He totally got sucked into it, unconsciously watching it again.

"Michael, whatcha doing?" she teased.

Horrified, he peered up at her and then back down at his phone.

She laughed. "Don't worry. I got sucked in at first, too. So, there may be a little human in me somewhere."

"Maybe this proves we won't have to worry about me. I have felt no changes or signs of my full transformation. So maybe I am half demon, after all."

"Just 'cause you felt nothing now doesn't mean you won't feel anything later. We don't even know how old you are."

She had to remember Michael knew nothing of his past. Thirty years ago, she found him being beaten by a Ganton—a gray creature with three arms—in Igoria, the realm of the forgotten. How long he'd been there was unknown, but immortality was bestowed upon demons and daimones like Michael.

He might have been only half-human since full daimones were rumored to be extinct. His motto was that since he was forgotten, what did it matter?

She often wondered who had forgotten him or who he'd pissed off enough to get sent there.

She had been searching for answers when she heard his cries for help and decided to intervene. After taking him back to Kilborn to heal, she discovered he had been wandering without any recollection of how he got there. Unlike her, his memories were completely gone, and he wasn't eager to discover what had happened to him.

They grew close over the months it took him to heal. Though he didn't want to learn about his past, he still encouraged her to seek her own. The strength and love he showed her gave her the courage to search for a way to stop the nightmares and unlock her memories. Unfortunately, he couldn't stay at the school—witches and demons were not on the best of terms. They had tolerated him until he outstayed his welcome.

When he gathered his bag to leave, she also packed hers. She couldn't stand the thought of them being separated. They had never been apart for more than a day or two. Their connection was strange—a demon and a witch, friends? It was unheard of, even in these modern times, but it didn't stop them.

As crazy as it sounded, they balanced each other out and learned from each other. She didn't know what would have happened to her if she hadn't found him.

After waking at Kilborn, Patience had felt lost and in pain. Until one day, she corrected a young girl struggling with her magic, teaching her how to trust herself. This made Patience realize she enjoyed teaching, and she asked permission to tutor others at Kilborn. Despite not unlocking her memories, teaching brought Patience joy and the chance to make a difference. She missed being a Mastria but wouldn't go back without Michael.

"I'll ask Missy where we should go. She knows where all the hottest places are." Michael closed the site and put his phone down.

"All right. I'm going to get ready for work."

"Yeah, me too." He leaned down and kissed her forehead. "We are going to figure this out. Have faith."

She smiled. "Why have faith when I have you?"

Shaking his head and smiling, he walked back into the apartment.

She sat outside for a few more minutes, enjoying the quiet early morning in Orendale. Out of all the realms, Eviathan was her favorite. There was something about the human realm that had always called to her. Maybe it was why she ended up here so long ago.

Red eyes flashed across her mind, ruining the moment.

It was frustrating, having this silent tormentor with no identity. She wanted to know who they were and why they were consistently in her nightmares. She wished she could remember one dream. Just one. So she could see the face.

Stopping her thoughts, she stood. It was too early to think about this, and today would be different. If she said it enough, maybe she would start believing it.

Walking back into the apartment, she headed to her bedroom to prepare for work.

"I'll see you later," she yelled to Michael as she walked out the door. She wasn't ready for the day but would make the best of it.

On her way, she stopped and grabbed another cup of coffee from the local shop and a pastry for her grumbling stomach, then headed to one of the best places she had ever worked, the Olde GreyJoy bookstore. It had been standing on this same spot—the corner of Irvington and Claude—for the past two hundred years. No one had considered how it had stood so long or why it had not been converted into a newer, spiffier bookstore. The best part about the bookstore was it was a magical bookstore. It ran itself as an entity all on its own.

Humans didn't even know the store existed. They walked past an abandoned building every day and didn't even perceive what stood inside it. Even in the old city records, it didn't exist. It looked like a deteriorating, outdated brick building from the outside until you stepped through the broken glass door.

When Patience first saw the bookstore almost five years ago, she had searched for the magical symbol but found none. The immense energy flowing from the place made her curious.

Certain races, whether witches or goblins... or vampires, owned immense places of power. Each race had its own emblem to identify themselves, like the vampire Black Ankh emblem. Patience didn't recognize the emblem on the bookstore door, so she entered in full defense mode, especially since her kind, Aberrants, were not always welcome in certain establishments because they weren't part of any covens, so she always had to be cautious. Those who chose not to stay with their kind were Aberrants and considered dangerous since they did not conform. Though she didn't consider herself one, they labeled her anyway.

When she woke, none claimed her.

The Mastria said her coven might have been destroyed, but she refused to believe it. She would continue to search until her very last breath.

Though here, she found a little peace from her problems. When she walked into GreyJoy five years ago, thinking they would turn her away, everything changed when a note floated down to her feet saying, "Welcome, Theá. I've been waiting for you. Please help me." She could not refuse.

Now, she sat here, looking out the window onto an empty street, waiting for a customer to arrive to distract her from her worries.

Her mind had been so chaotic even the book in her lap wasn't holding her attention. Coming to work was always a pleasant diversion from her lingering nightmares. However, she had no such luck.

Vivid red eyes flashed through her mind. She let them linger, feeling the intensity of their gaze. She often studied them, hoping they would reveal something about their identity, a clue as to what they wanted from her and why they seemed so desperate. The burning intensity of those eyes never faded, no matter how long she looked.

Thunder boomed, jolting her out of her thoughts. Lightning cracked the sky, illuminating the dreary city as the threat of water bursting from the dark clouds held everyone inside.

She glanced around at the rows and rows of bookshelves, sighing. From the outside of the building, the store was small, but because of magic, it expanded itself to hold its ever-growing knowledge of the realms and the species they held. It held so many vast treasures and... deep secrets.

Thankfully, she wasn't in charge of putting away books. Her job was to be the voice. Patience gave directions and cataloged all the books. She'd seen all kinds of Etherians, or non-humans, go into the shelves and come out weeks later, either joyful, sad or somewhere in between.

She generally remained in the shop's front. The one time she went exploring, she got lost for a few days, mostly because of all the distractions she encountered. No worries. GreyJoy kept her fed and hydrated by leaving platters of food and bottles of water near the shelves. Now, she waited for the books customers needed to appear on the counter instead of searching for them. She wouldn't trade her position for the world.

A note appeared on the counter at her elbow.

What is wrong, Theá? You have been distracted lately. You have not written to me.

She smiled, picking up a pen, remembering the one reason he hired her, the most important, was that she could read Olde GreyJoy's language. She didn't know the name or origin of his language, but it sounded ancient, and, to her surprise, she could understand it.

One day she brought a note home to show Michael how she communicated with her new boss. They realized she was seeing and writing the language without thinking about it - they both found it eerie.

Her memory was there, under the surface, as though small pieces had slipped through the cracks to her unconsciously. It was how she knew her memories were out of her reach.

She researched the mysterious language that GreyJoy knew but couldn't find books written in it. She tried to ask GreyJoy. He claimed he did not know. All he said was it was the language of the one who made him, which was someone he was reluctant to talk about. Just like he was unwilling to tell her what Theá meant, it was a cute nickname for her, so she didn't mind him calling her that.

She was about to write him back when a young female with dark curly hair streaked with silver wandered through the front door.

"Hi. How may I help you?" Patience smiled, hoping to wipe the cautious expression off the woman's face. The female also looked a little shocked to see Patience sitting there, which made her curious about who she was. The power flowed around her, informing Patience she was a witch.

Closing the door, she slowly approached. Patience hopped down from her stool and put her book away below the counter. "Are you searching for a specific book or just browsing?"

When Patience glanced up again, she found the female watching her intently. Her extraordinary silver-gray eyes seemed to pierce straight through Patience's soul, and yet there was something unnervingly familiar about her gaze. As Patience peered into them, she felt a strange familiarity ripple through her, though she was sure they had never met.

"I am looking for more information on the Orb of Gilean."

Interesting. She appeared a little young to be interested in such a powerful weapon. The Orb could control and manipulate people's memories. Luckily, it was lost so long ago in Enoch, the realm of the Dark. No one ever ventured to look for it.

Patience's curiosity got the best of her. "And what particular information are you looking for on the Orb?" she inquired casually, trying not to be too nosy. Some people didn't like it when she raised too many questions.

"I'm interested in knowing what it can do and where I can find it."

Patience searched the catalog for the title the female would need to read: The Book of Lost Orbs by Quinn Readily. She had already read it twice. Two entire chapters were dedicated to the Orb of Gilean.

One day, in desperation, Patience had almost gone to the dark realm to search for the Orb. She had created a portal and was about to enter when Silas intercepted her. Individuals who went into Enoch either didn't return or lost their minds from what they saw there. She thanked the Goddess every day he had stopped her.

Patience pulled out the card, strode over, and dropped it in the simple gold wooden box. The book appeared on the counter.

The female reached out to grab it. Patience placed her hand over it, preventing her from taking it.

"First, I am not sure why you are searching for the Orb, but I will tell you this because you look like an intelligent female. Don't go into the Enoch seeking this. It is not worth it. Dangerous weapons should stay lost."

"Actually, dangerous weapons should be destroyed so they won't hurt anyone ever again," she countered. Reaching into her pocket, she took out two gold coins.

"That is true. Second, we don't use that kind of currency here. You can sit and read it or exchange it for something equal to its value. He prefers personal items since it is a personal item of his own that he is giving away."

The female's fingers hesitated over her collarbone before she traced a delicate line down her neck. She unclasped a silver chain with a sigh, and a dazzling hammered pendant of purple Roman glass glinted in the light. It was beautiful. Patience almost reached up instantly to grasp it when she held it out. She had always wanted an Askarian necklace. Unfortunately, they were way out of her price range.

"You can place it on the counter."

The female gently laid her necklace down, and they both watched as it disappeared.

"Your payment was accepted." Patience slid the book toward her.

She looked like she would say something. Instead, she picked up the book, shuffled toward the exit, and hesitated to open it.

"Do you need something else?" Patience asked.

The young female turned to stare at her, several emotions running across her face. The only ones Patience could decipher were longing and grief. "Thank you," she spoke as she practically ran out the door.

"You're welcome," Patience replied to her lingering presence. "Not the strangest person to walk in here, but definitely amongst the top ten."

Making her way back to the counter, she picked up the pen and wrote GreyJoy back.

GreyJoy, I am sorry. I have been trying to distract myself from my nightmares, but I'm having no luck. I think I'll go home before the sky pours down its miseries.

She jumped down from her stool and put on her jacket. As she was turning to grab her purse from the counter, writing appeared below her note:

I am sorry. Thank you again for honoring me with your presence, and I hope to see you tomorrow. It is always a pleasure to serve you, Theá.

She took the note and placed it in her bag. "Remember that tomorrow is Saturday," she said aloud. The building audibly groaned. "No worries. I'll be here bright and early on Monday. We have a new shipment coming in."

Her favorite upbeat pop song played over the loudspeakers. Patience smiled and walked out the door.

As soon as she stepped onto the sidewalk, fat raindrops pelted her head and soaked her clothes. She felt something brush against her leg and saw a bright green umbrella lying abandoned at her feet. With a small smile, she opened it up to shield herself from the rain. Any sane person would think she was crazy for giving a thumbs-up of gratitude to an abandoned building like GreyJoy, but she didn't care.

She was halfway home when the torrential downpour began. The rain made her walk home slower than usual, with all the puddles she had to avoid and the cars she had to dodge. Water filled her sneakers, completely soaking them.

At least the top part of her clothes was semi-dry. She was grateful for the small things.

A strong gust of air swept the umbrella from her hand, and she hesitated, debating whether to run home or chase after it. Suddenly, there was an unexplainable tug in her gut that pulled her in the direction of the runaway umbrella. She usually would have resisted this magnetic attraction, but now she was intrigued as her strides increased against her will. This had to be an Allure of Soul charm like what she saw on the website, however this felt far stronger than any other allurement before. What lay ahead? The pull became stronger as she moved forward.

She let the compelling force at her core lead her to the front of the double doors of an old industrial building. It looked like a nightclub. Picking up her umbrella, she saw a sign above the doors that read Moarte.

Interesting. So this is Moarte. Club Death. Typical of vampires to name their club "Death." Strange creatures.

Realizing it had stopped raining, she folded up the umbrella. She must have become swept up in the enchantment because of the storm. Magic had a mind of its own sometimes. The weather constantly messed with enchantments, especially with lure charms.

Turning to walk away since the allure had done its job and got her here, she found her feet wouldn't leave.

"What the hell?" She struggled to leave, thinking it was a fluke. She tried moving toward the door instead of away, and it worked. Then she tried to turn away again. Her feet wouldn't move forward.

Fighting the enchantment became harder the longer she stood, so she gave in. Stepping up to the doors, she touched the handle. An image flashed through her mind.

It was too quick for her to see. A warm, familiar sensation washed over her, pulling at her memory. It ran through her body, brushing against her soul, then vanished as quickly as it came.

She pulled on the door. It wouldn't budge. She could unlock it, but there was a magical ward, and she didn't want to risk drawing attention to herself by blasting off the door to a vampire club.

Vampires and witches were still mortal enemies. Even with the law outlawing the killing of witches in place, vampires were to be avoided.

This time, when she turned to leave, nothing stopped her. Her feet moved forward without incident.

Her thoughts traveled in a million different directions.

The first being, what the hell kind of enchantment was that if it wasn't a lure charm? There were other enchantments that vampires used specifically to lure their victims into their clubs. It shouldn't have affected her, at least not this strongly. She could blame it on the rain. Another possibility was something else was leading her there.

Following clues to her past wasn't always easy. She went into many of her leads blind, knowing she would come out disappointed. She always told herself she had at least had to try. Her instincts told her there was a clue in the club.

Walking up the stairs to her apartment, she knew they would go to Moarte tonight.

No... I couldn't let that happen. She had followed too many clues already. Tonight was going to be about fun and doing something different. Remember: new energy in the air.

Though this differed from her dreams and nightmares, she had never seen a glimpse of memory or that warm sensation before, and it had never happened when she was awake.

No, she wouldn't think about it. Tomorrow was another day. She would chase it tomorrow.

She did this to herself all the time. All it did was add to her stress.

She promised herself she wouldn't go anywhere near the club tonight.

CHAPTER TWO

PATIENCE

"When I said I would let you choose the next club, I didn't realize you would be crazy enough to choose this place."

Michael clearly didn't appreciate her choice.

They had been to three clubs already. The first was a boring human club named Hypnotic—a trashy teen hangout that lived down to its name. The Pixie Dust had been amazing until Michael stepped on a pixie's wing and got them both kicked out. The third was a nymph bar that turned out to be a strip club with an orgy in the back.

"After that disaster, you lost picking privileges," Patience reminded him. "Besides, we got kicked out of the best club in the city. Where else are we supposed to go?"

Her mind kept drifting back to the afternoon—that strange pull toward Moarte, the flash of memory when she'd touched the door handle. This could finally be the clue she'd been searching for.

So here they stood across the street from Moarte. The line wrapped around the block, but the bouncer was letting mostly women inside, two at a time. The more revealing their outfits, the faster they moved through.

Luckily, Michael had convinced her to wear the black halter-top sheer-mesh mini-leather dress he'd bought her months ago. Her Kick-Ass spiked heels gave her the confidence boost she needed.

"So, for this to work, you're going to have to mask my powers," Patience told him.

"What? Oh, no!" Michael shouted. "Last time we did that, it wreaked havoc on your control for a week."

"That was ten years ago. You're stronger now."

"Patience, you want me to mask your powers so you can go into a vampire club where witches are prohibited. Have you lost your damn mind?"

"Technically, this is your fault. You stepped on a wing." She gave him her best doe-eyed look. "I promise I'm just here for fun."

"You aren't trying to look for a clue, are you?"

"No," she lied.

Michael stared at her, unconvinced, but her doe eyes always worked. "Fine. But don't say I didn't warn you."

He dragged her to a narrow alleyway and placed his palms on her shoulders. The incantation he whispered was one she'd taught him years ago when they'd been hiding from an Absergo—a devourer of magic. His hands glowed slightly as warmth flowed into her, making her magic resist before finally submitting.

"Okay, it's masked," she said. "Let's go."

Patience approached the bouncer with a grin. He stared at her breasts, smirked, and was about to lift the velvet rope when he noticed her hand in Michael's.

"Only you," he declared, refastening the rope.

Shit. "Do the thing," she whispered to Michael.

Michael's eyes glowed vibrant purple as he touched the bouncer's face. "You will let me in."

"Of course." The bouncer lifted the rope immediately.

As they approached the entrance, Patience read the illuminated red writing above the door—Epati, the language of Morian warlocks: "Only those who live by the night may dwell here. Witches prohibited."

She stepped through, waiting for the spell to react, but nothing happened. Someone would have to tell them they needed their money back on that ward.

Patience beamed, feeling badass in her kick-ass shoes. She'd passed through an ancient vampiric spell and lived to tell the tale.

"Two shots of tequila!" she called to the bartender.

"Relax, Michael. I can feel your tension." She downed her shot quickly. "We got in. We're good."

Michael knocked back his shot, visibly loosening up. The club was exactly what she'd expected—bars crowded with humans and Etherians, darkness shrouding tables at the edge of the dance floor, red strobe lights revealing hungry eyes searching for prey.

"This place is great!" she shouted over the music.

"Earth to Patience." Michael waved his hand in front of her face. "Are you alright?"

"I'm good." She accepted the apple martini he'd ordered.

From the corner of her eye, she noticed someone watching them. Not her—Michael. A gorgeous male with wavy shoulder-length jet-black hair sat in a booth across the room.

"I think you have an admirer," she said excitedly.

"I know. He's been watching since we walked in." Michael didn't look in the stranger's direction.

"He's devilishly handsome! What's wrong with you?"

"I can't leave you alone in here. You'll get into trouble."

Liar. She could see he wanted to go over there. "We came here for this. Go have fun. I promise to stay out of trouble."

She gave him a small push toward Mr. Gorgeous. Michael straightened his hair and ambled over, sliding into the booth across from the stranger. She'd never seen him act so shy before.

Satisfied they were hitting it off, she headed for the dance floor to work off some adrenaline before beginning her search.

She let the enchanting rhythm carry her away, finally allowing herself to just let go. When she closed her eyes, dancing to the beat, an image flashed through her mind—still unclear, but becoming clearer the more she ignored it.

Then powerful arms wrapped around her from behind, swaying with her without missing a beat.

She didn't tense. The arms felt familiar, their warmth making her feel safe and protected. Her body melted into his as they swayed together, his breath tingling her neck.

She wanted more. She craved to taste him.

She turned in his arms. Illuminating silver-gray eyes saw right through her, ensnaring her completely. The world around them melted away.

I belong to him... and he belongs to me. The thought rushed through her, making her shiver. This was why she was here. For him.

When his eyes lit with hunger, all rational thought disappeared.

"Mine," he growled, grabbing her hair and pulling her head back to expose her neck.

Heat burned through her body as his kisses trailed down her skin until she felt them—his fangs.

Vampire.

A moan escaped her lips as his fangs grazed her neck. She shouldn't let him bite her, but God, she wanted him to.

It terrified her.

Patience pulled away, heart racing. She stared at him—tall, devastatingly handsome, with dark hair that looked like he'd run his hands through it too many times.

This is bad.

She'd long awaited discovering a connection with someone, but not a vampire. The bad blood between their races was real and deadly. This had to be another enchantment, a trap to make her prey.

"Mine," he growled again, trying to pull her back, but she evaded him.

She had to find Michael. The bind on her powers wouldn't last much longer, and he didn't know she was a witch.

She rushed toward the restroom, sensing the vampire following. In the bathroom, she locked herself in a stall and called Michael. Voicemail.

Dammit, Michael.

She texted: **Where the hell are you? I need your help.**

No reply. When she found him, she was going to kill him.

She stepped out of the restroom, determined to find Michael and leave, when someone approached from behind.

"Dessa?"

She turned. A male with golden-brown eyes like hers stood there, surprise on his face.

"You have the wrong person. I'm not Dessa."

But hearing the name felt right somehow.

"You don't remember me?" Confusion marred his handsome features. "We were friends once."

Her curiosity got the better of her. "Who are you?"

"I'm Alden. I want to know where you've been for the last fifty years."

Patience's breath caught. This was it—the key to her past. But before she could respond, she bumped into something warm and solid behind her.

A growl sounded in her ear. "Mine."

One moment she was standing before Alden, the next she was pressed against a wall in what looked like an office, the vampire caging her with his arms.

Wetness pooled between her legs at the intensity of his stare. Before she could speak, his lips were on hers, devouring her mouth. The sensation was incredible—more than kissing, her soul begging to connect with his.

He stopped abruptly, disgust filling his eyes as her unbound magic rushed forth.

"Witch," he spat, his hand closing around her throat. "How did you get past the spell?"

"It won't work," she said confidently as he pressed against her mental barriers. "No one can penetrate my mind unless I want them to."

The strange part was that even with his hand around her throat, her magic hadn't instinctively defended her. Nothing in her perceived him as a threat.

"Everyone has a crack," he said, banging against her mental walls.

She kneed him hard and pushed away, but he blocked the door. Closing her eyes, she searched for Michael and found him in a private room down the hall. Something was wrong.

The vampire's lips crashed into hers again, and all thoughts melted away.

The banging against her mental barriers stopped. Instead, there was a gentle caress—warm, tender, familiar. *His* caress.

Her barrier cracked, and he slipped through. She followed him willingly.

A dark tunnel appeared before them, stretching into infinite blackness. The vampire—Lucius, her mind whispered—glanced back at her before disappearing into it. She chased after him, her footsteps echoing off stone walls that seemed to close in around her.

The tunnel led to a vast stone passageway carved from living rock. Ancient symbols glowed faintly along the walls, pulsing with a malevolent red light. The air was thick with despair and something else—magic so dark it made her skin crawl.

She followed the passage until it opened into a cavernous chamber. What she saw there made her soul recoil.

A dark-haired woman hung chained to the far wall, suspended by shackles that bit deep into her wrists. Her white dress—once beautiful, now torn and stained with blood and dirt—hung in tatters around her broken form. Light poured down from somewhere high above, creating a spotlight effect that made her look like a fallen angel awaiting judgment.

But it was the chains themselves that drew Patience's horrified attention. They weren't ordinary metal—they pulsed with intricate archaic symbols that blazed neon red against the darkness. The magic radiating from them was ancient, powerful, and absolutely evil. A binding spell unlike anything she'd ever encountered.

The woman's head hung forward, dark hair obscuring her face. Her breathing was shallow, labored. She looked moments from death.

Lucius moved toward her with desperate urgency.

"Mae," he whispered, his voice breaking as he dropped to his knees before her.

The woman slowly, painfully, lifted her head. When her face came into the light, Patience's world tilted.

It was her own face staring back—but wrong. This Mae looked older, more mature, with eyes that held depths of pain Patience had never experienced. But the features, the bone structure, even the way she held her mouth... it was unmistakably her.

When Mae finally opened her eyes, all the fight had left them. They were empty, hollow, like someone had reached in and torn out her soul piece by piece.

"Mae, how do I get you out of here? How do I break these chains?" Lucius pleaded, his hands hovering over the glowing shackles as if afraid to touch them.

Mae stared at him—or rather, through him. She didn't seem to recognize him at first, lost in whatever hell she'd been trapped in. When Lucius shook her gently, she didn't respond.

Patience almost stepped forward when he slapped her—not hard, but sharp enough to cut through whatever trance held her. It seemed to be the jolt Mae needed.

Her eyes finally focused. "Lucius?" The word came out cracked, barely a whisper.

"Yes, Mae, it's me." Relief flooded his voice as he pulled her against his chest as much as the chains would allow. Tears poured down her cheeks, and he held her while she sobbed.

"Oh, Lucius, it really is you." Her voice was raw from screaming. "I thought... I thought you were another vision. Another trick."

"I'm real. I'm here." His own tears fell freely now. "I know you're tired, but I need you to keep it together for me. Tell me how to get you out of these chains."

Mae took a shuddering breath, fighting to pull herself together. Even broken, even tortured, she was trying to be strong for him. "I can break them, but I need your blood. The symbols... they feed on magic, but vampire blood will corrupt the spell."

Without a second's hesitation, Lucius bit deep into his own arm, opening a vein. Dark blood welled up, and he pressed the wound to Mae's lips.

"Drink," he commanded softly.

Mae latched onto his arm desperately, drinking deeply. As the vampire blood flowed into her, the red symbols on the chains began to flicker and fade, their neon glow shifting to blue, then dimming entirely.

When the last symbol went dark, Mae went completely limp. The chains released with a resonant clang that echoed through the chamber. Lucius caught her as she fell, gathering her broken body into his arms.

He turned and walked toward where Patience stood, but when she waved her hand, trying to get his attention, he looked right through her as if she wasn't there.

As he carried Mae toward the passage exit, Patience heard her own voice, weak but urgent: "He wants her, Lucius. He will do anything to get her."

"Who?" Lucius asked, but Mae had already lost consciousness.

The scene began to fade around the edges, reality bleeding back in.

"Get out of my head, witch," the real Lucius snarled behind her.

Patience spun around, finding him standing in the memory-space with her, rage twisting his features.

She placed her hands on his chest and pushed with both physical and magical force, ejecting him from her mind. The effort sent her tumbling back as well, sealing the crack in her barriers behind them.

When she opened her eyes, she was back in the office, pressed against the wall. Lucius stood before her, his face a mask of fury and something else—fear?

She tried not to panic. Instead, she took a deep breath and reached out through her connection to Michael.

Then she vanished.

She reappeared outside a private suite, her heart hammering. The magical lock on the door was child's play—her magic flowed from her fingers, making quick work of it.

She opened the door and immediately wished she hadn't.

The scene inside was a nightmare of lust and transformation gone wrong.

Michael stood behind Mr. Gorgeous, who was bent over a mahogany table. But this wasn't the Michael she knew. Large, thick black horns curved from the sides of his head, and his fingers had elongated into razor-sharp claws that dug deep into Mr. Gorgeous's hips, drawing steady streams of blood.

Michael was fucking him with an animalistic intensity that spoke of lost control. His eyes had gone completely black—no iris, no white, just endless darkness. When he turned his head toward her, she saw his canine teeth had elongated into fangs.

The transitioning. It was happening now, and they weren't prepared.

The stench hit her—blood, sex, and something else, something wild and dangerous that made her magic recoil. Mr. Gorgeous lay face-down on the table in a pool of his own sweat, his eyes glazed and droopy. He looked like he'd been drugged, but she knew better. This was what happened when a transitioning demon claimed someone—their victim became intoxicated by the demon's pheromones.

"Michael, I need you to let him come to me," she whispered, trying to keep her voice calm.

Michael's head snapped toward her, and when he spoke, his voice was deeper, rougher—barely recognizable. "No. He is mine."

She could see the man Michael was still in there, buried under layers of demonic instinct. "I know you're in there, Michael. Just let the male come to me."

She took a step forward, but Michael's grip on Mr. Gorgeous tightened, his claws digging deeper. Blood flowed more freely, and the man whimpered in pain.

"No, he is mine. Get out!" Michael roared, his voice echoing with inhuman harmonics.

He moved toward her with supernatural speed, his hand closing around her throat. She beat her fists against his arms, but he was far stronger than he'd ever been before.

She was starting to see black spots when Mr. Gorgeous spoke.

"Don't hurt her," he said in a raspy voice, somehow finding the strength to stand despite his injuries.

Michael's attention shifted to him, his grip loosening slightly. In that moment of distraction, Patience acted.

She reached out with her magic and touched Michael's chest, feeling for the essence of his soul. What she found terrified her—his soul was fragmenting, pieces of it breaking away as the demon side took control.

She pulled at one of the loose fragments, drawing it toward her. The ethereal cord of soul-stuff glowed between them, and she pressed it to her own chest, trying to bind it to her soul. But it wouldn't connect.

Damn, why isn't this working?

She tried again, pouring more power into the attempt, but the soul fragment just wouldn't bind to her. Mr. Gorgeous still held Michael's attention, speaking to him in low, soothing tones.

Will it work? Only one way to find out.

She reached out and pressed the soul fragment to Mr. Gorgeous's chest instead. To her shock, it began to merge with his essence immediately. She quickly drew a corresponding piece of his soul and tethered the two fragments together.

Just as the soul-binding completed, the vampire from the dance floor—Lucius—crashed through the door with several other vampires behind him.

"What the hell is going on?" he demanded.

The soul cords illuminated brilliant white, then disappeared as the binding took hold. Michael's hand fell away from her throat as both he and Mr. Gorgeous collapsed unconscious at her feet.

She must have dropped her magical barrier in her exhaustion, because suddenly Lucius was approaching her. The last thing she saw was his aura flickering strangely from dark red to purple and back again as Alden entered the room.

Then darkness claimed her.

CHAPTER THREE

LUCIUS

The scent of magic still lingered in the air—ozone and copper, like lightning striking blood—when Lucius burst through the door. His brother lay unconscious on the polished floor, his usually pristine appearance disheveled, dark hair falling across pale features. The demon's clawed hand wrapped around Ian's wrist like a crimson shackle, its grip so tight that angry red marks had already formed on his brother's skin. Between them, the sorceress slumped against the wall, her emerald dress torn at the shoulder, revealing a glimpse of pale skin marked with what looked like silver scars. Her chest rose and fell in shallow, labored breaths.

Whatever spell she had cast was unlike anything he'd encountered in two centuries of hunting her kind. The very air hummed with residual power, making his desonite stone pulse warm against his throat.

"Wrap him in a blanket and take him to my car. Out the back," Lucius ordered his men, prying the demon's grip from Ian's arm. The creature's skin burned cold against his fingers.

He knelt beside the sorceress, studying her face in the club's dim lighting. Even unconscious, her features were striking—high cheekbones that spoke of noble bloodlines, full lips that had felt like silk against his earlier, and long dark lashes that cast shadows on skin like porcelain. Dark bruises were already forming around her throat—his doing, when he'd lost control seeing her invade Ian's mind. The sight should have satisfied him, yet something twisted uncomfortably in his chest, an unwelcome stab of what might have been regret. Her pulse fluttered against the delicate skin of her neck like a trapped bird, and memories of pressing his lips there earlier flooded back unbidden—the way she'd melted against him, the soft sound she'd made when he'd deepened the kiss.

Dangerous thoughts. Witches and their manipulations had cost him everything once before. His wife, their unborn child, his very soul—all lost because he'd trusted the wrong sorceress two hundred years ago.

"I'm taking her."

Lucius rose slowly, recognizing that pompous voice before he turned. "What are you doing here, Alden?"

The Head of the Council stood in the doorway like he owned the place, his pale eyes assessing the scene with calculated interest. Alden hadn't changed in the century since they'd first met—still tall and lean as a blade, with silver-white hair that made him look distinguished rather than old, and that same predatory smile that had charmed half the Council into supporting his rise to power. The scent of ancient magic clung to him like expensive cologne, marking him as far older than he appeared.

"As Head of the Council, I may go anywhere I please," Alden said, his cultured accent carrying the weight of absolute authority.

The same arrogance that had cost Lucius his seat. Alden had played politics while Lucius had spoken truth about the Council's corruption, and truth rarely won against well-placed bribes and whispered promises of power.

"That doesn't explain why you want the sorceress." Lucius stepped between Alden and the unconscious woman. "She trespassed on my property. We can discuss jurisdiction with the full Council if necessary."

Alden's composure cracked slightly. "As soon as your brother wakes, I'll collect her. Not a moment later."

Then he was gone, leaving only the lingering scent of old blood and older grudges.

Lucius gestured for his remaining man to step back. "I'll take her."

She felt lighter than she should in his arms, her dark hair spilling over his sleeve like liquid midnight. The sorceress was smaller than she'd seemed when facing him down in the club—perhaps five and a half feet to his six-foot-four frame—but even unconscious, power radiated from her like heat from a forge. Not the crude magic of hedge witches with their fumbling spells and kitchen-garden herbs, but something refined and ancient, like wine aged in oak or steel tempered in dragon fire.

At his car, thick rope waited in his men's hands, the kind used for restraining supernatural prisoners. The black sedan's trunk had been modified specifically for transporting dangerous cargo—soundproof, spelled against magic, and lined with iron mesh.

"Sir?" one of his men asked, nodding toward the sorceress in his arms while holding up the restraints.

Lucius found himself hesitating, his feet refusing to move toward the yawning trunk. The space looked cramped and dark, barely large enough for one person, let alone two. Something about putting her in there—this woman who had kissed him like she was drowning and he was air—felt wrong in ways he couldn't name.

She's a witch, he reminded himself. *She attacked your brother.*

He deposited her beside the demon and slammed the trunk shut.

Maxim waited outside the mansion's imposing front steps, his expression grim in the pre-dawn light. The neo-Gothic structure loomed behind him, all stone gargoyles and pointed arches, its windows glowing amber from within. After five centuries together, Lucius could read every nuance of his advisor's mood, and right now Max looked like a man preparing for war.

"Don't," Lucius warned, stepping from the car onto the circular gravel drive.

"Have you lost your mind? You can't antagonize Alden like that." Maxim ran a hand through his blonde hair, a nervous habit from their human days. "He could strip my Council seat as easily as he did yours. Five years of careful positioning, gone."

"He was there unofficially. His own decree states—"

"His decrees change when convenient." Maxim's green eyes flashed with old frustration. "You could have had his power if you'd listened to me last year."

The offer to rally support and reclaim leadership still echoed between them. But power without purpose was meaningless, and Lucius had lost his purpose the night his wife died.

"We have bigger problems." Lucius opened the back door, revealing Ian's unconscious form.

"What happened to him?" Maxim's anger shifted to concern.

"She happened." Lucius nodded toward the trunk as his men lifted out the sorceress and demon. "Chain the demon in the dungeon. The sorceress goes to the East Wing."

"Don't tie her up," Maxim suggested. "She might be more cooperative if we show courtesy. Light the fireplace—there's no electricity in that section."

Lucius nodded reluctantly. In his office afterward, surrounded by leather-bound tomes and the familiar weight of centuries-old furniture, he poured three fingers of Macallan and tried to make sense of the evening. The whiskey was older than most countries, a bottle he'd been saving for either celebration or catastrophe. Tonight felt like both.

Sorceresses were rare—powerful witches who could manipulate more than simple spells and herb-craft. They worked with the fundamental forces of magic itself, bending reality like heated metal. He hadn't encountered one in decades, which explained how she'd breached his wards. His protective spells were designed for common magic-users, not someone who could absorb and redirect magical energy like she apparently could.

But why had she chosen that particular memory when she'd invaded his mind? His wife's death was private pain, not strategic information. She had been mortal, vulnerable, and the sorceress who'd killed her had done it simply to hurt him. What could this new witch possibly gain from witnessing his greatest failure?

The whiskey burned, but not enough to erase the questions.

The East Wing hadn't been used since Maxim had modernized the main house with electricity and central heating fifty years ago. Dust motes danced in the firelight as Lucius entered his old bedroom, breathing in the familiar scent of aged wood and old leather. The room held memories—not all of them painful. He'd spent his first century as a vampire here, learning control, discovering his gift for hunting witches.

They'd placed the sorceress on his former bed, her dark form stark against the faded burgundy sheets. The four-poster had been carved from black walnut by craftsmen dead three hundred years, its posts twisted into spiraling vines that seemed to move in the flickering light.

She looked younger in sleep, almost innocent. Her face had a timeless quality that spoke of good breeding—the kind of bone structure that appeared in Renaissance paintings and medieval tapestries. Dark lashes cast shadows on pale cheeks, and her lips were slightly parted, revealing a glimpse of white teeth. No one would guess the power sleeping beneath that delicate exterior, or the way those same lips had set his world on fire just hours ago.

His fingers found the desonite stone at his throat—cold and still. No magic influenced him now. This pull he felt was entirely his own weakness.

He settled into a chair and reached out with his mind, testing her barriers. They stood firm as castle walls, impenetrable and smooth. An hour of careful probing yielded nothing.

The fire had burned low when she finally stirred.

———◆◇◆———

Patience

Crack. Pop. Crackle.

The sound of a fireplace made no sense. Their cramped Boston apartment had electric heating that barely worked in winter, and the ceiling above her was thick with cobwebs instead of familiar water stains and cracks in the plaster that she'd memorized during countless sleepless nights.

Patience sat up slowly, immediately regretting the movement as pain lanced through her skull like someone driving railroad spikes into her brain. The room swam into focus through waves of nausea—a massive four-poster bed with black walnut posts carved into twisting vines, moth-eaten burgundy curtains that might have been beautiful once, scattered leather-bound books on dusty mahogany furniture that looked older than her entire bloodline. Medieval luxury gone to seed, like a fairy tale castle left to rot.

The air smelled of old smoke, leather, and something indefinably masculine—sandalwood and steel.

"I wouldn't do that if I were you."

The voice emerged from the room's darkest corner, deep and gravelly. When she tried to sit up fully, agony exploded behind her eyes.

"What's happening to me?" The words came out smaller than she'd intended.

A figure moved into the firelight—tall and imposing, with broad shoulders that filled out his dark shirt perfectly. Lucius stood at least six-foot-four to her five-foot-six, with dark hair that looked like he'd been running his hands through it and those distinctive red eyes that seemed to glow in the dim light. His face was all sharp angles and masculine beauty—high cheekbones, a strong jaw, and lips that she remembered far too well. The vampire from the club, the one who'd kissed her like the world was ending.

He sat on the bed's edge carefully, as if approaching a wild animal, his face half-shadowed by the dancing flames. This close, she could see the faint lines around his eyes that spoke of centuries of experience, and the way his jaw tensed when he looked at her.

"You're experiencing magical backlash," he said, his voice surprisingly gentle for someone who'd had his hands around her throat not long ago. "Whatever you did to my brother and that demon created a three-way connection. Breaking it abruptly has consequences—think of it like magical whiplash."

When she tried to rise again, he pressed her back down with careful pressure. "Let me help."

His fingers touched her temples, and warmth spread through her skull like sunlight melting ice. The pain receded enough for her to think clearly.

"*Sunteți frumoasă,*" he whispered, his breath warm against her ear.

You are beautiful. The Romanian words sent heat racing through her veins, followed immediately by his lips on hers. This time she remembered—the club, the kiss that had made her forget her own name. Her arms circled his neck, pulling him closer as the kiss deepened, but he broke away abruptly.

The chill that followed his departure was like winter wind.

"You could have stayed to explain," she muttered, climbing from the bed. The door handle warmed under her touch—a containment spell, elegantly crafted but not unbreakable. She absorbed its energy, feeling the magic flow into her like water into a sponge.

The hallway beyond belonged to another century entirely. Torchlight flickered across stone walls lined with oil paintings of armored warriors locked in eternal battle, their faces fierce and proud in the wavering light. A worn red carpet stretched toward distant doorways, its once-rich color faded to the rusty brown of dried blood. Suits of armor stood at attention in alcoves between the paintings, empty helms turned toward her passage like silent sentinels.

The architecture spoke of old money and older power—the kind of family that had been wealthy when wealth was measured in land and titles rather than stock options. Gothic arches soared overhead, disappearing into shadows thick with the weight of centuries.

Voices drifted from a partially open door ahead, low and intense. Patience crept closer, her bare feet silent on the ancient carpet, curiosity overriding the caution that had kept her alive for twenty-six years.

"—tried to break into her mind, but her barriers held," the vampire was saying, pacing like a caged predator. "She's stronger than any sorceress I've encountered."

"Lucius." The blonde man on the velvet couch sounded patient but tired. "You know what you must do. Talk to her."

Lucius. The name fit him—formal, imposing, with sharp edges.

"This would be easier if I could simply extract the information," Lucius said, hurling an empty glass against the wall.

Patience flinched at the crash.

"Your witch-hunting days are over," the blonde man—Max, apparently—reminded him. "The Council forbade torture more than a century ago. You're no longer the Ragana Žudikas."

The Witch Hunter. Patience's blood turned to ice water.

She was in the home of the vampire who had slaughtered covens, who had driven her people into hiding for two hundred years. The desonite stone that amplified his power against magic-users would be around his neck, hidden beneath his shirt.

"What was the penalty for breaking that decree again?" Lucius asked with dark humor.

"Just talk to her," Max said firmly.

After Max disappeared through a hidden passage behind the fireplace, Lucius stood silhouetted against the window. Dawn was breaking, painting his profile in shades of gold and shadow.

Patience backed away from the door and reached out through her connection to Michael. His essence felt distant, muffled—somewhere deep underground. The dungeon, most likely, and his transitioning energy was making him harder to locate.

The door hinges squealed behind her.

"Eavesdropping, sorceress?"

Lucius gripped her arm, but she twisted free easily—her absorbed magic lending her strength.

"Looking for Michael. You know, the horned guy you threw in your dungeon?"

His eyes flashed with surprise at her easy escape from his grasp. When he lunged for her again, she let him catch her arm.

"So I'm a sorceress now, not just 'witch'? Progress." She smiled sweetly and pulled free again.

This time his hand closed around her throat. "My patience has limits. Tell me what you did to my brother."

"I need to see him," she gasped. "It's the only way I can help both of them."

His grip loosened enough for her to breathe. "If you've harmed Ian, I will kill you regardless of Council laws. Do you understand?"

At her nod, he released her and led her down stone steps to a bedroom where his brother lay shivering with fever. Ian was beautiful even in unconsciousness—angular features, dark hair, the kind of masculine elegance that ran in their bloodline.

"Where's Michael? They need to be together." She placed her hand on Ian's burning forehead.

"The demon stays chained until you explain what's happening."

"Then Ian dies." Patience pressed her palm against the stone wall, sending her magic through the mansion's bones. The ancient structure responded to her call, walls rippling like water. She stepped through.

"Sorceress!" Lucius's shout followed her into darkness.

The dungeon reeked of old blood, despair, and something worse—the lingering psychic residue of centuries of suffering that made her magical senses recoil. Her conjured light—a small orb of pure white energy she called Seckor—revealed stains on the rough stone walls that spoke of horrors she didn't want to imagine. The passages were carved directly from bedrock, creating a labyrinthine maze that extended far beneath the mansion's foundations.

She passed torture chambers that belonged in a medieval nightmare, where skeletons still lay shackled to iron tables, their stories written in rust and bone. One skull grinned at her from beneath a leather hood, its jaw wired shut for eternity. The air grew colder as she descended, until her breath misted with each exhale.

The maze of corridors would have trapped anyone else, but Seckor pulsed brighter as it sensed Michael's demonic energy, leading her through twists and turns that defied architectural logic. She found him in the deepest cell, chained to a weeping wall where moisture seeped between ancient stones in a constant, maddening drip.

His skin had turned from red to black—the transition was accelerating.

"Three spa days and unlimited milkshakes," she told his unconscious form, unlocking his shackles with absorbed magic. "You owe me."

She pressed her palm to the floor, asking the mansion to connect her with Ian's room. The stone shimmered, and she pushed Michael through the portal just as footsteps echoed in the corridor.

Lucius appeared in the doorway, fury radiating from every line of his body. "Where did you send him?"

"Where he needs to be." She backed toward the wall as he advanced.

"Bring him back. Now."

"No. They have to be together, or both will die."

He slammed her against the stone, and stars exploded across her vision. "You try my patience, sorceress."

"That's unfortunate," she managed, "because trying patience tends to make her irritable."

His growl of frustration preceded another impact with the wall. This time, the world went gray at the edges.

"Enough, Lucius!" Max's voice cut through the dungeon air.

Lucius released her immediately, and Patience pressed her palm to the wall. It shimmered like water, and she slipped through, leaving the Witch Hunter's curses echoing behind her.

CHAPTER FOUR

PATIENCE

The mansion's ancient stones had thankfully brought her to the same room as Michael. Patience took a moment to arrange both unconscious forms on the four-poster bed so they touched as much as possible—Michael's crimson hand resting against Ian's pale wrist, their foreheads nearly touching. The connection between their souls needed physical contact to stabilize.

Satisfied with their positioning, she approached the tall windows where faint golden light seeped between the heavy wooden shutters. Dawn had broken while she'd been navigating the dungeon's maze. She snapped her fingers, sending ribbons of magic toward the oil lamps scattered throughout the room, extinguishing their flames with small puffs of smoke.

"Daylight," she murmured, pressing her fingertips to the metal shutter mechanism. Her magic flowed into the ancient hinges, and she watched the heavy wood lift slowly.

"Close it!" Lucius's voice exploded behind her as he burst through the doorway and lunged toward the windows, desperate to block the golden streams from reaching the bed where his brother lay vulnerable.

Damn. She'd forgotten about Ian.

Patience threw herself between the sunlight and the bed, forcing Lucius back into the shadows as she slammed the shutters closed. Too late—the acrid smell of burnt flesh filled the room, and she glimpsed angry red welts forming on Ian's exposed skin.

Working quickly, she placed her palm flat against the carved bedpost and wove a protective shield around the entire four-poster, creating a barrier of shadow magic that would deflect any stray sunbeams. Fortunately, Michael's larger frame had shielded most of Ian's body from the direct light.

"Sorry about that," she called over her shoulder, then immediately re-opened the window she'd just closed. Her fingers snapped again, and magic zipped through the air like silver threads, throwing open the remaining two windows. Brilliant morning light flooded the room completely, transforming the dusty space into a golden cathedral.

"Sorceress!" Lucius hissed, instantly retreating to the room's single dark corner, as far from the bed as possible. He crouched low, using her body and the bed's bulk to create a pocket of protective shadow.

"Yeah, not so tough now, are we?" Though she had to admit he was impressive—most vampires would be unconscious by now from sun exposure. It had to be nearly mid-morning from the sun's position, and he was still awake and coherent. *One powerful son of a bitch.*

His long black sleeves had protected most of his torso, but she could see the flesh on his hands rapidly healing where the light had touched him. Steam rose from the regenerating tissue in thin wisps. She almost felt bad for about half a second, until she remembered him slamming her head against stone walls. Twice.

Patience ensured her shadow continued to protect him as she moved to check on Michael and Ian. Both their fevers had dropped significantly, and Michael's skin had returned from the alarming black to his natural deep crimson. Having them together was definitely working—she could feel the soul-bond strengthening with each passing minute.

His horns had grown another inch during the night, curving back from his temples like polished obsidian, and his muscle mass had increased noticeably. She wondered what he would look like in full demon form when the transformation completed. Unfortunately, they wouldn't find out until the process finished entirely.

Sighing, she leaned against the stone windowsill and bent to remove her Kick-Ass spiked heels, which had been torturing her feet for hours. The black leather was scuffed from her adventures in the dungeon, and her stockings were beyond salvation.

She glanced over at Lucius, who was staring daggers at her from his shadowy corner. "If looks could kill, I imagine I'd be dead right now."

"If only," he growled, his red eyes glowing like embers in the darkness.

She still couldn't believe she was in the presence of the Ragana Žudikas and still breathing. Witches told their children bedtime stories about him—or threatened that he would come steal their magic if they didn't practice their spells properly. She'd heard many of the Mastria at Kilborn Academy use his name to frighten lazy students. *If you don't master your barriers, the Witch Hunter will break through with his infamous word of power: Luzia.*

She'd always assumed the legendary vampire was an overdramatized myth because she couldn't fathom how the witches hadn't banded together to destroy him centuries ago. But here he was, cowering in a corner from simple sunlight. Not so terrifying after all, even with that dark red aura that pulsed around him like barely contained violence.

Patience moved back to the window, settling against the sill to observe his hunched form. "So, are you ready to listen, or do you plan to strangle me again?"

He continued to glare at her with the intensity of a caged predator. "Doesn't appear I have much choice," he said, his voice rough with barely suppressed rage.

"Strangled twice in one day... well, technically three times if you count Michael grabbing my throat at your club. That's a personal record." She rubbed her neck, which still bore faint bruise marks. "Do you strangle all the women you dance with, or am I just special?"

"I'd say you're very special," he hissed, putting enough venom in the words to kill a horse.

"Yeah, you're a real charmer. Now listen carefully, *idiot*, because I'm only explaining this once, and your brother's life depends on you understanding." Her voice sharpened with authority.

Lucius shifted in his corner, studying her with new wariness. "Get him killed? I'm trying to save him. Tell me what you've done to Ian and what that demon has to do with any of this."

"It's absolutely imperative that we keep both Michael and..." She paused, realizing she'd been thinking of his brother as 'Mr. Gorgeous' this entire time. "What's your brother's name, anyway?"

His face twisted with fresh anger. "What?"

"Your brother. He does have a name, right? Or do you just call him 'brother' for six centuries?"

"Ian," he spat out like the word burned his tongue. "His name is Ian."

"Right. Ian." She nodded approvingly. "When you separate them, you're essentially tearing their souls apart. I tethered their souls together using an ancient binding ritual."

He scoffed, disbelief written across his shadowed features. "You what? Without his permission?"

"I know how it sounds," she said, holding up a hand to forestall his outrage. "I was supposed to be Michael's anchor originally, but he rejected our bond and accepted Ian instead. I had to save my best friend—we'd discussed this possibility before, though we weren't sure it would actually happen. We thought we had more time since he hadn't shown any signs of transitioning yet."

"An anchor to maintain his connection to humanity," Lucius said slowly, understanding dawning in his voice. "He's a daimones."

"Yes. Ten years ago, when we were exploring the borders of Evictus, this appeared on his hand." Patience moved to Michael's side and glided her palm over his wrist. Magic responded to her touch, and a intricate symbol materialized on his crimson skin—a perfect circle bisected by a cross, the lines glowing faintly silver. "Michael is going through the final stage of transformation into a full daimones demon."

"The transformation takes nearly four hundred years, and they only anchor to someone they trust completely." Lucius ran his hands through his dark hair in frustration, the gesture making him look younger despite his obvious age. "Ian and your friend met last night. How could that possibly work?"

When he wasn't glaring death at her or attempting murder, she had to admit he was devastatingly handsome. The sharp angles of his face, those intense red eyes, the way his shirt clung to broad shoulders—if he weren't a legendary witch killer, she might have been interested.

"Stranger things have happened in the supernatural world," she said with a slight shrug. "Besides, Ian could be much older than he appears. Vampires age differently."

He looked skeptical. "So you're telling me my brother has become the soul anchor for a daimones—"

"His name is Michael," she emphasized firmly.

He shook his head in disbelief. "My brother is anchored to Mi—" He caught her warning glare. "To Michael. Last I checked, daimones were extinct."

"Clearly they're not, since one is lying on your bed." She gestured toward the unconscious demon. "Besides, there's at least one other still alive. A very famous one."

"King Kieran," Lucius said immediately. "Both he and his queen disappeared almost two centuries ago. What does the demon king have to do with your friend? And please tell me you have the soul gem needed to safely break their connection."

This was the part she'd been dreading. They'd focused so much energy on unlocking her lost memories over the past decade that finding a soul gem had become secondary, especially since Michael had shown no signs of transitioning. They'd hoped he might be only half-demon.

"Well..." she muttered, looking anywhere but at his face. "No."

One second she was leaning casually against the window; the next, she was flat on her back with six-foot-four of furious vampire pinning her to the stone floor. The impact knocked the breath from her lungs.

"What do you mean, *no*?" he shouted, his face inches from hers.

"Please don't strangle me again," she said rapidly, her voice coming out in a breathless rush. "My throat really can't take another round, and then I won't be able to give you the answers you desperately need."

He didn't move from on top of her, his weight pressing her into the cold stones. This close, she could see flecks of gold in his red eyes and smell his distinctive scent—sandalwood and steel with an undertone of something wild and dangerous.

"Calm down," she pleaded, very aware of how his body covered hers completely. "We can find the gem now that we know what we're looking for. We only thought he was half-demon and didn't realize he'd fully transform, though we knew it was possible. We believed we had more time."

"Why?" he growled, his voice a low rumble she felt in her chest.

"It's complicated, but the basics are that Michael can't remember his past. I found him in Igoria—the realm of the forgotten—thirty years ago."

Doubt flickered across his features. "The realm of the forgotten hasn't been accessible for centuries."

"Well, I got in," she said dryly. "Look, I know we only have four days to find the gem before the transformation completes. Technically three and a half now. Are you going to let me up so we can actually do something about it?"

She waited patiently for him to decide, trying to ignore their compromising position. He was settled between her legs, and her dress had ridden up considerably during their struggle. The stone floor was cold against her back, but he radiated heat like a furnace.

She tried not to squirm as inappropriate thoughts flooded her mind—how easy it would be to wrap her legs around his waist, how perfectly they seemed to fit together despite their size difference. Her thoughts were so intense she had to look away from his penetrating stare.

When she finally glanced back, his eyes had taken on an otherworldly glow, and she could feel him growing hard against her, evidence that he'd noticed their intimate positioning as well. They were directly under the open window—he couldn't stand without being burned by the streaming sunlight.

She could use magic to close the shutters, but she needed a better angle with her hands free. As it was, she was trapped beneath him just as surely as he was trapped by the sun.

Patience wrapped her legs around his waist and tried to shift their positions, but he was solid muscle and wouldn't budge. He gazed down at her with a mixture of curiosity and unmistakable desire burning in those crimson depths.

"If you help me roll us over," she explained, her voice coming out huskier than intended, "I can get on top and stand to close the shutters."

He nodded curtly, though the evidence of his arousal was still pressing insistently against her. She bit her lip to keep from making an embarrassing sound—the wetness between her legs was becoming impossible to ignore.

"Put your arms around me," he said roughly. "It'll be easier to roll that way."

"Okay." She slipped her arms under his, flattening herself against his broad chest. They lay still for a moment, and she found herself basking in his warmth and solid strength.

This should feel dangerous—lying in the arms of the most feared witch hunter in supernatural history. Instead, she felt safe and protected in a way that made no sense. She wanted to blame it on a spell, but all her magical senses told her this feeling was entirely real and entirely her own.

Just as she was getting used to the sensation of being held by him, he rolled them smoothly.

Patience stood from the floor and tugged her dress back down, her body protesting the loss of contact. She flicked her finger toward the windows, and magic slammed the shutters closed with a resounding bang.

As soon as the room plunged back into shadow, Lucius rose and moved to light the oil lamp beside the bed.

"This place has electricity," she observed, noting the modern fixtures mixed among the antique furnishings. "So you deliberately stuck me in the cold, lightless wing."

"Yes," he said simply, turning on two more lamps without a trace of apology.

Rolling her eyes, Patience settled into a cushioned chair near the window. Unfortunately, the ancient furniture was about as comfortable as sitting on rocks, but it would have to do.

Using so much magic in such a short time was taking its toll. Her body always grew weak and drained when she pushed her abilities too hard, too fast. Sometimes she felt like her mortal form wasn't designed to channel such vast amounts of power. Twice before, when she'd absorbed or used too much magical energy, her body had gone into what she called "magic shock"—all her abilities would suddenly leave her, making her completely vulnerable and essentially human. It had taken weeks to recover both times.

Now she tried to use magic only when absolutely necessary. Simple spells were fine, but tonight had been far too much.

She got as comfortable as possible in the torture device masquerading as a chair and leaned back, closing her eyes.

"What are you doing?" Lucius's voice was sharp with impatience. "We need to find a soul gem, and we only have four days."

"I know, *buddy*," she said without bothering to open her eyes. "Look, my body hurts, I'm magically drained, and I'm exhausted. In case you forgot, you threw me against stone walls multiple times. I need a few minutes to recover, then we can start searching. I know where to begin looking, which buys me at least a short rest."

She cracked one eye open to peek at him. "Besides, even if we found the gem right now, we couldn't use it yet. The transformation has to complete first. Only then can we safely break the soul bond without killing them both."

"True," he admitted grudgingly. "A few minutes. Then we start."

Through her half-closed eyes, she watched him settle into a chair on the opposite side of the room, positioning himself where he could watch her every movement. His red eyes never left her face, studying her with the intensity of a predator waiting for weakness.

Patience took a deep breath and tried to focus on relaxing, though it was easier said than done with the Witch Hunter glaring holes through her skull.

Lucius

Lucius stood on the mansion's roof, watching the sun set beyond the treeline as he waited. The evening air carried the scent of jasmine and approaching rain.

Footsteps echoed behind him on the slate tiles. He turned to find Estelle, Maxim's wife, emerging from the shadows. Even in the fading light, her beauty was breathtaking—golden hair that caught the last rays of sunlight, violet eyes that seemed to hold secrets.

"Estelle," he said, moving toward her. "Max has been searching everywhere for you."

She stepped back into the gathering darkness, just out of his reach. Something was wrong—her usual warm smile was absent, replaced by an expression he couldn't read.

"Lucius, where are you?" Another voice called out—Mae, his beloved wife. His heart leaped at the sound as she appeared at the roof's edge, moving toward him with that radiant smile that had captured his heart three centuries ago.

He looked back toward the shadows where Estelle had been, but found only empty air. "Estelle!" he called out, sudden panic gripping his chest. "Where are you?"

He turned back to Mae, fear crawling up his spine as he hurried toward her outstretched arms. She waited for him, patient and loving as always, her dark hair flowing in the evening breeze.

So focused was he on his wife's welcoming embrace that he didn't see the figure lurking in the darkness behind her until it was too late. Red eyes gleamed in the shadows—Estelle's eyes, but wrong, transformed into something predatory and cruel.

"Mae, run!" he shouted, but Estelle was already moving with inhuman speed.

Estelle's hands closed around Mae's shoulders before she could react. "No, don't!" Lucius ran toward them with all his supernatural strength, but the distance seemed to stretch endlessly. The closer he got, the farther away they appeared.

"Fight, Mae! Fight!" he screamed as his wife smiled sadly at him, accepting her fate with the grace that had defined her mortal life.

Estelle exposed Mae's slender neck and sank her fangs deep. The life drained slowly from Mae's eyes as her body went limp and crumpled to the roof tiles.

When Lucius finally reached them, he dropped to his knees and gathered Mae's lifeless form into his lap, her head cradled against his chest.

"Mae," he whispered brokenly. Her eyes fluttered open one last time.

"Lucius, I'm sorry. I failed you," she breathed, her voice barely audible.

"No," he said fiercely, tears streaming down his face. "It was I who failed you. All you ever did was love me."

She smiled with her final breath, reaching up to wipe away his tears. Then the light faded from her eyes forever.

A gentle hand touched his shoulder. He looked up to find Estelle gazing down at him, her eyes filled with sorrow rather than the predatory hunger he'd seen moments before. She reached down to touch his cheek, wiping away his tears with infinite tenderness.

She held out her hand to him, offering comfort he knew he didn't deserve.

He looked down at Mae's still form, not wanting to let her go, then back at Estelle's outstretched hand.

Rage exploded through him like wildfire. His hands shot out, wrapping around Estelle's throat and squeezing with centuries of grief and fury. "No, no, no, no!"

Lucius's eyes snapped open to find his hands wrapped around the sorceress's throat as she clawed at his arms, trying desperately to break free. Her face was turning an alarming shade of blue.

He released her immediately, jerking backward as if burned.

She gasped and coughed, dragging air into her lungs in harsh, painful sounds. "What the hell?" she choked out when she could finally speak. "I was only asleep for a few minutes."

"I didn't mean—" he started, then stopped. There was no excuse for what had just happened. "I'm sorry. I had a nightmare."

Without another word, he strode from the room, needing distance from both her and the lingering horror of the dream.

In his private chambers, Lucius found his bottle of blood gin and took a long pull, letting the alcohol burn away the taste of fear and grief. The nightmare had felt different from his usual torments—more vivid, more real, but definitely not a memory. Mae had never met Estelle, and his wife had died in their bed, not on any rooftop.

He glanced out the window through a crack in the shutters and saw the sun balanced on the edge of setting. Normally he only needed an hour or two of rest—a level of efficiency only the most ancient vampires achieved. Maxim believed it was due to all the witch magic he'd been exposed to over the centuries.

It shocked him that he'd left himself so vulnerable around an enemy, especially a witch. But she hadn't taken advantage of his unconscious state. She could have cast any number of spells that wouldn't technically break supernatural law, yet the most she'd done was that simple mind trick at the club.

Even when she'd opened the shutters, she'd used her own body to shield him from the worst of the sunlight.

She appeared no older than twenty-three, but her powers were vast for someone so young. The magical energy that flowed around her was intoxicating—it would drive a young vampire mad with hunger. Despite her obvious strength, she hadn't retaliated against any of his attacks.

Unless she was simply biding her time, waiting for the perfect moment to strike.

He settled into his favorite leather chair by the fireplace—old and worn, with seams coming apart despite Maxim's constant pleas to replace it. Running his hands over his face in exhaustion, he tried to make sense of the nightmare.

He'd never had that particular dream before, though similar visions had been plaguing him for weeks. The problem was that Estelle had been missing for months, and bringing up the subject with Maxim was... complicated.

A soft knock interrupted his brooding. "Come in."

Maxim entered, looking as perfectly groomed as always despite the late hour. "You look like hell," he observed, settling into the chair across from him. "Let me guess—the witch got under your skin."

If anyone else had made that comment, they'd be decorating the wall. As it was, Lucius merely glared.

"Have you learned anything useful from our unwelcome guest?" Maxim continued, apparently immune to homicidal stares.

"Ian is soul-bonded to a daimones," Lucius said bluntly.

Maxim's eyebrows shot up. "A daimones? I thought they were extinct. Well, except for—"

"King Kieran, yes." Lucius stared into the fireplace flames, considering the implications. "The situation is... complex."

"Please tell me she has the soul gem needed to break the bond safely."

"She doesn't." At Maxim's sharp intake of breath, Lucius held up a hand. "But she claims to know where we can find one. We have less than four days before the transformation completes and this Michael creature becomes a full demon."

"Shit." Maxim leaned back in his chair. "A powerful, fevered demon with a direct soul connection to Ian. That's not terrifying at all."

"The implications are staggering," Lucius agreed. "Daimones only bond with people they trust completely, yet Ian and this Michael met last night. There's something we're not being told."

"Have you found any information about the sorceress or her coven?"

"My contacts within the witch communities have never heard of her," Maxim replied, his expression troubled. "She doesn't seem to belong to any known coven."

"Contact Volt immediately. Have him investigate her background and see what he can discover about King Kieran's lineage—any children or siblings who might have survived."

Maxim raised an eyebrow but nodded. "Any word from Silas about identifying our demon guest?"

"He'll arrive tonight. In the meantime..." Maxim relaxed back into his chair with a knowing smile.

"I'll be working with the sorceress to locate a soul gem," Lucius said reluctantly, hating the idea even as he acknowledged its necessity. So far, she'd done nothing overtly threatening beyond trespassing and making his body react in ways he'd thought long buried. "She claims to have a lead."

"Stay cautious, Lucius. We don't know her true motives." Maxim's expression grew serious. "And keep that desonite stone close. Since Ian wasn't wearing his protection, we're already in this mess deeper than we should be."

"Even if Ian had been wearing his stone, it wouldn't have helped against a demon," Lucius pointed out. "We'd still be in exactly this situation."

"True enough." Maxim's smile returned, carrying hints of mischief Lucius didn't like. "It's been a long time since I've seen a woman affect you like this."

Lucius paused at the door, his hand tightening on the handle.

"She's either cast a spell on you—which I doubt, given your protections—or you're attracted to her. It's been two centuries since Mae died, Lucius. Maybe it's time—"

"Don't." The word came out sharp as a blade. "Mae has nothing to do with this situation. I'll find the gem, save Ian, and send the sorceress on her way. End of story."

He strode from the room, slamming the door behind him with enough force to rattle the frame. With the nightmares still plaguing him and the memory of his wife's death so fresh, he couldn't afford distractions.

No matter what his traitorous body suggested, nothing would happen between him and the witch. The soul gem was the only thing that mattered now.

CHAPTER FIVE

PATIENCE

Silver moonlight streamed through the tall windows, painting ethereal patterns across Patience's face as a cool night breeze whispered through the ancient castle. She stirred slowly, blinking away the last vestiges of sleep as she realized she was alone in the four-poster bed.

Standing and stretching her body, she marveled at how completely restored she felt. Every ache had vanished, all the pain from Lucius's rough treatment was gone, and her magical energy hummed at full strength once more. Sleep had worked its healing magic more thoroughly than she'd expected.

Most remarkably, she hadn't been jolted awake by nightmares or woken in a cold sweat. For the first time in months, she'd enjoyed truly peaceful, restorative sleep. Part of her wanted to burrow back under the covers, but time was their enemy now.

She moved to check on Michael and Ian, noting that their fevers had completely broken. Both looked healthier, though still unconscious. She lifted Michael's wrist and examined the mystical symbol—about a quarter of the circle had faded, leaving the lines slightly less distinct than before. Good. They still had time. The circle needed to disappear entirely before they could safely use the soul gem, leaving only the cross behind.

Time was indeed of the essence. But where had the infuriating vampire disappeared to?

Her stomach chose that moment to announce its emptiness with an undignified growl. She pressed a hand to her abdomen, suddenly ravenous. She wasn't sure if vampires bothered with actual food, but she was about to find out. Searching for soul gems on an empty stomach was asking for trouble—the last thing she needed was to become lightheaded during a fight or while trapped somewhere for hours. In enemy territory, maintaining her strength was crucial.

Patience made her way through what she was increasingly certain was an actual castle. The grand hall she passed through featured enormous tapestries depicting medieval battles, and the massive stone fireplace could have roasted an entire ox. But it was the family crest above the mantle that confirmed her suspicions—a magnificent phoenix rising from flames, with the words "Prin cenușă, ne vom ridica din nou" (From the ashes, we will rise again) inscribed below in flowing script. Above the phoenix, "Familia de Cordovan" was emblazoned in gothic lettering.

Cordovan. Why did that name tug at her memory like a half-remembered song?

Following her nose and instinct, she discovered a stone stairway leading down to what turned out to be a surprisingly modern kitchen in the castle's basement. The contrast was jarring—state-of-the-art appliances and sleek countertops surrounded by medieval stone walls. A massive walk-in refrigerator hummed quietly in the corner, and she sent up a prayer to the Goddess that it contained actual food rather than just blood bags.

Crossing her fingers, she pulled open the heavy door and nearly wept with relief. *Actual food!* The refrigerator was well-stocked with everything needed for a proper meal. She gathered bread, mayonnaise, lettuce, tomato, ham, and cheese, and—blessing of all blessings—mustard. She arranged her bounty on the granite counter like a shrine to sustenance.

This might legitimately be one of the happiest moments of her life, which would be pathetic if she thought about it too hard. She determinedly didn't think about it.

Patience was just finishing her first sandwich when Maxim wandered into the kitchen, looking surprised to find her there. He carried a jar of peanut butter and a spoon, which answered her question about whether vampires ate regular food.

"Hi," she said around a bite of sandwich.

"Well, hello," he replied, moving further into the kitchen. She watched with amusement as he discretely placed the peanut butter in a cabinet and blocked it with a bag of chips. Someone was protective of his snacks. She could relate—Michael was always raiding her food stash too.

"So, what are you, like... Lucius's lapdog or something?" The words left her mouth before she could stop them.

He smirked, approaching the table where she sat. "Believe it or not, he's my sire."

Interesting. So Lucius was powerful enough to create other vampires. Her knowledge of vampire society was admittedly limited to what she'd read about other creatures' encounters with them. GreyJoy had given her extensive texts on most supernatural beings, but for some reason, vampires had been notably absent from her education. She was beginning to wonder why.

"You've got to be kidding me," she said, pausing mid-bite. "You're stuck with him for eternity? Are you compelled to follow his orders or something?"

Maxim laughed, a genuinely warm sound. "No, surprisingly enough. He took pity on me and gave me a second chance at life. We're actually friends after all these centuries. Don't you have a sire? Or parents?"

She shook her head and continued eating.

Curiosity filled his green eyes as he studied her. "Lucius made it sound like you'd instantly bewitch me if I so much as looked at you."

"I'd laugh if his paranoia weren't so tragic," she said, biting into her sandwich with perhaps more force than necessary. "He's a complete ass. Plus, I don't do spells. Never have."

"He's been called worse. Much worse, actually." Maxim chuckled as he settled into the chair across from her. "But you don't use magic? That's... unusual for a witch."

She set down her sandwich, realizing she'd need to explain. "I do use magic. I just don't need spells for it." The confused expression on Maxim's handsome face was almost comical. She took another bite instead of laughing.

"That's impossible. I've never heard of a witch who doesn't use incantations."

"Well, I'm sure there are plenty of things that exist beyond your experience," she said dryly. "And I could think of several colorful words that would describe your sire perfectly."

He threw back his head and laughed, the sound transforming his features. "You're different from what I expected. I think you might be exactly what Lucius needs."

"Me? What he needs?" She nearly choked on her sandwich. "That's hilarious. More like the person he needs to kill."

"What are you doing?" Lucius's voice cut through their conversation like a blade as he strode into the kitchen, scowling darkly. Though he was ostensibly addressing her, his glare was fixed firmly on Maxim.

"Nothing," Maxim said, turning to face his sire. "We were just talking."

"I distinctly recall telling you not to speak with her."

Patience wanted to kick him somewhere painful. Hard.

"You told him not to talk to me?" she said, setting down her sandwich with deliberate care. "What the hell is wrong with you? Do you think I'm going to bewitch him? What exactly have I done to deserve this paranoia? I'm starting to think you're just an idiot."

Maxim tried unsuccessfully to hide his laughter as he stood to leave. His chuckles echoed up the stone stairwell long after he'd disappeared.

Patience concealed her own smile as Lucius continued glaring at her.

"And just for your information," she said, flicking her hand casually toward the scattered condiments. They all flew back to their proper places in the refrigerator and cabinets, the mustard jar sailing past Lucius's head close enough to ruffle his hair. "I don't need spells."

The shock on his face made the demonstration completely worth it.

"Are you planning to stare at me all night, or are we going to find that soul gem?" she asked, taking another bite of her sandwich.

"Let's go, witch," he said, moving to stand beside her in what she assumed was meant to be intimidating. If only he knew that he annoyed her far more than he intimidated her. She was never pleasant when annoyed.

"No need for the attitude," she said after swallowing her last bite. "This whole situation is your fault anyway. You were supposed to wake me after a few minutes." She punctuated each word by poking his broad chest with her finger until he caught her hand, stopping the assault. "You still haven't explained why you tried to strangle me just for falling asleep."

"I don't owe you any explanations, witch. Now let's go."

Thoroughly irritated, she yanked her hand free and smiled sweetly as she wiped her greasy fingers down the front of his pristine black shirt.

Before he could retaliate, she vanished and reappeared across the kitchen, but he was on her before she could teleport again. Vampire speed was definitely unfair.

"I've killed people for far less," he growled, pinning her against the stone wall.

He was too close again. She hated when he invaded her personal space like this—it scrambled her senses and made thinking clearly impossible. His scent was pure distraction, all sandalwood and steel and something uniquely him. Gazing into his red eyes, she realized she wasn't the only one affected by their proximity. Heat flared between them before he abruptly released her and stepped back.

"You said you had a lead," he stated, clearly trying to regain control of the situation.

"Yes, possibly. At least I know where we might find answers," she said, waving her hand over his shirt to make the grease stains disappear. She waited for a thank you that would probably never come.

"Where?" he demanded.

"GreyJoy."

"And where the hell is—"

"Not where. What. It's an ancient magical bookstore," she explained. "Think of it as a library that specializes in the impossible."

"And you're certain it contains the information we need?"

"Because we've been looking for exactly this kind of information. GreyJoy can at least point us in the right direction. Right now, we're wasting time with conversation when we could be—"

He grabbed her arm and pulled her along. The world dissolved into a blur of speed and shadow until they materialized beside his sleek black sedan in an underground garage.

"—on our way," she finished, rubbing her eyes to adjust to the sudden change of scenery.

"Get in," he said, opening the passenger door with surprising courtesy. "I'd prefer to have my brother back sooner rather than later."

"Agreed," she replied, sliding into the luxurious leather seat.

The car's interior was immaculate, all black leather and modern technology. She'd never been in such an expensive vehicle—it even had that coveted new car smell despite obviously being customized for supernatural needs.

When he started the engine, heavy metal music blared from the speakers before he quickly turned it down. Patience smirked. It was one of her favorite songs too. Maybe the legendary Witch Hunter wasn't quite as cold and emotionless as he pretended to be.

He activated the GPS system on the dashboard, and she typed in GreyJoy's address. As they pulled out of the garage, he reached into the backseat and retrieved a black cloth.

"Put this on," he commanded.

Her eyebrows shot up. "Are you serious?"

He met her gaze with an implacable look and held out the blindfold.

"Fine, but wait." She turned to study the imposing structure they were leaving behind. "I knew it. You actually live in a castle."

"Witch."

Rolling her eyes, she tied the blindfold around her head. "I don't care where you live anyway. When this is over, I won't be coming within a hundred miles of this place."

She felt him wave his hand in front of her face to test the blindfold's effectiveness.

"Satisfied?" she asked dryly.

He grunted and pulled onto what sounded like a gravel road. Given the dense forest surrounding his property, they were probably miles from civilization. Maybe she could nap during the drive.

They traveled in comfortable silence until the car stopped. "Are we there?"

"No, but we're in the city."

"Can I remove this thing now?"

"Yes."

She pulled off the blindfold to find them sitting at a red light on the edge of downtown, just a few blocks from GreyJoy's. The GPS screen was dark—she wondered when he'd turned it off.

Looking out the window, she watched a group of young humans pour out of a nearby bar, laughing and carefree. How she envied them. That could have been her and Michael in another life, if fate hadn't had other plans. Two young women broke away from the group to take selfies with their phones, grinning without a care in the world.

Speaking of phones, where was hers? He'd probably confiscated it, though it hardly mattered. The only person she ever called was Michael, making it useless now.

They turned a corner and drove past her apartment building. She gazed longingly at the familiar windows, wishing she were curled up in her own bed. A change of clothes would be wonderful, but she didn't need Lucius knowing where she lived.

After several more turns, they finally pulled up to Olde GreyJoy. The shop's windows lit up the moment she stepped out of the car—he always sensed her approach.

She smiled, breathing in the night air tinged with the scent of old books and ancient magic.

"Witch, no games," Lucius warned. "We find the soul gem information and then we're done with each other."

She frowned. More likely, he'd try to kill her the moment this was over, just as he'd attempted earlier. As the Ragana Žudikas, his hatred for her kind ran deeper than ocean trenches. It surprised her that he hadn't simply tortured the information from her, though she suspected his restraint had everything to do with Maxim's influence. Max seemed like the only reasonable person in that castle.

Her thoughts drifted, unbidden, to the feel of Lucius's lips on hers. Even after learning what she was, he'd kissed her with devastating passion. Maybe there was a possibility of something between them... No. She needed to focus. Finding the soul gem was all that mattered. Once this crisis was resolved, she'd escape and ensure they never crossed paths again.

Pulling herself from dangerous thoughts, she approached the familiar door and found it unlocked, as always. "Home," she whispered.

"Hi, GreyJoy," she called, holding out her hand. A note materialized and floated gently into her palm.

Good evening, Theá. Always a pleasure to see you.

"Always good to be here. I know I said I wouldn't visit until Mon—"

"Sorceress!" Lucius's voice exploded behind her.

She turned to see the vampire standing outside, pounding on what appeared to be solid air, his face twisted with frustration.

"GreyJoy, let him in," she called.

A new note appeared in her hands with a single word: *No.*

Shocked, Patience stared at the paper. She'd never seen GreyJoy bar anyone from his store before. To him, good and evil were meaningless concepts—information belonged to everyone, and what they did with knowledge was their choice. Free will in its purest form.

"GreyJoy, please let him in," she tried again.

Another note materialized: *I don't like him.*

Patience had to bite her lip to keep from laughing at the vampire's murderous expression. She held up one finger to signal she needed a moment, which only made his glare more poisonous.

"I know you don't like him, but he's seeking knowledge. We need to help Michael, and this man's brother is the only thing keeping Michael anchored to our world. Please let him in."

She waited. "GreyJoy, please."

Nothing.

She'd never encountered such stubbornness from the ancient entity. "GreyJoy, why won't you let him enter?"

A note suddenly appeared: *He wants to hurt you, Theá. All those who wish you harm are forbidden. He is not himself.*

She couldn't argue with the first part—he definitely wanted to kill her. But what did that cryptic last line mean?

"GreyJoy, what if he swears not to harm me? Could he enter then?"

Instead of a simple note, a thick stack of papers slammed onto the floor with an authoritative thud. A single sheet fluttered down on top.

He must sign this binding contract, swearing to do you no harm for the remainder of your natural life. Entry is denied until he complies.

Patience picked up the contract and skimmed the first few pages, fighting laughter. It was magnificently thorough—Lucius couldn't harm her in any way while on the property, and if he tried, he'd become GreyJoy's personal slave to be used as the entity saw fit. GreyJoy had essentially created her own personal sanctuary.

"I don't think he'll appreciate this, but I'll try," she muttered.

Moving to the door, she watched it dissolve into transparency. Lucius tried to step through but met an invisible barrier as solid as steel.

"So, GreyJoy refuses entry because you intend to harm me," she explained, holding out the contract. "He says you have to sign this first."

Lucius took the papers and scanned them rapidly. Then, to her amazement, the entire contract burst into flames and disintegrated in his hands.

"Absolutely not," he said flatly.

Interesting. So he wielded witch magic. Very few vampires could channel magical energy—they weren't natural conductors unless they had witch blood, and even then, only a handful achieved true mastery. For him to use magic so effortlessly demonstrated incredible strength, discipline, and control.

It was also completely arousing. An image of those flames consuming his clothes instead of the contract flashed through her mind before she hastily banished it.

"Well, he won't let you in without it," she said.

"I don't know what game you're playing, witch, but I refuse to become enslaved to some object."

"That's exactly why you're stuck outside. GreyJoy isn't an object—he's possibly a creature, but definitely not a thing. He already dislikes you, so I'd suggest being respectful. Besides, you're wasting precious time. He's the only one who can help us find that gem."

How dare Lucius call GreyJoy an object? The ancient entity deserved more respect than that.

"Tell him to let me in," Lucius demanded.

"That's not how this works. I don't control him."

The vampire's glare could have melted steel.

"Fine. Stay out there. I'm going to research while you waste time being stubborn."

She'd barely turned around when another contract slammed at his feet, accompanied by an ornate pen. A note floated down to land on top of the papers. He snatched it up before she could read it, scanned the contents, and scowled. The note caught fire and crumbled to ash.

With obvious reluctance, he picked up the contract and signed it with sharp, angry strokes.

He threw the signed papers through the barrier, where they vanished instantly. The door reappeared and swung open, allowing him entry.

What did that note say to change his mind so quickly?

"Could you understand his note?" she asked as he stepped inside.

He looked at her like she'd asked if water was wet. "Of course I can read it, just as you can. Where do we start searching?"

He didn't realize the note had been written in an ancient language, seeing it as English just as she did. Curious indeed.

"This way," she said, leading him to the green filing cabinets behind the counter. "GreyJoy, we need information about soul gems for Michael."

Drawers flew open and catalog cards shot out, arranging themselves in neat piles before her. She placed them in the golden request box, and each card instantly produced its corresponding book on the counter. Express service at its finest.

She pulled three more cards and fed them to the system. Twenty books materialized—enough reading to last until dawn.

"Ready to research?" she asked, settling at the reading table.

He didn't complain as she'd expected. "This is your lead, after all."

She gave him a brilliant smile. "You have a better one?"

He shook his head and sighed, picking up the first volume. "What exactly am I looking for?"

"Anything about soul gem locations, unfortunately. We don't have specific coordinates, but look for references to daimones or ancient binding rituals."

"We'll find something," he said with surprising confidence, already absorbed in his reading.

"We will?"

"Yes," he said without looking up. "The alternative is that I end your life if my brother dies."

Patience rolled her eyes and decided to ignore the threat. The faster they found their answer, the sooner she could escape him forever.

She'd worked through three volumes when she glanced over to see Lucius running his hands through his dark hair in frustration. The gesture was unconsciously graceful, and she had to admit he was devastatingly attractive when absorbed in research.

Damn. No man should look that good reading a book.

Shaking off the inappropriate thought, she picked up a tome about demon rituals and began reading. Twenty minutes later, her favorite rock song blared from somewhere nearby.

Lucius pulled her phone from his pocket and checked the caller ID before holding it up for her to see: *Bloody Wanker.*

"Are you going to let me answer it?" she asked.

He hesitated before handing over the device.

"Not a good time," she answered, trying to keep her voice steady.

"Where are you?" The voice was sharp, impatient.

"Why do you need to know?"

"Patience, where the hell are you?" he practically shouted, a tone she'd never heard from him before.

"The bookstore—"

The line went dead. She stared at the phone in disbelief. He'd actually hung up on her.

"Who was that?" Lucius asked, his dark eyes narrowing dangerously.

"None of your business," she replied, matching his stare.

He continued studying her with unblinking intensity.

"Fine," she sighed. "It was a friend of Michael's."

"And you gave him our location?"

"He asked," she muttered.

He rolled his eyes in exasperation. "Are you completely—"

Patience burst into laughter, the sound bubbling up from deep in her chest. "Oh my God, please do that again," she managed between giggles, wiping tears of mirth from her eyes.

"Call you an idiot?" he asked, clearly confused.

"No," she gasped. "Roll your eyes. It's so perfectly teenage angst."

Without warning, he pressed her against the bookshelf, silencing her laughter. But just as quickly, he vanished completely. Patience frantically searched the aisles, her heart racing.

"What the hell?" she called out. "GreyJoy, what did you do with him?"

A note materialized on the floor: *He knew the rules.*

The shop's door chimed, and a tall figure entered—bronzed skin, worn leather jacket, and a distinctive scar running from his left cheek to his left eyebrow.

"Silas," she breathed.

"Where's Michael? I've been trying to reach him."

"Hold that thought." She needed Lucius back, unfortunately. "GreyJoy, bring him back."

Another note appeared: *NO.*

"Please. I still need his help."

"Need whose help?" Silas asked.

Patience held up one finger. "I know you don't like him, and he's definitely an ass, but I'll make sure he behaves. Pretty please?"

A loud splash and creative cursing erupted behind her. She turned to find Lucius covered in what appeared to be green slime.

After composing herself, she waved her hand to clear away the mess. "You're welcome. He told you to behave, so don't anger him further."

"When this is over, I'll burn this entire—"

Patience clapped her hand over his mouth. "Please don't threaten him. I can't save you if you use that word. He has zero tolerance for threats."

Silas cleared his throat pointedly.

"So, Michael is—" she began.

"Potentially killing my brother," Lucius interrupted, addressing Silas. "Did you bring the information Maxim requested?"

"My lord," Silas said, dropping to one knee.

Patience blinked in shock. Silas—proud, independent Silas—was kneeling before a vampire.

"What the hell? You know him?" she demanded.

"He works for me," Lucius revealed calmly.

"No way! Silas, you traitorous bastard!" So much for trusting anyone. How was she going to explain this to Michael?

"How do you know him?" Lucius asked.

"I thought he was our friend, but apparently he works for the enemy."

"I'm still your friend," Silas said, rising at Lucius's nod. "My lord, may I speak freely?"

"Yes."

"Michael is my friend, and you are my friend, but I serve him because I owe a life debt."

"Oh, wonderful. So you're his slave after all."

"Patience, no. He saved my life centuries ago. Honor demands I repay that debt."

"Ugh, warriors and your codes," she muttered, returning to her book. "Why are you looking for Michael?"

"He's transitioning."

Her head snapped up. "How do you know that?"

Silas glanced at Lucius. "Volt told us."

The vampire nodded as if this explained everything.

"I need to understand what happened tonight," Silas continued.

Since Lucius remained unhelpfully silent, Patience reluctantly explained the entire situation, with him occasionally adding details or corrections.

"This is serious," Silas said, concern evident in his voice. "Without the soul gem, Michael won't be able to return to human form. His demon side will consume Ian's soul and take complete control."

"We know," Lucius said tersely. "We have less than four days. You can help search. I don't like leaving my brother vulnerable."

"We can't just take the books," Patience informed them. "GreyJoy requires payment—an exchange of equal value."

"What are you talking about, witch?" Lucius demanded.

A note floated down, which he caught and incinerated after reading. "This would have been useful information before we left the castle."

Silas exchanged a meaningful look with her—he understood the implications.

"You can read his notes?" Silas asked carefully.

"Of course. They're in English."

"They're not written in English," Patience said slowly. "They're in his ancient language. I've been the only one able to read them... until now."

Without hesitation, Silas pulled out his centuries-old emerald dagger—the weapon he never traveled without—and placed it on the counter.

"This should be sufficient," he said.

Damn. She'd been curious to see what Lucius would sacrifice, but Silas had beaten him to it.

The dagger vanished instantly. A note drifted from the ceiling, which Lucius caught and handed to Silas.

"Read it," he commanded.

Silas studied the paper and saw only meaningless symbols. "I can't read this."

"He can't read it," Patience confirmed. "Only we can." She placed the note on the counter. "Look at it carefully before you read."

Lucius examined the note, and she watched realization dawn on his face.

"You can actually read that?" he asked, stunned.

"And so can you, apparently." She studied him with new interest. How could they both understand GreyJoy's ancient script? This mystery would have to wait.

She read the note aloud. "The dagger is worth eight books. And Lucius, you're still an ass."

She selected the book she'd been reading plus three others, leaving him to choose the final three volumes.

Then, because they'd caused her nothing but stress and frustration, Patience stuck out her tongue at both men and vanished in a swirl of magic.

It was childish, but she didn't care. They deserved it.

CHAPTER SIX

PATIENCE

Patience reappeared in the familiar bedroom where she'd awakened to Lucius's kiss hours earlier. Sighing, she allowed herself a moment to remember the warmth of his palm against her face, the intoxicating taste of his lips claiming hers with such desperate intensity.

She couldn't afford these thoughts now. A metallic clatter behind her broke the spell of memory. Turning, she found Silas's emerald dagger lying on the dusty floor where it had materialized from thin air.

She picked up the ancient weapon, smiling at GreyJoy's unexpected generosity. The entity wasn't known for returning payments once accepted, which made this gesture particularly curious—though he did understand how much the blade meant to Silas.

Waving her hand over the dagger, she sent it back to its rightful owner through the magical connection that still lingered.

Her phone rang, the caller ID displaying *Bloody Wanker*.

"Hello? I—"

"Witch, when I find you, I'm going to skin you alive. Slowly." Lucius's voice snarled through the speaker, pure venom dripping from every word.

"You have such a way with words," she replied sweetly. "They just make a girl want to swoon." She hung up before he could respond.

Stepping into the hallway, Patience searched for a quiet sanctuary where she could read through the remaining books without discovery. She explored room after room—most filled with dust-covered furniture or wooden crates containing old silverware and forgotten household treasures.

Her phone rang again as she emerged from one particularly cluttered room. She ignored it, knowing it would be either Silas or Lucius, and she had no desire to speak with either traitor at the moment.

Continuing her exploration, she encountered the first locked door she'd found in the entire castle. Magic trickled from her fingertips into the mechanism, but the lock refused to yield. Strange. She tried again, pushing more energy into it to force compliance, but it remained stubbornly sealed.

A magical ward, perhaps? She placed her palm flat against the carved wood, asking it to reveal its secrets.

Three silver interlocking circles—blue, red, and purple—materialized on the door's surface, glowing softly in the dim hallway. She'd never encountered such a ward before, though the craftsmanship was exquisite. She'd have to research its meaning later.

Instead of forcing the lock this time, she laid her hand directly over the mystical symbol, channeling her magic into its complex patterns.

The door clicked open with a sound like a sigh.

Inside, a thick layer of dust coated everything—floors, furniture, even the air itself seemed heavy with neglect. Most items were so moth-eaten and deteriorated she could barely identify their original purpose. Yet underneath the choking dust lingered a light, perfumed scent that gave the space an unmistakably feminine atmosphere.

The fragrance tugged at her memory, hauntingly familiar yet impossible to place.

When she crossed the threshold, shivers raced down her spine like ice water, as if someone had walked over her grave. Every instinct screamed at her to seal the room and leave it undisturbed. She was turning to go when a silvery glint caught her eye from what appeared to be a vanity table.

Her feet moved of their own accord, drawn by an inexplicable compulsion toward the gleaming object—a necklace.

Setting down her stack of books, she lifted the jewelry and gently brushed away decades of dust. Her breath caught. It was Askarian work—similar to the piece the young woman had traded to GreyJoy for the Orb book, but this pendant was far more intricate, the Roman glass clearly ancient and infinitely more precious.

Patience had always coveted such pieces, but they remained perpetually beyond her means. They were rare as dragon's teeth and twice as expensive. Seeing two in as many days couldn't possibly be coincidence.

Moving to the window, she wiped away the grime and held the necklace up to the moonlight. It sparkled magnificently, revealing a delicate symbol etched into the glass—the Cordovan family crest she'd noticed above the great hall's fireplace.

Watching it catch and scatter the silver light filled her with inexplicable joy. It felt so familiar, so *right* in her hands. She should have replaced it and fled the room immediately. Instead, she fastened it around her neck, desperate to feel the cool metal against her skin.

The moment the clasp closed, sudden warmth enveloped her as happiness spread through her veins like honey. The necklace bore an enchantment—if memory served, a Vow of Protection spell designed to shield the wearer from harm. The question was: protection from what, exactly?

She didn't want to remove it. The sensation against her skin was too perfect, too familiar... too absolutely right. It felt as though it had been made for her, which was impossible.

Wasn't it?

Reaching behind her neck, she tried to undo the clasp, but it wouldn't budge. Panic fluttered in her chest. She tried again, forcing herself to breathe calmly, but the jewelry remained firmly sealed.

Shit. This is bad. Very bad.

After one final attempt, she surrendered to the inevitable. For now, she'd have to hide it. Placing her hand over the pendant, she wove a glamour around it, making it invisible to all eyes but her own. She'd figure out how to remove it later—hopefully before Lucius discovered her theft.

Gathering her books, she resealed the room and leaned against the door, trying to steady her racing pulse.

Her phone rang again. The caller ID showed *Unknown,* but she suspected she knew exactly who it was.

"Hello?" she answered in her sweetest voice.

"What did you do, witch?"

"I have absolutely no idea what you're talking about, vampire."

"What. Did. You. Do?"

"You must be so accustomed to getting your way. This must be pure torture for you." She ended the call with savage satisfaction.

Damn. The ward on the door—he must have detection spells in place. He'd know she'd been inside his wife's private sanctuary. If he discovered the missing necklace, there would be consequences she didn't want to contemplate.

Pushing away from the door, she continued down the hallway until she found a stone stairwell leading to a different floor. A few cobwebs decorated the corners, but very little dust suggested this passage was used, though not recently.

Like the floor above, torches provided flickering illumination along the stone walls. She searched room after room, finding them all empty, until she reached ornate double doors at the corridor's end.

Opening one side, she felt slight pressure as she stepped through—unusual, but not alarming. Stone steps descended into darkness, and she followed them without hesitation until reaching a landing.

"And let there be light," she whispered, magic spilling from her hands in golden streams. Cliché perhaps, but effective. Lights on tables and ceiling fixtures blazed to life one by one, illuminating the space. Fire erupted in the massive fireplace with a comfortable roar.

Holy shit... a library.

She walked into the room's center, momentarily speechless. It was magnificent—easily rivaling GreyJoy's collection. Rows of bookshelves lined the walls from floor to vaulted ceiling, while four polished wooden tables with brass lamps occupied the central space. Two butter-soft leather chairs faced the fireplace, and in the far corner, a large bay window with built-in seating beckoned like a perfect reading nook.

The moonlight streaming through that window would be ideal, and when dawn came, the sun would make it even better—a perfect hiding place from one irritated vampire.

She explored further, discovering a spiral staircase leading to an upper gallery that wrapped around the entire room. Books in dozens of languages covered every conceivable subject. A bibliophile's paradise, exactly like GreyJoy's domain.

Running her fingers along the elaborate spines, she was reminded of that night she and Michael had discovered what they'd believed to be the Goddess's lost library beneath Hellstone River Bridge. Rumored to contain texts on the darkest arts and secret histories of forgotten worlds and realms, it supposedly held ancient scrolls documenting the Goddess's mysterious disappearance.

They'd spent hours exploring until a heavy golden tome had beckoned to her, practically daring her to open it. The strangest thing was that she remembered opening the book but not reading it—they'd awakened outside the library hours later with no memory of what had transpired inside.

Nothing dramatic had happened afterward. She'd remained unchanged... though the witch communities had been in an uproar for weeks about rumors of the Goddess's return. The excitement had died down after a month.

Oops.

Continuing her exploration, she discovered that many of the volumes dealt with warfare and strategy in various languages. Clearly, Lucius believed in being prepared for any conflict.

In the library's back corner, she found an unexpected treasure trove—novels from the past two centuries, including one of her absolute favorites, Jane Austen's *Persuasion.* Examining the collection more closely, she realized most were romance novels, and they were predominantly titles she adored.

The library doors opened, and multiple voices drifted up from below. Patience quickly ducked behind the upper gallery's thick wooden balusters, praying the shadows would conceal her.

"Why do you think she'd be here, Lucius?" Maxim's voice echoed off the stone walls as the door closed behind them.

"Where else would she go? Her friend is still unconscious upstairs, and I know I should have double-checked that blindfold." Lucius paused, and she heard books being set on a table. "I know she was in Mae's room."

Patience unconsciously touched the hidden necklace. She'd forgotten he'd been married. His wife's death had triggered his transformation into the legendary Witch Hunter. Was this Mae's necklace? She prayed it wasn't, but instinct told her it had to be—which made her inexplicable connection to it even more disturbing.

"The door was still sealed, Lucius. How could she have entered? It's spelled to admit only you."

She pressed further back into the shadows as Lucius began searching the lower aisles. "The same way I know she breached Mae's room. She's a witch—she found a way. She's here somewhere. I can sense it. This is the only place we haven't searched except the dungeons."

"Silas already checked there. She's nowhere to be found. Besides, only those in your trusted circle can enter this library."

Patience glanced above the door she'd used and saw illuminated words: *Doar cei în care am încredere pot intra.* Only those I trust may enter.

That explained the pressure she'd felt crossing the threshold. But how had she bypassed such a specific ward? Especially one that recognized emotional bonds rather than simple magical signatures?

"She penetrated the wards at the club too," Lucius said, his voice growing closer to her hiding spot.

"She did?"

Patience wove a cloaking spell around herself and crept silently back to the balustrade. Lucius stood directly below her position while Maxim remained by the entrance, watching his friend's increasingly agitated search.

"Yes. Have you learned anything about her and the demon's origins from Volt or Silas?"

"Actually—"

A devastatingly handsome man materialized beside Maxim without warning. He could easily compete with Lucius for sheer masculine beauty—broad shoulders, razor-sharp cheekbones, and striking silver hair. However, the dark, impenetrable green aura surrounding him made him seem distinctly unapproachable.

"Volt's here," the newcomer announced.

Lucius emerged from the stacks, seemingly unsurprised by the man's sudden appearance within his private sanctuary. A trusted ally, then.

"Volt, report what you've discovered."

Patience leaned forward slightly to get a better view of this mysterious figure.

"They found the witch fifty years ago, unconscious on the steps of Gregory Kilborn Academy—the premier school of witchcraft. She had no identification, no possessions, and no memory. Their assessment suggests either a spell gone catastrophically wrong or intentional memory erasure."

Moving to a concealed panel in the wall, Lucius slid it aside to reveal two crystal decanters filled with amber liquid. He selected a glass and decanter, carrying both to the table before pouring himself a generous measure.

"Wait—she couldn't remember who she was or how she arrived there?" Maxim asked, clearly startled.

Waking up surrounded by strangers asking questions she couldn't answer remained the most terrifying moment of Patience's life, even considering all the deadly situations she'd survived since. She'd gladly erase that memory of absolute panic, dread, and vulnerability if she could.

"Correct, sir. When she regained consciousness, she awakened screaming. It required several witches working together to calm her because their individual spells were too weak to affect her. She didn't even know she was a witch until they explained it. She had to begin her education from the very basics, but once she started, they discovered she was exceptionally gifted—advancing rapidly and requiring no incantations to channel her magic."

"Fascinating," Lucius murmured, pouring himself another drink. He nodded for Volt to continue.

"After twenty years at the academy, she departed with the demon."

Kilborn would never admit they'd been expelled.

"And this demon's origin?" Lucius poured a third drink.

"Unknown. A few months after he appeared at the school, they both left."

Technically accurate, though missing several rather significant details. The academy kept the true story locked away tighter than state secrets. She suspected it had everything to do with Gregory Kilborn's hidden library of forbidden texts that opened portals to other realms—books that shouldn't exist and were undeniably dangerous. Still, she remained grateful for that library, since it had led her to Michael.

"No one knows where the demon came from?" Maxim confiscated the decanter before Lucius could pour a fourth drink.

"No, sir," Volt confirmed.

"Except possibly the witch herself," Maxim interjected. "Perhaps another conversation with her would prove illuminating."

"She mentioned finding him in Igoria," Lucius admitted reluctantly.

"The realm of the lost? Did she explain how he arrived there? Let me guess—you didn't ask," Maxim said, shaking his head in exasperation.

Lucius glared but offered no retort.

"They don't know how he got there," Silas revealed, entering through the library door. "He has no memories either. They've been searching for ways to unlock Patience's memories for years. Every spell and magical artifact they've tried has failed."

Lucius drained his glass and glared meaningfully at Maxim, who still controlled the liquor. "And no coven has claimed her?"

"Some have tried, drawn by her growing power, but she bears no coven mark."

Power. That's all any coven wanted from her—her abilities, not her heart or soul. As desperately as she craved belonging to a magical family, it wasn't worth being used and discarded. She could never be certain they'd truly accept her rather than simply exploiting her gifts.

Somewhere out there was her real family, her true home. She just had to find them.

"What about her magic? Is it confirmed she requires no spells?"

"Have you observed her utter a single incantation, Lucius?" Maxim asked pointedly.

Definitely my new favorite person. Apparently Lucius hadn't listened when she'd explicitly told him she didn't need spells.

"It's another reason covens pursue her. She channels magic without incantations, which terrifies many in our community."

Lucius sighed heavily. "Silas, I know the demon is a daimones. Is it possible he's the king's son?"

The same thought had occurred to her upon learning Michael's true nature. With his memories lost, there was no way to confirm such speculation. She'd never shared her suspicions with Michael—she couldn't bear giving him false hope. Besides, King Kieran had been missing for two centuries.

King Kieran, sovereign of Evictus and known throughout the supernatural world as the Demon King, had been banished from his kingdom by the Goddess herself. His gift of creation had been stripped away as punishment for his betrayal of her and her people. His insatiable greed for power had blinded him, causing the downfall of his entire race.

Only the king's queen, Circe, could reverse his banishment by pleading for forgiveness and earning permission for his return. Within Evictus, Queen Circe had created a new capital called Askaria, where they'd lived in peace until approximately two hundred years ago. Then rumors had surfaced about a son, though no one could confirm the child's existence due to their mysterious nature. No one could enter Askaria without the queen's explicit blessing.

Silas hesitated only briefly. "I don't know. The king has been missing for years."

"Fuck." Lucius hurled his empty glass at the wall near the fireplace, where it shattered into glittering fragments.

"You know, that's the fourth glass you've broken this week," Maxim observed dryly. "People might think you have anger management issues."

"Shut up, Max." Lucius's voice was sharp with frustration. "Silas, I need you to research everything available about daimones—find out if any others exist besides the king. Volt, locate the witch. If she's not here, I need to know where she went. And Max, don't you have responsibilities elsewhere?"

Maxim rolled his eyes before departing, taking the crystal decanter with him.

Before Volt vanished, he looked directly up at her hiding spot and smirked before fading away. Patience quickly checked her hand to ensure she remained invisible. She was still cloaked, yet somehow he'd seen through her concealment. She'd need to watch him carefully—he wasn't vampire, that much was certain. Vampires couldn't teleport like witches. They moved fast enough to seem like they'd vanished, but Volt had actually transported himself. He might have witch blood, but she couldn't be sure without closer examination.

Silas followed Maxim, leaving Lucius alone. He stood in brooding silence, running his hands over his face in exhaustion before turning to leave.

Patience thought she was safe until he stopped abruptly.

She raised her head slightly above the balustrade to see what had caught his attention. Following his gaze, she spotted the stack of books she'd left on the reading table.

Damn.

She didn't move, didn't even breathe.

Something clattered below. When she looked back, he was gone.

Shit.

I'm invisible. He can't see me. I'm invisible. He can't see me, she chanted silently while backing toward the nearest bookshelf.

"Witch. I can smell you," his voice taunted from directly below. *Fuck.*

Where could she hide? She looked left and crept slowly toward another bookshelf as his footsteps began climbing the spiral stairs.

She tried to control her breathing, but it was difficult, especially when he reached the upper landing.

Unless... did she want him to catch her? Unbidden thoughts of his lips claiming hers sent her heart racing.

Shit.

"I can hear you, witch," he taunted, moving closer to her position. "I can smell your arousal."

Heat flooded her cheeks as he whispered that last part, moving to stand mere inches away.

Before she could decide on a course of action, he positioned himself directly in front of her.

"Witch. Found you."

She could feel his warm breath against her skin as he gazed at her invisible form with predatory satisfaction.

"You can't hide from me."

He braced his arms against the bookshelf on either side of her, effectively caging her as her invisibility spell dissolved. He smirked with dark triumph.

How the hell—?

"You were somewhere you weren't supposed to be."

She resisted the urge to touch the hidden necklace. "I was only looking for a quiet place to read."

Anger clouded his features, transforming his face into something dangerous. "Not by invading Mae's room."

She looked away, shame burning in her chest. "I didn't know it was hers. I truly am sorry."

She needed to return the necklace immediately. She shouldn't have taken it—sometimes her curiosity caused more trouble than she could handle.

When she met his gaze again, fury still twisted his handsome features. He studied her in tense silence, the only sound her shallow breathing.

His silver-gray eyes held such profound pain. Without thinking, her hand rose to cradle his cheek. To her amazement, he leaned into her touch, closing his eyes and breathing her in as if she were oxygen itself.

In that moment, something extraordinary happened. His red aura faded to purple—a color she'd never witnessed in anyone before. Stranger still, the purple energy grew and reached toward her, surrounding them both and pulling her closer until she instinctively wrapped her arms around his neck.

When he opened his eyes, his anger had melted away, replaced by an emotion she dared not name.

Before rational thought could intervene, her lips pressed against his.

When he didn't respond immediately, she started to pull back. But before she could fully withdraw, his hands plunged into her hair, capturing her mouth with desperate hunger.

As passion consumed her, coherent thought scattered like leaves in a storm.

He trailed scorching kisses down her neck with urgent desperation. Fire spread through her veins, consuming her as she surrendered to his touch. She never wanted this burning sensation to end.

The straps of her dress gave way as his kisses found their way to her breasts. He cupped them reverently, slowly devouring each sensitive peak. When he paid particular attention to her nipples, pleasure shot straight to her throbbing core, drawing a helpless moan from her lips.

She couldn't remember the last time someone had touched her like this—if anyone ever had. It had been so long since she'd allowed herself such pleasure.

Still kissing her with consuming intensity, he gripped her thighs and lifted her. She wrapped her legs around his waist as his arm braced against the shelf for support.

Goddess, he tasted like heaven itself.

Her thighs clutched his hips as his hands slipped beneath her dress to squeeze her flesh. Her panties tore and fell away before his fingers roamed to the apex of her thighs.

If he touched her there, she was going to climax immediately and embarrassingly hard.

She should be mortified, but she didn't care. She never wanted him to stop.

When he reached between her legs, she moaned as he discovered her wetness.

"You're soaked," he murmured against her neck, stroking her heated flesh with maddening skill.

She trembled in anticipation as he adjusted his grip to support her weight with one arm while his fingers slipped between her folds to find her most sensitive spot. Two fingers entered her as his thumb slowly circled her clit, finding exactly the right pressure and rhythm.

Pleasure shot through her as his fingers discovered that perfect spot inside her, driving her toward the edge of sanity.

"I need you to come for me," he whispered against her ear, pressing a kiss to her racing pulse. His fangs scraped along the delicate curve of her neck.

The thought of him sinking those fangs into her flesh sent her over the precipice.

Lucius covered her mouth with his, swallowing her cries as she surrendered completely to the overwhelming pleasure.

When the waves finally subsided, he withdrew his fingers.

"Fuck. I love watching you come," he growled against her lips. "Let me taste you."

His words surprised and thrilled her. She still trembled from her climax, but the thought of his mouth on her most intimate flesh ignited fresh desire.

She couldn't trust her voice, so she nodded her consent. He captured her lips in another searing kiss before dropping to his knees, pressing a soft kiss against her core that reawakened her hunger.

Before his mouth could descend further, a voice called out from below.

"Lucius? Are you still here?"

They both froze like deer in headlights.

"Lucius?"

It was Maxim. They could hear him moving around the lower level before the library door finally closed.

They waited in tense silence to ensure he'd truly departed. Patience slowly released her held breath as she pulled up her dress. Lucius gazed up at her from his position on his knees—he looked magnificent kneeling before her like a supplicant at an altar.

His purple aura gradually faded back to dark red as he rose and leaned against the bookshelf, clearly struggling to regain his composure.

"What are you doing to me?" He ran his hands down his face in confusion and frustration.

"I don't know," she admitted, retying the straps of her dress with unsteady fingers. "I don't understand this any more than you do."

After composing himself, he turned to face her fully. "This can't happen again. I don't know what spell you've cast, but I need you to undo it."

He reached out to touch her cheek with surprising gentleness, then leaned in to brush his lips against hers in a kiss so tender it nearly broke her heart.

Then he turned and walked down the stairs, leaving her alone with her chaotic emotions.

"I wish it were a spell," she called after him, turning her back as he exited the library. "At least then I could undo it."

But her words echoed in the empty space—he was already gone.

CHAPTER SEVEN

PATIENCE

After pulling herself together and smoothing down her disheveled dress, Patience returned to check on Ian and Michael. They remained peacefully unconscious on the four-poster bed, their breathing steady and synchronized. She lifted Michael's wrist to examine the mystical symbol—the quarter section had almost completely faded.

The day was nearly gone. They'd wasted precious hours on research an d... other activities, but Michael was still deep in his transformation. They weren't ready to sever the soul-bond yet. Only three more days remained.

There was no time to dwell on what had happened in the library, but she couldn't dismiss his purple aura from her mind. She'd never known auras could behave that way—transforming colors, expanding outward, pulling her in like a mystical tether.

Everyone possessed an aura, but they never changed colors completely. They might brighten or darken with emotion, but never shift to an entirely different hue, let alone reach out with apparent sentience. She wondered if GreyJoy might have answers, though since only witches could perceive auras, his knowledge might be limited.

Sighing, she moved to the tall window to gaze out at the star-filled night sky. Something profound was happening between them that neither was ready to acknowledge, but part of her—a significant part—hoped that someday they would be brave enough to accept it.

Walking to the wall near the bed, she placed her palm against the cool stone. When the surface shimmered and became permeable, she stepped through and back into the library.

She found Maxim flipping through the books Lucius had abandoned on the reading table, his blonde hair catching the firelight as he studied the ancient texts.

Moving as quietly as possible, she tried to retrieve the books she'd left earlier, but he lifted his head before she could take a single step.

"I'm sorry," she said softly. "I didn't mean to disturb you. Just collecting the books I brought."

"So it's true—you can bypass the ward?"

"Apparently. I know it's... unusual." But if he didn't trust her, how was she able to enter so easily? The ward was specifically designed to admit only those Lucius trusted completely.

"That son of a bitch was right," Maxim said with an amused smile. "You were here the entire time during our meeting."

"Yeah, I overheard the whole conversation." She changed her mind about leaving and settled into a chair at the table. "I see he has information gatherers."

"You were actually in here? The whole time? And they're not spies—more like intelligence collectors," he said, clearly astounded.

She rolled her eyes. "Same difference. Out of curiosity, who created this ward?" She gestured toward the illuminated words above the entrance.

"Lucius designed it himself."

"It might have a fundamental flaw."

Maxim laughed heartily. "You don't say."

She smiled back, remembering the book she'd dropped on the upper level during their passionate encounter. Climbing the spiral stairs, she found it on the floor beside her torn underwear. Glancing down to ensure Maxim remained absorbed in his reading, she waved her hand to make the evidence disappear, then searched for any other incriminating remnants.

"Looking for something specific?"

She turned to find Maxim leaning against a bookshelf, watching her with knowing eyes. His aura glowed bright gray with amusement. She held up the recovered book as explanation.

He smiled warmly. "Ah, I see you discovered Mae's collection."

"Oh." Patience didn't elaborate, but Lucius's wife had possessed excellent taste in literature. "How did you end up befriending such a colossal idiot?"

Maxim grinned, understanding she meant Lucius. "We've been friends since before my turning. He's not as terrible as you think."

"Well, he's certainly fooled you, because I'm fairly certain he's a complete ass."

Maxim chuckled and shook his head as they descended to the main floor together.

"It's true. He's been nothing but rude since we met. Well, except when he kisses me," she said with studied nonchalance.

"Lucius kissed you?" He looked genuinely shocked by this revelation.

"Several times," she mumbled. They had been spectacular kisses, though. She could still feel his lips burning against hers. "I'm sure they meant nothing, so it doesn't matter."

"It's rather curious that someone who claims to despise you has kissed you multiple times. Do you honestly believe it was meaningless? Have you considered why he's so adamant about maintaining distance from you?" He gestured for her to sit in one of the leather chairs facing the fireplace.

He made a valid point, but there was no sense entertaining impossible scenarios. "Well, I am devastatingly beautiful. It's possible he's simply attracted to my gorgeous body." Sarcasm dripped from every word.

Maxim laughed appreciatively.

"Honestly," Patience continued, settling into the comfortable chair, "I don't understand it myself. Maybe you could enlighten me. I know he's the Ragana Žudikas, and he hates witches because one murdered his wife. Didn't he kill that witch? And wasn't this centuries ago? He can't possibly think we're all evil, right?"

Maxim considered his words carefully before speaking. "Lucius will murder me for sharing this, but I believe you deserve the truth. A witch named Arabella did kill his wife centuries ago. However, what most don't know is that Mae was... pregnant. We've kept this from the historical records because the loss devastated him. He rarely speaks of it now."

Surprise and horror washed over her face. She'd known her kind had killed his wife, but his unborn child as well? Guilt crashed over her like a tidal wave. The necklace hidden against her skin suddenly felt like a brand of shame.

His rage made perfect sense now. If vampires had slaughtered her family, no realm would be safe from her vengeance. The difference was, her reign of terror would have ended once justice was served—his hadn't.

"Why did he continue killing witches even after Arabella's death?"

Maxim sat in contemplative silence before responding. "Because he became consumed by power and blood rage. I wish there were a more noble explanation, but there isn't."

"And the witches simply allowed him to live?" This question had been burning in her mind since learning his identity.

"Yes and no. I pleaded for his life and accepted his punishment instead."

"What? He let you take his punishment? What kind of—"

"No, he never knew. It took Michael and me working together to bring him back from the brink. He wouldn't have survived the penalty in his condition. His mind had shattered from grief and rage—it required time and careful healing to piece him back together. I intervened when the witches finally decided to act."

That vampire had better understand how fortunate he was to have a friend like Maxim. "What did they do to you?"

"Three hundred lashes and the Blessing of Ashes."

"What?" The so-called blessing was actually a curse—he could never father children or create vampire offspring. He could never have a true blood family. "I'm so sorry."

"He would have done the same for me."

"Would he really?"

"Yes. For all his flaws, he's fiercely loyal and a good friend, despite your current impression. If he were still the Ragana Žudikas, you'd be chained in the dungeons right now instead of freely roaming his home."

He knew his friend better than anyone. Who was she to argue, having known Lucius for less than twenty-four hours?

"I suppose I have no choice but to believe you, given our circumstances."

"He might eventually grow on you," Maxim suggested with a slight smile.

"Possibly. He makes it difficult to like him, even though I barely know him. But I must admit there's a connection between us. I feel it every time we kiss. Yet what he did to my people... makes it complicated. Even setting aside his generally unpleasant demeanor."

Patience stood and walked to the fireplace, losing herself in the hypnotic dance of flames. She pushed thoughts of their library encounter from her mind.

"If he hadn't killed your kind, would you like him?" Maxim pressed gently.

"Maybe. There's potential there." She needed to change the subject—she wasn't ready to explore deeper possibilities that might never materialize.

She couldn't believe she was having this conversation at all, but Maxim was the only person in this castle who didn't seem to hate her.

A glint on his left hand caught her attention. A wedding band. "You're married?"

"I am." He looked down at the ring and touched it tenderly. Sadness crept across his handsome features.

"What's her name?" Patience moved to a nearby bookshelf, running her fingers along the leather spines until one caught her interest.

"Estelle."

"If you don't mind me asking, where is she?" She pulled the book from the shelf and flipped through its pages.

"I don't know."

Patience stopped her browsing and stared at him. "What?"

"One day she simply vanished without explanation and never returned. I believe she was frightened of Lucius during his darkest period, but it's been over a century. Nearly two, actually."

"I'm so sorry, Maxim." She replaced the book and turned to see sadness wash over his face before he masked it with practiced composure.

Her hand had landed on another volume—*Regna Universi* (The Realms of the Universe), written in Latin. She returned it to its place. "Any idea where she went?"

"I searched for her extensively, but eventually... I gave up. I hope she's safe and happy somewhere."

She could only imagine the pain of having someone you love simply disappear. The lingering sadness in his expression revealed how deeply he still loved and missed her. Perhaps she could help.

"This might sound presumptuous, but have you ever enlisted a witch's assistance in your search?"

He looked taken aback, as if the possibility had never occurred to him.

"I gather from your expression that's a no." She probably shouldn't make this offer—it could complicate everything. "If you have something that belonged to her, I could try to trace her essence or teach you a simple locator spell."

She could see his mind working, various emotions playing across his features, including uncertainty and hope.

"You don't need to answer now. Just consider it."

She turned toward the bay windows, leaving him to contemplate her offer, when that particular idiot strode into the library.

"Witch, have you discovered anything useful?" Lucius's voice was ice-cold from the doorway.

"I could ask you the same question," she countered.

"She came to retrieve her books. I engaged her in conversation," Maxim said, rising to her defense.

"Leave. Now."

"Why?" Patience asked, genuinely curious why a library would be forbidden to her. His prohibition only increased her interest. "Obviously your ward has flaws."

"She has a valid point," Maxim observed.

Lucius ignored her question entirely. "Leave immediately."

"This is the ideal place for research. It is a library, after all."

His shoulders tensed and his jaw tightened. He was furious.

Patience collected the books she'd left on the table, noting how his aura darkened to an even deeper red. She had yet to see it lighten. "Fine. I only came to collect my books. I'll respect your home—for Maxim's sake."

Maxim smirked with satisfaction. Lucius snarled in response. Patience smiled sweetly, then vanished.

Lucius

Lucius watched her disappear, and immediately an unbidden image flashed through his mind—her lying naked in his bed, trailing her lips down his body with deliberate, torturous slowness. Heat surged through him before the vision scattered.

"Interesting," Maxim observed, studying him with obvious curiosity.

"You continue engaging with her despite my warnings." The statement came out as an accusation, accompanied by a withering glare.

Maxim laughed and settled back into his chair.

"She's dangerous, Max. You must stay away from her." Lucius sat heavily beside his friend.

"I think she's far more dangerous to you than she'll ever be to me." A knowing smirk played across Maxim's features. "You kissed her? Multiple times?"

Lucius remained silent. He was still trying to comprehend what had possessed him in the library. He wanted to blame pure lust, but this was something far more complex. It had overtaken him, seized control, yet remained fundamentally *him*. Perhaps he was losing his sanity.

He couldn't explain it to himself—how could he possibly explain it to Maxim? It might have been a spell, except his protective stone hadn't burned in warning, and she'd seemed equally affected.

"Nothing to say? I suppose you don't hate her as much as you pretend."

Lucius stood and began pacing the length of the room.

"The kiss—"

"Kisses," Maxim corrected with emphasis.

"Were never intended to happen." He stalked to the concealed bar and poured himself three generous fingers of scotch, downing it in one burning gulp. "They were completely beyond my control."

"Somehow I doubt that. It's been quite a while since I've seen you drink this heavily. I think she's getting under your skin," Maxim mused, more to himself than to Lucius.

"She's fortunate to still be breathing." He slammed the glass down with enough force to crack it. "Once Ian awakens, I have other plans for her."

"And what plans might those be?"

"I don't think I should discuss such matters with a Council member."

Maxim's expression darkened. "Tell me. Now."

Lucius poured another drink before returning to his seat. "At the club, she invaded my mind and found the memory of Mae's death."

"What? How is that possible? Didn't your stone protect you?"

"I don't know," he said, sipping his scotch more slowly this time. The desonite stone was supposed to shield him from witch magic, yet it seemed to fail him consistently where she was concerned. She shouldn't have been able to breach any of his barriers—mental, magical, or emotional—yet she'd slipped past all of them with apparent ease.

"If that's true, you have much to consider. She makes you feel more than you have in centuries—whether it's lust, hatred, or something deeper. I know you're not ready to examine these emotions, but you need to before you do something irreversible."

Maxim stood and left Lucius alone with his turbulent thoughts.

He stared into the fire long after Maxim's departure, lost in contemplation. He could admit one truth: the witch made him *feel*. It had been so long since powerful emotions had overwhelmed him like this. After their encounter in the library, he was completely uncertain of himself around her.

He hungered for her with an intensity that both thrilled and terrified him, cursing the very thought of her even as he yearned to possess every inch of her.

Mae and their child were gone. The rage and pain had dulled to a manageable ache. Moving forward was possible, but beginning a relationship with a witch would betray their memory and everything he'd stood for these past centuries.

He prayed for the stone around his neck to burn, revealing whatever spell she'd cast over him. Instead, it remained cold against his skin, confirming his worst fear.

This attraction was genuine. It was his own conflicted feelings that complicated everything.

He finished his drink and collected the books from the table, skimming through them methodically, searching for any reference to soul gem locations.

After an hour of reading, he finally discovered a promising lead, but further research revealed that particular gem had been destroyed half a century ago.

Frustrated, he left the library to find the witch and see if she'd made any progress. The day was ending soon, and he desperately wanted a concrete location.

He entered Ian's room, unsurprised to find her reading in the chair by the window. She was completely absorbed in her book, occasionally biting her lower lip as she turned pages—a gesture that made his body respond with unwelcome intensity, especially knowing she wore nothing beneath that dress after their library encounter.

The urge to brush the curl that had fallen across her face behind her ear was almost overwhelming, just to see her features more clearly.

Control. He had to regain his control.

"I assume you're here to check on me?" She didn't look up from her reading. "I've decided you're right. This is your home, and I should respect it. I'll remain in this room until we find the gem. I only ask for food when I'm hungry. Deal?"

"Don't you have spells to conjure sustenance?"

Patience rolled her eyes, clearly exasperated. "For the last time, I don't *need* spells." Setting her book in her lap, she held out her hand, and an apple materialized in her palm. She offered it to him, but it crumbled to dust before he could reach for it.

"I can conjure food, but it never properly nourishes me."

"Fine." Lucius couldn't believe she was agreeing to confine herself to this room. Suspicion immediately flared. "What changed your mind?"

"If I were in your position, I wouldn't want a vampire roaming my home, invading my privacy, rifling through my possessions. I'll behave myself. Do we have an agreement?"

So the witch possessed some wisdom after all. He'd see if she could be trusted to keep her word. "Very well. It's a deal."

She extended her hand for him to shake. He stared at it for a moment before clasping it, intending a brief, formal contact. Instead, he found himself stroking his thumb across her silky brown skin, mesmerized by its softness.

"May I have my hand back now?"

He hadn't realized he was still holding it, savoring the contact and craving more. Instead of releasing her, he pulled her up from the chair, forcing her to drop her book as he wrapped her in his arms. The way this felt so natural, so familiar, was the most terrifying aspect—as if he'd held her like this countless times before.

Her heart raced as she moistened her lips with her tongue. Desire flared in her dark eyes as her lips parted slightly, releasing a soft moan that went straight to his groin.

He growled low in his throat before capturing her mouth with his.

Fuck. He shouldn't be kissing her, but she tasted so incredibly good he couldn't pull away.

He lifted her effortlessly, and she wrapped her legs around his waist in one fluid motion. His feet carried them until her back met the wall. He continued devouring her mouth until her hands pressed against his chest.

"We have to stop. We can't... we don't have time."

The witch was absolutely right. They didn't have time to spare, but he couldn't stop himself from trailing burning kisses down the elegant column of her neck. It would be so easy to lift her dress and claim her completely.

"Stop," she said, finally using enough force to push him back.

Reality crashed over him like ice water. He let her feet touch the floor slowly and stepped back. She looked at him with an unreadable expression as she smoothed her rumpled dress.

"If we continue like this, we'll never find the soul gem before time runs out," she said, struggling to control her breathing. "I hate that you stand there looking completely unaffected."

"I wish that were true," he muttered, his voice rough with suppressed desire.

She studied his face intently, as if searching for cracks in his composure.

"I came here because my research yielded nothing useful. I hoped you might have found something by now."

"Nothing yet. I thought I'd discovered a promising lead—a gem owned by a nymph named Sarilla—but reading further, I learned she cast it into the middle of the Heaving Deep. I doubt we want to navigate those treacherous waters unless absolutely necessary."

"Agreed. Those currents have claimed more ships than storms." Anything else?" he asked, maintaining careful distance even though he yearned to fall to his knees and bury his face beneath her skirts.

His hand touched the desonite stone at his throat—still cold. *Damn.*

"No," she said, though a strange expression crossed her features.

"You're not withholding information, are you?" He moved closer, drawn by an invisible force. "Because I've been remarkably patient so far, though that could change rapidly if I discover you're lying to me."

Her pulse quickened visibly. "I wouldn't give you that satisfaction."

Her tongue darted out to moisten her lips again, tempting him beyond reason to kiss her once more.

He could not touch her again, no matter how desperately he wanted to. He would not allow it to happen.

"Inform me the moment you find anything useful, witch. We've wasted enough time already," he said before forcing himself to leave the room, abandoning her to her obvious frustration.

But as he walked away, he couldn't shake the feeling that she was indeed hiding something important.

CHAPTER EIGHT

PATIENCE

Patience took a deep, much-needed breath as the door closed behind Lucius, leaving her alone with her chaotic thoughts. *What the hell was that?*

His aura had shifted to that impossible purple again just before he'd pulled her against him with desperate intensity. One moment he was devouring her mouth like a man starved, the next he was pushing her away as if she'd burned him. The hot-and-cold treatment was confusing as hell and wreaking absolute havoc on her already frayed emotions.

She could be home right now, safe in her cramped Boston apartment, curled up in her own bed instead of dealing with this supernatural soap opera. But first, she desperately needed a shower and clean clothes. The events of the past day had left her feeling grimy and emotionally drained.

Moving to the antique dresser, she began methodically opening drawers in search of suitable clothing. In the bottom drawer, she discovered a pair of black jeans and men's briefs that were close enough to her size to work with some magical adjustment. The adjoining walk-in closet yielded a soft gray knitted sweater that would serve her purposes perfectly.

She laid the borrowed garments out on the Persian rug beside the four-poster bed. Conjuring clothing from nothing required too much magical energy—energy she needed to conserve for more important tasks—but resizing and reshaping existing items was relatively simple magic.

Placing her palm against the denim, she watched the jeans shrink to accommodate her smaller frame. With a flick of her wrist, she transformed the masculine briefs into comfortable panties, then enlarged the sweater to provide adequate coverage for her braless situation. The familiar tingle of magic flowing through her fingertips was oddly comforting after the emotional turbulence of the evening.

When the clothing modifications were complete, she headed for the en-suite bathroom and turned the shower to near-scalding temperature. Stepping under the punishing spray, she let the hot water cascade over her body, washing away not just the physical grime but the lingering confusion and frustration of her encounters with Lucius.

This was the cleansing ritual she desperately needed—a moment of solitude to center herself before facing whatever came next.

Fresh from the shower and wrapped in a plush towel, she felt ready to take on the world again. But as she moved toward the mirror to comb through her damp hair, the necklace caught her eye, glimmering against her skin like captured starlight.

Mae's necklace. Guilt twisted in her stomach as she reached behind her neck, attempting once again to unfasten the ancient clasp. As before, it refused to budge, as if it had fused with her very flesh.

Frustrated, she channeled a small jolt of magic into the pendant, hoping to disrupt whatever enchantment kept it sealed. Instead of releasing, the magical energy bounced off the necklace like light off a mirror, ricocheting around the room in a brilliant arc before striking her squarely in the rear.

"Ow!" she yelped, rubbing her left buttock where the redirected magic had made contact. The sensation was like being snapped with a rubber band made of lightning.

She tried again with an even smaller magical pulse, but the result was identical—the energy bounced harmlessly off the necklace before being absorbed into the stone wall with a faint shimmer.

Interesting. Perhaps the necklace was designed to protect its wearer against magical attacks. That would explain the deflection, though it still didn't clarify why she couldn't remove it through normal means. The Vow of Protection she'd sensed earlier might be more comprehensive than she'd initially understood.

For now, the mystery would have to wait. Thankfully, her concealment spell remained intact—the necklace was still invisible to everyone but herself. She wasn't sure what she'd do if the vampire discovered her theft of his wife's most precious possession. The consequences would likely be swift and unpleasant.

Sighing, she glanced over at Michael and Ian, still unconscious on the bed. Their breathing remained steady and synchronized, the soul-bond holding strong. Michael's transformation was progressing exactly as it should, but time was running out faster than she'd hoped.

Later, she would deal with the consequences of her impulsive jewelry acquisition. Right now, she needed to focus entirely on finding that soul gem.

After dressing in her magically altered clothes, she settled into the uncomfortable chair by the window and picked up one of the books from GreyJoy's collection. This particular tome was written in ancient Epati—her favorite of the old languages, though Orese and Eusian tied for second place.

She'd often wondered how she could read so many dead languages fluently, especially considering her complete lack of memories from before

Kilborn Academy. It was just another mystery in the ever-growing collection of questions about her identity and origins.

Some people romanticized memory loss as a chance for a fresh start, and in some ways it was. But her particular fresh start had come with the unwelcome baggage of nightmares and those terrifying red eyes that haunted her every time she closed her eyes to sleep. She hated those visions more than anything—the fear, the sense of running from something unspeakable, the feeling that she'd lost something infinitely precious.

More than anything else, she wanted to understand her past and discover where she truly came from. Most importantly, had she left anyone behind who might still be searching for her?

It was a question that had plagued her with increasing frequency lately. The more attempts they made to breach her memory barriers, the more convinced she became that someone had deliberately locked those memories away. An even more terrifying possibility was that she had done it to herself—that her past contained pain too devastating for her psyche to handle.

"Shit." A sudden memory struck her like lightning. The man from the club—the one who'd approached her before all hell broke loose. She was supposed to find him. He'd claimed to know exactly who she was, had called her by a name that wasn't Patience.

What had he called her? She closed her eyes, reaching for the fragmented memory.

"Dessa." The name emerged from her lips like a prayer, and a profound sense of familiarity washed over her. Was this her real name? The identity she'd carried before waking up on Kilborn's doorstep?

The name Patience had been given to her by the academy administrators—a placeholder to help give her a sense of identity during those first terrifying days of consciousness without memory. But hearing this other name, *Dessa*, filled her heart with something she'd almost forgotten how to feel: hope.

She had to discover who that man was and how he knew her true identity. Unfortunately, the only person who might have answers was the insufferable vampire. The prospect of asking Lucius for help was about as appealing as voluntarily entering a dragon's lair, but he might be the only thing standing between her and the truth about her past.

Once she finished reading the remaining books, she would swallow her pride and question him. Finding the soul gem's location was still their primary objective—the portal conjuration would be simple enough once they had coordinates. The challenging part would be negotiating with or stealing from whoever currently possessed it.

Buckling down and forcing herself to concentrate, she dove into the ancient text, hoping that somewhere in these pages lay the key to a better future for both herself and Michael.

Lucius

This unnatural attraction was going to be the death of him—literally and figuratively.

The temptation to lock her in the dungeons and throw away the key grew stronger with each passing hour. Another witch could potentially locate the soul gem, but that would require approaching the Witches' Council for permission and assistance. His hunting days still cast a long shadow over supernatural politics, and asking Maxim to return to face those who had punished him so severely was absolutely unthinkable.

Every time he closed his eyes, visions of her beckoned him—images of wrapping her in his arms, holding and kissing her, never letting her go. The intensity of these fantasies was unlike anything he'd experienced, even during his mortal years. *What the hell was happening to him?*

He touched the desonite stone at his throat for the hundredth time that evening. Still cool to the touch, offering no explanation for his unprecedented behavior.

Alecia. He needed to contact her immediately.

She was the only person who could provide answers, the only witch he trusted even partially—and that trust existed solely because she was half-vampire. Alecia despised her witch heritage with a passion that rivaled his own.

As soon as she'd grown powerful enough, she'd systematically eliminated her warlock father and then magically imprisoned her witch mother in an endless sleep to live out her remaining years in dreams. Alecia was indeed a deadly creature, but one whose motivations he understood completely.

Their paths had crossed frequently during his hunting days. They'd even collaborated on eliminating several particularly dangerous covens, their combined skills making them nearly unstoppable. He'd also supported her bid for a seat on the Council. The Drath—half-vampires who renounced their witch ancestry—were numerous and deserved representation, and Alecia served as their fierce advocate.

She'd established an orphanage specifically for Drath children, helping those with magical abilities learn control while creating a formidable clan of her own. He was nearly proud of her accomplishments over the past few centuries, though he'd never admit it aloud. Alecia was determined to prove her independence from everyone, including old allies.

She was now one of the most powerful supernatural beings in existence and one hell of an ally to have. She could determine if his protective stone was malfunctioning and whether the witch had somehow bespelled him despite his defenses.

Volt materialized in his study just as Lucius reached for his phone, appearing from shadow with his characteristic silence.

"You're late," Lucius snapped, his frustration evident. "I've already located her."

"I'm aware. I decided you were perfectly capable of handling the situation yourself."

Fuck. Volt must have witnessed their passionate encounter in the library. He trusted his Khedian spy implicitly, but he hated that anyone now possessed this compromising information. As a member of an ancient shadow-walking race, Volt's ability to move undetected combined with his photographic memory made him invaluable for intelligence gathering.

A witch had kept him caged in her attic for years like a exotic pet until Lucius had discovered and freed him during one of his raids. The grateful Khedian had sworn a life debt, vowing to repay his liberation. He'd fulfilled that obligation tenfold years ago, yet he remained, continuing to serve without payment or complaint.

"You must have learned something significant, or you wouldn't be standing here."

"Silas spoke truthfully. She possesses no memories of her past, and no coven has successfully claimed her. She's been desperately searching for methods to unlock her lost memories."

"Silas wouldn't lie to me," Lucius retorted. "Why waste time verifying his report?"

"I don't trust him completely. I sense he's withholding crucial information."

Lucius shared that intuition. He trusted Silas to a certain extent—the warrior's loyalty was unquestionable—but the male definitely harbored secrets he hadn't yet revealed. The only reason he hadn't ordered Volt to investigate Silas's background was that unwavering loyalty. Some secrets were worth preserving if they didn't threaten his interests.

"Silas is my concern to manage. Is there anything else?"

"Her power."

"What about it?"

"Surely you can sense the magnitude of what dwells within her."

Of course he could sense it—the magical energy radiated from her like heat from a forge. What troubled him was that she'd used virtually none of this immense power against him, even when he'd threatened her life.

"It could be a deception—making her appear defenseless when she's actually incredibly dangerous."

"My thoughts were identical until I heard about the Milchan Coven incident."

"The ones cursed by their leader to experience endless suicide cycles?" Lucius's interest sharpened. "What about them?"

"The witch freed them. All of them."

"What? How is that possible?" It was supposedly an unbreakable curse, woven with blood magic and sustained by the dying leader's hatred. The spell should have been impossible to reverse. "She couldn't be that powerful... could she?"

"Everyone in supernatural circles has been trying to determine her methods. No one in the freed coven will discuss specifics—they're too grateful to her. They attempted to make her their leader in gratitude. She refused."

Fascinating. A witch with no memories who could shatter supposedly unbreakable curses. Who was she really, and where in all the realms had she originated?

"Investigate further. Go to Umber." He opened his desk's bottom drawer and retrieved an Astral Coin from its velvet-lined case. The ancient currency gleamed with otherworldly light. "Give him this and discover what he knows about the witch."

Volt nodded, accepting the precious coin before melting back into shadow and disappearing completely.

Umber was an ancient Eviathan Troll whose existence predated human civilization. Legend claimed he'd witnessed the birth of magic itself. His network of Makas—small, goblin-like informants—kept their ears pressed to every corner of the supernatural world, gathering intelligence for their master. If a being possessed the right currency, Umber would divulge certain secrets in response to carefully worded questions.

He was the same source who'd provided the location of Arabella, his wife's killer, all those centuries ago. The Astral coin would purchase approximately three questions from the ancient creature. Hopefully, Volt would return with answers about the mysterious witch currently disrupting his carefully ordered existence.

Sighing heavily, he picked up his phone and dialed Alecia's number.

"To what do I owe such an unexpected call?" she answered, suspicion evident in her cultured voice.

This conversation wouldn't be pleasant, but it was necessary.

"I need you to return to Orendale tonight."

"And I would do that because—?"

"I need to determine if a witch has bespelled me," he admitted, hating every word.

Her melodious laughter echoed through the line. "There were rumors about your brother being under enchantment, but not you. Has the famous Witch Hunter finally been bested by his prey?" she teased mercilessly.

"Alecia, my brother has been soul-bonded to a daimones, and the witch currently residing in my home is helping locate the soul gem needed to separate them. I need to know if she's placed some spell on me, since my protective stone hasn't reacted. She's... extraordinarily powerful."

Silence stretched across the connection. Finally, she sighed with resignation.

"Very well. I'm en route, but you owe me significantly for this favor."

The line went dead before he could express gratitude.

Alecia would extract a high price for this assistance—she'd been coveting his sword, Luzia, for decades. Surprisingly, she hadn't demanded it immediately, which meant she was planning something elaborate. She would arrive with questions, and he needed to prepare himself to answer them truthfully.

His thoughts inevitably drifted back to the witch upstairs.

In the past, situations like this had been simpler and more efficient. He would have extracted answers through fear and pain, methods that had served him well for centuries. After Arabella murdered his wife and un-born child, he'd killed every witch within his considerable reach—hunting them relentlessly, torturing them for information, slaughtering them to make them suffer as he had suffered. Mercy had been a foreign concept.

He'd killed until it became as natural as breathing again, for destroying witches was literally in his blood.

His lineage descended directly from Lilith, the first vampire and creator of their entire race. His great-grandfather Dracul had shared stories of walking beside her, drinking from her power until the Goddess of the witches had imprisoned her in the demon realm of Evictus and cursed all vampires to eternal darkness. To compound their suffering, she'd created witches specifically to hunt and destroy vampires.

His grandfather Xavier had captured Thalia, one of the first and most powerful witches, forcing her to create the twelve rose desonite stones that granted vampires the ability to wield witch magic. Those artifacts had leveled the supernatural playing field, ensuring vampires no longer had to hide in fear.

Lucius had planned to follow his grandfather's legacy in leading the vampire clans until Mae had changed everything. His focus had shifted to protecting his small family, and he'd willingly set aside his sword to embrace domestic tranquility. But they'd stolen that happiness from him—ripped away the only peace he'd ever known.

Memories and emotions still flowed through his mind like poison, making him crave those simpler, more violent days when problems had clear solutions.

The witch would never have survived leaving his club back then.

He'd brought her here specifically for Maxim to serve as his conscience, to prevent him from simply killing her outright. Now everything had changed in ways he couldn't fully comprehend.

The witch frustrated him beyond measure, but strangely, the thought of ending her life hadn't seriously crossed his mind—which was completely unlike him. Her inexplicable allure grew stronger with each encounter, drawing him to her despite every rational instinct screaming warnings.

This had to be magical manipulation. Whether the spell was her conscious creation or some natural phenomenon remained to be determined. If she'd deliberately enchanted him, the consequences would be devastating for her—she would learn exactly why they'd called him the Ragana Žudikas. But if these feelings were genuine...

He honestly didn't know what that would mean for either of them.

A sudden, powerful urge to see her struck him like a physical blow. Deliberately ignoring the compulsion, he left his study to seek out Maxim instead. Perhaps his oldest friend could provide some clarity in this increasingly complicated situation.

But even as he walked away, part of him remained acutely aware of her presence somewhere above, like a magnetic pull he couldn't quite resist.

CHAPTER NINE

LUCIUS

In pure frustration, Lucius slammed his fist against the stone wall down the hallway from Ian's bedroom. The ancient masonry absorbed the blow without so much as a tremor, but his knuckles protested the violent contact.

On his way to find Maxim, thoughts of her crept into his mind again like smoke through cracks, drawing his feet inexorably back toward her. He found himself striding toward Ian's bedroom until sheer force of will made him stop mid-step.

He turned away from the hallway and went to locate Maxim instead.

A strong drink—or several—was exactly what he needed.

Lucius discovered him in his private study, absorbed in reading notes from the Council meeting he'd attended three nights prior. Maxim's blonde hair caught the lamplight as he frowned over the documents, occasionally making annotations in his precise handwriting.

"Have you found anything useful yet?" Maxim asked without glancing up from his papers.

"Unfortunately, not yet—except possibly one lead in the Heaving Deep. The witch has several more books to examine. Hopefully we'll discover something before dawn." Lucius settled into the comfortable chair facing Maxim's mahogany desk. "Anything noteworthy at the meeting?"

"Nothing particularly exciting, unless you count Lady Alecia staring daggers at Lord Christian throughout the entire proceedings. Unfortunately, there was no bloodshed," Maxim said with dry amusement.

"I assume she learned about him discarding her proposal on female vampire rights?"

"Oh, she found out, all right. Rumor has it she attempted to castrate him in his sleep, but you know I don't indulge in gossip." Maxim's tone suggested he absolutely did indulge, frequently.

Lucius laughed despite himself. He couldn't fathom how those two had remained married for centuries. Their relationship defied all logic.

"Speaking of which, where have you been?" Maxim asked, finally looking up from his notes. "I was searching for you earlier."

"Volt visited. I sent him to consult with Umber."

Maxim's eyebrows shot up as he leaned back in his leather chair. "You sent him to Umber? You actually used an Astral coin for that?"

"I need more comprehensive information about the witch."

Maxim rolled his eyes expressively. "Normal people have conversations instead of consulting thousand-year-old trolls."

"She liberated the Milchan Coven."

"She what?" Maxim's voice sharpened with surprise. "That's impossible. Those witches have been imprisoned for over two centuries."

"Now you understand why I used an Astral coin. She's an enigma, and I despise mysteries—especially when they're wandering freely through my home." Lucius stood and moved to his prized sixteenth-century Ufreti globe bar, pouring himself a generous measure of whiskey. The familiar burn provided momentary comfort.

"Fascinating. I still maintain that a direct conversation with the witch would prove more productive."

"Unless she's a manipulative liar," he said, taking another deliberate sip.

"Care to elaborate on that accusation?"

Lucius remained silent, unwilling to voice his suspicions. He'd share his concerns once Alecia confirmed what was happening to him—until then, Maxim could speculate all he wanted.

"Clearly there are matters you're not prepared to discuss. As always, when you're ready to address those bottled-up emotions, I'm available." Maxim returned his attention to his notes, effectively dismissing him.

Lucius watched as Maxim continued reviewing his Council documentation, remembering their long history together.

He'd known Maxim for approximately five hundred fifty-eight years now—nearly his entire vampiric existence. The year had been 1464, he believed, when that fool had tried to stake claim to the Eviathan realm. Lucius had been acquainted with Maxim for several years before turning him, and the man had possessed such remarkable vitality then—eager to explore unknown territories until the day he died.

Lucius vividly remembered their first encounter.

Centuries before meeting Mae, he'd been returning to his secluded cabin for a few months of solitude. Taking a shortcut through dense woods to clear his troubled mind, he'd stumbled upon Maxim engaged in passionate congress with a young woman against an oak tree.

He wouldn't have interfered until she produced a knife and pressed it to Maxim's throat while he was still moving within her. That had given Lucius pause.

He'd watched, fascinated, as the woman struggled between maintaining the blade's pressure and moaning with pleasure as Maxim brought her to climax. Afterward, he'd calmly withdrawn a leather pouch of coins from his pocket and tossed it at her feet, completely unfazed by the weapon at his neck.

Lucius had laughed silently at the poetic justice—it served her right for attempting highway robbery mid-coitus. He'd planned to continue his walk when the cold barrel of a shotgun was pressed against his spine. The only mortal who'd ever caught him off guard.

Maxim had assumed Lucius was complicit in the robbery until realizing he was vampire—unsurprising, given Ian's recent habit of terrorizing the local villages. His brother would kidnap, bite, and deflower the villagers' sons and daughters in the middle of the night, then send them home naked at dawn. Ian claimed it kept the populace "on their toes," but for Lucius, it was merely a nuisance when seeking peace.

Maxim had shot him in the shoulder, and Lucius had nearly killed him from pure instinctual reaction. Not wanting another death burdening his conscience, he'd given Maxim his blood to heal the wound. That should have been the end of their interaction—except Maxim had the audacity to follow him home, ensuring he hadn't been turned vampire. The man was either incredibly brave or remarkably stupid.

Lucius could have easily lost him if he'd chosen to. But he'd understood his own loneliness at that point in his existence. He hadn't yet found his mate, his father pressured him to join the Council despite his reluctance, and he genuinely needed companionship.

After a night of heavy drinking, Lucius had made the questionable decision to return Maxim's weapon. They'd discovered friendship and camaraderie in the most unlikely circumstances. Five years later, Maxim had pleaded with him for the turning, wanting their friendship to endure eternally. Lucius had capitulated because he couldn't imagine his existence without this steadfast companion.

Now, observing Maxim's refined demeanor, one would never suspect he'd once been the man fornicating against trees with knives at his throat.

He'd transformed into the epitome of gentlemanly sophistica-tion—managing Lucius's vast finances and currently representing him on the Council. Lucius wasn't certain how he'd managed his affairs before

Maxim's influence, but he couldn't conceive of operating without him now, especially since Maxim consistently kept him from making catastrophic mistakes.

Speaking of the Council, he realized Alden hadn't created significant trouble regarding the witch incident. At least, not that he'd heard.

"Alden wants the witch," Lucius informed Maxim, hoping his friend would reveal any behind-the-scenes political maneuvering.

Maxim stared at him in confusion before comprehension dawned. "Alden wants the witch specifically?"

"Yes. He intended to take her from the club."

Maxim set aside his notes, giving Lucius complete attention. "For what purpose?"

"Unknown, but we need to discover his intentions." Lucius rubbed his chin thoughtfully. "He was conversing with her at the club, though I couldn't overhear their discussion."

"Intriguing. Do you think she knows him personally?"

"From her expression, I'd say no—but he definitely knows her." Lucius finished his drink and sat in contemplative silence. "I can't imagine why he'd need a witch, particularly this one."

"We both recognize her considerable power. Perhaps he's attempting recruitment... or requires her to craft a specific spell."

"Uncertain. We must learn his motives quickly. He cannot be allowed to claim her." Lucius ran his hands over his face in frustration and exhaustion. "At least not until we've freed Ian from the daimones."

Maxim leaned back, studying him with obvious concern. "When did you last feed properly?"

"None of your damned business."

"You're looking rather pale. It might be time to seek sustenance again."

Lucius ignored the observation and rose to leave.

"Lucius, I must say—I like her."

"Like whom?" Though he suspected the answer.

"Patience. She doesn't seem malevolent."

"Max, she's a witch, which makes her inherently dangerous." Anger filled his voice, though strangely, he didn't feel the emotion—which was deeply concerning.

"When this crisis ends, simply let them depart," Maxim pleaded earnestly.

Lucius moved toward the door without responding.

"Consider it, for my sake," Maxim called as he departed.

Lucius spent the next two hours pacing his study, alternating between whiskey and restless movement. He'd sent word to Alecia immediately after his conversation with Maxim, knowing he needed answers about what was happening to him. The witch's effect on him defied every logical explanation, and if it wasn't magical in nature, then the alternative was far more terrifying.

The sound of the front door's heavy oak panels swinging open echoed through the castle's stone corridors, followed by the distinctive click of Alecia's heeled boots against marble. She never knocked—after five centuries of friendship, such formalities were unnecessary.

"So explain why you believe a witch has bespelled you despite wearing rose desonite?" Alecia demanded the moment she swept into the foyer, not bothering with pleasantries. Her emerald eyes were already assessing him with the sharp intelligence that made her one of the Council's most formidable members.

She appeared deceptively delicate in her pink pencil skirt and auburn hair arranged in a pristine bun, but Lucius knew better. Her temper burned as fiery as her vibrant red hair and emerald eyes, and she was absolutely lethal with her signature double-edged sword.

"Let's discuss this in my study." Lucius led the way to his private office, closing the door firmly before touching the wall. Crimson light spread from his fingertips, sealing every crevice against eavesdropping. He poured himself a glass of premium liquor, turning to offer Alecia one before remembering she'd abandoned alcohol decades ago. Perhaps he'd follow her example someday—just not today.

After finishing his first drink, he poured another and settled behind his desk.

"Please, have a seat." He gestured to the chair facing him.

"It's irrelevant how powerful she is. If a spell were cast against you, the stone would reveal it immediately." Alecia settled into the offered chair with predatory grace.

Lucius recounted the club incident and his inexplicable reactions to Patience ever since. When he concluded, he sipped his drink while awaiting her assessment. She raised one perfectly sculpted eyebrow in surprise.

"So you're attracted to the witch?"

"I wish it were that simple. It's more like... I crave her." He admitted this while finishing his drink and slamming the glass down with enough force to crack the crystal.

"Fascinating. Your aura appears... different," she observed with curiosity.

"What do you mean?"

She shook her head dismissively. "Never mind. Hand me the stone."

Setting down his glass, he touched the clasp at his neck's base, speaking the unlocking spell before the chain loosened and fell into his palm. He placed the precious desonite in Alecia's outstretched hand.

She examined it meticulously—checking for fractures, cupping it between her palms, and speaking an incantation Lucius had never heard. Her hands glowed with golden light before fading.

Dread bubbled up in Lucius as he awaited her verdict.

The necklace dangled from her fingers like a judge's gavel. "Lucius, there's absolutely nothing wrong with this stone. It will fully protect you against any witch's magic."

Fuck. He'd known it, but hearing confirmation still felt like a physical blow.

"The magic she wields is beyond supernatural manipulation. There's no spell to defeat natural attraction," Alecia smirked with obvious amusement. "What an interesting predicament you've created for yourself." She returned the necklace.

He accepted it and spoke the binding spell to secure it around his neck once more.

"Your best option now is to bed her thoroughly, then eliminate her before this develops into something beyond your control. Law be damned, darling." She leaned back, crossing her legs with elegant nonchalance.

"As I mentioned, Ian is currently soul-bonded to a daimones named Michael."

"I thought they were extinct. Well, except for—"

"Our assumption as well."

"And you can't simply kill the witch because—?"

"Because you know I cannot approach the Witches' Council requesting another to locate the gem."

Her eyes danced with mirth. "But why is she here originally?" she asked with genuine curiosity.

"According to her testimony, she and the demon are friends." He stood and poured another drink. "She claims she attempted to anchor herself but was rejected, so she bound Ian to the creature instead." He consumed the entire measure in one burning gulp.

"Remarkable. A witch befriending a demon? None of this follows established patterns..." She trailed off, becoming lost in thought.

"Many aspects aren't making sense, hence your presence here," he said, pouring yet another drink. The alcohol wasn't helping significantly, but it provided momentary solace.

"I want to meet her."

Lucius stared at her as if she'd lost her sanity.

"Why?" he demanded, immediately suspicious.

"I want to encounter this witch who befriends demons and has rendered you utterly besotted. My curiosity is thoroughly piqued."

There was no inherent danger in Alecia meeting the witch, but he couldn't risk any "accidents." Sighing, he warned her: "This witch differs from others you've encountered."

"That's what they all believe—"

"She doesn't require spells to channel magic."

"What?" Genuine shock registered on her features. "That's impossible. All witches need incantations to access their power. Are you certain she's actually a witch?"

The possibility hadn't occurred to him—especially since she possessed no memories of her origins. What manner of creature could she be? Other covens recognized her as witch, unless she'd somehow deceived them all.

"As certain as possible under the circumstances."

"Now I absolutely must meet her." She rose eagerly from her chair.

He fixed her with his most serious expression, ensuring she understood every word. "You may meet her, but if you harm her before Ian awakens, you'll face the fight of your existence—because I will kill you without hesitation. Understood?"

She raised an eyebrow at his vehemence but nodded. "Understood."

Lucius led her through the castle's winding corridors, their footsteps echoing off ancient stone walls. As they approached Ian's room, he could hear the soft rustling of pages—the witch was still reading, still searching for answers they desperately needed. He paused outside the door, suddenly uncertain about introducing these two formidable women. Alecia was unpredictable at the best of times, and Patience had already proven she didn't respond well to perceived threats.

"Remember," he warned quietly, "she's not like other witches you've encountered. She's... protective of those she cares about."

Alecia's smile was all sharp edges. "How delightfully refreshing."

He led her to Ian's room, where the witch sat gracefully on the windowsill, gazing out at the star-filled night sky. Only a few hours remained before dawn's approach.

Her book lay abandoned on the nearby chair. She looked breathtakingly beautiful silhouetted against the window, studying the celestial display. Everything seemed hauntingly familiar for a moment—as though he'd experienced this exact scene before, watching her contemplate the night sky while wishing desperately she were anything but a witch.

She turned her head slowly as they entered. "A guest? How unexpected. I must have done something right. Who do I have the pleasure of meeting?"

She stood, extending her hand toward Alecia, who stared at the offered appendage with obvious disgust. "Well, I suppose the pleasure is entirely mine." Patience let her hand drop gracefully.

"Well, hello, witch." Alecia began moving in a predatory circle around her.

Patience pivoted carefully, never exposing her back to the potential threat.

"She is indeed powerful," Alecia noted clinically. "I can sense it radiating from her. Now I understand why covens would compete for her allegiance."

"You're quite powerful yourself, and... ancient." Patience crossed her arms defensively when Alecia completed her inspection.

"Why, thank you. Most vampires and witches aspire to achieve my longevity," she replied with obvious pride. "Lucius tells me you and the demon are friends. Is this accurate?"

"What if it is? It's not illegal," Patience said defensively.

"No, merely unusual. He also claims you don't require spells to access magic?"

Patience smiled with wicked delight. Alecia's pink suit transformed to bright orange, and a small cloud materialized directly above her head.

"Witch, stop immediately," Lucius commanded.

"What? She requested a demonstration."

The moment Alecia glanced upward, rain poured from the cloud, thoroughly soaking her before the precipitation vanished.

"Oops," Patience said with mock innocence.

"Witch," Lucius snapped. "Enough."

"You're absolutely no fun." With a casual gesture, Alecia was completely dry, though her clothing remained orange.

Lucius scowled at Patience, then noticed Alecia's attire had returned to its original pink.

"Interesting," Alecia murmured, moving toward Ian and Michael as if nothing had occurred. "Has there been any change in their condition?"

"None that I've observed." Lucius looked to Patience. "Witch?"

She shook her head, clearly annoyed. "Is there a particular reason she's here?"

"This is my home, last I checked," Lucius grumbled.

"No concerns. I'll be departing your space shortly, witch." Alecia approached Ian's side and simply placed her palm against his arm. Brilliant golden light emanated from her hand, pulsing with ancient power.

As the light faded, Alecia cried out and collapsed. Lucius caught her before her head could strike the floor.

"What did you just do?" Patience shouted, rushing to Michael's side to ensure his welfare.

"I needed to examine something. They're both perfectly fine, and so am I, Lucius." Alecia stood and walked toward the door with determination.

"You'd better not have harmed either of them!" Patience's voice carried genuine threat.

Alecia didn't bother acknowledging the warning as she departed.

Patience ran her hands over both unconscious males, finding nothing amiss. She released a breath of relief. "Your friend is peculiar. If she'd hurt them, I might have killed her—or made her wish I had."

She continued examining Michael and Ian for any signs of damage. Finding none, she returned to her chair and resumed reading. Lucius followed Alecia into the hallway.

"She is indeed a witch," Alecia confirmed, "though something about her is... anomalous."

"Are you going to explain what happened in there?"

Alecia merely smirked in response.

"I take that as a refusal."

"Lucius, she's extraordinarily powerful. I don't know how you became entangled with her, but she's unlike any witch I've ever encountered." The warning in her voice was unmistakable.

Lucius was surprised by her serious tone. Alecia touched his cheek gently. "I understand your attraction to her, but I'd exercise extreme caution—and eliminate her at the first opportunity, because if you don't, the consequences will exceed your ability to manage them."

She paused, studying his face intently. "Now I must depart. Do give Maxim my regards. I look forward to seeing him at the next Council meeting."

As she walked away, Lucius contemplated everything she'd revealed. The only thing truly resonating was the confirmation that his attraction was genuine—and therefore infinitely more dangerous than any spell.

He stood in the hallway long after Alecia's departure, staring at Ian's door and fighting the overwhelming urge to return to the witch who was systematically destroying every defense he'd built around his heart.

The most terrifying realization was that part of him wanted her to succeed.

CHAPTER TEN

Patience

Patience sighed deeply, walking over to check on Michael and Ian for the third time since that strange woman had departed. She still had no idea what Alecia had done to Ian with that golden light, but both men appeared stable for now—their breathing remained synchronized, their skin no longer feverish.

She lifted Michael's wrist to examine the mystical symbol once more. The quarter section had completely vanished now, leaving only three-quarters of the circle remaining. They had exactly three days left before the transformation completed.

She was curious why Lucius had brought a Drath to examine the situation—probably attempting to find an alternative method to break the soul-tether, which was utterly impossible. Only a genuine soul gem could safely sever the bond. Any other approach would risk either Michael or Ian dying, or both perishing in the process.

He should have consulted her before involving outsiders, but of course, he didn't trust witches. Well, apparently not full-blooded witches, anyway.

Before returning to her research, she added an extra layer of magical protection around the four-poster bed, weaving the spell through the existing wards until it hummed with power. Then she picked up her abandoned book and settled back into the uncomfortable chair.

So far, the ancient text had yielded nothing valuable to their desperate situation. She still had two more volumes to examine, and she hoped that insufferable vampire had discovered something useful instead of simply calling in more supernatural backup.

She attempted to read a few more pages, but concentration proved impossible. Her mind kept drifting to Lucius's purple aura and the way his hands had felt against her skin. Closing the book with frustration, she glanced at the remaining two volumes on the side table.

"Which one of you will actually be useful?" she asked the books aloud. "*Demonology* by Kyros, or *Cazador de Demonios* by Esteban Figueroa?"

The Demon Chaser sounded infinitely more promising than poring over dry demon terminology and classifications. She made herself as comfortable as possible in the torture device masquerading as furniture and opened the second book.

Four chapters in, she discovered something genuinely intriguing. She needed a reference text to verify the information, though—the claim seemed almost too good to be true. Her first instinct was to transport herself directly to GreyJoy's, but then she remembered spotting a relevant book in Lucius's extensive library.

She could slip in and out without anyone knowing the difference. Standing, she touched the wall and felt it shimmer beneath her palm before stepping through the stone barrier.

The moment both feet touched the library's polished floor, deadly silver-gray eyes locked onto hers with predatory intensity. She braced herself, fully expecting his fingers to curl around her throat at any second.

"Never trust a witch."

"I only came to retrieve a reference book for my research," she said defensively, then couldn't resist poking him firmly in the chest. "I may have found something important. Besides, you're a complete hypocrite. What, you only associate with Drath now?"

"She has an excellent point, Lucius," Maxim observed from his position by the reading table, an open book spread before him. "You should at least grant her unrestricted access to the library."

His presence made this confrontation significantly easier—less chance of an actual physical altercation.

Lucius grunted but offered no verbal response to either of them.

Taking his silence as grudging permission, she moved to the bookshelf where her hand had previously grazed the title she needed: *The Realms of the Universe*. She pulled the leather-bound volume from its place and quickly skimmed through the pages until she found the relevant section.

Lucius mumbled something to Maxim, but she didn't bother listening because she'd just discovered exactly what they needed to save Michael.

"See? If I'd had to wait for you to find this, it would have taken forever to solve all our problems."

She laid both books open on the central table, pages spread to display the crucial information.

"I know where to find this." She pointed to an illustration of a brilliant blue gemstone that seemed to capture light even in the static drawing. "She has it." Her finger moved to indicate a terrifying creature depicted in the other volume.

"We need to acquire this soul gem from the demon goddess—" Maxim paused to read the nameplate beneath the illustration. "Sucora?" He continued reading, his expression growing increasingly alarmed. "You realize this text states that she slowly peels the flesh from her victims, one small patch at a time, until they're completely skinned alive, then—" His voice caught as he read further. "Then she carves the meat from their bones and roasts it, consuming it while they watch. She keeps her victims conscious throughout the entire ordeal."

"Then I suppose we'd better not get caught," Patience said with forced lightness, taking the book from his trembling hands to read the passage herself.

"Would you please talk some sense into her?" Maxim appealed desperately to Lucius. "This plan is absolutely suicidal."

But Lucius remained silent, clearly lost in strategic thought.

"According to this, she keeps the gem somewhere in her private chambers," Patience continued reading aloud, "which are located in the highest tower of her fortress. See? We have a specific location to target."

"Lucius," Maxim's voice carried genuine panic now. "Surely there are other soul gems in less... lethally defended locations."

Lucius snatched the book from her hands, his eyes scanning the text rapidly. "Do you genuinely believe you can retrieve it without detection?"

"I believe I can," she replied with more confidence than she felt.

He flipped to the next page, studying the detailed information. "It states here that she resides in Calidium, a realm within Evictus, and we'll require a gl—glop—"

"A glopinian," she corrected, retrieving the book from his grasp. "Fortunately, I know exactly where to acquire one, because we absolutely need it to safely contain the gem. Only the anchor and the daimones can physically touch a soul gem without catastrophic consequences."

"Are we certain the gem will actually be there?" Maxim asked, still clearly opposed to this dangerous plan.

"There's only one way to find out definitively. We have to make the journey."

"For once, we're in complete agreement, witch. Now let's acquire this glop thing so we can claim the gem and return home."

"It's called a glopinian," she corrected with exaggerated patience, "and we need to visit GreyJoy to obtain one."

"Wonderful. I'll drive us there."

"No, I can transport us much faster." Patience was about to place her hands on his shoulders when Maxim interrupted.

"Wait—I'm accompanying you both." He placed his hand on her shoulder with obvious enthusiasm. "Silas told me about this remarkable bookstore that despises Lucius, and I'm genuinely curious to meet this entity."

The moment Maxim's fingers made contact with her skin, Lucius's eyes blazed with sudden fire, glowing with supernatural intensity before he blinked and the light vanished. Patience almost convinced herself she'd imagined it, but she was certain she'd witnessed that flash of possessive fury.

"No. Stay here to protect them," Lucius growled, his voice rough with barely controlled emotion.

"No one will breach the mansion's defenses while we're gone," Patience assured him. "I placed a comprehensive protective barrier around Ian and Michael after your Drath friend departed."

Lucius scowled, but before he could voice another objection, Patience grabbed his muscular forearm and triggered her transportation magic.

They materialized directly in front of the familiar bookstore, the familiar scent of ancient parchment and magical ink filling her lungs like coming home. Patience immediately released Lucius's arm and stepped through the always-unlocked door.

"Hello, old friend," she called warmly.

Smiling, she held out her hand as a note floated gracefully down from the vaulted ceiling with GreyJoy's characteristic elegant script: *"Hello, Theá."*

"This place is absolutely incredible," Maxim breathed, his green eyes wide as he took in the seemingly infinite expanse of books and scrolls that defied the building's modest exterior dimensions.

Before she could respond to his amazement, the familiar prickling sensation at the base of her skull told her that Lucius was glaring daggers at her from outside.

"Witch!" His voice carried clear frustration through the barrier.

GreyJoy had locked him out again, just as before. She exhaled slowly while Maxim chuckled with obvious delight.

"GreyJoy, I understand you don't approve of him, but remember—I need him for this mission, at least temporarily," she called to the entity. "Please grant him entry. I promise he'll behave himself appropriately. He did sign your binding contract, remember?"

The door shimmered and became permeable once more. Lucius stepped through, radiating fury like heat from a forge.

She held up her hand before he could unleash whatever venomous comment was forming. "You will behave yourself and keep whatever rude observation you're about to make firmly locked behind your teeth. GreyJoy will banish you to whatever unpleasant dimension he sent you to before, and I lack both the patience and time to persuade him to retrieve you."

Lucius appeared thoroughly disgruntled but kept his mouth shut, which was probably a minor miracle.

"I've never witnessed that level of restraint from him in all my centuries of friendship," Maxim whispered behind her, his voice filled with amazement.

She suppressed her satisfied smirk. "Now then, this way, gentlemen and beast."

Lucius's sneer could have frozen water, but he followed silently as she led them down the final aisle—the only section she ever visited—to the very back of the store where a plain brown door waited.

She slid her finger down the right side of the doorframe, and mystical symbols blazed to life one by one, each character pulsing with silver fire.

"The language of the Silverlands," Maxim said with genuine awe. "Ancient Argian script."

Patience turned to face him, surprise evident on her features. "You can identify what these symbols represent?"

Maxim approached the door for a closer examination, his scholarly curiosity clearly piqued. "Not their specific meaning, unfortunately. The language has been lost for millennia, existing now only in the most ancient texts."

"They simply came to me when I wanted to secure this space," she admitted, disturbed by this revelation. "I didn't consciously choose this particular magical script."

She remembered that day clearly—when she'd first stored her most precious treasures behind this door. After carefully arranging her collection, she'd instinctively slid her finger along the doorframe without conscious thought, and these symbols had appeared. She'd assumed GreyJoy had provided the security, but perhaps not.

"The symbols just manifested spontaneously? You created these seals? You actually know this ancient magical language?"

"Apparently so, though I have no memory of learning it." An ancient seal crafted in the language of the Silverlands terrified her, but it also intensified her curiosity about her mysterious past. The Silverlands was the realm where the Goddess herself resided—the source of all magic and the nexus that connected every dimension in existence. How could she possibly have learned such sacred knowledge?

Maxim continued studying the symbols as if they might reveal their secrets through intense observation.

"As fascinating as this linguistic mystery is, time remains our enemy," she said, stepping through the now-open doorway into her private sanctuary.

The space beyond was filled with treasures she'd collected over five decades of adventures—some valuable to the wider world, like the legendary Daggers of Kronin that every Elevian thief coveted for their power to grant the wielder the abilities of the master assassin himself. Others held value only for her and Michael, like the eternally blooming Lilies of Flora that provided beauty without ever wilting.

She walked past her other precious artifacts, her fingers trailing over the iridescent Feathers of Gamira as she searched for her target. Now, where had she stored the glopinian?

"You possess the Sword of Hemala?" Lucius asked, genuine surprise coloring his voice.

She turned to see him carefully holding the ornate weapon that had been gifted to her by a grateful orc warrior after she'd located his kidnapped child who'd been taken by malicious heffalings.

"Yes," she confirmed simply. She and Michael had shared quite a few adventures over the years, though she couldn't pinpoint exactly when their focus had shifted entirely to unlocking her memories. After this crisis ended, regardless of whether they recovered her past, they needed to embark on another grand adventure together.

"How did you acquire this particular blade?" Lucius pressed, and she detected suspicion in his tone—he clearly thought she'd stolen it.

"It's a long story, but the sword was a gift."

"A gift?" Lucius held the weapon as though it were a natural extension of his arm, testing its balance with practiced movements. He sliced through the air with fluid precision, evaluating its weight and responsiveness before carefully returning it to its sheath.

She lifted the precious Fleece of Gilahein—a gift to Michael from the Queen of the Nymphs—and finally located the glopinian concealed beneath its shimmering folds. The artifact appeared to be nothing more than an ordinary red velvet pouch, but it was infinitely more sophisticated than its humble appearance suggested. Crafted by the master artisans of Gilahein specifically to contain powerful magical stones like soul gems, it completely masked the gem's energy signature so it wouldn't affect whoever carried it.

"Found it. Let's proceed," she announced, turning to show them her prize.

Lucius was now examining the twin daggers mounted on her wall while Maxim played with the Orb of Hindalin—a powerful artifact capable of granting prophetic sight and breaking through even the most sophisticated illusions.

"Maxim, please set down the Orb and let's depart. I promise I'll allow you to explore my treasure collection properly later."

"But this artifact is—"

"Yes, I'm well aware of its significance, and it was incredibly difficult to obtain, but we don't have time for lengthy explanations right now."

He reluctantly replaced the Orb on its pedestal.

"Anduril Blades," Lucius observed as she approached him.

"Actually, Silas gave those to me as a birthday gift when Michael decided I needed to celebrate my birth anniversary."

"That sounds exactly like something Silas would choose," he said, following Maxim toward the exit.

As she watched him leave, she could have sworn his aura shifted to that mysterious purple hue momentarily before reverting to its usual dark red.

She desperately needed to find a comprehensive book about auras and their meanings. She wanted to understand what the color changes signified—perhaps she could find a way to help him, to heal whatever was causing him such constant anger and sadness.

Sighing, she followed them out, sealed the door behind her, and rejoined them at the front counter where Lucius waited with obvious impatience.

"I have the glopinian," she announced, displaying the innocuous-looking pouch.

He extended his hand expectantly, and for one joyous moment she thought he was reaching for her. Then reality crashed down—he was simply requesting the magical container. As she handed it over, his fingers grazed hers briefly, sending an unexpected shudder of pleasure racing through her nervous system. She hoped desperately that he hadn't noticed her reaction.

One glance at his face told her he absolutely had noticed. Desire burned in his silver-gray eyes with such intensity that she was forced to step backward.

"I just need to retrieve one additional item, then we can depart," she said, her voice slightly breathless.

She moved behind the counter and knelt to remove a specific floorboard, revealing a hidden safe built into the foundation. Her fingers traced the top of the vault, and mystical symbols appeared in response to her touch, unlocking the mechanism with a soft click.

She opened the safe and withdrew a massive tome bound in what appeared to be dragon leather, then carefully closed and resealed the vault.

"And what exactly is that monstrosity?" Maxim asked, leaning over the counter to get a better view.

"What do we need to safely reach Sucora's realm?" She hefted the enormous book onto the counter's surface with a grunt of effort. "Come here so we can finish this mission."

She positioned herself beside the tome and placed her right palm flat against its ancient cover. "I'll transport us back to the library." She held out her left hand toward them.

Lucius placed his hand over hers while Maxim grasped her upper arm. The sensation of Lucius's skin against hers was deeply disconcerting, especially with him standing close enough that she could feel his body heat. It took several moments of concentrated effort before she could focus enough to close her eyes and trigger the transportation spell.

They materialized in the library, but Lucius's hand remained covering hers, warm and solid and infinitely distracting. She turned to look at him, finding him standing close enough that she could detect his distinctive scent—sandalwood and steel and something uniquely masculine.

She gazed into his eyes, seeing flames of desire raging within their silver-gray depths. She found herself leaning closer, wanting to be consumed by those flames, to lose herself in the heat building between them.

Maxim cleared his throat pointedly, shattering the spell. Lucius immediately stepped away while Patience shook her head, trying to clear the sensual fog from her thoughts.

She placed the massive tome on the table and opened it to the relevant section. "The spell we need should be right here."

Maxim approached to stand beside her. "So you do use traditional spells?"

"I *can* use spells when necessary. I simply don't *need* them for most magic," she clarified. "There's a significant difference. But I need a guide for this particular transportation, or we could end up in a completely different realm entirely—like Astrona, the realm of eternal lightning storms."

"This is your personal spellbook?"

"Let's just say I'm... borrowing it," she replied evasively. More accurately, Selene, a powerful witch from the Silverlands, had entrusted it to her for safekeeping years ago. She probably shouldn't be using it for personal missions, but this qualified as an emergency situation. Selene would understand. "We're going to need a mirror for the portal."

She flicked her wrist, and an oval silver mirror materialized on the table.

"Borrowing it?" Maxim questioned with obvious concern. "The owner won't come searching for it? I don't want to be dismembered while you're both gone."

"That's a valid concern," she acknowledged. "Though I would be incredibly surprised if she came looking for this particular tome."

Patience paused in her reading and walked to the library wall, placing her palm against the cool stone. She closed her eyes, intending to place a comprehensive protective barrier around the entire mansion, similar to the ward she'd created around Ian and Michael's bed.

But there was already a barrier in place—the exact same type of protection she'd planned to weave. How curious.

She'd possibly placed the ward around the entire mansion earlier instead of just their bedroom, though this particular barrier felt somehow different. She'd investigate that mystery later. The existing protection would hold until their return.

Shrugging off the coincidence, she returned to the spell tome. "Don't worry—you're completely safe here."

She read through the transportation incantation carefully, then realized they needed one crucial component. "You wouldn't happen to have a drop of Verdian on hand, would you?"

"I don't believe we—" Before Maxim could complete his sentence, a small vial of luminescent green liquid appeared on the table beside her.

She hadn't even realized Lucius had left the room until he was standing close to her once again, close enough that breathing in his intoxicating scent made her lose all concentration. She almost leaned into his solid warmth until he stepped away, leaving her feeling oddly bereft.

She shook her head to clear her thoughts and forced herself to focus on the task at hand.

Patience read through the spell one final time, then approached the conjured mirror.

"*Aperi ad notum ostium in Calidium realm Evictus,*" she intoned clearly, then placed a single drop of Verdian onto the mirror's surface.

The glass rippled like disturbed water, the reflection transforming to show endless golden sands beneath an alien sky.

"The portal is now active and stable."

"Is this gateway simply going to deposit us in the middle of a desert?" Maxim approached the mirror cautiously. He reached out to touch the shimmering surface, but she caught his wrist before he could make contact.

"Yes and no. The spell will transport us near the closest sentient inhabitant. Hopefully, that will be Sucora's fortress."

She turned to see Lucius waiting with obvious readiness, a sword now strapped across his broad back. Not just any blade—he carried Luzia, his legendary weapon.

The sword was magnificent, with her long, thin, slightly curved silver blade that seemed to capture and reflect light with supernatural beauty. Legend claimed that the words "*Prin cenușă, ne vom ridica din nou*" (From the ashes, we will rise again) glowed crimson along her blade whenever Lucius killed a witch and absorbed their magical essence. Seeing the famous weapon in person was breathtaking, and she felt an almost irresistible urge to reach out and touch the legendary steel.

"Could you specify a more precise landing location?" Lucius asked, interrupting her fascination with his sword. "Particularly regarding the sun's position?"

It took a moment for coherent words to form in her mind. "Unfortunately, no. If we discover we're too far from Sucora's stronghold, I'll need to determine our exact position within the realm before creating another portal to transport us closer. As for the sun..." She attempted a reassuring grin that felt more awkward than confident. "Let's pray it's nighttime there."

"Not amusing, witch." His expression remained deadly serious. "We should return within twenty-four hours," he informed Maxim. "If we're not back within thirty-six hours, send Silas to retrieve us. If she returns without me, kill the demon immediately."

"You realize that action could kill your brother as well," Maxim pointed out.

"*Could* kill him, not *would* kill him," Lucius corrected grimly. "Now, is there anything else you believe we'll need for this mission?"

She wanted to be childish and stick her tongue out at him for his perpetually serious demeanor, but she couldn't afford such behavior now. Lives hung in the balance.

"Actually, yes." She waved her hand over the floor, and a well-worn leather backpack materialized. "My survival pack is filled with essentials that will keep us alive in hostile territory. I never venture into other realms without it."

She picked up the pack and opened it, withdrawing her crescent-shaped silver dragon talisman and her last precious vial of Night Vow potion.

"Give this to Silas if we're delayed beyond the deadline," she said, offering the talisman to Maxim. "It will transport him directly to our location. Hopefully, he won't need to use it."

She held out the dark vial to Lucius. "And this is for you. Night Vow will protect you from direct sunlight for approximately six hours, give or take a few minutes depending on the intensity of the solar radiation."

Maxim accepted the talisman while Lucius took the vial, slipping it carefully into his pocket. She shouldered her backpack, adjusting the straps for comfort.

"I'll see you on the other side," she said, then stepped through the mirror's shimmering surface.

Immediately, she was falling through absolute darkness, the sensation of plummeting through space both terrifying and exhilarating as the portal carried her toward whatever dangers awaited in the realm of Calidium.

CHAPTER ELEVEN

PATIENCE

U ntil she landed on something unexpectedly soft—a mountain of silken pillows in varying shades of crimson and gold. The rich scent of vanilla, musk, jasmine, and exotic spices enveloped her like a perfumed embrace, confirming they were definitely no longer in the familiar atmosphere of their home realm.

Daylight streamed through an ornate window on the opposite wall, illuminating a striking painting of a fierce male warrior clad in ceremonial onyx armor. Serpents were embedded in the vambraces, and his piercing green eyes and raven-black hair seemed hauntingly familiar, though she couldn't place where she might have encountered him before.

As she moved off the luxurious bed to examine the portrait more closely, a heavy thud followed by an agonized groan echoed from the bed's far side. Peering over the silk-covered edge, she discovered Lucius holding his head with both hands, clearly having had a much less cushioned landing than her own.

The vampire rose from the marble floor just as she slid gracefully off the bed. She almost asked if he was injured but bit back the words—he didn't deserve her concern or kindness.

The chamber was sparsely furnished, containing only the massive bed, the compelling painting, an elaborate Venetian red armoire, and an ornate vanity table inlaid with precious stones. Walking to the armoire with curiosity, she discovered it filled with extravagant gowns that would have cost a fortune in any realm.

Lucius approached until he stood directly behind her, close enough that she could feel his body heat. She turned to face him, catching a fleeting emotion in his silver-gray eyes before it vanished too quickly to interpret. Her fingers itched to touch the hidden necklace at her throat, but such a gesture would immediately alert him to something invisible around her neck.

"Where exactly are we, witch?" He rubbed his head while surveying their surroundings, and she felt a flutter of relief that his tone held more curiosity than accusation.

"Somewhere within Sucora's stronghold, I believe. I hope we're close to her private chambers, though I don't think this particular room is hers."

"Then why are you searching through the wardrobe?"

She shrugged with forced casualness. "Wishful thinking?"

The sharp sound of a door slamming echoed in the distance, followed by voices growing steadily closer. They were clearly approaching this chamber, since the entrance was nothing more than flowing curtains of red and gold silk.

Lucius moved with lightning speed, closing the armoire and pulling them behind a heavy tapestry near the window mere seconds before a man and woman entered the room.

"She's such a vindictive bitch," declared a short, curvaceous woman with cascading blonde curls as she swept through the doorway. She removed her white silk shawl and tossed it carelessly onto the bed. "Remind me why we continue to endure this torment."

A imposing bronze-skinned man with auburn hair followed her, his height making her appear even more petite. "Circe, you know perfectly well why we must persevere. We need her army—it may be our only hope of defeating him, unless the Goddess can be located."

Circe sighed dramatically, moving to the vanity and removing elaborate silver earrings. "I only tolerate this situation because you deem it necessary. We could simply eliminate her and commandeer her forces."

The man placed gentle hands on her shoulders, pressing a tender kiss to the crown of her head. "Shh... you mustn't speak such thoughts here. She has surveillance everywhere—eyes and ears in every shadow."

"I don't care if she hears me. I despise her, and she's well aware of my feelings."

He pressed his forehead against hers with obvious affection, sighing before claiming her lips in a passionate kiss. Then he moved toward the window, and Patience's heart began racing with panic.

Shit. She should have cloaked them immediately. If he drew the curtain aside, they were completely exposed.

Her pulse thundered as he approached their hiding spot.

"We are cloaked," Lucius whispered directly into her ear, his warm breath sending shivers cascading down her spine. His finger began tracing slow, hypnotic circles against the sensitive skin of her neck.

Her racing heartbeat gradually slowed as the man reached the window, but instead of fear, Patience found herself entirely focused on how calming Lucius's touch was and how desperately she didn't want him to stop.

"I understand your hatred of this place, Circe," the man said, gazing out at the landscape. "Soon it will be time, and I promise you can return to do whatever you wish with her."

A satisfied smile curved Circe's lips as she approached him from behind, encircling his broad frame with her arms. "Kieran, you always know exactly what to say to restore my happiness. Now, let's find proper sustenance before she forces us to consume that revolting gruel again."

Patience hadn't even realized the couple had departed until Lucius ceased his maddening circles and a door slammed shut somewhere in the distance.

"That was the king," he informed her as he stepped from behind their concealment.

"Huh? What king?" Patience emerged from the tapestry, genuinely confused by his declaration.

"King Kieran of Evictus. The missing Demon King."

Oh. Holy shit. "What's he doing here?"

"Unknown, but the gem remains our priority."

Patience could barely comprehend it—they'd discovered the missing monarch and his queen. Though the royal couple didn't seem to realize they were considered missing, but time flowed differently between realms. Perhaps they were unaware of how long they'd been absent, or maybe they simply didn't care.

Were they here seeking Sucora's army? And why did they need to find the Goddess? Her curiosity was absolutely killing her, but unfortunately, the vampire was correct—the soul gem took precedence over everything else.

"Let's move, witch. We need to determine our exact location and find that gem. I don't want to remain here longer than absolutely necessary."

Ignoring his command, she headed toward the vanity table, hoping the gem might be concealed within one of its drawers. She was systematically searching when Lucius spoke again.

"I doubt we'll find it here. She would never store something so precious this far from her personal quarters. However, I'm certain we're in the correct stronghold."

She paused in her investigation and joined him at the window. The sun blazed high overhead, but the building's shadow covered their vantage point, allowing the vampire to observe without risk of burning.

A vast courtyard stretched below them, featuring a beautiful white fountain—bone dry but the only aesthetically pleasing element visible. Guards and servants moved about like industrious ants, attending to various tasks. From their perspective, they appeared to be four stories above ground level. The tower she'd seen illustrated in the ancient book rose from the opposite side of the complex, and she could see their escape route—the path into the desert lay to the right of the fountain. Massive wooden gates stood open, allowing people to pass freely. Beyond those portals, crimson sand stretched endlessly toward the horizon.

"Well, we're definitely not in our home realm anymore," she announced.

"Obviously. We need to evacuate this chamber before they return. The cloaking may conceal our visibility, but these overwhelming fragrances won't mask our scent much longer."

A brilliant glint from the tower's highest window caught her attention. The gem was there—she could feel it calling to her with supernatural certainty. She wasn't sure how she knew, but she'd learned to trust her instincts implicitly over the years. "At least we can agree on something. We need to reach that tower." She pointed toward their target. "I'm convinced she's keeping it there."

Moving to the heavily curtained doorway, she peered through the silk barrier. Intricate geometric designs covered the polished marble floors, and the red clay walls were clearly designed to maintain coolness in the desert climate.

The corridor appeared empty. She gestured for him to follow as she slipped through the curtains.

She chose the direction opposite to where the king and queen had gone, with Lucius moving silently behind her as they made their way down the elaborate hallway.

They were slightly more than halfway to their destination when voices echoed from behind them. Lucius immediately grabbed her and sprinted down the corridor, darting into the first curtained doorway they encountered.

They found themselves in an antechamber with a darker curtain concealing a second entrance. She prayed to the Goddess that no one occupied the space beyond as the voices passed directly outside their hiding place. The sounds grew distant before stopping at the room they'd just vacated.

"We must locate them," they heard clearly. "She'll be furious that we allowed them to escape our surveillance."

As they remained motionless, the voices grew closer again. "Let's check the gardens, then the dungeons. Perhaps they went seeking food."

Patience and Lucius waited until the sounds faded completely into the distance. She released a breath she hadn't realized she'd been holding. "That was far too close for comfort."

"We need to find concealment until nightfall, unless you can shield me from direct sunlight. How are your magical reserves, witch? I exhausted mine creating our cloaking."

She closed her eyes momentarily, reaching for the familiar wellspring of power within her core. It was present but severely diminished—something was actively blocking her access to most of her abilities.

"I can sense it, but something is interfering with my connection to it."

Voices in the distance began moving toward their location again. Lucius pulled them through the black curtain without hesitation.

Ten pairs of eyes met them as they turned to survey the room, seeking another hiding spot. Some eyes held terror, others burning hatred, and only one pair showed genuine curiosity. Everyone froze as the threatening voices passed by outside.

Voluptuous, scantily clad men and women lounged around a cascading waterfall pool adorned with floating water lilies and lotus blossoms. They were drinking exotic beverages and consuming delicate foods as though waiting for something specific. Then understanding dawned on her with uncomfortable clarity—they were waiting to be selected for intimate encounters. This was a harem.

They weren't waiting for Patience and Lucius, however. As soon as the voices passed, the occupants returned to their leisurely activities of lounging and fanning themselves with broad leaves. All except the curious observer, whose piercing green eyes seemed remarkably familiar. A young man rose gracefully and walked to a curtained doorway on the chamber's opposite side, beckoning for them to follow.

She stepped forward when Lucius caught her arm, stopping her progress.

"What do you think you're doing?"

"What does it look like I'm doing?" She attempted to free her arm from his grip, but he held her firmly. From his expression, he clearly thought she'd lost her sanity. "Look, he might have a safe place for us to hide, and he may also have answers to my questions. Besides, he looks familiar somehow."

She tried pulling away again, but his grip remained unbreakable. "Could you please trust me on this one thing, even if you can't trust me regarding anything else? I have a positive feeling about him. Trust me, please."

She attempted to free herself one final time, and he finally relented.

"I don't like this situation at all," he informed her, but still followed despite his obvious reservations.

She walked in the direction the young man had gone, which led them into a cramped room no larger than a storage closet, with a single small window. It was an extremely tight fit for three people. The man had donned simple brown robes to cover his nakedness, which Patience appreciated, even though he was quite pleasant to observe.

"What are you doing back here?" he asked, peeking through the doorway to ensure they hadn't been followed. "If she discovers you both, she'll execute you without hesitation."

Patience and Lucius exchanged confused glances.

"Wait, what do you mean 'back here'? We've been here before?" Did he mean they'd both visited this place individually, or together? That seemed impossible since she'd only met Lucius yesterday. She still couldn't believe this was where her simple night out had led her, but what he was suggesting couldn't possibly be true.

Could it?

"Yes, don't you remember? It's been over two thousand moon rotations since you freed me and I helped you escape from this place." He moved away from the doorway and retrieved a makeshift knife fashioned from broken glass and hardened leather from behind a clay urn.

Before he could say more, Lucius grabbed the man and captured his wrist, forcing him to drop the improvised weapon.

"You can understand him, witch. What is he saying?" Lucius growled menacingly.

"What do you mean, what is he saying? He's speaking perfectly clearly." Her brows furrowed with genuine confusion.

The man continued struggling until he released the knife.

"What did he say to you?" Lucius demanded, his voice dripping with venom. "I know you can understand him. Tell me immediately, or I'll kill him."

"Wait—can't you understand him?"

"No."

The man suddenly ceased struggling and spoke in a trembling voice. "He doesn't know our language as you do. The last time you were here, you made him understand our words."

"Could you understand the guards when they passed earlier?" she asked pointedly.

"No," Lucius admitted with a frustrated scowl.

How was it possible that only she could understand him? Just like with GreyJoy—her mind was automatically translating the language without her conscious awareness. As much as this should disturb her, what bothered her more was why he looked so familiar. She searched her fragmented memories until realization struck like lightning. "You're the man from the painting."

His distinctive green eyes confirmed her suspicion. His raven hair was much shorter now, and his nose appeared crooked as if he'd endured multiple beatings.

"Yes, I am Jafa. I was once the proud ruler of these lands until she stole my power and cursed me to the eternal darkness of Cavella. You were the one who freed me from that torment. Now I dedicate myself to rescuing those who wish to escape Queen Sucora's tyranny."

Another crucial key to her mysterious past. But what connection did this have to Lucius? The situation was becoming increasingly complicated.

"Witch," Lucius rasped impatiently, "what is he saying?"

"Shh... he's explaining who he is and how we know each other."

Lucius grumbled inaudibly but remained quiet, though his tension was palpable.

"Are you claiming that we were here together over one hundred and fifty years ago, by our time or yours?" she pressed.

"Yes, by your time calculation. Don't you remember any of it?"

"No, neither of us do," she replied, addressing both men.

Silence filled the cramped space as she absorbed the shocking revelation. How could it be possible for them to have visited this place together? She couldn't be that ancient. It would mean they'd been here a century and a half ago in their timeline. *Holy shit.*

At least, she didn't think she was that old.

"Witch, I'm growing impatient and hungry." Lucius's fangs descended as he gazed at Jafa's exposed neck with predatory interest.

"Let him go. He means us no harm. Trust me."

Lucius reluctantly released his captive, retracting his fangs. Jafa retrieved his makeshift blade and wrapped it carefully in his robes.

"Listen, I don't have time to explain everything now. We must get you to the sigra before she discovers your presence here."

"What is a sigra?" she asked, though the word seemed familiar somehow.

"It's what you call a tree, I believe."

Trees. Ancient portals between time, worlds, and dimensions—similar to mirrors but far more powerful. The crucial difference was that trees drew their magic directly from the planet's ley lines, whereas mirrors required active spellcasting to function.

"He wants to take us to a tree," she translated for Lucius.

"That makes sense, but we're in the middle of a desert, if you hadn't noticed. Trees don't typically grow in desert environments," Lucius pointed out as he overturned a bucket and used it as a makeshift seat.

"He's correct about the terrain, but there's one tree nearby. You created it during your previous visit," Jafa informed them.

"I did?"

"You're the one who taught me about sigras and how they serve as portals to different realms."

"Witch, you need to translate immediately."

She ignored his demand, focusing on Jafa.

"Why isn't my magic functioning properly here?"

Jafa placed his finger to his lips, motioning for silence.

Guards shouted in the distance. "Someone must have observed you entering the harem, or the concubines alerted them to your presence." The sounds of armed guards grew closer to their storage room. "Follow me quickly."

Jafa ran toward the small window and leaped without hesitation. Patience stood gaping for a moment before following his example, jumping out after him. She landed in a pile of fragrant hay, though the overwhelming smell of horse manure immediately assaulted her nostrils.

Lucius flew through the window after her, landing gracefully beside her in the hay.

Jafa quickly pulled them both upright and pushed them behind a large stone watering trough. Seconds later, a massive, burly guard with two small thick horns protruding from his forehead and draconic scales covering his skin stuck his head through the window. He scanned the area thoroughly but failed to spot them in their concealment.

"Area clear," the guard reported before withdrawing.

Patience barely noticed the guard's departure—she was entirely focused on Lucius's exposed skin. Sunlight was touching him directly, yet he showed no signs of burning.

"You're not burning," she whispered, mesmerized by the impossibility.

"What?" He kept his head lowered defensively.

She grasped his hand and slowly extended his finger into direct sunlight. Nothing happened—not even the slightest singe. She pulled his entire hand into the bright rays, and still nothing occurred.

"The sun cannot affect him in this realm," Jafa explained as he leaned over the water trough. "Come quickly. They suspect intruders now, so we must leave this area immediately."

"Wait. We came here specifically for her soul gem. We need it desperately."

"The gem you gave her?"

"I gave her a soul gem?"

"Yes, in exchange for my life. You promised you would return for it someday. We'll retrieve it before you pass through the sigra."

She rose and followed Jafa stealthily through the courtyard, with Lucius close behind, until they reached a small hole in the outer wall. She was about to follow Jafa through when Lucius held her back.

"Witch, what about the gem?"

"Jafa says he knows about the gem we're seeking, but the guards suspect intruders now, so we can't attempt to retrieve it immediately. To return home, we must use a tree portal. The closest one is heavily guarded, so we'll have to wait for the right opportunity."

"I don't like this plan. Where is he taking us?"

"Let me ask him." Through the hole in the wall, she found Jafa waiting beside two magnificent horses.

She approached him. "Where are you taking us?"

"To my village. We'll arrive there before the moon rises and darkness falls."

Lucius came up behind her, and she turned before he could voice another objection. "He's taking us to his village, which is several hours from here. We'll reach it before nightfall. You don't happen to know how to ride a horse, do you?"

"Witch, this had better not be a trap, or—"

"Yes, I know. You'll kill me or torture me until I beg for death. Listen, you really need to develop more creative threats." Moving to the beautiful Arabian mare, she ran her hands through its silky mane and down its elegant neck. It was a magnificent specimen, at least she thought so—she knew relatively little about horses. The mare nuzzled her cheek affectionately in response to her gentle touch.

She stepped back and tried to figure out how she would mount the animal when Lucius lifted her from behind with effortless strength.

"Swing your leg over," he instructed, lifting her as if she weighed nothing. Then he climbed up behind her, taking the reins and enclosing her within his strong arms, surrounding her with his warmth and distinctive scent. She kept her spine rigid, not wanting to lean against him and reveal how much his proximity affected her.

"We'll have to ride hard toward the east. The guard has changed shifts," Jafa explained, pointing in the sun's direction before galloping away on his mount.

With practiced ease, Lucius directed their horse and followed at full gallop, staying close behind their guide while Patience struggled to maintain her upright posture.

In the distance, she spotted a large rock formation. Jafa galloped directly toward it, then seemingly vanished. Lucius slowed their horse just before reaching the stones and carefully maneuvered around them. On the far side, they discovered a hidden watering hole where two fresh horses waited patiently.

He dismounted and brought their lathered horse to drink, then lifted her down without comment and placed her gently on the ground.

"We must change mounts. We won't push these as hard for the remainder of the journey," Jafa explained.

She turned to translate for Lucius, but before she could speak, he said, "I understand the general idea." She closed her mouth and introduced herself to the gray mare who would carry them the rest of the way.

Lucius lifted her onto the fresh horse with the same effortless grace as before, catching her off guard. He mounted behind her, took the reins, and followed Jafa at a more sustainable pace, heading west this time.

Only an hour into the ride, her back began aching terribly. She tried to shift positions but had limited space to maneuver.

"Stop squirming, witch."

"I'm sorry. I can't seem to find a comfortable position." She attempted to adjust again when his arm came around her waist, shifting her back against him, then leaning her fully into his broad chest.

Patience made no comment, not wanting him to change his mind about the arrangement.

She settled more comfortably against him, and a profound sense of familiarity washed over her. Had they truly been here together long ago? If it were true, why couldn't either of them remember?

She wasn't sure whether she should tell him about their supposed shared past—about being here together over one hundred and fifty years ago. Could it possibly be true? She didn't remember any of her history, but surely she couldn't have forgotten something so significant.

He wouldn't believe her anyway, even if she told him. To him, she was just another lying witch. He'd probably kill her before trusting anything she said.

She would have to learn more from Jafa before making any decisions. This mission was becoming exponentially more complicated by the hour. This was supposed to be simple: acquire the soul gem, awaken Michael, and return home. Simple and straightforward.

Instead, this was neither simple nor easy, especially when she had the most infamous witch hunter in supernatural history at her back—a man who didn't trust her as far as he could throw her.

She took a deep, steadying breath before panic could set in. One crisis at a time: soul gem first, then deal with everything else. It was a perfect plan.

Now she just had to find the strength to stick to it.

CHAPTER TWELVE

LUCIUS

The witch had finally drifted off to sleep, relaxing against him. Strangely, it brought him comfort to know she was resting. What was most unsettling was how familiar this felt—as though he had been here before, done this all before with her. Even the odd native seemed familiar, like déjà vu.

Lucius didn't want to think about it, but her resting comfortably in his arms brought to the surface a nostalgic feeling of joy he hadn't felt in a long time. He wanted to say it was because of being in this bizarre land where the sun didn't burn his skin, but he knew it wasn't.

Part of him was disgusted with himself for being attracted to her, but another part—which he wanted to bury deep inside—wanted to explore the feeling. She made him *feel*. After his heart had been dead for so long, this made him pause in his anger and disgust.

She differed from any witch he'd ever encountered. She hadn't tried to use her powers on him, but it wasn't simply that. She also treated him like a male and not a feared hunter. She didn't cower in his presence, even knowing how deadly he could be. It was refreshing.

If Maxim hadn't interrupted, he would have taken everything she gave him.

Part of him still wanted to believe it was a spell, even though Alecia told him differently, because if he believed this was real, then... he was afraid to admit the possibilities. He missed Mae every day, but he also missed companionship, joy, and laughter—all the things she made him love and then took away.

Everything in him wished she was anything but a witch so he would be free to explore his feelings for her. Ultimately, this could not be... no matter how much a small part of him wanted it. Once his brother awoke, he would be rid of her, and these feelings would disappear. First, they needed to get through this alive so they could return to their realm.

Though Lucius had a distinct feeling these emotions would not just disappear.

Tents appeared on the horizon in the distance—the village the male was taking them to.

As the witch slept peacefully, he looked at her. He had the urge to lean down and kiss her, but he resisted. Instead, he awakened her roughly.

"Up, witch! We are almost there."

The male looked at him strangely. The witch took her time waking, stretching and yawning, forgetting where she was until she saw him. She smiled at first, then caught herself. Her back straightened, and distance grew between them.

He hated it when she pulled away, even though it was because of him. He despised these feelings she caused.

The male slowed until his horse was walking alongside theirs, then spoke to the witch in a language that sounded familiar to Lucius, though he couldn't place it.

"His village is just ahead," Patience translated.

"Yes, I figured."

The closer they got, the more people gathered, waiting for them. As they approached, the male spoke again.

"These are the Kaverian, and this is their camp. He's telling them to welcome us and that you don't understand the language, so be cautious around you."

The loud clang of cheers echoed around the bustling encampment. His voice sliced through the chaos with a sharp edge. "How come I don't think that's what they said?"

"Well... that was the gist of it."

"Witch, if I find out it was something different—" he threatened, his tone low and menacing.

She nodded quickly. "Yeah, yeah. I know."

The male climbed off his horse, and Lucius followed suit, helping the witch down. He didn't even realize he'd done it until he noticed how close she was to him. The way she gazed at him made him want to drag her into his arms and capture her lips.

The male spoke to the witch, interrupting his thoughts, then gestured for them to follow. An image of the male's head on a pike flashed through Lucius's mind as he growled angrily. The witch laughed, looking pleased with herself for affecting him, as she walked in the direction the male went.

Lucius grunted and followed them through rows and rows of tents until they reached the center, where women gathered around a fire pit with bowls of grains and water—their evening meal preparations.

The male stopped at a tent near the edge of the center and lifted a flap. The witch walked inside. Lucius was about to follow when the male stopped him, shaking his head.

"Witch."

She popped her head through the flap. "He wants to separate us."

The male spoke, and she replied, then smiled. "He doesn't like how you spoke to me earlier and thought I would want distance from you."

She spoke to the male, and he nodded before turning and leaving.

"Come on. I told him you were just grumpy due to lack of food."

When he'd told the witch earlier he was hungry, unfortunately, he wasn't lying. His hunger had grown exponentially since she'd shown up, even though it was usually months between feedings. For now, he had it under control. Max's warning to feed before he left echoed in the back of his head. There was nothing to be done about it now. Soon, this would be over, and he would feed once he returned.

Stepping into the tent, they found a small fire pit in the middle with an opening above it. Fur pallets lined both walls, and woven baskets lay about, giving it a nomadic feel.

"Well, this is comfy," she remarked.

"When darkness falls, we leave."

"Why must you always call me 'witch'? I have a name, you know," she retorted, irritated.

"You are a witch, aren't you?"

With a sigh of defeat, she conceded, "Fine, vampire. Call me what you wish."

She plopped down on a pallet and crossed her arms in contempt.

If she wanted to be a child, then so be it. She was a witch, and nothing would change that. He continued to remind himself of that fact.

"What are we doing here?"

She glanced up at him as he towered over her. "We're waiting for it to get dark. It's safer to wait here since the guards are on high alert. The darkness will give us a better chance of getting the gem, getting to the tree, and going home."

It made sense. "Good."

He went to sit near the fire pit, now with nothing to do but wait for darkness to come. His hunger grew as his fangs itched to sink into her pulsing veins.

The flap opened, bringing Lucius to his feet as the male and a young, white-haired, slender female came in with a platter of meats.

They tried to step further into the tent, but Lucius held up his hand. "Tell them to give us a minute."

She told them as she stood. "And why do you need a minute?"

"Does your magic work?"

She looked confused, then thoughtful. "I—that's an excellent question. Let me try."

She closed her eyes and placed her hands on her sides. After a moment of awkward silence, the sweater she wore transformed into a black T-shirt with the words "I'M A WITCH, BITCH. Deal with it" written on the chest.

If he hadn't wanted to strangle her, he would have laughed.

"I guess I have my magic back."

"Good. Now make it so I can understand the language."

"That would involve me touching you," she said, raising a brow, waiting for his permission.

"Do I have a choice?"

"No."

"Then let's get it over with."

The witch stepped closer. Her scent—vanilla with a hint of honeysuckle—wafted through his nose, driving his senses crazy. His fangs involuntarily descended as he remembered the taste of her lips and his hands on her body. He hid them as she lifted her hands and gently touched his temples.

"You're going to feel a warm, tingly sensation."

He nodded slightly, not trusting himself to speak with her so close.

She closed her eyes to concentrate. He gazed freely at her face, drawn to her lips, wanting to trace every curve with the tip of his tongue. She would taste exquisite.

Warmth, then a tingling sensation crept into his temples. A pleasant feeling washed over him, relaxing him and causing his eyes to fall to her lips. He remembered tasting them, sucking them, licking them. He had the urge to capture them again.

"Are you done?" he forced out. As soon as the words escaped, the sensation stopped, and the witch moved back. They stood in silence. Lucius was trying to get himself under control. If he moved, he would grab her and kiss her. He closed his eyes and took a deep breath. When he opened them, he had more control.

She took another step back, understanding the danger she was in.

"Did it work?" he asked when he felt fully in control.

"Let's find out." She lifted the flap, gesturing for the male and female to enter.

The female set the meats by the fire pit and grabbed tinder to light the fire.

"Please speak to him. My magic works so he may understand now," she said to the male, who turned and looked at Lucius.

"My name is Jafa."

It worked. He could understand him. "Lucius."

Excitement lit up Jafa's face. "Excellent. This is Taki. It's a Kaverian custom for us to cook for our guests." He pointed to the woman lighting the fire. "She will make your meal," he explained to the witch. "Then she will be your meal," he told Lucius before bowing slightly and leaving.

Taki sat quietly as she prepared the witch's meal. Her chestnut skin glowed against the fire as she skillfully added meat to a bowl with sauce. It was odd to see a woman with white hair—it made her elegant. His fangs didn't ache for her, even as his hunger grew. She would do, for now.

He sat back down to wait until the witch's movement caught his eye. She knelt next to Taki.

"May I ask what you're making?" she whispered.

"Yes, I was told our bread dish would be most pleasing to you." Taki pierced the meat and hung it over the fire, then sliced round loaves in half.

Lucius tried to concentrate on their conversation until the witch pulled back her hair to taste the sauce Taki offered, exposing her neck. Her blood pulsed through her veins, drowning out all conversation, all of his thoughts. He dragged his gaze away and tried again to focus.

"Thank you," Patience said as Taki handed her the bread with meat and something white melted on top.

Patience took the pronged utensil and bit into her meal. A moan escaped her lips as juice from the meat ran down her chin, down her neck and over her pulsing vein. His fangs strained against his lips. She tried to catch it with a cloth Taki handed her, exchanging words as she took her meal back to her pallet.

As Taki cleaned, his eyes moved to the witch as she continued to enjoy her meal. He had the urge to clean up the juices himself, to run his tongue over her pulse, to feel it beating before he sank...

Taki knelt in front of him, obscuring his view. She moved her head to the side, exposing her neck.

His fingers itched to push her out of the way and reach for the witch. Then he came to his senses.

Taki reached forward to touch his clenched fists—he hadn't even realized he'd tightened them. She smiled timidly before pulling her long, silky hair aside with no fear, revealing her curved neck. He glanced at the witch, still devouring her food and paying no mind.

Part of him wanted her to stop this moment. For her to be the one in front of him. He was being ridiculous. He grabbed Taki and pulled her between his legs.

Her earthy scent drifted to his nose, causing his fangs to retract. Disappointment hit the pit of his stomach. This wasn't who he wanted.

Of their own accord, his eyes moved to the witch. Her food lay abandoned next to her as she watched them. Several emotions ran through her eyes as they stared at each other, but when doubt appeared, he looked away. He didn't want to know what she read in his.

This was crazy. He needed to feed and not think about the witch.

When he looked up again, the witch was moving toward them. She touched Taki's shoulder.

"You can leave," she commanded.

Taki gazed at him, then nodded and stood, leaving them alone.

The witch's heart raced as she stood above him. Dropping to her knees, she moved between his legs, taking Taki's position and moving her curls aside. Her pulsing vein drew his eyes as he gently pulled her close, running his nose over her neck, taking in a deep breath of her scent—vanilla with a hint of honeysuckle. There it was—the scent he wanted to taste.

He could take it no longer. When his fangs elongated and sank into her neck, her blood poured into his mouth, making its way throughout his body. The world ceased to exist. It was only him and her.

His eyes closed as he savored her sweet, addictive taste, becoming lost in the sensation.

CHAPTER THIRTEEN

Patience

"Dessa, love, wake up," Lucius called from the distance.

Patience slowly opened her eyes and found Lucius looking at her strangely.

"There you are. I thought you would never open your eyes," he smiled.

She sat up slowly and looked around the room. They were in a bedroom in the mansion. How did they get here?

"Dessa, are you okay?" He touched her arm gently. She closed her eyes for a minute and opened them again. He was still there, kneeling beside the bed, looking up at her with love in his eyes.

"Why are you being so nice to me, Lucius? Why are we here? Where are Ian and Michael? I'm so confused."

"Nice to you? Dessa, my love. You are my everything. I'm going to be more than nice to you. Ian and Michael are in their bedroom. You've been through a lot. You need to rest."

Patience's world spun. *Dessa? My love?* What the hell was going on? Someone had to be playing a trick on her. This man would never love her. He hated her.

She looked toward the door as it opened, and the most beautiful little girl she'd ever seen ran into the room. She had silver-gray eyes and curly black hair just like... hers. "Mommy! Daddy!" She jumped onto the bed and crawled right into Patience's arms.

The little girl hugged her tightly and then looked up at her. "You're finally awake! Can we go play outside now?"

"Now, Munchkin, you know Mommy just woke up. Let her eat first. Then we can go," Lucius said, taking her from Patience's arms and setting her down. "Now go find your Uncle Ian and Uncle Michael and tell them Mommy is awake."

She ran out of the room screaming Michael's and Ian's names. Ian and Michael were awake? She needed to see them. She tried to get up, but Lucius stopped her.

"Hey, hold on. Where are you going?"

"I need to see Ian and Michael," she said, trying to get up again.

"They're giving us some time alone first, then they'll be here."

This was all becoming too much. What was going on? Patience laid back down and pulled the covers over her head. She hoped if she went back to sleep, this would just go away.

"Why are you hiding from me?" Lucius said, sitting on the bed and pulling the covers off her face. This is what it would be like if Lucius didn't hate her kind... hate her... if he loved her.

"I'm not hiding from you. I was just waiting for you to find me," she laughed. "I see you have. Finally."

He leaned down and pressed his lips against hers. He suckled her bottom lip, causing her to shudder. Warmth spread over her body as he devoured her lips, deepening the kiss. Then he pulled away, looking at her.

"I love you so much and am glad you're home safe. I don't know what I would have done if I had lost you."

"Don't," she said, grabbing his shoulders and pulling him back to her for a kiss.

"I wish we could stay like this forever," she said as she came up for air. He moved to lie in the bed next to her, and she snuggled closer to him. "I wish this wasn't just a dream."

"A dream?" he said as he buried his nose in her hair, inhaling her scent. "This isn't a dream. Dessa, you're here with me."

"If only that were true." Patience closed her eyes, enjoying the feel of him.

"I'm never going to let you go," Lucius said, then kissed her. "You are mine. Forever."

Warmth surrounded her as she snuggled closer, rubbing her cheek against him, loving the feeling of him against her skin. He was even comfier than her bed. Her hand reached up to touch her chest and met real, live flesh. Her eyes flew open.

Her dream—she remembered it.

She took a moment to replay it before slowly gazing up and seeing the outline of Lucius's face. His eyes were closed. Maybe she was still dreaming. She opened her eyes and looked up again. She was definitely here.

How the hell had they gotten into this position? She remembered talking to Taki, then she was on her pallet eating, then she... walked over to the vampire and took Taki's place. Holy shit!

She sat up abruptly. The vampire slept peacefully beside her, his arm wrapped around her tightly. She touched her neck and found two little healed holes in her artery. Why the hell had she let him do that?

Is this why she remembered her dream?

After this breakthrough, questions raced through her head, but the only one at the forefront was: Was he the key?

Unable to tear her gaze away from his face, she wanted to move away but couldn't. The aura surrounding him was purple again. So strange. It was rare to see him so at peace. The urge to trace the contours of his face overwhelmed her because the chances of getting this opportunity again were slim. Patience leaned over him and gazed upon his face, noticing the faint scar on his chin. She wondered if she would ever learn how it had gotten there. To think the key she'd been looking for might be sitting right in front of her.

A sigh escaped his lips, drawing her eyes. Licking her lips, she couldn't help but reach down and kiss him. Her lips gently pressed to his, but his hand grabbed the back of her head as she was about to pull back. She waited for the pain.

To her surprise, he deepened the kiss. She became so lost that she failed to notice Taki and Jafa banging against an invisible wall. It wasn't until the vampire let her up for air that the electric energy ran through her.

"Shit. Damn."

"I kind of wish I got that answer every time I kissed a female." Lucius smiled, distracting her from the problem at hand. His smile was devastating. She wished he would smile at her all the time like this.

"As much as I want to lie here with you, I may have erected a protective barrier while we slept." She stood and saw Taki and Jafa banging against the barrier.

She gestured to them, indicating they were both okay. They nodded understanding. She touched her hand to the barrier and tried to get it to fall, but nothing.

"Shit."

The vampire stood behind her. She already missed his warmth. She tried to dismantle the barrier, but it wouldn't budge.

"Witch."

She cringed at the contempt in his voice. She had a feeling his aura had turned back to dark red.

"Take down the barrier."

"What do you think I'm trying to do?" Instead of trying to dismantle it, she tried to absorb the barrier, but it zapped her, causing her to fly back. The vampire caught her.

"Doesn't seem like it's working." He lifted her back to her feet.

"Thank you, Captain Obvious." She walked back to the barrier, examining it. "Maybe it's not mine—"

"It's not." The vampire put his hand on the barrier, and it dropped. "It's mine."

What the hell? Why did he put up a barrier? And why couldn't she take it down? She sensed her magic within the barrier.

As soon as the barrier fell, Jafa rushed to them. "Nightfall has come. We must go. We've lost some time already."

The vampire was behind her, and she could only imagine what his face looked like after hearing the news.

"Are the horses ready?" he demanded.

"They will be, momentarily."

The vampire grunted as Taki lifted the flap, leaving.

"We'll be right out," she let Jafa know. She needed a moment with the vampire.

Jafa nodded and left.

As soon as the flap closed, he spun her around.

"You will tell no one of what occurred here last night."

Pain flared in her arms from where he gripped her. "You're hurting me."

"Do you understand me, witch?" He spat the word as he abruptly let her go.

She didn't know how to respond. Should she tell him? Would he believe her? This was getting complicated. Of course, he didn't want anyone to know how he smiled at her or that she'd willingly given him her blood. She would have to figure out how to approach this with him. Or just get him to bite her again...

"No worries. I wouldn't dream... of it."

Something flashed in his eyes, then was gone. Patience thought it looked like regret but couldn't be sure.

"Let's just go so we can get back home."

"Agreed."

She picked up her knapsack and walked out of the tent, finding Jafa waiting outside. "We're ready," she said.

"The last time you—"

Patience put her hand over Jafa's mouth quickly. She looked behind her, relieved that the vampire was still in the tent. She took Jafa's arm and walked away, slipping into another tent, out of Lucius's earshot.

"Look, I really don't want him to know we were here before. I'm not sure his puny little brain can handle it."

"I understand. He didn't know of your life before."

"Tell me why we were here. You know, back then."

"You were here looking for a man. He had something important to both of you, but you wouldn't say what it was. You knew he was working with Sucora. You were hoping to find some clue to his whereabouts."

What would have been important to both of them? Unless this man had Michael and Ian, this didn't make sense. The child from her dreams... or memories? This was getting stranger by the minute.

"Do you know what this man looks like?"

"Possibly. If I saw him again, I may know him, but it's been many moons."

"Witch, you have ten seconds to show yourself!" the vampire yelled in the distance.

Patience rolled her eyes, then whispered to Jafa. "Keep this between us for now."

"Of course. I can see your relationship has changed significantly since you were last here."

"Changed? How?"

"Witch," the vampire yelled in the distance.

She needed to have a longer conversation with Jafa later. "Come before the baby cries." She lifted the flap and walked back to the vampire.

The angry death stare was back.

"No games, witch."

"We were just gathering supplies for our journey. Let's go."

She let Jafa lead the way to the horses. She was curious about how her relationship with Lucius had changed. Was it for the better or worse? She would have to figure out how to get more answers from Jafa without the vampire knowing.

When they got to the horses, she realized there were two. Shit. That meant she would have to ride with him again, but maybe she could ride with Jafa. Before she could think more about it, he lifted and deposited her on a brown chestnut mare. Then, the vampire was behind her. Well, there went that worry.

"We must ride fast. These horses will take us all the way to the hole in the palace wall. Do you remember where it is? Make sure you're not spotted," Jafa said as he got on the black mare.

The vampire nodded.

Then Taki jumped on the back of Jafa's horse, and they galloped off. Patience expected them to get moving, but the vampire did nothing.

"Hello?" She tried to turn, but then his arm came around her front and pushed her back completely against him.

"I'm going to need you to hold on to me and squeeze your thighs tight against the horse," he softly whispered into her ear. "We're going to be going fast." He gave her a minute to readjust herself. "Are you ready?"

No, I'm not. She nodded anyway. She grabbed hold of his arm. Then they were off.

Holding on for dear life, the scenery blurred as they moved as fast as the wind. She gripped him tighter, and he pulled her closer until he enveloped her, safe and warm in his arms. The dream drifted through her thoughts again—seeing the love in his eyes and the way she responded to him, how happy she was with him.

Ever since she met him, she'd never dreamed of red eyes. She remembered the words he spoke: "I'm never going to let you go. You are mine. Forever."

They weren't the exact words that tumbled through her mind when waking from her nightmares, but they were close. Was he red eyes? Was this a trick? None of this made sense. It was confusing as hell. This would be so much easier if she could unlock her memories; sitting right behind her was the key to that possibility.

His arms squeezed her a little closer to him, and pure euphoria spread through her. This ride was going to kill her. Distracting herself with somet hing... anything, her brain cleared of its euphoric fog, and she remembered the male from the club. Alden? She believed his name was. He knew her, and Lucius knew him. How did he remember her but not Lucius? She had to get answers. This wasn't the best time to ask, but who knew when would be suitable?

Gathering courage, she yelled. "Who was that male at the club?"

"WHAT?" he yelled back over the wind.

"WHO WAS THAT MALE AT THE CLUB?"

"YOU'RE ASKING ME THIS NOW?"

"SEEMED LIKE A GOOD IDEA AT THE TIME!"

The vampire ignored her and continued to ride through the moonlit desert, following Jafa and Taki. She would have to wait. Clearly, he didn't plan to answer her questions on the back of the horse at breakneck speed. Unintentionally, she snuggled closer until her bottom rested against his rock-hard bulge, loving the feel of him. All thoughts of memory, dreams, and mystery men went out the window when his nose buried into her neck and inhaled. The need to see his face overwhelmed her.

She summoned Seckor, her favorite pathfinder, then placed her hand on the horse, sending a soothing magical command for him to slow to a walk and follow Seckor.

As the horse slowed, she lifted her leg over the horse's head to sit sidesaddle, with no fear of falling, to face him.

"Witch, what do you think you're doing—"

Pushing aside all thoughts about the danger they were heading into, her lips crashed into his in a frenzy. She caught his bottom lip, sucking it until his tongue invaded her mouth, exploring every crevice. She knew this was crazy, but she couldn't help it. The urge to kiss him wouldn't go away until she got her fill of him.

The horse continued to walk across the desert toward the palace as she devoured him until she finally managed to break them apart. Putting her hand on the horse, she sent a magical command for it to stop, even though the palace was still miles away. They stared at each other as they caught their breath.

"What was that, witch?"

She wanted to kiss him again. Her hand went to the bite on her neck, drawing his eyes to it. She wondered if this was because he bit her.

"We don't have time for this—"

"Who was the man at the club?"

"Is that why you kissed me? So you could get an answer to your question?"

It was a good excuse until she figured out what the hell was happening between them. For now, maybe she could get some answers about her past. "No, but I thought I would ask since we're here."

"Witches and their games. Why do you want to know who the male from the club was? Who is he to you?"

"Possibly the key I've been looking for."

For a moment, she thought he would yell at her and call her a cruel name, but he surprised her.

"His name is Alden, and I'll tell you more about him when we return, but for now, we must go. They're waiting for us. We've lost too much time."

She had no choice but to believe him; they'd lost too much time already.

"Okay, you're right. I'll trust you to keep your word."

He nodded as Patience slowly lifted her leg back over the horse, turning around, ignoring the rising urge to kiss him again.

"Follow Seckor. He'll show you the way." She pointed to the ball of light.

Lucius took up the reins, following Seckor as they raced through the night undetected until they reached the hole in the wall where Taki and Jafa were waiting.

The vampire removed himself quickly from the horse. She believed he would abandon her, but his hand gripped her waist, bringing her to the ground.

"Good, you're here," Jafa said, smiling. "The tree is heavily guarded, so we'll need a distraction, but first, we must get you to the tower for the gem. Taki will show you the way. Once you get the gem, you must be quick. She'll know it was taken."

He moved closer and looked up at the top of the wall. "The guards are changing shifts. Follow Taki and do as she says. I'll see you soon, my friends."

Jafa disappeared through the wall. Shouts and a grunt could be heard, then silence. Taki gestured for them to follow her.

Moving through the wall, two guards lay unconscious on the ground. Taki pulled them aside, sticking them behind barrels near the wall. Holding up a hand to wait, she ran toward the fountain, peeking around until two guards passed. She motioned for them to follow.

They moved silently behind her, sneaking past more guards until they approached a door. Taki picked the lock and peered through. She turned to nod, letting them know the coast was clear when a guard appeared in the doorway and grabbed her, pulling her through the door. Before she could blink, Lucius appeared behind the guard, his eyes illuminated, snapping the guard's head clean off. Another guard emerged, and without hesitation, Lucius grabbed the guard and plunged his teeth into its neck, ripping out its throat.

The image before her reminded her why he was the Ragana Zidikas. His eyes illuminated brighter, and his fangs grew sharper. Blood dripped down his mouth, and an evil grin formed. He pulled Luzia from his back, and two more guards emerged behind him.

Taki quickly closed the door, shielding her from seeing what happened next. She grabbed Patience's hand and led her to hide behind a wagon. Four guards passed by them, unaware of their companions' deaths.

"Shouldn't we go help him?"

"No, he comes now."

Patience glanced at the door and, just as Taki said, Lucius appeared without a scratch. Using his sleeve, he wiped the blood from his mouth and then used the guard's shirt to wipe the blood from Luzia as his eyes searched the courtyard, almost passing over the wagon, until they hastened back, locking onto them. With no fear of being caught, he strode over and reached out his hand for her to take.

Patience gazed at him, loving the power radiating from him and hating how delicious he looked now. *Fuck. If only there were time.*

She couldn't help when her tongue darted from her mouth to lick her very... parched lips.

"Witch," he growled as his silver eyes illuminated.

"More guards come. This way," Taki informed them, breaking the spell and moving back toward the door.

Patience grabbed his hand, and he led her across, swiftly moving her through the door and past the six dead guards. She tried to ignore the blood on the walls, but she couldn't miss the torn limbs on the floor. Someone had some anger to let out.

They moved through the halls silently, not encountering any more guards, until they found the steps leading to the tower.

"She's at dinner, so the room will be empty," Taki informed them. "Find your way into the room. Be quick about it. I'll wait right here for you."

They crept up the stone steps until they came to a simple wooden door. The vampire was about to reach for the handle when the witch stopped him.

"The door is spelled," she whispered.

More like cursed.

She placed her hand an inch from the handle. Power emanated from it. The spell was powerful and would resist her. She could touch the door and absorb the curse, or she could...

She tried to go through it but couldn't. Then she tried to absorb the magic, but it didn't work. What the hell?

"What's the problem, witch?"

"I can't... I can't open the door. My magic isn't working again."

He glanced at her strangely. Then he touched the door handle. The stone on his neck glowed as he opened the door. She hoped it was just the place and not anything else. She remembered not being able to dismantle his barrier earlier. It should have been easy work for her, no matter whose barrier, but she couldn't absorb the magic. This place had to be affecting her powers.

Lucius cautiously walked into the room. She followed him.

A dark purple king-sized four-poster bed sat in the middle of a large black room. Chains hung from the top of the bed, but nothing else was in the room—except the gem.

A blue marquise-cut gem sat right there, embedded in the headboard, gleaming at them. It was so inviting, begging for them to take it.

Patience climbed onto the bed, but he pulled her back before she could grab the gem.

"What are you doing, witch?" The vampire stood at the edge of the bed.

"What does it look like I'm doing? I'm taking the gem." She tried to reach for it again, but he pulled her back.

"Something doesn't feel right," he said. "Get down now. My stone is burning. A spell is being cast."

"Let me just grab the—wait, don't touch the bed!" she cried. *Fuck!* The bed was enchanted. She looked down and saw his leg touching the bed. *Shit.*

It was too late. His eyes illuminated as desire sprang into them. "We don't have time for this."

They were screwed. She knew this enchantment. An old friend wanted her to put this enchantment on his bed, but as she read up on it, she realized it enslaved people. Anybody who touched the bed would succumb to instant lust for the person on the bed, which was her. Shit, he was totally going to blame her for this.

"There is always time for this, Zeita." He pulled her down hard onto the bed and covered her body with his.

"Lucius, you must fight the enchantment. Remember, you hate witches. I'm a witch. Fight it."

Ignoring her pleas, his lips descended upon hers, consuming them completely. She needed to fight him. It was hard for her to resist when she didn't want to stop. *Focus. Stay focused.* "Stop this."

"I could never hate you, Mae. You are my everything."

Surrendering to the enchantment and his touch, she let his hands move over her body, driving away all thoughts of resistance.

No, they needed to stop. She had to stop this. The enchantment was consuming her mind. They would lose themselves if she didn't stop.

"Zeita, I finally have you where I've wanted you since I first saw you." He captured her mouth, sending shivers down her spine.

She wanted him inside her right now. Flipping him over, she climbed on top of him and unbuttoned his pants. Something gleamed out of the corner of her eye. She turned and gazed at the beautiful gem on the headboard.

Why did it look so familiar?

Lucius pulled her down to him and had her under him. "Stay with me, love."

She needed to be somewhere... someone needed her. Michael. It all came rushing back to her. She grabbed the vampire immediately, rolling them off the bed.

They didn't move for a moment.

Several emotions crossed the vampire's face: desire, confusion, then anger. He lifted her off him, then stood, buttoning his pants and checking to make sure his sword was still on his back.

She stood, straightening out her shirt. She dared to look in his direction and saw him easily reach for the gem, plucking it from its resting place.

Next time, she wouldn't be so fast to touch foreign objects. She took the glopinian out of her satchel. She cautiously approached him and removed a tiny feather from his shirt. He flinched, grabbing her hand.

"I have the glopinian."

He slowly let go of her hand and placed the gem in it. She was surprised to see no emotion in his eyes when he looked at her.

"We have to go. Taki is waiting for us."

He nodded and led the way out of the room. They made their way back down the stairs but found the hallway empty.

"Where did she go?" Patience asked. "Shit. What do we do now?" They looked both ways, but there was no sign of her.

"Do you have the gem?"

Taki appeared behind them, startling Patience. "Don't do that!"

"Do you have the gem?" she repeated, ignoring Patience's outburst.

"Yes," Lucius said, unfazed by her sudden appearance.

"Good. Let me see so I know you have the right one."

"You mean there's more than one here? Jafa never mentioned that."

"Yes. A decoy. I need to see that you have the real one. Why do you think he sent me with you? I'm the only one who can tell you if it's real."

Patience pulled the gem from her satchel and opened the glopinian to reveal the gem. "Is it real?"

"Yes." Suddenly, Taki opened her hand and blew dust in their faces—a sleeping powder.

"What the hell?" Patience tried not to breathe it in, but it was too late. Her world tilted, then spun. "Sorry, I need this more than you." Taki slipped the glopinian right out of Patience's hand.

Patience turned to find the vampire already passed out on the floor.

"You're much stronger than him." She blew more dust into Patience's face.

Unable to stand upright, she slid to the floor as Taki walked away with the gem in hand.

She strained to stay conscious as the guards arrived moments later. She tried to reach for the vampire, but the last thing she remembered was being lifted before she fell unconscious.

"Theá." Someone called. "Theá, is that you?"

Patience sluggishly opened her eyes. Darkness surrounded her. She tried to bring her hands to her face, but found them chained to the wall behind her. "Damn."

"Theá, is that you?" the voice repeated.

"GreyJoy?"

"No, it's me. Jafa."

He called her Theá. Only GreyJoy called her that. She tried to make out his shape before her, but no light was seeping in from anywhere. "Jafa? Where are you? I can't see a thing."

"I believe I'm a few feet from you."

"Where are we?" She pulled on the chains, praying for a miracle. They held fast to the slimy wall. Part of her was glad she couldn't see where they were. From the sludge she was sitting on, she had a feeling she wouldn't like what she found.

"We were betrayed. Taki betrayed us." Jafa said, his voice guilt-ridden.

"Well... I figured that when she blew the dust into my face. So where are we?"

"In her dungeon."

"How do we escape?" She pulled harder at her chains as she tried to call forth her magic, but it still wasn't working. "Damn."

"Shh... Theá. They come."

CHAPTER FOURTEEN

Lucius

"Lucius. Oh, Lucius. It's time to wake up."

Lucius slowly opened his eyes and lifted his head to find himself bound with elvan rope, sitting at a long, elegant dining table surrounded by strangers. The oak oil made the rope grow tighter the more the victim struggled. He had used it on many witches.

A goblet of thick blood sat in front of him. The smell wasn't human. He looked up and saw two pairs of eyes staring at him—the king and queen, who sat sipping their wine, watching him with curiosity.

"Ah, finally, we can have some fun."

He turned his head, following the voice until his eyes landed on a beautiful green-haired female. He didn't like the mischievous smile on her face.

"Who are you?"

"You come back to my kingdom and have the audacity to ask who I am?" She stood and strolled over to him. Her fingers ran through his hair, grabbing a fistful and pulling his head back, forcing him to stare into her strikingly purple eyes.

"Oh, Lucius. How naïve and foolish of you not to remember." She let go. "Now, the real fun can begin."

Lucius paid no mind to Sucora's rambling. Lies. He had never been here before.

He searched the table for the witch or the native. They were nowhere to be seen. They might have escaped, or she had them locked away somewhere in this damn place. He glanced around for an escape route. Guards stood at the exits in front of him.

"Ah, there you are." Sucora held out her hand as Taki walked out of the wall to his right and handed her the gem. "Good girl."

"May I have it now?"

"Get on your knees, child."

Taki immediately obeyed, dropping to her knees in front of Sucora.

"For being an obedient child and doing as you're told, I'll grant your wish." A small glass bottle filled with black liquid appeared in Sucora's hand. "Open your mouth."

Taki opened her mouth and let Sucora pour all the black liquid down her throat. Taki immediately cringed and held her stomach.

"You asked to be immortal like me, and now you are."

Taki's skin turned stone gray, and her eyes went completely black.

"Guards!" Two guards appeared immediately. "Throw her in the Gorganite's pen." The guards dragged her lifeless body out.

"Now that unpleasant business is done, we can have some real fun." Guards moved to his side and turned Lucius's chair so he could face an open room. A striking throne of onyx sat on the opposite side, with crystal skulls adorning its legs and back. A stained-glass window sat behind the throne, depicting the horror queen herself. Luzia leaned against it in her sheath, awaiting his grasp.

The floor in front of the throne opened, and a platform rose from the dark below. Her scent hit his nose, letting him know the witch was on the platform before it reached the surface. Patience and Jafa sat on two chairs, tightly bound with rope.

"Finally, she joins us. Come to steal from me again." Sucora said as she moved over to the platform.

The witch glanced around the room until her eyes finally landed on him. Relief washed over her face before she turned and whispered something to Jafa. Then her shoulders squared as she took a deep breath.

"You make it so easy. I couldn't resist," Patience taunted.

"Well, there's no one here to help you escape now. You're all mine."

"You will not touch her! She is sacred, and you will be punished by—" Jafa yelled, but the back of Sucora's hand silenced him as she slapped him hard.

"Kaverians. So easily breakable. Now, where were we? Ah, yes."

The platform turned. Lucius and Patience now faced each other with distance between them. "Now your lover can watch as I slowly bleed you." A sharp, curved knife appeared in Sucora's hand as she moved in front of the witch. Her cackle echoed throughout the room as she raised her hand and cut two thin slashes across the witch's cheeks. Droplets of blood formed, dripping down her cheeks.

"Fuck you!" Patience screamed.

Sucora smiled, reaching out a finger and wiping a droplet of blood off the witch's cheek. She stuck out her tongue, placing the droplet on her long, snake-like tongue.

"You taste even better than before. This time, I'll taste your delectable flesh." Sucora grabbed the witch's head and licked the blood directly from her cheek. "Mmm... delicious. Let us bleed you more."

Slowly and meticulously, she sliced her knife across the witch's flesh, creating deadly lacerations. Blood ran down her cheeks, staining her shirt. The blood on her arms dripped down, soaking her pants and pooling on the floor. The witch struggled, trying not to cry out, but she lost the battle when Sucora sliced through her shoulder. Her scream resounded through the room as the smell of her blood permeated the air. Every time she cried out, his rage grew, bringing to the surface a deadly fury he had only experienced once before—when his wife died.

He struggled against the ropes, needing to get to her, not caring that they dug into his hands, causing them to bleed. His sole focus was reaching her as he continued to struggle, feeling the rope grow tighter and tighter. His fingers were growing numb as it cut off his circulation.

"Oh, look, I think he's getting upset," Sucora said, turning away from the witch. "I think he'll feel differently once I get him into my bed." She laughed, slicing the knife too close to the artery on the witch's neck, giving him her back as she continued to make the witch bleed out. Only her evil laughter filled the room. No more screams could be heard from the witch.

His fangs descended as the rage became uncontrollable. He continued to pull, losing all feeling in his hands until a gentle hand landed on his shoulders.

"Calm, my friend. We'll get you all out of here." The queen. He had forgotten they were behind him, watching this all. She looked over, and he followed the direction of her gaze. The king stealthily moved toward Sucora. Too consumed in her torture, she didn't see him until it was too late. He placed a knife at her throat. "Drop it."

"Never." Sucora stabbed the witch in her leg too close to her artery. Lucius snarled, wanting to rip her throat out. If the king didn't kill her, he would. Lucius quickly glanced around for the guards. They all lay dead at the exits.

"Drop it or lose what's most precious to you." The king pulled out another knife and placed it against Sucora's belly. She immediately dropped the knife. The king kicked it away.

"How could you?" she asked vehemently.

He grabbed her head. "Bitch, you had this coming to you. My wife doesn't like you very much." The sound of Sucora's neck snapping as he twisted it didn't calm Lucius's rage.

"Wife, work quickly. We may only have minutes before she awakens and is royally pissed." He tossed a knife to his wife. She caught it and cut the ropes off Lucius.

He grabbed the knife from her and ran to the witch, pushing the king out of the way. The king moved to the other side, and Lucius swiftly cut the ropes, releasing the witch and Jafa. He gathered Patience into his arms. Her heart was still beating, barely. She was losing too much blood.

The queen knelt near him. "Lay her down. We need to stop some of the bleeding."

Lucius placed her gently on the ground.

"Rip these the long way." The queen handed him a small pile of cloth. He ripped them into long pieces as she took them and wrapped them around the largest cuts. She tied two pieces together to wrap the wounds around her neck and leg. "That should hold her for now." She stood.

"We need to get her out of here now," the king said, throwing Jafa over his shoulders.

"This way. Follow me," the queen yelled, already having moved across the room, where she dispatched a few guards coming through the door, stealing their swords.

Lucius gently gathered the witch into his arms, holding her tightly against him as he blindly followed them through the castle. His thoughts were consumed with the witch's slow-beating heart.

The queen used her dual swords to take out guard after guard as the king followed silently, carrying Jafa over his shoulder while wielding a sword, killing any guard she missed.

Lucius gazed down at the witch when he almost thought her heart stopped, not seeing the guard come up behind him. A dagger flew past his head. He saw the queen nod, taking out two more guards. Lucius glanced behind to see the dagger protruding from the guard's head.

"This way," the king yelled from the doorway. Lucius continued to follow until they reached the stables.

The king put Jafa on the back of a gray spotted mare. "I'll hold her while you get on the horse."

Lucius hesitated.

"I promise I'll give her right back to you."

Lucius handed her over, got on the horse, and reached for her. The king handed her up. Lucius tried not to think about the relief that spread through him when she was back in his arms.

The queen dropped from the wall above—Lucius hadn't even known she'd separated from them. "We must go now. The gate is open." The queen leaped onto the back of a white mare the king had secured for her as the king climbed on the spotted mare. "Let's go."

Taking the lead, the queen raced through the gate as a dead guard dropped from above. The king and Lucius followed her through.

The gates closed behind them slowly until guards on horses burst through. They lost the guards as they raced across the desert toward the rising sun.

It was well above their heads when they reached Jafa's village. The witch's heart was growing faint. As soon as they rode into the village, the Kaverians came to help. They took Jafa from the king and tried to take the witch from him, but he refused. His grip tightened as they reached up to grab her. "Get back. Leave her."

The queen climbed off her horse and walked toward Lucius. "Hand her to me. They need to give her to the village elders so they can save her."

"No." His hands refused to let her go.

"Please trust me," she pleaded.

He handed her over and watched as they carried her to the village elders, controlling himself not to go after her. He climbed down from the horse and saw the king. He strode over to him.

"Thank you," Lucius murmured, bowing his head respectfully before the king.

The king nodded. "I am—"

"King Kieran and she must be your wife, Queen Circe." Lucius interrupted, recognizing them.

Circe gracefully joined her husband's side. "You know who we are?" she asked, surprised.

Lucius gave a knowing nod. "Yes. I met you both a long time ago when you met with my great-grandfather, Dracul Cordovan. I am Lucius Cordovan."

"He's a descendant of Lilith," Kieran added, giving Circe a look he couldn't quite decipher.

"We believe the female with you can help us get out of here," Circe revealed.

"What makes you believe she can help you?" Lucius questioned.

"She's a witch. Quite a powerful one if my senses are correct," Circe replied confidently.

Before he could question them further, Jafa appeared and dropped to his knees in front of Circe and Kieran.

"Thank you for saving us. We're completely at your service," Jafa declared fervently, his eyes brimming with sincere gratitude.

Circe reached out a hand to help him up, her expression softening. "Please stand up. There's no need for such formality." Circe helped Jafa to his feet.

"Let me show you more comfortable accommodation as we wait for Theá to recover." Warm hospitality radiated from his words.

Jafa led them away toward a tent. *Theá?* The bookstore had called her the same.

He wondered what it meant. He would have to ask the witch. If she survived...

Pain pierced his heart. She wouldn't die. They would save her.

He shouldn't care, but rage still burned inside him. He wanted to rip Sucora apart limb by limb for daring to even touch her. His irrational thoughts made little sense to him, but his rage was real. His worry was genuine.

One of the Kaverians found him pacing near the edge of the village and brought him to the tent they'd used before. He could still smell Patience's scent in the air.

They brought him food and drink, but he couldn't touch it. His worry consumed his thoughts. At some point, he tried to convince himself his worry was only because she was his way home, but in his heart, he knew it was more.

Finally, Jafa emerged from the tent, his face etched with worry. He stood immediately.

"How is she?" Lucius asked, his voice tight with concern.

"I'm afraid she's not doing so well. We've done all we can, but the bleeding won't stop," came the grave reply.

"Take me to her," he commanded, striding forward purposefully.

Jafa led him to a small tent tucked away at the edge of the village. The sound of distant drums and chanting filled the air.

"She's in there. I must gather herbs to see if we can stop the bleeding." Jafa said before he hurried away.

Lucius moved the flap aside and stepped inside. They had laid her on a table and removed her clothes, leaving her naked except for her privates, which were covered with cloth. He didn't realize how extensive and deep the cuts were. The wounds continued to bleed even though they'd been cleaned and cauterized.

There had been poison on the blade. He bent close to one wound, sniffing. Crimson Clutch. It was meant to hold its victim's death at bay by giving them a long, slow, agonizing death. *Fuck.*

Her heart still beat even though it was slowly fading.

"You have a connection to her," Circe said as she walked in and touched his shoulder. "I can feel it even now."

"It's a lie. I don't know her."

"That may be, but the connection isn't a lie. You know you can save her."

"I cannot..."

"You can, but it's your choice."

The flap lifted, lighting up the witch's face as Circe left, leaving him to decide.

He stood gazing at her, listening to her slowly fading heart, debating whether to save her or let fate take its course. Then he remembered his dream as she slept in his arms, of the girl with silver-gray eyes like his and curly black hair like hers. He reached out, moving a curl from her face. He didn't know if fate showed him his future or if his dreams were trying to tell him what his heart already knew; either way, he had already decided.

Taking a deep breath, he placed his hand on her arm and whispered a healing spell he'd learned long ago from a witch who tried to use the spell to bargain for her life. After giving him the spell, he killed her anyway. She'd been killing children to gain youth—he couldn't let her live no matter the bargain.

The stone on his neck grew cold as he drew magic from it. His hand glowed white as magic flowed from it, spreading over her body and pouring into the wounds. He suddenly pulled his hand away, halting the spell.

His nostrils flared as anger seized him; the spell healed the cauterized skin over the wounds, reopening the cuts.

"Damn witch magic," he yelled, slamming his fist against the wood of the table.

Her heart continued to grow faint. Frustrated and panicked, he made a split-second decision, not thinking of the consequences.

Lucius opened her mouth, then lifted his wrist to his mouth and bit down, opening a wound. He held his wrist over her mouth and let the blood drip down her throat. She didn't respond at first, but then her hand shot up and gripped his wrist, bringing it to her mouth.

Her soft lips sucked the blood from his veins, giving him pleasure he hadn't felt in so long. This was sacred and not shared with anyone except someone he trusted. It was unthinkable for him to do this, but they needed her... he needed her. Reluctantly, he pulled his wrist away. His blood did its job as the cuts on her body ceased bleeding and closed. Her silky brown skin was once again smooth.

Her heartbeat was strong when she opened her eyes. They pierced through him as though she were seeing his soul and all his desires. She slowly sat up, her eyes never leaving his.

"Lucius." She held the piece of cloth to her breasts, drawing his gaze to them. Glancing away, he saw a blanket lying in the corner. He picked it up, handed it to her, and then turned his back.

"What happened?" she whispered, voice barely audible.

"Her blade was poisoned," he replied, voice strained. "Your wounds wouldn't stop bleeding. I healed you."

"You did?" she asked incredulously, looking down at her now clean and unblemished arm.

He nodded solemnly. "Yes, you forget I—we still need you."

Patience gently tapped his shoulder. "I'm all covered. Now tell me how we got out of there?"

Lucius turned to find she'd wrapped the blanket around her body, shielding her completely from his view. "Believe it or not, the king and queen helped us escape."

"Did Jafa make it?" she asked, concern filling her voice.

"Yes. He's fine. You were the only one badly hurt." Sucora's words came back to him. "Have you crossed paths with her before?"

"That's a good question. I don't know. She seemed to think I had, so it's possible. All I know is I couldn't help but taunt her. If I was here before, I definitely didn't like her and still don't. Did you get the gem?"

The gem. He'd completely forgotten about it. He'd been too busy trying to protect the witch and Luzia... "Shit. Get dressed. I need to find Jafa."

He rushed out of the tent in the direction he'd seen Jafa run off.

"Could I get my clothes, at least?" she yelled.

He ignored her and strode between tents, trying to determine which one the native was in. All the tents looked the same. "Shit. Fuck." He turned around and headed back.

What did I do? A few feet away from her tent, he paused. Glancing down at his wrist, he touched where the witch had drawn his blood. This changed everything, which should have made him regret it, except it didn't. The dream kept drifting to the front of his mind. The image of the little girl wouldn't leave him. It was already beginning to take effect since he was already contemplating a future with her. He couldn't deal with this now. He had to return for the gem. Their time was running out. He moved to lift the flap until footsteps approached. It was Jafa and another Kaverian.

"Is she awake?" Jafa asked cautiously.

"Yes."

A smile grew on his face as he dropped to his knees. "Thank the almighty."

The other Kaverian smiled and ran off—Lucius assumed to tell the others. "We need to go back, Jafa."

"Back?" Jafa seemed confused, and then sudden realization dawned on his face. "Yes, for the tree. Unfortunately, you'll have to wait until she's no longer on high alert. There are too many guards."

He'd forgotten about the tree being their way home. This didn't bode well for them.

"We must go back for the gem and my sword. This entire trip is pointless without the gem. Where are the king and queen?"

"I'll take you to them."

Lucius followed Jafa as he brought him to a large tent at the end of the camp. Before Jafa could even announce their presence, the queen called them to enter. Jafa lifted the flap, and they entered.

"Ah, wonderful. I just heard you decided," she exclaimed, moving toward him, clapping her hands joyfully. King Kieran nodded to him in acknowledgment but continued to eat his food by the fire.

"Come sit. Join us." Queen Circe patted the stump next to the king and offered Lucius a bowl of soup. He kindly declined.

"I need your help. I need to go back. We need to retrieve what we came for."

The king leaned over to the side, picked up something, then threw it at Lucius. He caught it. It was the bag with the gem. "Is that what you needed to retrieve?"

Lucius opened the bag, revealing the gem. "Yes."

"Good. Now, we can leave as soon as the witch recovers."

"I also need to go back for my sword."

The queen approached a cloth and pulled his sheathed sword from under it. "Is this the sword you're talking about?"

Grabbing the sword, he pulled it from its sheath. There she was, in all her marvelous glory. "Yes."

He put her back in her sheath and strapped her to his back as the witch stepped through the tent's flap.

"I take it we got lucky, and the gem was recovered?"

In one instance, the king was sitting; in the next, he was standing in front of the witch—an electric blue barrier erected around her.

"Now your point has been proven." Circe stood on her tiptoes and whispered something in his ear. He visibly relaxed even though the scowl never left his face. He stepped back, but the witch's barrier didn't drop.

"I'm grateful you helped us," she began politely, "I know he's the king of Evictus, and you must be the queen. Why do you want to go back to our realm? What were you doing here?"

Circe walked in front of the witch but kept her distance. "Yes, I'm Circe, his wife."

"Queen of Evictus," the king interjected.

"We were here to obtain her army," Queen Circe announced, "though it seems we won't need her army anymore."

The witch leaned forward curiously. "And why is that?"

"Because we may have found allies who may help us."

"And who may that be?" the witch inquired.

"You and the Ragana Zidikas." Circe replied, a glint of determination in her eyes.

Lucius turned to look at the witch, and at the exact moment, she looked at him.

The witch's eyes widened in astonishment. "What?" the witch exclaimed, clearly taken aback by their proposition.

CHAPTER FIFTEEN

LUCIUS

Before Lucius could respond, Silas appeared in the tent before him. "Your twenty-four hours, and then some, are up. You must return."

"I said thirty-six," the witch said.

"Thirty-six hours is too long. His circle is fading faster, so you're needed back."

"Silas, we have guests." Lucius pointed out. He turned to see King Kieran and Queen Circe.

"Silas?" the queen asked as she walked up to him. Silas froze when she gently touched his face. "Little brother?"

"Sister?"

"Yes."

They stared into each other's eyes, and then Silas pulled her to him, wrapping her in his arms. "I thought you were dead. How is this possible?"

Silas had thought his sister had been lost to him for all these years. Yet here she was, standing in front of him. The queen of Evictus was his sister after everything that had happened. This didn't surprise him.

"It's a long story. All that matters is we found each other." Tears streamed down her face as she took a step back from Silas.

"Well, if this isn't a change of events. How do we know this isn't a trick?" the witch asked suspiciously. Lucius had to admit she made an excellent point.

Silas turned and looked at the witch. "This is no trick. This is my sister. If you must, you can check." He held out his hand to her.

Her shield stayed in place as she approached him. She allowed an opening just enough for his hand to fit through. He placed it within. She touched it, closing her eyes.

A moment later, she let go of Silas and opened her eyes. "He speaks the truth."

"Show me."

The witch gazed at him, a little shocked, but quickly recovered. With her shield still up, she allowed an opening for his hand. He reached within, and as soon as they clasped, the shield expanded around him.

Her scent was everywhere within the shield, causing his nostrils to flare as his desire ignited. An electric warmth spread over his skin, making him feel safe, which was foreign to him. "What the hell? Witch, what are you doing?"

"I don't know. I didn't do it on purpose. It did it itself."

"They're your powers," he argued.

"Sometimes they have their own mind," she argued back.

"Just show me."

She closed her eyes and projected what she saw within Silas. Images of Silas and Queen Circe as children playing in lush green grass with a Novarian castle in the distance, then as adolescents hiding in a dark Novarian cavern, their faces illuminated by a dying torch, flashed through his mind. They were Novarians, skilled warrior assassins, part of the nation of Sabia that was lost long ago in the realm of Enoch. The city of light in the realm of darkness. Lilith destroyed their kind. Not all of them, apparently.

"Are you sure these weren't implanted?"

"Yes, I easily accessed them, and there were no spells, enchantments, or magic residue to break through. Trust me, I would have found it if it were there."

"If you're wrong—"

"I'm not." She dropped the shield and stepped away as warmth escaped him. He hadn't realized they'd gotten so close.

"All right, people. It's time to go. Since it's too dangerous to go back through the tree, I'll have to create a portal here." The witch flicked her wrist, and a mirror appeared before her. She didn't have the tome or a drop of Veridian, so she would have to improvise. *I hope she remembered the words.*

Jafa dropped to his knees in front of the witch. "Please, please, I beg you to take me with you! I will serve you forever, Theá."

A sharp intake of breath from Queen Circe drew Lucius's attention. King Kieran touched her hand, and they glanced at each other, silently communicating, then brought their attention back to the witch.

"Jafa, stop. Please stand up. Of course, you can come. Sucora may come looking for you."

He stood and smiled.

"Speaking of, we need to protect the village," the witch remarked, dropping to her knees, placing her hands on the ground, and closing her eyes. They all watched as her hands emitted a glow, and power shot out like roots on a tree. The power crackled around them as it spread throughout the tent and across the village. The glow faded, and she stood. "Now that's done, let's go."

She ambled over to the mirror. She grabbed some sand from the floor and poured it over it, hoping that would ground it. Then she placed her hand on it. "Now, what were the words to the spell?"

"Witch."

"Shhh... I'm thinking. Aperi ad notum ostium in Calidum realm Eviathan—Michael." The image of his house appeared in the mirror. "Yes!! Come on, people, look alive. Time to go. Silas, you first."

He went through, followed by Jafa, Queen Circe, and King Kieran.

"Go, witch."

"No, I have to make sure the portal is sealed, and all traces of my magic residue are gone." Leaving her behind didn't sit well with him, meaning it was already beginning.

"Then I guess I'll wait."

"You're one stubborn bastard." She glared at him, but he made no move to go through. "Fine."

She waved her hand over the floor, and her bag appeared.

"And how the hell did you get that back?"

"It was never lost. I can always get it back. It's my bag. Only me or Michael can open it. Can I place the gem within it for safekeeping?"

Lucius hesitated, then realized she needed the gem just as badly as he did. Their purpose was the same. He handed it to her.

Opening her backpack, she placed the gem inside and pulled out some Glendale weed—magic eraser—throwing it into the fire. It immediately smoked.

"Come on, quickly now." She held out her hand to him. "Hold my hand."

He grumbled but took it. She placed her hand on the mirror.

"Pull us through. Fast. Now."

He yanked them through the mirror.

———◆◇◆———

She fell through the darkness until she landed hard on something warm and soft in front of the mansion. She realized that something warm and soft was the vampire.

Sandalwood. She rubbed her face into him. She wanted his scent all over her, which was weird. His scent smelled magnificent, but not enough for her to be rubbing herself all over him. She wanted to feel his flesh against her skin. Her hand reached into his shirt.

"Witch. Stop."

She paused all movement and lifted her head. His aura was purple, and his eyes were aglow as they bored into hers. All she could think about were his lips and how they would feel right now, brushing against hers.

"You need to get off me. You need to get off me right now."

"And if I don't?" She didn't know what force made her say it, but she was glad when it came out.

Before she knew it, she was on her back, and his lips were devouring hers. Her hands tangled in his hair, and her legs wrapped around him. She couldn't breathe, yet she couldn't find it in herself to pull away. The connection they had before was stronger now. His soul brushed against hers in a gentle caress, causing a shiver to move through her. Both an exciting and frightening feeling, yet it was something she didn't want to run away from.

Lucius broke the kiss, finally letting her up for air. He stared straight into her eyes. "I don't understand this," he whispered as he kissed her neck. "But I want—"

"If you guys are finished, your friend and brother would like to be woken up," King Kieran interrupted them.

Lucius moved away from her fast, disappearing into the house and leaving her cold on the ground. He wanted what... her. *Ugh.* She lifted her head and saw Kieran standing over her. He held out his hand. She eyed it suspiciously before she grabbed it, letting him lift her off the ground.

She scanned the area for any sign of Lucius, but he was nowhere to be seen. Kieran reassured her, "No worries. He won't be able to stay away from you for long. The connection between you two is strong."

"Yeah, well, maybe not strong enough."

She still couldn't believe she was in the presence of King Kieran, the infamous king of Evictus, the now not-missing king. If someone told her this is where her night out with Michael would lead her, she would have laughed and called them insane.

She had thought her life was complicated enough without her memories. Now, she would pay to go back to that being her only problem.

Patience walked toward the house. Kieran strode behind her until she reached the door, and then his presence slipped off into the night.

The eerie quiet of the mansion surprised her when she strolled inside. She closed her eyes and let her magic reach out and search for everyone's presence. Michael and Ian were still here. As were Maxim, Jafa, Silas, and now Circe. Kieran and Lucius weren't in the house.

She could sense Lucius was close like he was standing right next to her. A shiver went through her as she remembered the feel of his kisses trailing down her neck. She shook the memory from her head before she got lost in it.

Taking a deep breath, she went up the stairs. She needed to check on Michael and Ian, though they still had time. It never hurt to double-check.

Making her way to their room, she found them just as she'd left them. She lifted Michael's wrist, and the cross had faded. It was now a dark X through a disappearing circle. The third quarter of the circle had just faded. The transformation would be almost complete once the circle of the last quarter was half gone. They needed to put the soul gem on and untether the souls.

Thankfully, she had the chance to rest since it would be a few more hours before it occurred. She didn't have any energy. Exhaustion was hitting her badly. All she wanted to do was drift off to sleep.

She moved a chair to sit in front of the window, flicking her wrist to lift the shutter to watch the setting sun. She leaned her head against the windowsill, liking how the moon could be seen. It was rare for them to be out simultaneously, a sign of change. The moon was always comforting to her, especially when it was full; it gave her a feeling of warmth and safety.

Remembering the necklace, she pulled it out and let it gleam in the moonlight. The colors were mesmerizing and beautiful. As she placed the pendant in her palm to better gaze at it, a slight breeze blew through the room, whispering the words: *For you, my love. You will feel my love burning for you every time you touch this.*

The necklace grew warm in her hands, and a tear escaped her eye. Those words weren't meant for her. She never realized the necklace had a simple enchantment on it, meant just to bring comfort to a loved one.

Patience pondered if the other necklace also had an enchantment. She wondered if GreyJoy would let her see it, just to compare.

Sighing, she needed to put the necklace back. There would be trouble if the vampire caught her with it. She placed the necklace back into her shirt, vowing to return it as soon as possible.

She rubbed her face and sat back in the chair, closing her eyes. The image of the little girl drifted into her thoughts. She was beautiful. She wanted to have the dream again, just to remember it again.

Between Lucius and Alden, one of them was the key, she just didn't know how and why only one remembered her. Honestly, she wanted Lucius to be the key more than anything. She wanted the future she saw with him.

Even though her memories should be the most important, she couldn't help thinking about Lucius and her connection with him. How could it be stronger? Even now, the feel of his presence was so close, even though he was nowhere near her.

They needed to figure this out, or this lust—no, this desire—would never go away. Why could she feel this connection to her soul? It was too scary to think about... too hopeful.

It was her last thought before her eyes grew heavy, and she drifted off to sleep.

"I will kill him. You are mine. Forever. Come to me."

CHAPTER SIXTEEN

PATIENCE

"P atience! Wake the hell up!" Lucius screamed as he shook her awake. Her eyes flew open.

"Witch! Do something! They've been trembling like that for the past five minutes!" Lucius pointed to the bed where Ian and Michael were convulsing, causing the entire bed to shake.

She shot off her chair and moved to the bed. She touched Michael, who was hot to the touch.

"Shit, he's burning up." She touched Ian, but he was cool to the touch.

"What the hell is going on, witch?" Lucius demanded.

"I don't know!" He was making her panic. "Calm down so I can figure it out."

Taking a deep breath, she stared at Ian and Michael. She realized their hands were no longer clasped, and their bodies weren't touching. Grabbing Ian's hand, she placed it on Michael's arm. The trembling instantly stopped.

Relief washed over her. "Okay, that's one thing figured out. I think it's time to wake them up."

"Are you sure it's time?" Lucius came to stand next to Ian. "I don't want you harming my brother."

She glared at him before she moved around the bed and lifted Michael's hand. The symbol on his arm had changed. The circle had almost faded to half-quarter, and a thick X interconnected with a cross, creating a star, which wasn't like any daimones symbols she'd seen before.

"Yes, the circle has almost faded. We need to get him out before it completely disappears," she proclaimed.

Kieran walked into the room with the queen, Maxim, and Silas trailing behind him. Silas immediately assessed the situation, grabbing Patience's bag and handing it to her. She took out the glopinian and opened it, letting the gem fall into her hand.

Before she placed it over Michael's heart, she summoned the spell book. Appearing before her, she flipped through the pages until she found the spell.

She placed her hands on the gemstone and read the words:

"Gem of Souls. Snälla hjälp den förlorade själen med att hitta sin väg hem. Hjälp den att hitta sin väg genom mörkret och bli förenad med sitt sanna jag igen."

Gem of Souls. Please help this lost soul find its way home. Help it find its way through the darkness and be united with its true self again.

Power flowed through her into the gem, but it didn't glow. "Shit, it's not working."

Patience tried again.

"Fuck! I don't know what I'm doing wrong!" Her frustration caused tears to emerge and flow down her cheeks until a hand pressed to her shoulder. Patience turned.

Circe smiled apologetically at her. "I know you're frustrated. If you allow me, I may have an idea. Trust me, okay?"

Patience nodded. She was open to anything at this point. She didn't understand what she was doing wrong.

Circe cautiously took Lucius's hand. Patience glanced over at Kieran, seeing the tension roll off his shoulders as he prepared himself to fight if Lucius made one wrong move toward his wife.

She stood in front of Lucius, staring into his eyes like she was trying to communicate something to him. Then, holding his hand, she walked over to Patience, grabbing her hand and placing it within his.

"Trust me. You're the two people they trust the most. You must do this together. Close your eyes and try again." Circe dropped her hands away and moved back.

Patience understood what she was getting at. Michael and Ian were two different people, and the gem needed someone they could trust to wake them. She glanced at Lucius. She squeezed his hand for reassurance, and to her surprise, he squeezed it back before she closed her eyes and placed her hand over the gem.

Taking a deep breath, she said the words again. This time, when she opened her eyes, the gem was aglow. So much excitement rushed through her that, without thinking, she hugged Lucius. She instantly realized what she'd done and let go of him, stepping back.

"What do we do now?" Maxim walked to the opposite side of the bed, checking for any sign of Ian's waking.

"Now, we wait. We must let the gem do its job."

Lucius moved to Ian's side of the bed to wait without a glance in her direction. Disappointment washed over her. This was almost over, and their paths wouldn't cross again. Just the thought alone broke her heart. She still didn't understand what was happening between them, but it didn't matter. It would only be a matter of time before they went their separate ways.

She moved from the bed and headed to the window to watch the dawn break before the shutters closed.

Hours passed as they all sat around, waiting for a miracle to happen. She wasn't even sure if this would work. She only prayed to the Goddess that it did. She wasn't sure what she would do if this didn't work.

"If this was going to work, shouldn't it be done by now? You're a dai-mones. Can't you help?" Maxim directed this toward the King, going over to Ian for the hundredth time. Impatience grew by the hour, and everyone was becoming antsy.

"The only time I've gone through this was when I transitioned, which was before all of you were even a thought in anyone's mind. A Silverite Priestess, who are all dead, has always done this ritual. The witch currently knows more than I do."

The vampire's eyes bored into her back every minute that went by without a change. When the clock struck 11:30 p.m., she finally gave in. She couldn't continue waiting for something to happen. She knew what she needed to do, and she absolutely hated delving into people's minds, especially people she knew. It was always messy, plus she never wanted it to happen to her.

She put her book down and went to the bed. She stared down at them, resisting what she knew she had to do.

His presence slowly descended upon her, taking up space behind her. "Witch."

"I'm going to wake them up."

She reached to touch Ian's forehead when he grabbed her hand.

"If I don't do something, we'll just sit here, not knowing what's happen-ing in there. The circle on his wrist faded an hour ago," she said, concerned. "Something could be wrong, and we would never know."

"She's right. They should have woken up already. You're lucky she even has the ability." Kieran spoke from the corner of the room where he and his wife had been vigil for the past hour.

The vampire groaned, but he released her hand. Touching Ian's fore-head, she closed her eyes, descending into his mind. She barely had to break through any barriers.

When she appeared in his mind, Ian was holding Michael in his demon form in the middle of a great stone hall. The Cordovan tapestry was hanging over an enormous fireplace, and the walls were crumbling around them.

She paused momentarily, realizing this place seemed familiar to her, which was curious since this was Ian's mind. She wanted to explore but had to be cautious when being in someone else's mind. For now, she carefully made her way toward them as the world rumbled.

"Is he okay?" Patience shouted. Ian looked up and clutched Michael tighter, baring his fangs. His eyes were bloodshot, and his clothes were in tatters. He looked like he'd been through hell.

Patience stepped back a little and held up her hands. "I'm not here to hurt you. I'm Patience. Michael's best friend. I'm here to help you. I need to know if he's all right."

Looking down at Michael, she saw that he had bat-like wings, his black horns had grown longer, and his skin had darkened to red. He looked like the picture she saw in a book about the daimones, a very faun-like demon, though he looked like he had more muscle. "Is he okay?" she yelled again.

She didn't think she got through to Ian until his fangs retracted.

"I don't know. He collapsed when that appeared on him." Ian looked relieved to see her once he realized she was real. "I had to tear it off." He pointed to the blue glint, which was a few feet away. *Shit*, it was the gem.

She quickly grabbed the gem before the crumbling rock crushed it. Then she made her way back over to Ian.

"Okay, I'll need you to place this back on him to get you two out of here, all right? Trust me, please."

Ian looked down at Michael, then nodded. Patience handed Ian the gem and showed him where to place it on Michael's chest.

Nothing happened. Patience could see the frustration growing on Ian's face. She touched Michael's forehead, sending a small jolt of electric warmth to let him know she was there. "Please wait."

His horns shrank as his skin changed to its normal shade of peach. Patience put her hands on both of them, then closed her eyes, bringing them back to the surface and severing the link between Ian and Michael.

Patience opened her eyes to find her hands still interlocked with Lucius's. They both looked down simultaneously, but she was the first to let go as Ian opened his eyes little by little, letting his eyes adjust to the light in the room. Lucius rushed to his side.

Patience gazed down at Michael and saw him staring up at her. "About time you opened your eyes. I've been waiting out here for you forever."

She grabbed the glopinian, took the gem off his chest, and placed it inside. Then she placed it inside her backpack. She waved her hand over the bag, sending it to her vault along with the spell book.

"How long was I out?" Michael yawned and stretched.

"Just a couple of days. You don't know what I had to endure to get you back. I have some hilarious stories that I can't wait to tell you."

Michael chuckled.

"I'm so happy you're awake. How do you feel?" she asked him.

"Like I got run over by two trucks twice in a row. I need water."

Patience helped him sit up, leaned his head against the headboard, and then handed him some water left on the bedside table.

He took a sip, then turned toward Ian, who was looking at him already. They smirked at each other.

"Thank you." Michael reached out and grabbed his hand. Ian squeezed it tight and didn't let go.

"I know you've all been through a lot. Would it be okay if you guys give us a minute, please?" Ian asked Lucius in particular, who looked reluctant to grant his request, but after a minute, he nodded. Everyone cleared the room.

"I'll go get you some blood so you can regain your strength," Lucius informed Ian as he moved out the door.

Before she could move to leave, Michael motioned for her to come closer. "Who are all these people?"

Laughter bubbled up and spilled out. "As soon as you recover, I'll explain everything."

Patience squeezed Michael's arm, then followed Lucius out. She let the door close behind them.

This was her chance. She had to return the necklace. She headed toward the library so she could make her way back to that room. Then, she would find Jafa. There was a lot they needed to talk about. Halfway there, she froze.

A jolt of fear surged through their connection. Without a thought, Patience placed her hand against the wall and walked through. She stepped out in front of Ian's room, coming face to face with Lucius.

"You felt it, too." They spoke in unison.

They both rushed toward the door. Instinctively, she pushed the vampire out of the way as a dagger whizzed past their heads, embedding itself in the door. Lucius stared at her strangely until they heard footsteps behind them.

They both turned to find a hokima, an Askarian assassin. Covered head to toe in thick black cloth, only their luminescent white eyes could be seen as they threw another dagger at them.

This time, Patience was prepared. She lifted her hand, deflecting the dagger with her magic. The assassin ran toward them as she erected a shield around her and the vampire.

"Where is the king?" Lucius asked. "Why is there a hokima assassin in my house trying to kill us?"

Patience was about to reply when the assassin pulled a dagger made of red glass from behind their back. "Oh, shit. I don't know what kind of magic you hold, but whatever it is, I need you to fortify this shield with it, or they'll get through."

Lucius touched her shield, adding his power, which turned it from blue to violet. At the same moment, the assassin stabbed it with the red dagger.

"Fuck." The assassin tried to cut the shield, but it wouldn't move. Whatever magic, either vampire or witch, did the trick for now.

"This won't hold long. You're right," Patience told him. "Where is the king, and why would he send an assassin?"

"I don't know, but we need to get—"

The shield tore in two, then disappeared.

"Lucius, where is your sword right now?"

He hesitated as the hokima regarded them.

"I need you to trust me now so we both can get out of this alive. Very few people have faced a hokima and lived to tell the tale."

"In my bedroom, sitting above the fireplace."

As soon as the silver handle of his sword appeared in her hand, she threw it toward Lucius, then ducked as the assassin threw another dagger toward her. She rolled to a stand, throwing a ball of electricity at the hokima before she ran toward Ian's bedroom door. She tried to open it but found it locked.

The vampire used Luzia to deflect daggers as she tried to open the door. "Witch! Get that door open!"

"What the hell do you think I'm trying to do?" Patience tried to use her magic to open the door and even go through it, but nothing worked. She banged in frustration.

"Unless you're trying to break the door, I... suggest... you... help me... kill... this thing." The vampire said, this time deflecting poisonous spikes.

Patience turned and threw another ball of electricity at the assassin, who dodged it easily. "You know you just can't kill them. You need—"

"The Blades of Flux. I have one. We need Max!"

The assassin took out their double-edged Blade of Valhal, ready to cut the vampire in two. The vampire stood ready with his sword.

"Find Max!" he yelled before he charged at the assassin.

How the hell was she supposed to find Max? She couldn't leave Lucius like this, and they needed to get in the room to find out what was happening to Ian and Michael.

Patience slammed her hand to the ground, sending a signal to the whole mansion for whoever was in and within the surrounding area to come to this location. She needed to buy time, if only a few seconds, for more help. She had to think back to the books she'd read about the hokima. *How do I slow them down?*

Truesilk. She needed something made of Truesilk. The Fleece of Gilahein. She wasn't sure if this would work since technically it belonged to Michael, but she waved her hand over the floor, summoning the Fleece to appear. Nothing after the first try. She waved her hand again. Still nothing. *Shit.*

"Witch!"

She glanced up to see Luzia glow red as Lucius brought it down against the hokima's leg, dealing a deadly blow that would have crushed any enemy but only fazed it momentarily. Lucius sidestepped to avoid a deadly blow to his shoulder, and the assassin's blade hit Luzia instead.

Patience became mesmerized as his fluid movements turned into dance. He dodged, sidestepped, and dealt blow after blow, none hindering the assassin until Lucius got the hokima onto its knees. She threw another electric ball, hitting the assassin in the side and only deterring him momentarily.

She was about to try again when Maxim appeared next to Lucius. Patience used her magic to throw them both out of the way, then she threw a ball of wind, knocking the assassin on their ass. She tried to summon the Fleece again, and this time it appeared. Using her magic, she pulled Lucius and Maxim back to her, then lifted the Fleece in the air above the assassin.

Just as they were running toward them, she slammed the Fleece down upon them, wrapping it around them. Using her magic, she threw their sword from their hands, flinging it across the room.

She turned, blasting Ian's bedroom door open, shattering it to pieces. She was done being nice.

"We need the Blades of Flux," Lucius said to Maxim as she walked through the door.

She couldn't believe what she had walked into. Michael was pinned against the wall with a black spike, unconscious—a Tral'goth demon. Four thick horns sat atop its head. Its reptilian body rested on Ian's chest as it used its long, slithery tongue to suck the life force from his body.

Patience summoned an Anduril blade and cautiously made her way over to the thing. She would only get one chance at this because the bastards were quick. She stood over the demon, about to bring the knife down, when she heard a noise behind her.

Patience turned to see Lucius striding toward her with fury in his step and Luzia at the ready. Before he could get to her, he found his way blocked by a knife to his throat.

Kieran's knife. "I wouldn't do that."

The vampire moved toward her, not caring that the knife pressed into his neck, cutting him. Blood dripped down from the cut. "Witch, if you harm him, I'll kill you."

Harm him? She was trying to save his brother's life... again.

"I'm trying to stop you from making the biggest mistake of your life," Kieran tried to warn him, but the anger never left the vampire's face.

She turned to find two ghastly eyes staring at her. *Shit.* She moved to stab it when it pounced onto the wall.

The vampire tried to grab her, but Kieran got to him before he could touch her, throwing him against the wall. Maxim came running into the room with the Blades of Flux in his hand and the assassin on his heels. The Tral'goth jumped onto him at that moment, taking him to the ground.

Patience had to make haste. Moving out of the vampire's reach, she used her magic to throw the Anduril blade at the demon, hitting it in the side before it could get its tongue on Maxim.

She didn't have time to watch as it exploded on Maxim. She rolled, grabbing the dagger Maxim dropped and throwing it to Circe, who stabbed the assassin from behind. They instantly dropped, turning into ash.

Patience almost collapsed in relief. She turned to find the vampire standing bewildered, looking at the dead demon splattered on Maxim. She didn't have time for this.

"I need that blood. Maxim, come here."

Without hesitation, he got up from the floor and approached her. She touched Ian's chest and then placed her hand on the blood splatter on Maxim's chest. The warm and gooey green substance almost made her want to throw up, but she sucked it up and concentrated. She pulled the life essence from the blood the creature took and put it back into Ian. Life flowed back into his pale body. He gasped awake, panic in his eyes.

"Michael!" he screamed.

"It's okay. It's dead," she reassured him, then moved to Michael. Kieran grabbed onto Michael as she used her magic to pull the spikes from his shoulder gently.

"Those are Gutrend spikes. The assassin must have pinned him." Kieran moved Michael, placing him on the bed next to Ian.

She placed her hand over the holes, letting her magic seep into his wounds, healing them as Michael regained consciousness.

"Patience." He opened his eyes and smiled when he saw her. Then panic set in. "Ian."

"I'm right here." Ian placed a hand on Michael's arm, reassuring him he was all right.

"Why did you send an assassin to kill my brother?" The vampire's nostrils flared as he stood, planted chest to chest with the king.

Circe moved to stand next to her husband. "We didn't send any assassins. I need you to trust us. They're after us. There are many things we need to talk about. Now isn't the time. These two need to rest, and she needs to rest before she collapses."

Patience felt she was talking about her, especially since they all turned her way.

Maxim placed a hand on her shoulder. "Patience? Are you okay?"

"I'm—" She moved to walk toward the bed when she fumbled, almost falling. To her surprise, Lucius was the one to stop her from falling. "Th-thank you. I'm fine."

She took a step back from him, feeling completely drained. She'd used too much of her magic too fast. Moving through realms wasn't a simple task, other than fighting off an assassin plus a Tral'goth demon. Sleep would be wonderful.

Circe came to her side, smiling as she took her hand. "Come on, darling. How about you rest? When you wake up, can we answer any questions you may have? And maybe you can answer a few from us."

"Okay, that sounds like a good idea." Sleeping for a few hours would help her regain some of her energy.

When Maxim spoke up, Lucius looked as though he was about to say something. "You can stay in my room."

"Maxim, I couldn't. I can just—"

"Yes, you can since you just saved my life."

"Theá, can I be of any help?" Jafa asked, hovering in the doorway. *Jafa.* She'd forgotten about him for a moment.

"Jafa, I'm okay. I just need some rest."

"Come, I'll walk you to my room," Maxim said graciously.

Patience nodded, then touched Michael's hand in reassurance before she quietly followed Maxim to his room. She was lost in her thoughts about everything that had just occurred, but her mind kept going back to Lucius and his intention of killing her even after everything they'd been through.

CHAPTER SEVENTEEN

LUCIUS

Lucius's blood boiled in his veins as he sat in his office and poured himself his third drink. When the witch left with Maxim, he'd wanted to question the king more. Before he could say anything, they took Jafa and left the room, promising to answer their questions once everyone rested.

He should go after them and question them further. That should be his focus. The witch clouded his thoughts. He'd almost killed her. When he saw her standing over his brother with a knife, he'd almost plunged Luzia into her. If the king hadn't stopped him, she would be dead.

He needed to hit something—something hard. Anger boiled through him, causing his vision to go red. Everything was in chaos, and nothing made sense except... except for her blood flowing through his veins.

He downed the drink and poured another.

"I'll take one of those." Maxim walked in, grabbed a glass, and set it in front of him. "What the hell happened tonight?"

"I have no fucking clue." Lucius poured him a generous amount before pushing it toward him.

Maxim finished his drink, and Lucius poured him another.

Lucius sat back in his chair and assessed his friend. "How can you be so calm? A Tral'goth demon attacked you, and I almost killed the witch before she could kill it. Fuck." A Tral'goth demon he'd failed to see. He'd forgotten about the hokima's creatures.

He downed his drink. Maxim held his glass toward him, indicating to pour him another. "Îi datorez viața mea," Maxim said before he took a sip. *I owe her my life.*

"I know. She saved Ian's life again. I owe her for both of your lives."

"Yours as well."

Lucius had ignored the fact that he'd saved her life until her blood moved through his veins, reminding him that technically, she'd repaid a debt to him. Now he owed her again for his brother's life and now for his friend's life.

"Veşnic îndatorat cu ea," Maxim added. *Forever in her debt.*

"I know."

As much as Lucius hated witches, Maxim had a point. They were eternally in her debt. "How could this have happened?"

"I have no fucking clue, Lucius. Part of me is happy it did."

"You wanted to get attacked by a demon?" Lucius poured himself another drink, preparing for whatever nonsense was about to come out of Max's mouth.

How did his life come to this? Being indebted to a witch? But she wasn't just any witch. Lucius had to admit she'd done nothing to harm him or his family. Thinking back, she'd only protected them. She'd gotten under his skin, and now she was in his blood. It would be easy just to kill her, but now he couldn't. He hated owing debts, especially to a witch. A debt was a debt, and he had to pay it whether he liked it or not.

The glass broke in his hand, and Maxim stopped to look at him. "I bet a particular woman made you break that glass."

Lucius glared.

"I bet I can guess who." Maxim raised his glass to Lucius, then realized he no longer had a glass. He pushed the bottle toward him. "I think you need this more than I do."

Lucius took the bottle and took a long swing. As pissed as he was, the alcohol wasn't helping. After getting up, he left the bottle with Max.

He didn't know which direction he was going. All he knew was he didn't like how her blood beckoned him to find her. He should have never given it to her.

Breaking a blood bond was tricky and almost impossible because once the blood got into the system, it was hard to remove, especially when they continued to strengthen their connection. It would be nearly impossible, but he would try anyway.

The real problem was just the idea of removing the bond—her blood from him—was killing him.

He didn't even realize his hands had connected with furniture until he smelled blood and realized it was his. Blood covered his hands as he looked around him and saw he'd destroyed the living room. The sofas were torn apart. The glass antique cabinets and all the lamps were shattered. He'd even destroyed the paintings on the wall.

Lucius slid down the wall, sinking to the floor. He hated her, and he hated himself more. He hoped he could break their bond, even though it was a slim chance since it wasn't complete. He hoped the witch would never realize it because he would be enslaved to her forever.

A few hours later, Ian walked through the debris. He'd finally emerged from his room, looking refreshed.

"What did I miss?" Ian said, moving through all the broken glass on the floor. "You realize we've had these for centuries, right? They were worth a fortune."

Lucius didn't even bother looking at his brother. He didn't have the energy to argue with him. Ian sat next to him. "Do you plan on filling me in on what happened while I was locked away? And telling me about what the hell just tried to kill me?"

"As for what the hell attacked you, I'm just as lost as you. This whole thing has been a whirlwind that hasn't slowed since that night, but we'll have answers soon. As for what happened, a witch saved your life. The details mean nothing."

"They mean something since it caused this." Ian gestured toward the debris.

Lucius glanced at his brother and realized he was being selfish. His brother had been through an ordeal, and here he was, wallowing in his self-hatred.

"How bad was it?"

Ian sighed and ran his hands through his hair. Rubbing his face, his eyes went distant as his hands clenched together. "Something happened there that I just can't explain. It was like..."

"That bad?"

"It was bad but not as bad as you think."

Lucius's curiosity was now piqued.

Sighing, Ian ran his hands through his hair again. Obviously, he was nervous. "I have to tell you something, but you have to promise me you won't flip out on me, okay?"

Lucius could count on his hands how often he'd seen his brother this serious. He wondered what it could be. He would listen closely. Maybe he would get to shed some blood tonight, after all.

"I'm listening."

Ian stood and paced. "Being anchored to a transitioning demon is intense. Intense as hell, and apparently very intimate. Well, at least, ours was." He ran his hand through his hair again, which made Lucius tense up. "I know we were only there for a few days, but for us, it was forever."

"Okay? What are you trying to tell me? I get to kill a demon tonight?" He tried not to sound too hopeful, though he couldn't help it.

Ian stopped in his tracks and turned to him with a seriousness that scared Lucius. "No, you don't kill anybody tonight. Besides, if you did, you'd kill me, because he's my mate."

Lucius couldn't understand what he was saying. It made little sense to him. "You soul-bonded with it?"

"Him."

Lucius didn't know what to say. To soul-bond with someone was sacred and forever. Both parties would have to be willing, and the ancient sacred words would have to be spoken. Unlike the blood bond he and the witch now shared, when a vampire bonded their life, it fused two souls together, including their life force—meaning if one of them died, they both died. Blood bonding was rarely done nowadays. Soul bonding was practically never done.

"What were you thinking? You know you can't take it back," he chided sternly as he stood.

"Yes, I know, Lucius. It was stupid, but I thought it would save him. I love him."

Lucius couldn't believe what he was hearing. "You love him? How? You just met him. You barely know him," he argued. How could Ian love someone he didn't know?

"I know this makes no sense to you, but everything I say is true." Ian stood directly before him and looked him straight in the eyes. "I'm not under any spells, and no one controls my mind. As soon as I saw him, I knew he was the one."

Love. Lucius couldn't believe his brother was standing in front of him, declaring he not only soul-bonded with a demon but was also in love with him. What was happening to this world? First the witch, now this.

"She did something to you while you were in there. I'm going to kill her." She could have put a spell on his brother without him knowing. He would sort this out. Lucius tried to push past Ian. He stopped him.

"Would you listen to me for once in your goddamned life? I am not under any spells. I am me!" Ian was furious, which made Lucius pause. Ian hardly ever became angry.

"I know this will take some time for you to get used to, but I need you to support me and be by my side like I have always been for you. I love him. You need to believe me."

Lucius had no actual choice in whether this was real. He needed to support his brother because he was right—Ian had always supported him—his damn soft spot.

"I believe you."

"Good. But I have more."

Lucius crossed his arms and tried to prepare himself. It couldn't be worse than him being soul-bonded to a demon. "And what is it you have to say to me?"

"I know you. You won't like this," Ian advised, running his hands through his hair again, which made Lucius tense up.

"You can't kill Patience or harm her," Ian said.

Lucius glared daggers at him. The truth was, he no longer had the urge to hurt her. He couldn't anyway, not until he paid his debt. Killing the witch was the fastest way to break their blood bond. But he always paid his debts.

"Don't look at me like that. I know you hate witches for what Arabella did... it was unforgivable. She's dead. You killed her. She no longer exists. I think Mae would want you to move on. To be happy. The world is different, and this witch is different. She's Michael's best friend and his only family. As my bond mate, I'm sworn to protect him and his family. I don't want to fight you on this," Ian pleaded.

His wife and child... Ian didn't understand. Lucius could never let what was done to them go. They were dead, and the witch who he'd killed was also dead. Wrapped in the thickest of gendleweed and secured with chains dipped in the oil of a sundown flower to make sure her soul never found peace as her bones lay eight feet underground. The memories of her screams as the smoke suffocated her were ingrained into his memory.

He was unsure he could truly trust a witch, especially after all these years. He also understood not every witch had evil intentions, and he was willing to give this witch a chance for his brother's sake. It was time he let go of some of his hatred to make room for his brother's happiness. He ignored the part of him waiting for an excuse to give in to the witch. The image of the little girl floated through his mind again.

"Lucius. Lucius. Come back to Earth." Ian waved his hands in front of his face.

"Do I have a choice in this situation?"

Ian just smiled at him, knowing his brother was about to consent to his terms.

"No. No, you don't."

Lucius smiled. His brother's happiness meant the world to him, and he would give it to him, even if it killed him.

"The witch is safe from me, but if she does anything to harm this family, I won't hesitate to kill her. Do you understand me?"

Ian nodded happily and hugged Lucius, catching him a little off guard.

"Whoa, there." Lucius clapped him on the back. "Come on. Let's go properly introduce me to your mate and get some answers from the king and queen."

CHAPTER EIGHTEEN

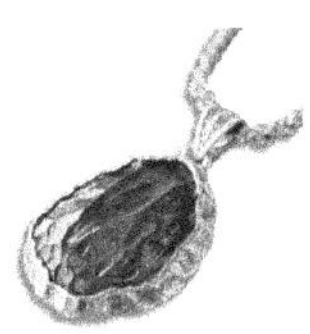

PATIENCE

Patience tried to fall asleep but couldn't. Too much adrenaline ran through her body, and she couldn't get the look Lucius had given her out of her head. After everything they'd been through, he still thought she would harm him and his family. She shouldn't have even cared what he thought, but unfortunately, she did.

"What is wrong with me?" Patience yelled, throwing a pillow across the room.

"Well, I always thought you were too crazy for your own good," Michael replied from the doorway.

Patience immediately jumped up and ran to him. "Michael!" she squealed, jumping into his open arms. He embraced her, hugging her tightly to him. "I've missed you so much!"

"I bet you did." He smiled, then became serious, pulling his head back to look her in the eyes. "I heard a bit of what you've been through. I'm sorry I wasn't there to protect you."

Her smile faltered, and she moved from his arms to sit on the bed. "There was nothing you could have done about it. You needed to concentrate on yourself."

Michael sat next to her. "I know, but I still should have been there for you."

"Look, I'm fine. How are you feeling?" she asked, concerned. He'd been through an ordeal.

"I feel fine. Nothing really feels different except... that I can feel my powers coursing through my body. Like, literally. It feels weird but good."

Patience looked at Michael. She reached out and touched his arm. Energy pulsated through him. Raw power, similar to hers. Now, that was interesting.

"Have you seen yourself in your full form?"

"No, but Ian has, and that's all that matters."

"Well, your horns are way bigger, and you have wings."

Michael's eyes widened in amazement. "Wings? Really?"

Patience nodded eagerly. "Yeah... wait, why is Ian seeing you all that matters?"

Michael shifted uncomfortably, avoiding her gaze. But she wasn't going to let him off the hook that easily.

"All right! Spill it. I know I won't like it, so just say it."

Taking a deep breath, Michael finally confessed, "Okay... Ian and I are mated... bonded."

Her heart skipped a beat as she processed his words.

He cannot be saying what I think he is saying. "What? Explain."

"Well, I'm not sure how it happened exactly," Michael began hesitantly. "All I know is I wanted it to happen... no, I needed it to happen. When our souls converged, it was the most beautiful and wholesome experience.

I don't even have the words to explain it." The intensity of his voice both scared and intrigued her.

"Well, please try." She knew what he was going to say, so she prepared herself.

He looked at her nervously. "Well... it means when he dies, I die. We're stuck together for life."

Patience stood and paced. When he said their souls converged, she knew what he meant. She'd just needed him to clarify so she wasn't mistaken. This news didn't surprise her. A part of her had always known he would find someone to love him. She just hadn't wanted to admit it out loud.

She wanted to be happy for him, but the only thing she could think about was how his soulmate had a brother who wanted to kill her.

Patience stopped pacing and looked over at Michael. "Does Lucius know?"

Michael stood up and walked over to her, putting his hands on her shoulders. "Yes, he knows, and he agreed not to kill you."

"Well, gee, that's encouraging." She couldn't help but roll her eyes.

"If he harms you, I'll have to kill him, but he won't risk hurting his brother."

She sighed deeply and sat back on the bed. "So, what happens now?"

"I'm not sure. I don't know what it means. Being with him feels right."

"I'm so happy for you. I truly am. It's worth everything I had to put up with to see you this way." She threw her arms around him, hugging him tightly. "You deserve this more than anyone."

"You'll find happiness too, you know."

"Yeah, we shall see. Maybe one day... for now, we must figure out why a hokima and its Tral'goth attacked us." Patience dragged her hands down her face and slowly shook her head.

"I don't know," Michael began. "I hope this king and queen have some answers for us. I can't believe you found them."

"More like they stumbled upon us and saved our lives... or, at least, mine."

"Jafa told me a bit about your adventure, but there are definitely some pieces you need to fill in."

Patience laughed. Of course, he wanted to know all the juicy details. "Trust me, I'm still dissecting that trip in my head. I'm simply happy I got back in one piece."

They sat there silently for a moment, lost in their thoughts, realizing they'd both been on journeys for these past few days.

"So much has happened. I don't even know where to begin."

"Well, I'm not going anywhere. Fill me in."

Patience told him about Alden, her crazy attraction to a killer vampire, and the vampire's strange changing aura.

"What? His aura changes? That's impossible."

"I know, right?" Patience touched his wrist, showing him her memories of Lucius's changing aura.

"I want to ask Greyjoy. I'm not sure if he'll have an answer. I might have to contact the witch council to see if they'll grant me access to the Library of Divinity."

"You think they'll grant it to you, and will it be worth the price they ask?"

They would ask her a steep price. They'd been after her powers for a long time, wanting her to serve as a Sentinel of Light, a.k.a. a Guardian of the Witch's Council. Did she really care that much? No, not after he tried to kill her.

"Not worth it. I'm just so damn curious."

"So Alden and Lucius may be the keys you're looking for? The question is, which one can truly unlock your memories?"

A knock at the door sounded. Michael jumped up to answer it like he knew exactly who it was.

Which, it turned out, he did. It was Ian. He walked into the room straight to her and dropped to his knees.

"I want to apologize on my brother's behalf. He doesn't like your kind due to his past, which is why he's hostile toward you."

Patience smiled. It was adorable how he was apologizing for his brother's behavior.

"Please stand up. You don't need to apologize for him." She didn't want to tell him the apology meant nothing to her since it wasn't coming from the source. If he wanted to say sorry to her, he knew how and where to find her. "Thank you for the thought. I really appreciate it."

Ian stood. "I understand. I've spoken with my brother, and he will no longer try to harm you."

She highly doubted it, but she smiled and nodded anyway.

"I'm truly sorry we weren't properly introduced. I'm Ian Cordovan."

"Yes, my brother-in-law and I'm Patience Harrington. Now, your sister-in-law."

He smiled. "It's a pleasure to meet you finally."

"Yes. Yes, it is." He had a devastating smile. The name Mr. Gorgeous definitely fit him. "Look, I need to go home to get some rest. I feel I won't get any here. Nothing like the comforts of your home to bring sanity back into your life. I will—"

"Not yet." Circe glided into the room. "Sorry for interrupting, but Kieran and I wanted a minute to talk with you and Michael."

As usual, Kieran walked in behind her, and Silas followed immediately. Well, judging by the tense look on Silas's face, she wasn't going home soon.

Patience sighed. "Perfect. We need to talk to you as well."

Jafa, Maxim, and Lucius strolled through the door.

Being in the same room as Lucius right now wasn't helping her sanity. Her eyes met his. The urge to walk right up to kiss him flitted through her mind. She craved to see him smile again. It was stupid to have these feelings, but there they were, and it didn't look like they were going anywhere soon. *Fuck.*

"Since this seems to be a group meeting, let's get this conversation over with so my life can return to some form of normalcy. Why did the hokima attack? We know they're Askaria warriors, only controlled by the king. Why help us just to kill us?" Patience fired her questions off, hoping to get some much-needed answers.

"First things first," the queen said earnestly. "I'm Circe, and this is my husband, King Kieran of Evictus."

"Queen Circe," the king interjected.

Patience was curious why Circe never referred to herself as queen.

"Thank you for taking us from that horrendous place," Queen Circe said sincerely. "That woman was a real bitch. She had no useful or relevant information to help us. I know you have questions about the hokima. Let me reassure you we didn't send them. We would never risk harming you," she said adamantly, "before we can give you any more information, we have something you might help us with. It will let us know if we can trust you and let you know you can trust us."

Patience's ears perked up when Circe glanced at Michael.

"What information could I possibly have for you?" Michael asked nervously. Ian placed his hand on Michael's shoulder to help ease his tension.

"Michael. Kieran and I have been looking for two things for a long time. We might have found one, but we have a few questions before confirming anything."

Confirm... confirm what? What do they need Michael to confirm? The suspense was killing Patience. The pressure of Lucius's eyes on her begged her to look in his direction. She refused.

She had no answers for him and was afraid of what she might see in his eyes.

"How did you and Patience meet?" Circe asked Michael.

Michael glanced at Patience before answering. She nodded.

"Patience found me being beaten by a Ganton demon in Igoria."

"How would that be possible? How would you have ended up there?"

Michael thought a minute, then said, "I'm not sure how I got there, and I'm not sure how long I was there. My memory... I don't have any memories from before thirty years ago. When Patience found me, I was trying to escape. That's why they were beating me."

Circe's skin glowed red until Kieran touched her shoulder, and she calmed.

"So both you and the witch have lost your memories?" the vampire asked from the corner of the room.

"My memories aren't lost," Patience said, "just buried in my brain, and I need to find the right key to unlock them. But his memories are gone. Trust me, I've looked, and his are gone. Why do you need to know all this information?" Patience asked Circe curiously.

"Because we've been looking for our son for over a century, and we believe it's possible Michael is our son."

Holy shit. Over a century? "What? Seriously?"

"Yes, we've been looking for him for a very long time." Circe took a step toward Michael with such hope in her eyes.

"Why do you think he's your son?" Maxim asked.

Circe turned to look at Silas.

Silas stepped forward. "I was assigned to be their son's personal guard when he was a boy. As the queen's brother and her son's guard, I swore to protect him, and if he died, I would die. Since I'm alive, I know the boy lives. It was a royal blood oath, I swore, and I sensed my blood in Michael."

"Is that the reason you befriended us?" Michael asked, clearly shocked to learn Silas was related to the queen.

"Yes, I was unsure where to look for your parents," Silas offered. "I didn't know where they were, but I knew if you were truly the royal son, my nephew, I couldn't lose you again."

This was all blowing Patience's mind, and if she were feeling this way, she couldn't imagine how Michael felt. She could see he was barely holding it together. Ian silently slipped his hand into his.

"Why didn't you tell us who you are, or at least, whom you thought Michael was?"

"I wanted to tell him so many times, but when I learned he had no memory of his family, and he was found in Igoria. I knew someone had put him there on purpose, but I had no proof of my story. I thought it would be better to remain friends to watch over him to see if someone would reveal themselves as the culprit, and I'd hoped once the king and queen returned, I could reunite my sister with her son."

Patience stood feeling herself getting anxious, which was never good. "So how do we find out if he's truly your son, other than the word of Silas over here?"

"The symbol on his wrist means he's daimones royalty," Queen Circe explained, "but to prove he's our son, Kieran will need a moment alone with Michael."

"Not happening." If they thought she was just going to easily leave them alone together, they'd lost their damn minds. Michael was still vulnerable after the ordeal he'd just gone through.

"Patience." Michael looked at her with hope in his eyes. "I would like to know."

"But there are so many questions they haven't answered, like why were they in Sucora's realm working with her? We can't just let that go."

"Working with her? Far from it." Anger filled Circe's voice. "We went there seeking information about a powerful demon, and clearly, we didn't find what we were looking for, but we may have found something better. Not only do we think we may have found our son. We also think we found the witch who can help find the demon we're looking for."

Patience peered around the room for a minute and realized she was the only witch there. "And how do I fit in with all of this?"

"If you give Kieran a moment alone with Michael, I'll explain it to you."

Patience was skeptical, but it wasn't her choice. "It's up to you, Michael."

He hesitated for a moment, then nodded his consent.

"Fine, but if he harms a hair on your head, he's dead. King or not."

Michael smirked, knowing how protective she could get.

"I promise no harm will come to him," Kieran declared.

Everyone cleared out of the room. Patience was the last to leave, and it was on the arm of Circe, who practically dragged her out.

"So, explain." Patience let Circe lead her into the hallway, but she would go no further. "Why do you need me to find a demon? Any witch can help you do that."

"The demon we're looking for isn't your ordinary demon. He's but a half-demon. His other half is unknown. He's powerful. Powerful enough to lock us out of Askaria and set Lilith free."

"Lilith? As in the creator of the vampires? As in the one locked deep in the prison of Euphoria in Askaria?"

"Yes."

Patience couldn't believe what she was hearing. "I'm not understanding. What do Lilith and this demon have in common? And why do you think he's powerful enough to free her?"

"We believe he's Lilith's son, and he's been hiding in Evictus, growing his powers for these past centuries. We also know he's the one who stole our son. He knew we would look for him, and now he controls the hokima."

"Well, ain't that just peachy?" Patience needed a drink. A very God-dess-damn strong drink. Patience grabbed Circe's hand, touched the wall, and then stepped through to the library, dragging Circe after her. She went straight to the liquor cabinet and poured herself a glass of whiskey, then gulped it all down. She was turning into Lucius. He was a bad influence.

Then she poured herself another glass and took a seat. "If he's hiding in Askaria, technically, you need any witch to do a locator spell."

"No. We need a witch from the Silverlands."

"Silverlands? I'm not from the Silverlands." Patience took a big gulp of her whiskey, no longer feeling the burn. "I'm not the witch who can help you."

Confusion marred Circe's face. "But I saw your eyes. They glow silver when you use your magic. The mark of the Silverlands witches. How do you know if you can't remember?"

Patience took a sip from her whiskey. She hated it when people asked her that. "I've already been told by the witches I'm not one of them, so it's just me and Michael." She drank down the rest of her whiskey. "Look, I'm not a Silverlands witch. My eyes only change when I do powerful magic, and my skin doesn't glow with the symbols of the land. Besides, the Silverlands witches haven't claimed me. So I'm not the witch you're looking for. I'm an Aberrant. I have no coven."

Circe didn't look convinced. "Hmm... okay."

When Patience first heard of the Silverlands and their witches, she'd thought the same. That it was possible, especially since her eyes glowed silver. When she sent a message to the coven, they never replied. She'd thought her message wasn't received and sent another. Then, in their travels, they found a Silverlands witch, Selene, who they were still unsure if they found her or if she found them either way. She helped to get them out of trouble with the grumpy gremlin. When asked what coven she was part of, she spilled it all. Admittedly, she was three cups into a bottle of Ginnili, which loosened her tongue quite a bit. She told her she was looking for a Silverlands witch, and Selene said she'd be happy to help her. Three bottles of Ginnili and a hangover later, they woke up sprawled across a haystack in that same gremlin. Selene made a great hangover drink before she handed her the stone of Juprium and told her to speak three words: Stuulus Elementelio Focuictus. The stone didn't glow, and her skin didn't illuminate with the symbols of the Silverlands. It devastated her for weeks.

"I could help you find a Silverlands witch," Patience said, "but why do you need one specifically from there?" GreyJoy knew where Selene could be found. Hopefully, she could help.

"Silverlands? What about that dreadful place?" As usual, Lucius walked into the library with a scowl on his face. "Some of us would have liked to know the rest of the story before you rushed off."

Patience rolled her eyes. "Probably because it's none of your damn business."

Lucius glared at her but didn't move to harm her, which surprised her.

"How about I let her catch you up while I check on my friend?" Patience strode over to the wall, brushing shoulders with him. His scent drifted up her nose, causing her to pause momentarily before her hand touched it.

Stepping through, she found herself in front of Maxim's bedroom door. Without thinking, she walked in, finding Michael embracing Kieran with a smile.

"I'm taking it as if this is good news."

Michael let go of Kieran and ran to her.

"Yes, I'm his son. He's my father! I can't believe this." His happiness was so contagious that she couldn't help but catch it.

Circe wandered through the door and found them jumping for joy, literally. Michael ran to her and embraced her. "Mother!"

Patience wasn't at all surprised by this news. Her concern was the information that Circe had just spilled to her, especially because she thought she was a Silverlands witch. What she really wondered was why she thought this. She was about to ask when Ian joined them. Michael ran to him, spreading the joy. Even Silas and Jafa smiled when they walked into the room, but all humor died when Lucius came in.

"As joyous as this reunion is, Circe tells me we have an even larger problem." Everyone turned and looked at Lucius. "A powerful half-demon has taken over Askaria and plans to free Lilith."

"Taken over?"

Lucius raised his brow at her. "Clearly, you missed that part of the conversation."

"I did." Patience turned to look at Circe, waiting for her to explain further. Kieran spoke instead.

"As we were searching for Michael, this demon unknowingly slipped into our kingdom and took over in our absence. Before you criticize my oversight, I had protection in place to prevent such an event, but he had inside help. He's the one who sent the hokima and the Tral'goth. He, somehow, must have found out who and where Michael was. It would explain why the hokima tried to kill us, but not Michael.

"As soon as we heard what he'd done," the king continued, "we tried to return. We found ourselves barred from our kingdom. We knew we needed to find our son more than ever now. With the true heir of Evictus, we could regain control of the kingdom."

True heir? This was getting more curious by the minute.

"Why do you need a witch from the Silverlands?" Patience asked.

"Because if he sets Lilith free, only a Silverlands witch can imprison her again. Or the Goddess herself, but the Goddess hasn't been seen in quite a long time. Not even by the Silverlands witches."

Oh, then she really needed to find Selene.

"Why do you need my help?" Lucius asked.

Patience was surprised to hear Circe had asked for Lucius's help.

"As a direct descendant of Lilith's, you would be the only one to match her in strength and possibly give her pause enough to see reason."

Direct descendant? Of Lilith? Shit. Cordovan. He is a Cordovan. Oh my god! Why am I only making this connection now? Lilith was his great-grandmother. She'd known he might be related to a descendant of Lilith, being a Witch Hunter, but she hadn't known he was a direct descendant. Maybe it was time for her to brush up on her vampire history.

"They're going to need all the help they can get," Patience said. "I know where to find at least one Silverlands witch."

"We should inform the Council of this. They may help," Maxim said as he strolled into the room.

"I take it you were eavesdropping?" Lucius asked, not surprised at all.

"I can't help it if I have great hearing." Maxim shrugged sheepishly.

"That sounds wonderful!" Circe exclaimed. "Kieran and I have been trying to fix this ourselves until now. Both Councils have denied us a hearing."

"That's because King Kieran tried to murder us all," Maxim informed them.

She really, really needed to brush up on her history.

Circe pleaded Kieran's case. "Yes, but he helped to imprison Lilith, knowing her reign needed to end. He's more than made up for his crimes."

"Okay. Do we think it's a good idea to inform the Council about this? Some people wouldn't mind freeing Lilith." As Patience said the words, she looked directly at Lucius to gauge his reaction, but he was stone-faced.

"It's a risk, but it's a bigger risk not trying to elicit their help in case she gets free. We'll need an army to stop her," Circe advised.

"I'll get word to the Witches' Council," Patience told them.

Lucius grimaced, not liking that.

"Before we get ahead of ourselves, we have a ceremony to conduct," Maxim said, breaking the silence. "The Sacru de rit Legare, or the Sacred Binding Ritual, must be performed, and paperwork must be filed. Once that's complete, we can go back to saving this world."

"Why the rush?" she asked.

"What we did is kind of illegal," Michael chimed in.

"Illegal how?" Patience said in surprise.

Ian answered, "We were supposed to file paperwork before we soul-bonded. We could go to prison if they find out we bonded before getting their approval or pay a huge magic fee, and with Michael just coming into his powers, it wouldn't be ideal."

"Yes, he's correct," Maxim confirmed. "The council likes to keep track of all soul bonds. It helps clear up other deaths, especially if someone were to drop dead without explanation. Not to worry. Lucius and I will go now to start the filing process and prepare for the ceremony."

Maxim pushed Lucius toward the door.

"Ian, Michael, come along. We'll need your signatures," Maxim called from the doorway. Michael kissed her forehead and was about to follow Ian when Patience stopped him.

"Wait. I'm going to head home for a little. I need to sleep, shower, and change."

"I don't want you to go alone."

"Don't worry. I'll take Jafa with me."

Michael glanced at Jafa, who stood in the doorway patiently waiting, then nodded. "Okay. But I'm sending the cavalry if you're not back in a few hours."

"Deal."

Michael followed Ian.

"All right, Jafa," Patience said. "Ready to see the sights?"

He grinned. "Yes, Theá."

The expressions on Kieran's and Circe's faces changed. They quickly masked it before she could interpret it. She needed to ask him about the name; maybe he would tell her the meaning, unlike GreyJoy.

"Will you two be able to keep yourselves occupied until I get back?"

They both looked at each other and smiled. "I'm sure we can think of something to do to fill the time," Circe smirked.

Patience grabbed Jafa and disappeared.

CHAPTER NINETEEN

PATIENCE

Too many people take home for granted. Being able to take a nice, steamy shower and put on fresh clothes was a luxury.

She'd sent Jafa to GreyJoy after asking him about the name Theá, and just like GreyJoy, he had no suitable answer. There were questions she had to ask him, but she needed some time to herself after being around so many people and dealing with all the drama. She was drained—magically, physically, and mentally.

Too much had happened too fast. Crazy how her one night of fun turned into days of craziness. When this was all done, she thought she should stay in for a while. Maybe years. If this ever would be done.

Fresh and clean and more herself, she climbed into her cubbyhole with a skylight where she stared up at the stars and tried to find her center so she could heal herself, except it wasn't working. She couldn't determine if it was because of the loud music the neighbor was currently playing or possibly the fact she'd almost died. But she knew it was him. He consumed her thoughts, preventing her from resting.

She should stop thinking about things that would—could—never be.

Looking into her dresser mirror, she could still see his bite marks on her neck. If he healed her, why were they still there? Tracing over them, she remembered her surprise when his fangs penetrated her neck. She'd expected pain. Instead, pleasure had spread through her, surprising her and making her want to experience it again. It sounded crazy.

Placing her finger against the marks, she sent healing magic into them. When she moved her fingers away, she found the marks still there.

"Ugh!" Patience slammed her body back against the wall, frustrated. *Of course, it won't heal. Fuck.*

She needed to stop thinking about him. Even though she'd washed, she could still smell him all over her.

It was insane even to think this way since he'd tried to kill her. Only Goddess knew how many times. She couldn't help it.

"What the hell?" Patience shouted. Something was seriously wrong with her. The proof was that she was still wearing the necklace she'd found in that room. She never returned it.

Patience let it dangle in the skylight, letting the moon's light shine through it. Even though it belonged to his wife, she wasn't sure why it seemed familiar. A part of her was curious about his wife and what she was like, but she would be the last person in this realm he would talk to about his wife.

Sighing, she played with the necklace, watching the colors fill her reading nook.

Letting it fall against her skin, she grabbed the book on vampire history off the shelf near her head. She promised herself that for the third time, she would figure out how to get it off and return it. For now, she had been serious about brushing up on her history. She flipped through the chapters until she found the one on Lilith.

She'd read some information about her, though at the time, she'd only thought she was a myth, just like she thought he was. She was real, just like the Ragana Zidikas.

Reading, she discovered Lilith had been born in the Dark Realm of Enoch. Her mother, Catlith, was a succubus demon from Evictus, and her father was a Silverite, whom they didn't name. *Oh, wow.*

Silverites were the original wielders of magic from the Silverlands. They were the first to use magic to create. They were all gone now. Though Patience was sure she'd read somewhere the Goddess was one or a descendant of one. She continued to read. According to the book, Catlith tried to kill the Silverlands queen, Queen Layana, and was banished to the Dark Realm while she was with child.

Why would Lilith's mother try to kill Queen Layana? She read the paragraph again, hoping to see if she missed something. Maybe GreyJoy had another book on it. She continued reading.

Lilith was born with eyes that were so pale that many believed she was blind and silver hair. When she came of age, she left Enoch and returned to the Silverlands. She claimed to be the rightful heir to the throne, though she brought no genuine evidence. When her claim wasn't taken seriously, she tried to kill the Goddess but failed. The Silverlands guards, the Hallows, wanted to catch her, but she evaded them and hid in Eviathan, the realm of the humans, where she now lived. Though it was no longer the realm of humans, other creatures, including vampires and witches, lived there.

With revenge in her blood, Lilith wanted back into the Silverlands at any cost. Lilith heard King Kieran, the king of the demon realm, Evictus, was unhappy with the Goddess and wanted her off the Silverlands throne. The king wished to receive more power—magic—to his realm, but the Goddess refused him.

Ah, so this is where King Kieran comes in.

Lilith went to him with a deal. If he gave her an army, she would remove the Goddess from her throne and give him all the power he wanted. Kieran laughed at her and revealed that demons couldn't enter the Silverlands because of the Silverite barrier. But Lilith knew humans could get past the barrier. King Kieran and Lilith created what are now known as vampires. With her blood, they took demon souls and placed them in human bodies. They were strong and fierce. They only lasted a few days, and then they died suddenly.

He helped to create vampires... so if Lilith was the mother, which meant... King Kieran was like their father... whoa.

It was one of the first vampires, named Dracul, Lucius's great-grandfather, who discovered they needed blood to sustain themselves. Once that was learned, her army grew quickly, and they invaded the Silverlands by storm.

The Goddess and the Hallows fought them for three long years, but in the end, Lilith was so focused on defeating the Goddess that she didn't see the betrayal until it was too late. With the help of King Kieran, Lilith was imprisoned.

Dracul evaded capture, but the Goddess created a spell, cursing vampires to live by the night, making the sun deadly to them. The Goddess then gave select humans magic to protect themselves. She called them witches, and they were charged with killing vampires. For hundreds of years, witches tried to eradicate vampires, even recruiting humans. Vampires banded together, realizing they were stronger in numbers. They formed covens of their own called clans.

If Lilith were released, all hell would break loose, especially since the Goddess hadn't been seen in centuries.

Patience continued to read until her eyelids grew heavy.

"Come to me," A voice whispered as she drifted asleep.

Lips brushed against hers, waking her. She smiled, opening her eyes, but no one was there. She stuck her head out of her nook and found her room empty.

Strange. Lips had brushed against hers. Familiar lips. His lips. Perhaps it was a dream, even though it had seemed real. Maybe she was losing her mind.

Her stomach grumbled in protest, reminding her she needed to eat. How long had she slept? She looked up through her skylight and saw it was still dark outside.

She got up and stretched. It wasn't as comfortable as people thought, falling asleep in a reading nook.

The words "Come to me" floated through her mind, causing her to pause.

Red eyes appeared in front of her, then disappeared. Jumping, she closed her eyes to calm her nerves. She missed the damn vampire. At least he was good for keeping the fucking red eyes away.

She peeked through the slants of her eyes, glancing around the room. She was relieved when she didn't see any red eyes. Getting up, she went to the kitchen to scrounge for some food.

Sauntering into her kitchen, she realized she wasn't losing her mind. Lucius stood there, leaning against her counter, casually waiting for her. So she wasn't alone after all, and the kiss was... real.

"Fuck," Patience said under her breath, realizing he now knew where she lived.

"Well, nice to see you again, too," he said sarcastically.

Why did Michael's soulmate have to be related to him out of all the vampires in the universe? Then she remembered they were in this situation because of her impulsive idea to go to a vampire club. She was going to suck it up and be nice, even if it killed her.

"I wish I could say the same, asshole." *Shit. Well, that went out the window.*

"Now, now. We're supposed to be playing nice. Aren't we? That's why I won't kill you for stealing this."

He pulled the necklace out of his pocket.

"Are you always keen on taking things that don't belong to you?" he fumed.

The necklace. Shit.

She reached up and touched her neck. "How did you get it off?"

His left eyebrow raised.

"In my defense, I didn't know how to take it off. I tried several times. It wouldn't come off. I know it belongs to your wife..." she trailed off, feeling completely guilty.

She stared at the floor, not knowing what else to do except say, "I'm truly sorry for taking it. I know it means a lot to you."

"How did you even get it on?" he asked through clenched teeth.

"I unclasped it easily and put it on." He glared at her skeptically.

"The necklace has an Arnon lock on it. It's spelled to only lock and unlock with one specific word of the wearer's choosing."

Now, that made so much sense. She would have never gotten it off without his help. Though, it didn't explain how she unclasped it. "Maybe you should get it checked. The lock may have worn down since I unclasped it with no problem."

"Witch, you're lucky. I promised my brother," he said, placing the necklace in his pocket.

Watching it disappear into his pocket caused her to cringe inside. Her neck felt empty without it against her skin. *It is mine.* Her feelings were wrong. In her heart, it belonged to her. She was unsure why, but her instincts screamed for her to take it back. Instead of listening, she pushed it down, burying it with all her feelings about the vampire.

She was possibly losing her mind, especially since all she wanted to do was kiss him and slip the necklace from his pocket.

"I know again. I'm sorry," she grumbled. "I know we must tolerate each other. I apologize for taking what isn't mine. It was a complete accident."

"This is the one time I'll let this go for the sake of my brother. If it happens again, I make no promises."

Patience nodded before she opened the fridge. "Thank you. I won't bother to ask how you got into my apartment, but may I ask what you're doing here?"

"I'm the cavalry. You've been gone the full day. I was the only one available to come and find you. Michael gave me the key."

She must have been exhausted to have slept the full day away. "Well, gee, he just sent my would-be murderer to check on me."

"He had no choice. Until the legătura sufletului is complete, he won't be going much of anywhere."

"The what?" she said, pausing to glance at him. *Soul-bond ritual?*

"The legătura sufletului."

"Huh?" Patience took out some leftover Chinese food. She sniffed it and made a disgusted face, then threw it away.

"The soul-bond ritual. They can't be away from each other for too long. Their bond is still weak. It'll grow stronger once the ritual is done."

Patience looked through her cabinets, searching for something to settle her rumbling stomach. "So what exactly is involved in this ritual? We won't be sacrificing any animals, will we?" Patience finally found a bag of Doritos to eat. "Yay!"

Lucius shook his head. "Animals? No. We don't sacrifice animals for this ritual, but occasionally, we sacrifice a human or two."

She glared at him until she saw the smirk on his face. He was joking—the ass.

"You're an ass. And that's good to know." Patience hopped onto the counter and opened her bag of chips. Lucius wrinkled his nose in disgust. "What? Don't like the smell of powdered cheese?"

"No. Not particularly."

Patience laughed at him and ate her chips. She couldn't believe he was in her apartment, let alone in her kitchen. It was probably taking all his self-control not to kill her right now. He would succeed eventually, especially with her being around him like this. It was like dangling a mouse in front of a cat. He was patiently waiting for the opportunity to get the mouse. He didn't realize this mouse could bite back. It could bite back hard.

"Look at me being rude. Would you like something to drink?"

Lucius jerked his head toward her and smiled viciously. Patience realized what she said instantly. "Not that kind of drink, you bastard." Though, she was tempted to see if another memory would surface.

"Well, you so graciously offered," he said, still smiling viciously as he ambled toward her, and her heart sped up. He looked like a predator about to pounce on his prey. "You seemed to enjoy yourself the last time..."

"I'm warning you now. Don't do anything crazy because you might not like the results..." She tried to say it bravely, but she faltered. As he got closer to her, her heart pounded harder against her chest, and he could hear it by the intensity in his eyes. She hoped he thought it was out of fear. When he reached her, warmth rose into her cheeks, making her blush as she realized he was standing between her legs. She hoped he would think it was because she was afraid.

He stood there, gazing at her. He was so close to her that she could smell him—sandalwood. He smelled like sandalwood. Looking into his eyes momentarily, she didn't see hatred in them. She saw something else.

Patience glanced down at his lips. His fangs were out. She wasn't terrified at all. She only wanted to know what it felt like to have him look at her with...

Lucius pulled away. "Checking on you wasn't the only reason I came here. I need to go to the bookstore, and since it doesn't like me much, I'll need your help to get in."

"Shit. Jafa." She totally forgot she'd left him at the bookstore. Lucius looked confused, especially when she suddenly grabbed him.

She transported them to the front of the bookstore.

"We could have driven."

"But this was faster." Patience walked into the bookstore with Lucius right on her heels. She was a little surprised GreyJoy let him so easily enter. "Hi, GreyJoy. Where's Jafa?"

A note floated down, but before she could grab it, Lucius snatched it. *The ass.*

Lucius read the note. "He's in the ancient tomes section."

Of course, he is. "I need to find Jafa. You can ask GreyJoy for what you need, and maybe he'll give it to you." He glared at her as she strolled away. He made her want to stab his eyes out. Always glaring at her. She hated that she also enjoyed it. It was sad how much she craved the feel of his eyes on her, even if it was a death glare.

Sighing, she made her way to the ancient tome section, praying she wouldn't get lost or distracted as she sought to see what Jafa was up to.

She found him sitting on the carpet near a fireplace that had never existed, with his head in a book about enchanted sandstorms.

"There you are. Sorry I took so long."

He looked up from the book with a smile on his face. "Theá! No worries. Ustafa has been showing me incredible things like this. How to defeat the ancient sandstorms of our realm so my people may find a new home further away from that evil place."

"Ustafa?"

"We're in Ustafa's home now."

Confusion distorted Patience's face.

"You didn't know his name."

"I thought his name was GreyJoy."

A note floated down from the ceiling. She caught it.

I am known by many names.

"Of course you are. Jafa, we've been summoned back to do their bidding. And they sent the devil to take us there."

Jafa closed the book. "Ustafa, it would be a great favor to me if you could send this to my people to help them." Jafa held the book out in front of him.

Patience waited for a note to float down, asking for a sacrifice, but nothing came.

"Yes, I know this will be the eighty-fifth favor I've asked you, but you still owe me ninety-five favors, especially after Cadive."

Confusion marred her face again. Did Jafa and GreyJoy know each other? Which made sense of why they called her the same name, but how did they know each other? But the more important question—

"Is he talking directly to you?"

The book disappeared from Jafa's hands.

"Yes," Jafa said. "Does he not talk directly to you?"

Another note floated down from the ceiling. Patience caught it, almost wanting to crush it in her hands, but she also wanted to understand.

You still have not unlocked that memory to understand. I will rejoice in the day you do.

"Okay." Patience was still confused. "So you two know each other? How? I wasn't gone that long for you to do him that many favors."

Jafa stood and walked over to her.

"Yes, we know each other. As for how, Ustafa said it was best for you to unlock your memory before we tell you anything further."

"You said you knew me before. That I saved you."

A note floated down, and Jafa caught it and read it.

Be patient, and everything will be revealed soon.

"GreyJoy. You know something about me and my past?" This was all getting confusing. She'd saved Jafa once, so she must have been in his realm before, but why was she there? And what did GreyJoy know about her that he wasn't telling? She had so many questions, and no one gave her any answers—at least not the ones she liked.

"Come now. You said we were being summoned."

Patience let Jafa guide her to the front of the bookstore, where they came upon the vampire with three books in his hand and the necklace disappearing. She couldn't believe he'd given it to GreyJoy. She wondered what was so important he gave up his wife's necklace for it. When he heard them walking toward him, he turned the titles away so she couldn't see them.

"Are you ready, witch? I got what I came for."

"I can see." Patience walked up to him and put her hand on his arm. He tensed. "Relax. I'm just bringing us back to your car. Will you be coming with us, Jafa?"

"No, I'll stay here with my friend for now."

She nodded and transported them to the front of his car.

He shook off her hands and unlocked the doors. He placed the books in the trunk and got in the car. Patience got in the back, not wanting to be near him.

She settled into the back, getting comfortable. She closed her eyes and made her mind blank. Her mind would go on overload if she thought about anything, and she needed to stay focused.

⚬

Lucius

The king and queen of Evictus were in his home. His brother was illegally bonded to their son. A half-demon had taken over Askaria, the capital of Evictus, and was trying to set their creator, Lilith, free. Her sole purpose in life was to build an army to take over what she believed to be her home realm. If she were set free, she would wreak havoc on this world to get what she wanted.

All this was happening. All he could think about was the witch's blood coursing through his veins, enticing and drawing him to her even more. His blood in her body called to him. Things couldn't get any worse. He had a feeling there was more to come.

Lucius still didn't understand how she could wear his wife's necklace. He and his wife were the only two who knew the word to unclasp it. *Lubire pentru totdeauna.* (Forever Love)

He'd given it to her for her birthday. He'd noticed her admiring it when they'd gone to the jeweler to find a gift for his mother. He'd surprised her with it. He still remembered the look of pure happiness on her face.

As much as he hated sacrificing it, he needed the books, but they were the only thing he had of equal value. The store assured him that he would receive the necklace if he returned the books. He promised to burn them to the ground and curse the ashes if they didn't.

Looking in his rearview mirror, the witch slept peacefully. She had no clue what kind of havoc she brought into his life.

When he found her sleeping, he couldn't stop himself from kissing her. He wanted to do more until the necklace caught his eye. At first, he thought his eyes were deceiving him, and maybe it was a different necklace. The necklace seemed to belong to her until he spoke the word, and the necklace was unclasped. He surprised himself. Anger didn't surface as quickly as he thought it would. Part of him almost left it on her, liking it around her neck. His feelings for the witch were getting to him. He had to undo this bond before things got worse and he did something that would be nearly impossible to take back. He wouldn't let it get that far. He promised himself as he glanced in the rearview mirror at her sleeping form.

Silence and her shallow breathing filled the car as they drove into the night.

When they reached his home, he left the witch. He had more important things to do. He grabbed the books from his trunk and walked inside. Glancing back at her only once.

He dropped the books in his safe and then went to his office.

He discovered Max filling out the paperwork for the ritual.

"Did you find her, and is she still alive?"

Lucius poured himself a drink before answering. "Unfortunately, she's still breathing."

"You must learn how to live with her now that she's your sister-in-law."

"She'll be no relation of mine."

"Well, that may be, but on paper, she will be."

Lucius finished his drink. "Where are the king and queen?"

"I believe they're resting in their room."

Lucius still couldn't believe he had demons in his household, even if they were the king and queen. Demons weren't overly fond of vampires. But now his brother was bonded with one, and he couldn't be simple or bonded to any plain old demon. He had to get hitched to the demon king's son. How the hell was he supposed to explain this to the Council? Though maybe he wouldn't have to.

"I know what you're thinking, and I'm not explaining shit to the Council," Maxim said grudgingly. "That's all you. It's about time you took your place on the Council back from Alden."

Damn. "I'll consider it."

"Lucius, I'm serious. You're supposed to be head of the Council. Not him."

Lucius blatantly ignored him, changing the subject. "When can we have this ritual done?"

Maxim glared at him but answered his question. "Well, a courier is coming to pick up the paperwork as we speak, so it must be done by the end of the week."

A week of having her in his house. He would have one week to get it done. She would stay near the demon... Michael. It would be his only chance.

Silas entered the office.

"In walks the traitor."

"Lucius, you're unfair. Besides, you're in the presence of royalty," Maxim chided.

"Not only royalty. A Novarian. It explains many questions we've had about you."

"I can explain," Silas said with conviction. "I came to apologize for not disclosing my past, even though, at the time, it didn't seem necessary. The dynamic between us hasn't changed. I still serve you." Silas knelt near Lucius.

Maxim glared at Lucius.

Lucius was being an ass. He trusted Silas like a brother, and nothing would change it.

"Get up. Your loyalty has been tested, and you haven't failed. You've found the family you thought was lost. I won't fault you for that."

Maxim nodded in approval and came from around the desk to hold his hand to Silas. He took his hand and stood. "Thank you," he said.

Lucius stood as well. "Besides, we have a bigger problem now that my brother is awake. Silas, I'll need you. We have some council members to visit."

"As always, I'm at your service, except the king would like a word with you."

Kieran appeared in the doorway. "May I come in?"

Lucius gestured for him to step in as he eyed him, only slightly curious about the man who was their creator but would never acknowledge them as such.

"Thank you for allowing us into your home. I know how it feels when unwanted strangers invade your home. Trust me. That's why I hope to resolve this as quickly as possible."

Lucius glanced at Maxim, who bowed to the king.

"It's a pleasure to have royalty in our home, no matter the lineage," Maxim said respectfully. "I'd like this issue solved as well. Having Lilith go free wouldn't go well for anyone. We need to locate the half-demon and get you and Circe back into Askaria before he does the unthinkable. It will take convincing the Council members of this. Do you have any proof?"

"We've been barred from our kingdom. No doorway will allow us through."

"The Council would say it's a trick," Lucius stated.

"Why would we trick you into thinking we can't enter our kingdom?"

Maxim chimed in. "Some Council members are old fools who hold on to grudges."

"Still, we need to figure out a way to prove your story true. Can anyone get out of Askaria? They could confirm this," Lucius probed.

"The only person who can get into Askaria is my son and, possibly, the witch."

"She's claimed she isn't a Silverlands witch."

"She also doesn't have her memory, so it's possible she could still be one," King Kieran offered.

"Even if she shows no signs or traits of being one?"

"It's possible she may not show the traits because of her lineage. Lilith only had silver hair, and she's a Silverite descendant."

Lucius wanted to laugh because if it were true, she would be a formidable foe to take down in battle. *Damn, his promise to his brother and his fucking feelings.*

"We need to know what's going on there," Lucius said. "We may have to use your son—or the witch—to find out. For now, Silas, we have a few

Council members to talk to. It's possible to convince a few, and we can convince the rest."

"Then I'll leave this to you until the ceremony is complete. Now I must return to my wife and son," King Kieran said before he stepped out the door.

Lucius nodded, then headed out the door with Silas right behind him.

CHAPTER TWENTY

LUCIUS

Having only been able to convince less than a handful of council members about the happenings in Askaria, Lucius was pissed. With no proof, a few thought he was ridiculous, and it was impossible to set Lilith free, while the other half thought it was none of their concern. They didn't care if she killed the witches' Goddess.

Silas tried to explain to the idiots that it wasn't about their Goddess being killed. It was the fact that Lilith would enslave every vampire to build her army, and she would kill all those who resisted her. And more than half, if not all, of them would die trying to fight the Hallows, the guards of the Silverlands. All so she could claim a throne that may or may not be hers.

Leaving Silas, he convinced two other Council members about the situation. All they could tell him was if he wanted people to take him seriously, he should take his rightful place as the head of the Council, which was true but also bullshit. However, the one he really needed to talk to was Alden, who could easily make the council listen. Unfortunately, he wasn't ready to take that step yet.

He had more pressing matters to deal with, like breaking the blood bond between him and the witch before she discovered it.

Speaking of the object of his thoughts, she was coming down the stairs as he walked into the foyer.

"There you are," she said gleefully.

"Here I am."

He tried to keep walking past her, but she followed him.

"I heard you went out to convince some Council members of our cause. Any luck?" She followed him right into his office and sat in the chair in front of his desk.

He should toss her out, except... he wanted to talk to her—and he loved how her scent filled his office. *Fuck.*

"Not our cause, and no luck." He pulled out two glasses and poured them both a drink. He handed her the glass. She hesitated momentarily before she reached for it. Their fingers slightly grazed as she took the glass. A shiver went through him. He ignored it as he took a sip of the whiskey.

"True, it's not really yours," she said matter-of-factly, "since it's not your Goddess whom she wants to murder."

"But unfortunately, it is my people she wants to use to kill your Goddess."

"So, technically, that would mean it is partially your cause." She smiled at him before taking a sip from her glass. He could see the discomfort on her face as the liquor burned down her throat.

"It takes some getting used to."

She nodded and took another sip. "I know."

Walking around his desk to stand in front of her, he leaned in toward her. "Is there a reason you followed me in here?"

Her lips parted slightly as desire filled her eyes.

"I... uh, I... um... I—"

"Yes?" He placed his drink on the desk, leaning even closer. Her legs parted, inviting him.

"I... I wanted to talk about the man at the club."

Alden. She wanted to talk about Alden. He pulled back and went to sit back in his chair.

"Why are you interested in Alden? You seemed like you knew each other already."

"No, I'd never seen him before that night. Who is he?"

Lucius was reluctant to tell her for some damn reason. There was no harm in telling her about him. He should warn her to stay away from him. He still wasn't sure what Alden wanted from her, but he would see him soon now that his brother was awake, especially since they filed the paperwork.

He took a sip of whiskey. "He's the head of the vampire Council and not someone you should associate yourself with."

"Well, that's going to be hard since he seems to know who I am and my past. He may be the key to what I've been looking for."

How the hell does Alden know about her past? He needed to learn more about her and what she wanted from him.

He pulled out his phone and sent a quick text to Volt.

I need more information on the witch and Alden's connection to her.

"The head of the vampire Council. Seriously?" She took another sip of whiskey, shocked to hear the news.

"Yes. Trust me, this is one thing I wouldn't lie to you about. He's very dangerous, and you should keep away from him."

"Wow. Warning me to stay out of danger. You must really care." She took another sip of her whiskey, finishing it. She stood.

"You're technically now under the protection of the Cordovan clan, or you soon will be once the ritual takes place."

"Well, isn't that nice? Does this mean you can no longer kill me?" She leaned over his desk, placing the glass in front of him. Her proximity stirred his desire. His fangs elongated, wanting to taste her again.

"Do not. Push. Your luck."

As they gazed into each other's eyes, they didn't move. She licked her lips, drawing his eyes to them as she leaned closer. Her hand lifted, accidentally knocking the glass off his desk. He caught it.

"Oops." She leaned back. "Luck, huh? It seems to me it could be more." She went to leave, but she turned to look back at him before she got to the door. "I never got to thank you for saving my life. You didn't have to, but I'm glad you did."

"Don't thank me for it."

"Why?"

Because I should have never done it, I let you in, and I don't think I will ever be able to let you go. The words were on the tip of his tongue, but he held them back and said, "I only saved your life so we could get home."

"Oh."

He ignored the sadness in her eyes as he purposefully hurt her even when all of him burned to go to her and wipe it away.

"Well, thank you anyway. No matter the reason you did it." Sighing, she placed her hand on the door handle when he moved, without thinking, and pinned her against the door.

"What are y—"

His lips crashed into hers in a vicious kiss. He didn't care if it was the blood bond or his attraction. He had to have her.

As he kissed her, she wrapped her legs around him. Her moans were driving him crazy as he gripped her ass and moved from her lips to her neck. His fangs pressed against his lips, urging him to sink them into her succulent vein.

"Lucius," she moaned. His name coming from her lips almost made him explode like a schoolboy. What was she doing to him? *Fuck.*

A knock sounded on the door. *Shit.* He wanted to kill whoever was at his door. They needed to go away.

"Lucius, I know you're in there. I need you to sign this before I send it off."

It was Max. He would plan his funeral.

"Give me a minute." He groaned as she unwrapped her legs from around him and placed her feet on the floor. He reluctantly removed his hands from her ass and took a step back as his fangs retracted.

She seemed as confused as he appeared. At that moment, he wanted to tell her about the blood bond, but he didn't want Max to hear. Instead, he leaned forward and gently kissed her on the mouth.

Pulling back, a small smile appeared on her lips. She touched his cheek. He pressed his face against her hand, enjoying the warmth. Taking it away, she placed her hand on the wall near the door and stepped through.

Lucius stared at the wall after her, wishing her to return. Instead, he opened the door for Max. He felt like a lovesick puppy, but then again, he would have to be in love, and he wasn't.

"How can I help you, Max?" Leaving the door open for Max to walk through, he grabbed his abandoned drink and finished it before he poured himself another, using the glass she'd left behind.

"You drink from two glasses now?"

"Max, I'm not in the mood. What do you need me to sign?"

"This." Max placed a document of authenticity in front of him. "They want you to sign to guarantee the union's legitimacy."

Lucius laughed. "Alden basically wants to make sure the ritual isn't fake. What bullshit is this? Why would I want to fake a ceremony for my brother to marry a demon? The idiocy." He grabbed a pen from his desk and signed the document. Things like this almost made him want to take his Council seat back.

He could get the support. Since they'd outlawed the killing of witches, he had more time to think. The guilt of how he'd abandoned his duties and his people to become the Ragana Zidikas still plagued him. However, it looked as if he would have to put his guilt aside and take his place back because Alden was becoming tiring to deal with, and if he couldn't see this as a problem, he would be forced to remove him, peacefully or violently—his choice.

Lucius handed the signed paper to Maxim.

"We should be able to have the ceremony tomorrow night," he told him. "We need to have witnesses. Is there anyone, in particular, you'd like me to add to the guest list?"

"No, there's no one I can think of other than the usual. I'll try to convince them again. Will my mother be joining us? I need to know if I must prepare for her theatrics."

"According to your father, she's off in Italy somewhere. You know how your mom is. She may show up late and make a big scene."

Their mother loved to be the center of attention, so she always had to cause a scene that made Lucius cringe inside. She would bring the theatrics when she found out Ian was soul-bonding to a demon.

"If you see her before I do, bring her to me," Lucius advised. "Preferably before she causes a scene."

"I'll keep an eye out for her, as always. Also, a request came along with the document as well. The Council is asking to attend the ceremony, which could be because it's rare for a demon and a vampire to do the ritual."

"You know damn well it isn't. Is the request deniable?"

"I'm afraid not."

Lucius nodded. He would throw something if he spoke, and he'd already done enough damage to this house.

Maxim nodded in return and walked out the door without another word, closing the door behind him.

Lucius stared after him, moving to the wall beside the door, hoping she would reappear. When she didn't, he ran his hands through his hair in frustration, then walked over to his safe, pulling out the books.

It was time he found a way to break the bond before he ultimately succumbed to it.

———◆○◆———

Patience

"Why do I have to dress up for this again?"

Michael wanted Patience to dress up for the ceremony. He was currently in her new room, courtesy of Maxim, helping her pick out a dress. She despised all the dresses he'd laid out on the bed for her. They looked like runway-model dresses she would never be able to fit in.

She'd hoped trying on dresses would distract her from thinking about Lucius. She wasn't having any luck so far. All she could think about was his lips trailing down her neck, leaving her yearning for more. She wanted to feel his bite again to see if it would bring to light another memory, but she would be lying to herself if she didn't also want the pleasure it brought her. It was seared into her memory as a pleasure she would never forget that spread throughout her body until it went straight to her core. She swore she could still feel it even now.

Focus. Don't think about it. Don't think about him.

"Patience, Ian wants you to look your best. That's why he sent you these."

Michael had been trying to convince her to try one dress on at least, but she couldn't get herself to do it. Nothing looked like her style.

"I don't need to wear a ball gown to look my best, and what kind of ceremony is this, anyway?"

"Their kind of ceremony and only one of these is a ball gown, which we've already taken out of the pile. Patience, you told me you would try, and this isn't trying. This is just you being a baby."

"Me? A baby? That's just low." Patience didn't mean to make a big deal about this, but she realized she would be around people she didn't know. Also, they were all her mortal enemies. *Cannot forget that little tidbit.*

When she woke after being abandoned in the car, Michael had found her and given her the wonderful news that the ceremony would be tomorrow night with a few of Ian's and Lucius's close friends. If the people who showed up tomorrow were anything like Lucius, she was in trouble. She would have to keep herself in check, especially for Michael's sake. Hopefully, no one would try to kill her.

"Well, if the shoe fits," Michael taunted.

Patience gasped. "Rude," she humphed and continued to look through the pile of dresses Ian had dumped on her bed. "Are you going to talk about what it feels like to find your parents?"

Michael lifted a green sleeveless gown with a heart-shaped neckline, which looked decent until she saw the split up the back of the dress. She could magically alter it, but dresses weren't her forte. She would wind up making it uglier than it already was. So it wasn't worth the magic.

"Not happening. So—?"

"I still can't fully process it, Patience. I found my other half and my parents, all within a few days. It sounds too good to be true. And I'm afraid something is going to come along and screw it all up."

She stopped looking through dresses and went to sit next to him. "Aw, Michael. It's real."

"But how do you know? This could all be an illusion."

"Seriously, I think I, of all the people here, would know if this was an illusion. Besides, who would conjure a reality in which my best friend's fiancé's brother hates me and wants to do nothing but murder me? If this is an illusion, I'll kill the person casting it." This would have to be some person's sick joke to cast an illusion like this. It was too elaborate, and illusions didn't last this long. Only possibly the Goddess would have enough power to sustain an illusion like this. However, she should double-check.

"But you haven't hurt him," Michael declared. "It's curious to find you haven't used your powers against him. Especially since he's threatened to kill you, how many times already? And you saved his life the other night."

"I know. He's not my enemy, even though he thinks he is. And he may come around. He saved my life, after all." She was trying not to think about him, and here Michael was, bringing him up when all she wanted to do was go back to his office and finish what they started.

"Here, try this one on." Michael pulled a beautiful sangria-colored satin sheath dress out from under an ugly pink frilly dress. "It doesn't look too bad. Go try it on for me, please!"

"Fine! I'll try it on just for you." Patience took the dress from Michael, went into the bathroom, and changed into the dress.

When she came out, she found Ian and Michael making out.

"Really, guys?"

They stopped themselves, for which Patience was incredibly grateful.

"Oh, my Goddess... you look beautiful." Michael gazed at her with his mouth open.

Ian was staring at her as well.

"Ha ha, you two are funny. There's no way I look that good."

Ian got up, took her hand, and brought her to the floor-length mirror. "Look." He turned her toward it.

Patience realized it had been a long time since she really looked at herself. It had been a while since she'd washed her hair. It was becoming a curly mess. She was thinking about cutting it but never got around to it. There were bags under her eyes. She could blame that on Lucius. A good night's—or a week's worth of—sleep was what she needed; either would work for her. She wouldn't say she was beautiful, but the dress made her feel good, and she liked it. With a few adjustments, she could feel sexy in it.

When she turned around, she found three pairs of eyes looking at her.

"You look absolutely beautiful, Patience." Maxim smiled at her from the doorway. "I see you tried on one of them."

"Yeah, he finally guilt-tripped me enough to try one on."

"Well... it worked." Michael always knew how to get to her. He was the only one who knew, but she felt Lucius might as well.

"Let me get out of this before I ruin it." Patience walked into the bathroom but took her time to change. It had been a while since someone other than Michael called her beautiful. It made her feel good to be noticed. She couldn't help but wonder what Lucius would think of her in this dress, which was completely and utterly stupid of her.

When Patience walked out of the bathroom, she had a solid plan. Stay the hell away from Lucius. Being near him would only cause her trouble and possibly heartbreak. Maxim was still in the room, talking to Michael and Ian about the ceremony.

"How about we continue this discussion over a round of cards?" she proposed. "And possibly the bottle of bourbon I saw earlier?"

She could see the hesitation in their eyes. "Come on! It'll be fun! I need fun after the week I've had. The week we've all had."

"Remember, that's how this all started," Michael reminded her.

"Which led to you finding the love of your life. Who knows, maybe this night we could find yours, Maxim."

Maxim smiled as if he liked the sound of that. "Fine, but just one round."

Ten rounds and a 150-year-old bottle of scotch later—they couldn't find the bourbon—they finally headed to bed around 4 a.m.

"Shit. Where was my room again?" Patience asked.

"Doesn't matter. Pick any room. There are so damn many." Maxim was so far gone; she wasn't even sure how he would make it up the stairs. He answered her question and then laid back on the couch, closing his eyes.

Ian and Michael had disappeared a few minutes earlier, pulling off their clothes as they went upstairs. She gave them a few more minutes before she made her way up. Unsure of where to head, she let instinct take over. She stumbled upon a room that looked like it belonged to Maxim. She didn't care. Taking off her shoes and pants, she got under the covers. Warm and comfy.

Patience had closed her eyes when she was jerked out of her sleep.

Red eyes floated above her. "Come to me."

She rolled from the bed onto the floor and cautiously glanced at the ceiling. No red eyes. *Thank fuck.* She took a deep breath and laid her head against the side of the bed. Did she have a nightmare? It didn't feel as though she did. She closed her eyes and took another deep breath before she opened them. She glanced up at the ceiling one more time before she got up.

A part of her was tempted to find him just to lie in bed with him so he would keep the nightmares at bay. He would keep her safe.

She laughed out loud to herself as she sat on the bed. Maybe she drank just a little too much last night. Laying back down, she was about to close her eyes when the energy in the air shifted. She sat up as her powers stirred. Something called to her, urging her to embrace the force that was coming. A force she didn't think she was prepared to face. None of them were.

CHAPTER TWENTY-ONE

Lucius

"**A**lden, I didn't know you would grace us with your presence tonight," Maxim said as Lucius observed him from the landing near the stairs, hidden from their view.

He'd had a feeling the bastard would show up to collect her. He was actually surprised he hadn't shown up sooner, but this would be the best excuse he had for showing up in his territory. He would have to handle this carefully so the imbecile wouldn't ruin his brother's night.

"Lucius knows why I'm here. I also couldn't resist when I heard one of the infamous Cordovan brothers was getting soul-bonded to a demon." Maxim was trying to figure out why Alden was here. He would come to the same conclusion as him: the witch.

Lucius continued to watch intently. Ian would say Alden oozed sexiness and intimidation all at once. Maxim said his build reminded him of a Saxon warrior. He wore his long hair back into a ponytail, and his suits were always black and immaculate. Lucius could never place his accent since it appeared to change all the time. There was also something off about him that Lucius could never put his finger on.

"Well, I hope you enjoy yourself this evening, and if you need anything, please ask," Max said, pointing to the dining room.

"I shall not hesitate at all. Please let Lucius know I'm here."

Alden entered the dining room, and Maxim ran upstairs to find him. When he reached the landing, he stepped out of the shadows to meet him.

"We've got a problem, Lucius."

"I know."

"Alden's here. He's here for—"

"Patience." Hearing her name coming from his mouth sounded strange. He realized he liked how it sounded.

Surprise dawned on Max's face, but he said nothing about it. He was more concerned about the matter at hand. "What? Why?"

"I don't know what he wants with her, but she told me he knew who she was earlier, and he may be the key to unlocking her memory."

Maxim was relieved to hear it. "Do you want me to tell her he's here? And is Ian ready?"

"No, don't. I'll deal with it. And I don't know if he's ready. I was about to head to his room before you stormed here."

"What will we do about the king and queen?"

"Shit. Alden can't know they're here and Michael is their son. Not yet."

"Okay. I'll go warn them."

Maxim left, leaving Lucius to find Ian.

He wasn't sure he was ready for tonight. He was happy for his brother. He deserved to find love, even if it was with a demon. If Lucius could set aside his disdain, maybe he could move on and find happiness again. He shook himself of the ridiculous thought. He'd had his happiness, and it had been snatched away. This infatuation with the witch was temporary.

They would go their separate ways once this bond was broken and this debt was paid. The thought didn't sit well with him. He ignored it.

After watching a few more guests arrive, Lucius searched for his brother. He was relieved when he found him alone in his room, trying to put on his tie.

"We've got a problem, little brother."

Ian stopped struggling for a moment to look at him. "What problem could that be?"

Lucius walked over to him, took the tie from his hand, and tied it correctly. "What? Are you so nervous you forgot how to tie a tie?"

Ian looked at him thoughtfully. "Yes. Yes, I am."

Lucius couldn't help but smirk as he took the tie from his brother. His brother, who was born with a steely confidence that sometimes scared Lucius, was nervous. Maybe then, what he found with Michael was real—at least Ian thought it was. That was enough for Lucius because all he wanted was for his brother to find happiness the way he had once found it, and if anyone impeded him, then he would kill them no matter who they were.

Ian ran his hands through his hair as Lucius tied the tie and stepped back from him. "Alden's here."

"Shit, why?"

"He's here for her."

"Patience? Why? Why does he want her?"

"I don't know what he wants from her, but I'll find out. You just concentrate on getting through the ritual, and I'll watch him tonight."

Lucius could see the concern still in his eyes. For as long as Lucius could remember, Alden had hated Ian. He wasn't even sure why. Any chance Alden could get, he would go after his brother and the fucked-up part. There was nothing Lucius could do about it since Alden sat on the Council. He'd repeatedly asked his brother what he'd done to Alden to make him hate him. Ian insisted he did nothing. Then again, his brother was in a rage for a few centuries after an old boyfriend slept with his best friend.

Lucius would have to make sure nothing went wrong. This was his brother's night, and he wanted everything to go well for him, at least for today.

"Look, don't worry about him. I promise not to let him ruin anything, okay? Do you trust me?"

Ian smiled. "Of course I trust you. You're my brother. Who else am I going to trust? Have we told Michael's parents that Alden's here?"

"Max will warn them now and suggest they don't attend the dinner."

"Suggest?"

Maxim would have difficulty convincing the king not to come to dinner. He hoped the queen would be more reasonable, but he wasn't sure. "Yes, suggest. We must pray Alden has never met them and that this will be a peaceful dinner."

"I trust you."

"Good. I'll meet you downstairs so you can introduce your fiancé to the world."

Ian's smile grew wider. Just as Lucius was about to walk out the door, Ian stopped him.

"Hey, wait. I need you to do me a favor."

Lucius had a strange feeling he wouldn't like the favor. "And that is?"

Ian ran his hand through his hair.

I will not like this.

"I need you to escort Patience to dinner tonight."

"That's not a good idea." His brother squared his shoulder, meaning he knew how Lucius would answer and had prepared a counterargument. Lucius wouldn't like this, but, fuck, he would give in. He always gave in.

"It's my night, and it will make me very happy if you do this."

Lucius loved his brother. Sometimes, he asked too much of him.

"I know you don't want to do this," Ian started. "I can't have her walk in there alone. She's still an Etherian, and no one will touch her if they know she's under your protection. Besides, I don't want her to hurt anyone, either. The goal is to keep the peace—just for tonight."

Lucius needed to make him realize how much of a mistake it would be. If he did this, everyone would know a witch was now under the Ragana Zidikas's protection. He wasn't sure he was ready to take that step. "You ask too much."

"I know it may be too much to ask, but it'll show me you really are trying and not planning to kill her at a later date."

Lucius would have no choice but to walk her in. That smart little fucker. His brother was so lucky he loved him. *Shit.*

"Fine. I'll escort her in. You owe me for this."

Ian grinned as Lucius walked out, slamming the door behind him.

Lucius couldn't believe he'd given in. He would do this, though his brother didn't realize how much he was going to owe him. He refused to admit how a small part of him was thrilled to do this to be near her. He was losing the battle.

Patience

"Are you uninviting us to our son's ceremony?"

Maxim had a bad feeling about this. "Um... we just think it would be better if you didn't attend with a Council member here."

Kieran stared daggers at him. Maxim looked to the queen for help, but she simply walked into the bathroom. Maxim guessed she didn't want to ruin her dress with the bloodbath that was about to happen if the look on the king's face was any sign.

"I won't hide from anyone. I'll be at my son's dinner whether you or Lucius like it."

"It may ruin our plans to go to the Council for help."

Kieran grabbed him by his shirt and lifted him off the floor. "Do I look like I give a shit? I just found my son and am happy to celebrate this joyous event with him."

"Maxim's trying to say that it may look like you're in league together, especially with two powerful species and families joining." Patience placed her hand on Kieran's arm to get him to lower Maxim.

She'd been going to see the king and queen to ask if they needed anything. As she was heading down, she walked in and overheard their conversation.

Kieran looked at her, anger still on his face, but he lowered Maxim to the floor. "Is that what you meant?"

"Yes, it is."

Kieran let go of him. Maxim straightened up and said, "I just want our request for aid to work."

"But I'd also like to be there for myself," the king said adamantly.

"And I may have the solution."

They both looked at her, curious about what solution she could offer.

"I'll disguise you so only we will recognize you so that you may attend. If that's okay with you."

Kieran looked at his wife, and she nodded. "That'll be okay with us as long as we can attend."

Maxim took that as his cue and slipped out of the room.

Patience walked toward Circe and held out her hands. "Let me see your hands."

Lucius

"Guests are arriving, and there's already gossip about why Alden's here," Maxim confirmed as he entered his office and found Lucius closing his safe. "What are you doing? We're ready."

"Nothing. Come on, so we can get this night over with."

They found everyone standing at the bottom of the staircase except for Patience.

"Where is she?" Lucius asked, trying to keep the anger from his voice. He didn't enjoy being late.

"She's coming. She's not used to wearing what she's wearing, so give her a minute or two." It was Michael who spoke, but it was Ian who pierced Lucius with a menacing look. "Wait for her," Ian added.

Lucius had forgotten how much of an ass his brother could be.

"All right. I'll go in first to make my speech. When it's over, if Patience gets here, she and Lucius will go in next, followed by Ian and Michael. They'll come in last if she's still not here."

Maxim proceeded into the dining room. They could hear him speaking about why they were there and the festivities for the night.

He was more than halfway through, and she still hadn't arrived.

Lucius was losing his patience fast. "It shouldn't take this long for her to get down here. What the hell is she doing up there?"

"I'll go get her." Michael was about to walk up the stairs when Ian grabbed his arm.

"You can't. We must go in now."

Maxim had ended his speech, and they could hear people clapping.

"Come on. He'll wait for her." Ian pulled a reluctant Michael along. Michael smiled at him apologetically before entering the dining room.

They walked in as his rage grew. He waited a few more minutes and walked up the stairs to find her. Before he made it up one step, she appeared at the top of the stairs.

"I'm so sorry I'm late." She rushed down the stairs toward him, trying to hold her dress in one hand, but she was going too fast and tripped.

He rushed up to her, and before he even realized it, his hands were out catching her. She fell right into his arms, and for a moment, he didn't want to let her go. He wanted to kiss her... again.

Her dress hugged her curves in all the right places. The image of them entwined together in the darkness flitted through his mind as he gazed into her eyes.

He set her on her feet.

"Thanks. I'm sorry I'm late. I forgot I needed to do my hair." She glanced around and realized it was just Lucius waiting for her. "Where is everybody?"

"They're already inside, and since my brother talked me into escorting you in, I've been out here waiting for you. Now, we're more than fashionably late, and all eyes will be on us when we walk into the room, so be prepared."

She slipped her arm through his. He tried not to dwell on how good and... natural it was to have her by his side. He didn't want to think about why as they entered the dining room.

CHAPTER TWENTY-TWO

PATIENCE

The silent hush that momentarily swept through the dining room when they walked in was nerve-wracking. Patience hated being the center of attention. She could feel the intense stare of everyone's eyes on her and Lucius. It made her want to turn around and run, or at least make herself invisible. She took a deep breath and tried to concentrate on walking and not tripping.

"Relax, no one is going to bother you," Lucius whispered to her as the noise in the room picked back up. The comment surprised Patience, and it calmed her nerves a little.

She finally relaxed when they reached Ian and Michael, standing near a window, talking to Maxim about how the rest of the evening would go. After grabbing a glass of champagne from a tray, she leaned against the wall to watch the crowd.

There were many people here. Vampires and some humans. Patience thought they were more for entertainment than guests. She saw the dining table had been removed, and they brought in little cocktail tables. People were standing around them, drinking their blood wine.

She continued to gaze around until her eyes landed on Kieran and Circe. Her glamor was working well. No one recognized them so far. Sometimes, her magic could have a mind of its own, but she'd spelled it to work all night. She hoped it wouldn't be the case tonight.

Patience continued to look around until her eyes landed on Alecia, walking into the room with a young woman who wasn't as young as she looked. Her eyes said everything. She looked like Ian, with her long wavy hair and slender body, as though she'd just stepped off a fashion shoot. She held herself with elegance, and Patience envied her. This woman was in charge of her own life.

Patience finished her champagne and took another off a tray, continuing to be a silent observer.

The woman walked over to Ian, hugging him. Patience could tell he had mixed emotions about her being here. He put on a smile and introduced his fiancé to her. Her beautiful face turned into a scowl as she looked at Michael in disgust. She also saw Maxim make a beeline toward her. She would make a scene when he took her to the side. Whatever he was saying to her, she didn't like. The woman was getting ready to throw a tantrum until Alecia intervened.

Patience was so busy watching the scene unfold that she didn't even hear or feel him standing beside her until he spoke.

"To gain knowledge, one must study, but to gain wisdom, one must observe," an enthralling voice said beside her, making her jump.

"I didn't mean to startle you."

Patience turned to find the man from the club standing next to her. He was dressed immaculately, as she remembered, with his long, dark hair tied back. The only thing different, she realized, was his eyes were light brown with specks of gold—not golden like hers. They gave away his real age, which had to be over a thousand years. Eyes tell no lies.

Alden. Lucius had said his name was Alden. This was the man who knew her past. Possibly the key to unlocking her memories.

"I never met anyone who could sneak up on me and quote Marilyn vos Savant simultaneously."

A vibrating caress ran through her. His powers were stroking her, caressing her, and calling her to embrace him. He was the jolt of power that had awakened her last night, but what about the red eyes? Does he have something to do with them?

"There's always a first time for everyone. Besides, you were so absorbed in watching everyone that I was surprised my voice pulled you out." He smirked.

"How do you know me?" she blurted. "I'm sorry. That was rude."

"No, it's not. You're eager to learn about your past, and I'm eager to know what happened to you."

He was right. She was eager to have some answers. Before she could ask anything, Maxim hushed the guests.

"Ladies and gentlemen, if you follow me this way, we shall get dinner underway." Maxim led them through a set of double doors beside the fireplace.

Patience set her glass on the tray as Alden leaned to the side to whisper in her ear. "I'm Alden, by the way. I wouldn't mind escorting you in if you don't mind," Alden offered.

"I know. Now, I must go find..." Patience was about to say her escort when she saw Alecia had already taken Lucius's arm and was headed through the doors. "Never mind. That would be wonderful, and I don't mind."

They were the last ones to walk into the room.

They had transformed what she assumed was a ballroom into a grand dining room. Candlelit sconces lined the walls, creating a dark but warm ambiance. A long mahogany table sat in the middle of the room with finery suited for royalty. A massive archaic stone fireplace with the Cordovan family crest above it reminded her of a certain someone. Her eyes unwillingly searched around for him. She discovered him sitting at the head of the table with Ian and Michael on his right. Alecia sat to his left. She wanted to sit at the opposite end of the table to piss him off, except she really wanted to talk to Alden. She needed to speak to him.

"Would you like to sit with me?"

"I thought you would never ask. Be forewarned. I have many questions." Patience chuckled. She realized this evening might not be as dreadful as she thought. They sat at the opposite end of the table just as the music began. Maxim sat at the head.

Scantily clad men and women poured into the room from a side door. They held carafes of wine as they circled the dining table.

"Ladies and gentlemen, please take your seats. Thank you for joining us in witnessing the legătura sufletului between Ian Cordovan and Michael Black." Maxim tipped his head toward the servers, and they poured everyone wine—except for Patience.

Alden must have seen her expression or her empty glass. "I don't think you'll enjoy this type of wine. I think it might not be suited to your taste."

"Oh, now that makes complete sense." She touched the side of her glass and watched as it filled with her favorite wine—the only edible thing that didn't disintegrate or go sour. *Now, this is more to my taste.*

"Please raise your glass to the happy couple. May their love bloom for all eternity."

Patience clinked her glass with Alden's before taking a sip.

"We'll begin momentarily. Please enjoy the first course."

First course. Damn, he meant their wine.

She hadn't even asked if real food would be at this dinner. Already on her second glass, she would need to sip this slowly before she became utterly intoxicated. Even after all these years, she was still a lightweight. And she had too many questions to ask him. What she really wanted was to find a quiet place and ask him all about her past. The most important question was, what happened to her? She just needed to get through the ceremony, and then she would fire away.

"Who are you friends with? The groom or the groom?" Alden gestured toward Michael and Ian. Patience laughed.

"I'm definitely friends with the groom."

Alden smiled, which made him look devilishly handsome.

"Michael is my best friend. We've been best friends for years now."

"So, this must be an absolutely joyous occasion for you."

"It is. I'm thrilled for them."

A young man approached her and placed cheese, crackers, grapes, and a small carafe of white wine in front of her.

"At least someone thought of me," she said, a little irritated. "I take it you know how this ceremony works because I have no clue. I hope that'll be the only blood spilled tonight and that it'll satisfy everyone's hunger." Patience gestured toward his glass of blood wine.

"I know what will happen. I can walk you through it if you like. Unfortunately, more blood will spill tonight. Willingly, of course. Also, I haven't felt genuine hunger in a very long time, so this will suit me fine. Besides, you're the only one in here good enough to taste."

Patience stopped mid-sip to stare at him. He was completely serious.

"Um... I'm unsure how to take that, especially since you know me, but I don't know you."

"Well, if you knew how to, as you say, 'take that,' I would be a little concerned." He smiled. He was teasing her. She laughed.

"And now that I found you, we'll have plenty of time to get to know each other again."

"You're quite charming for an old vampire, you know that?"

"That's exactly what you told me when we first met."

"And where exactly did we meet?" Patience asked eagerly, awaiting his answer.

"At your birthday party, I believe," he said, picking up his wine glass and taking a sip, then he wrinkled his nose. "This is almost as dreadful as the wine served at your party, but I only remember half the night since you hosted a drinking contest for a kiss."

Patience threw her head back and laughed, which caught the eye of everyone in the room. It sounded like something she would do. The joy and happiness that spread through her when she heard about her past were intoxicating.

"You poor thing. Here, let me make it better." Patience placed her hand on his glass and changed the wine to something more suitable for his tongue. "Now, take a sip."

He brought the glass to his lips and cautiously drank. Then, his face lit up in surprise. "This is delicious." He swallowed the whole thing down.

Patience laughed, then placed her hand over the cup to have it refill itself with more delicious wine. "Now, the cup will refill all night."

"Always trying to get me drunk." Smiling at her, he drank more. "I forgot how resourceful you can be."

"Oh, Alden. I think I can see why we were friends." She consumed the rest of her drink and enchanted her glass to refill automatically, just like his.

"I'm glad to hear that." He clinked his glass against hers in a toast and smiled at her. She became completely mesmerized by his eyes. His magic caressed her, luring her toward him, begging her to let him embrace her. She wanted to let it consume her as it flowed around her, but she didn't dare let it in. She leaned closer to him, wanting to touch him.

Maxim stood. "Now, let the ceremony begin."

Michael and Ian stood and walked over to a raised platform at the back of the room that she hadn't noticed before. A tall brunette in grey robes with dark blue symbols on the chest already stood on the platform with an open book. They joined her.

"Today, we're here to witness the bonding of these two souls. Could you please bring the cup?"

A server brought a golden goblet, and the woman took a silver dagger from her back. "Please hold out your arms." Both Ian and Michael rolled up their sleeves. She handed the dagger to Ian.

"What exactly is happening right now?" Patience whispered to Alden.

He smirked. "It's a simple ceremony. It should be over in a few minutes. They'll both bleed into the cup and drink it while saying the words to seal the bond."

"That's it?"

"Oh, they must also sign the bonding certificate. To make it official," he said, winking before turning to watch the rest of the ceremony.

Blood dripped from Ian's arm into the cup. Ian handed the dagger over to Michael as the wound on his arm sealed. Michael cut his arm and let his blood drip into the cup. His wound was slower to seal, but it sealed.

"Now, place the cup in both of their hands." The server placed the cup into their hands. "Repeat after me," the woman said to the couple.

"Te voi iubi pentru totdeauna. Eu sunt al tau si tu esti al meu. Eu îți dau de bunăvoie sufletul meu, astfel încât sufletele noastre să fie pentru totdeauna una. Moartea nu ne va ține niciodată separați." *I will love you for all eternity. I am yours and you are mine. I willingly give you my soul so our souls will forever be one. Death shall never keep us apart.* Patience followed along.

"With this cup, I give my blood freely to you so it may bond us and bridge the connection between our souls forever and always."

They repeated after her, and they each took a deep drink.

"Your bond is sealed. May the Queen Mother bless your union forever."

The words were familiar to Patience. An image appeared in her mind. She was standing at the altar with a cup in her hand, and someone was holding it.

Suddenly, there was a loud commotion across the room. The image disappeared.

She turned and saw Lucius storming out of the room. Looking down at her hand, Alden was holding her cup with her. She smiled, took it from his hands, and put it down.

Is he the person in the image?

She looked at Ian and Michael. They were already locked in a passionate kiss.

"Now, since it's their union, we're celebrating. They, of course, get the first pick." Maxim stood and motioned for the servers to line up against the wall. "Now, now, don't be shy. Take your pick. We're all hungry, too."

The tension in the room grew as fangs appeared. They all eyed their dinner with growing hunger. Ian selected a young girl who looked to be in her twenties. She was topless, and her undergarments left nothing for the imagination. He brought her over to Michael, who only had eyes for Ian.

"Great choice. Now, the rest of you may take your pick, and please, no fighting, only sharing. There should be no need to remind you about the rules."

Patience didn't know how she would feel about seeing Michael drink anyone's blood. He had fangs, but those only ever came out when he was in his demon form. Seeing that might take their friendship to a whole different level.

It would be nice for someone to have warned her about this.

The assholes.

"It looks as though something interesting is going on."

Patience glanced at Alden and saw he was looking at the front of the room, where Ian and Michael were. Clothes were now being ripped off, and Michael's horns were appearing. Patience noticed everyone had stopped what they were doing and began watching them.

"I can't be here for this."

Before Patience could even think of what to do next, Alden gently took her by the arm and escorted her out the door the servers had come in from. They found themselves in a hallway, and he led her down until they entered the foyer. That was when he finally let her go.

"Thank you."

"I understood that was uncomfortable for you."

Patience smirked. She was way beyond uncomfortable in there. She didn't want it to be awkward between her and Michael later if he knew she'd seen him. He was going to be embarrassed about the fact he was about to have sex in front of all those people.

"Yeah. No need to see my best friend having sex with his mate."

"I agree."

He grinned, holding out his hand for her to touch. She placed her hand in his, touching palm to palm. His powers flowed through her, caressing her everywhere. It was intoxicating.

Lust burned in his eyes as his hands slowly moved up her arms, moving closer to her. He pulled her closer, slanting his mouth over hers. He was going to kiss her. She should stop this right now, but she couldn't look away. She wanted to feel his lips. He moved his lips toward her, giving her time to refuse. When his lips almost made contact with hers, she stopped him.

"I'm sorry."

"There's no need to apologize. I got carried away—"

Footsteps approached. They had an audience. Alden took a step back, frowning. She turned to see what... who had interrupted them.

Lucius stood at the front door with anger on his face—no, not anger. Pure rage. His silver-gray eyes blazed, and his fangs protruded from his mouth, sharp and ready to attack.

Patience moved from Alden's embrace, and the exotic feeling dissipated. Lucius glared at them. Anger marred his face, and then he was gone.

Patience gasped, surprised by his anger. Unexpectedly, Alden pushed her out of the way as Lucius grabbed him, smashing him into the foyer wall, sending paintings crashing to the floor and creating a large dent.

Patience swore the house shook.

Alden still hadn't gotten over his shock as Lucius pummeled him. Lucius punched Alden in the face, causing him to bleed. Alden wiped the blood away, pulled his fist back, and sent Lucius flying across the foyer with an uppercut. It didn't slow Lucius down. He was right back on his feet.

Lucius rushed toward him. Alden tried to dodge him, but Lucius was faster. He caught Alden in the middle and slammed him into the marble floor. Not giving him a chance to recover, Lucius picked him up and hurled him across the room. Alden's back hit the upper banister, and then he dropped to the floor.

Lucius then turned his attention to her. He stalked toward her with menace in his eyes.

Running would be a good idea right now. But she couldn't get her feet to move as he came toward her.

Before he could reach her, Alden caught him from behind and threw him against the wall. Moving fast, he pinned Lucius to the wall and pummeled him with his fists.

Patience would have to intervene soon, or they would kill each other.

Lucius took each blow without flinching to her amazement. He deflected the last blow, taking out Alden's legs and causing him to drop. Before he could hit the floor, Lucius lifted him and threw him when she finally intervened.

She caught him with her magic before he hit the wall. She placed Alden on the floor and erected a barrier between them.

"Witch, let me out!" Lucius hit the barrier hard, trying to break it.

Alden stood, straightening his clothes, and tried to dust himself off. Rage and annoyance contorted his face as he moved toward her barrier. She moved toward him cautiously, placing a hand on his shoulder. He twisted, grabbing her until he realized it was her. He let go, his rage disappearing from his face.

"Nice barrier." He placed his hand against the energy barrier, pushing. It wouldn't let his hand go through. "I'm pretty sure I can't walk through this without your blessing."

"Practice makes perfect." She grinned, proud of her barrier. "You should go. I'm not sure what has him so enraged, but I'm sure he'll blame it on me. I don't look forward to him trying to kill me." Lucius struggled against the barrier. His stare bored into her, pressuring her to look at him. She concentrated on Alden, knowing he would make her pay for this. She wasn't exactly sure what she did to anger him. Unless it was the kiss, could he be jealous? No, that would be crazy for her to think.

"Witch, let me out now. My brother can't protect you," Lucius slammed his fist against the barrier, causing her to jump.

Fuck. This wasn't good.

"Has he tried to hurt you?" Alden asked.

Patience glanced away sheepishly.

"Look at me, Patience."

She gazed up at him.

"No one will ever harm you again. Do you understand me?"

She'd never seen such intensity before. He genuinely cared about her safety and well-being.

"I can take care of myself. I have been for years." She turned her head away from him. He grasped her chin and made her look into his eyes.

"I know you can, but you shouldn't have to." He pulled her close and softly kissed her on her lips. His arousal pressed against her belly shamelessly, and then his fangs scraped against her lips, startling her back to reality.

She pushed against his chest, stopping him. Lust filled his eyes.

Her barrier pulsated for a moment as Lucius almost broke through.

"You don't have to say anything at all," he said.

She smiled. He let go of her chin and stepped back from her.

He then took a necklace from around his neck. It had a beautiful silver pendant attached to it. It looked like a lightning rod encircled around words she didn't know. He leaned in close and whispered into her ear.

"This will keep you safe, and if you ever need me, just hold it close to your heart and whisper this: aparator. Protector. And I will come anytime. I'll be back for you, Zeita. We have much to discuss."

Alden took the necklace and walked behind Patience to place it on her. When he finished clasping it, he kissed her neck, sending shivers down her spine.

"Thank you for this, even though it's unnecessary. We still need to talk about my past." She turned around. He was no longer there. "That's one way to leave an impression on a girl."

Damn. She didn't get to ask him questions about her past. He was too damn charming for his own good. At least she had a way to contact him, she thought as she touched the necklace.

"Let me out now!" Lucius continued to push on the barrier; the crazy part was that her barrier was thinning. He would get through it soon, all on his own.

"Only if you promise not to attack me."

Lucius roared. "Let me out!"

She'd never seen him so enraged before. His vibrant silver-gray eyes were more illuminated than she'd ever seen them. She really looked at him. He was so handsome, even in this enraged form. Perhaps since he was so disheveled, she ran her finger down his face against the barrier, looking into his eyes. What she saw scared her and drew her in.

Patience placed her hand against the barrier. His aura changed to purple as he calmed, and his fangs retracted. There was a connection between them. It had always been there. Now, it was like a tether pulling her to him, except it wasn't strong enough.

"Let me out. I need to touch you. I need to make us whole." His voice was calming and alluring. "Let me hold you and keep you safe."

She couldn't believe the words coming out of his mouth. She wanted them to be real. Needed them to be real. Fifty years was a long time to be alone.

But it wasn't real, and he would regret it. He'd probably try to kill her as a bonus. When the barrier dropped, she vanished.

She appeared in the library. It wasn't the best place to hide but the farthest from the foyer. She hoped by the time he got to her, his head would be calmer.

Sighing, she browsed the books left on the table, thinking about what had happened and why Alden had kissed her.

She wondered if they had been more than just friends. She could see it with him. He was charming, and maybe he didn't want to tell her because he didn't want to frighten her or move too fast.

Ugh... she didn't know.

This handsome man who knew about her past kissed her tonight, but all she could think about was Lucius. She hadn't wanted Alden to kiss her. It was the reason she'd stopped. When his lips pressed to hers, she'd let it happen because she wanted to know if it would be like kissing Lucius. It wasn't anything like it at all. Now, all she wanted to do was go back out there and kiss Lucius so he would erase Alden's lips from hers.

A loud boom echoed in the distance, startling her and causing her to drop a few books off the table. As she was picking them up, the title of a book caught her eye. It looked familiar. Another loud boom sounded in the distance, just a little closer.

She picked up the book and looked at its spine. It was the same book the vampire had gotten from the bookstore.

She ran her fingers over the words: *Almas divididas. Souls Divided.* She let the book fall open to the last page and was about to read it when Lucius kicked the library door open.

"Witch!"

She dropped the book.

CHAPTER TWENTY-THREE

Lucius

"**F**uck!" he shouted.

So many emotions were running through Lucius that he would lose his mind. It had been a long time since he'd had rage coursing through him like this.

It wasn't supposed to happen like this. He was supposed to have more time before his blood called to hers. "Fuck!"

The blood bond shouldn't have gotten to this stage. "Fuck!"

When Patience and Alden walked into the dining room together, he was upset, yet he let it go, trying to ignore it even though his eyes were drawn to her, especially every time she smiled at him. It was her laughter that twisted him up inside. He wanted to march over there and tear them apart. *Mine* had flitted through his mind.

Then, seeing them holding the cup together was the start of his sanity unwinding. He'd needed to leave, or he was going to kill them both.

He'd stormed out of the room and headed outside, overwhelmed with the feeling of going back in there and dragging her out and... kissing her. Again, *mine* had flitted through his brain. He ignored it.

He was not being rational, blaming it on the bond. It shouldn't be this strong since it was only a blood bond.

But what pushed him over the edge was when he returned inside to find Alden's lips pressed to hers. Something inside him twisted, causing rage to surge in him. He wanted to call it jealousy, except he knew jealousy, and this wasn't it.

He hadn't realized his fangs were out until he pummeled Alden.

Unfortunately, it wasn't the worst part of his night. The worst part happened after she disappeared, and he still... burned for her.

He'd stormed off to his office and downed the last of his scotch when he remembered he had a house full of guests and needed to kick them all out. The ritual was complete.

He had to calm down so he could find Max.

He left the office and thought he was walking toward the ballroom. Instead, he found himself in front of the library doors. She was in there. He could smell her through the door.

Without thinking, he kicked in the door. His blood called for him to take her and make her his.

"Witch!"

He moved toward her, grabbed her arms, and pushed her against the wall. Looking into her golden eyes, he searched for something to make this urge disappear. He needed to see the hate, the evil. All he saw was the same yearning that was reflected in his own. She wanted him as much as he wanted her, and that was all it took.

He touched her face, moved his thumb across her lips, and wiped away her lipstick. She gazed into his eyes, waiting. When it was all gone, he captured her face and kissed her.

He took this kiss slowly. Unlike the others, this was a kiss he wanted to savor. This kiss was different because it wasn't a forced kiss. It was a kiss he wanted. A kiss he craved to taste, to learn every curve and crevice of her lips. Deepening the kiss, his fingers slid into her hair as his tongue slid past her lips to explore the warm depths of her mouth.

She responded sweetly to him as if her lips were made specifically for him. Her hands moved as a few buttons came undone, allowing her to reach the warmth of his chest, which was his complete undoing.

Wanting to feel her, Lucius pulled down her dress, exposing her luscious plump breasts. Her nipples stood taut against her dark areolas. His mouth watered, eager to taste them. Gently, he ran his fingers around her left areola. Patience moaned softly, the sound making his cock grow harder before he sucked her nipple into his mouth. He swirled the tip of his tongue around her, then sucked hard. Her moans filled the room as her body trembled with pleasure.

It was so good to have her in his arms, to know she quivered with pleasure because of him.

He ignored the nagging voice in the back of his mind, begging him to stop before it was too late as he switched to her right breast, giving it all his attention. Her hands ran through his hair, holding him to her. A growl escaped him, loving the way she held him as he lapped at her, giving her everything she needed.

Before pulling away, he nipped at her breast, causing her to gasp. He smiled capturing her lips again, pouring himself into it, never wanting this moment to end.

Gripping her dress, he slid it up her leg until he met her delicious soft flesh that he burned to taste. His hands slid further until they found her voluptuous ass. He wanted to flip her over and bite it. Instead, he kneaded her ass, giving it a slight slap as she jumped and moaned softly.

"Lucius, we should—" He captured her lips again, not wanting to hear her say they should stop. He knew they should, but he squished that voice to the ground as he tore her panties so he could reach those sweet lips.

Pushing her legs apart, he sank his fingers through her folds. Pure agony tore through him when he found her dripping wet. His cock barely contained itself as it pushed against the fabric, screaming to be let out.

"Fuck, you feel so good." He placed his mouth on her left breast and sucked before he slid his fingers into her. Her pussy sucked him in as he buried them deep within her. She moaned as her pussy clenched tight around his fingers. *Fuck.* She needed more. She was so close.

He gently nudged her legs open wider, and then he wrapped his arm around to support her better before his thumb found her core. Her moans grew louder, filling the library as he slowly circled her sweet nub and moved his fingers inside her.

"Please...," she begged. "Please. Lucius."

He sucked her nipple harder as he flicked her nub. Her body trembled in his arms as her orgasm ripped through her. He kissed her lips to silence the scream that escaped her.

He watched as she slowly came back to him. Removing his fingers from her, he gazed into her eyes intensely.

"I want you, Patience." The words were out of his mouth before he could think about them. All of his instincts were screaming at him to make her his. Damn the consequences. He didn't care if she was a witch. All he cared about was making them whole again.

"I... It is not..." She struggled to find the words. "We shouldn't. We—I want you too."

He lifted her into his arms, bringing her over to the window seat, and gently put her down. Grabbing his arm, she pulled him to her, kissing him. She gently pushed him down before she straddled him. Entwining her hands around his neck, she kissed him again, driving his senses crazy.

This is what he was missing. This was what he needed.

No, they needed to stop this. Never. She would be mine. Forever.

His thoughts were chaotic, but he could only concentrate on her lips devouring his. Her hands moved down his chest to his pants. Unbuttoning them, she reached in, wrapping her warm hands around his cock, releasing it from its confines. He groaned. *Goddess, yes.*

Then she stopped, surprising him and leaving him in agony. She gazed into his eyes and asked, "Are you sure about this? Because—"

He crushed his lips against hers, silencing her doubts and not giving voice to his own. There was no stopping him now.

Reaching down, she grabbed his cock, and brought it to her wet folds. He loved the feel of her warm hands on him as she squeezed gently before she pressed it to her flesh. Slowly, she rubbed herself against him, causing a delicious friction. He could already feel his pre-cum slipping out and joining hers.

"Patience," he moaned as her name escaped his lips. "So damn good."

Not being able to take it anymore, he removed her hands and thrust into her. She cried out in pleasure as he pulled out and thrust into her again, burying himself deep within her. Her inner muscles strained and throbbed around him as she got used to his broad length.

"Ride me," he whispered to her, barely able to restrain himself. Wanting her to reach pleasure as well. She placed her hands on his shoulders and lowered her eyes to where they connected.

"Patience, ride me. Please."

Capturing his bottom lip, she sucked on it as she slowly moved up, then down, on his hard cock. Her fingers dug into his shoulders, telling him how much she enjoyed herself. He gripped her hips, pulling out of her and slamming into her again and again. Her inner muscles clenched him tighter with each thrust. She spread her legs wider, taking him deeper.

Groaning from the pleasure, he wrapped his arm around her, bringing her closer to him and giving her a better position to move as she continued to kiss him. She rolled her hips in a slow rhythm, driving him insane.

"Harder," she moaned as he moved his hips to match her rhythm, thrusting harder with each stroke. "Goddess, yes. Lucius."

He couldn't take it anymore. Clutching her hips, he pulled out of her and then slammed into her, causing her to cry out. He loved hearing her cries of pleasure. He wanted to hear it more.

Lucius continued to thrust into her, deep and deliberate, fucking her until she was riding with her own carnal need to release. She cried out his name as her strokes increased and her muscles contracted around him. He rocked his cock deep within her, thrusting as she bit down on his shoulder, causing him to explode within her. Ecstasy spread through him as her name tumbled from his lips. Breathing hard, they gazed into each other's eyes, enjoying the serene moment.

"That was incredible." She leaned against his forehead as they both tried to catch their breath.

He didn't move, wanting to stay buried within her warmth so the reality of what he'd just done didn't come crashing down around him. They wouldn't have to face the world if he stayed here within her. They could shut it out together.

He looked into her eyes, seeing her warmth and happiness as she smiled at him. He shouldn't want her, but he did, and that was something he could no longer deny.

"Patience."

She looked away from him. "We should probably move."

Neither moved to leave as he continued to hold her in his arms.

The sound of footsteps could be heard coming toward the library door. Sighing, they both reluctantly moved. He hated the loss of her warmth.

Silently, she fixed her dress as he buttoned his pants and tucked in his shirt. He was buttoning his shirt when she bent over, picked up her torn panties, and smiled. "This is the second pair you've torn. I'm going to have to charge you."

He pulled her close, kissing her. "I'll gladly pay it anytime."

She smiled. Letting her go, he turned to see Max stroll into the library. He hadn't seen them yet, but she was gone when he turned back to her.

Damn. All he wanted to do was go after her. He would have to wait. He stepped away from the window and walked further into the room so Max could see him.

"There you are. What the hell happened to the foyer and the door?"

"Alden."

"What did you do?"

Of course, he would blame him. Max had little faith in him lately, though he didn't blame him.

"Nothing he didn't deserve. As long as I have her, he won't complain."

Max looked worried. Again, he didn't blame him because if Alden touched her again, he wasn't sure what he'd do.

"And I guess I'll have to get the foyer fixed?"

"I need a drink." He left Max standing in the library, not caring to answer his questions. Her blood was alive within him. He could feel her everywhere. She yearned for him still. *Fuck.*

He needed to distract himself, or he would find himself in her room.

Lucius made his way back to the guests, making sure they found their way out of his damn house. He even ensured the newlyweds found their way to their room with their clothes even though every inch of him burned to see her and bury himself in her again.

"Well, I won't ask what happened to your foyer," Alecia said as she stepped into the hall, "but that was quite entertaining to see a vampire and demon fuck."

"That wasn't supposed to happen. Though, when the Council asks for authenticity, no proof is better than a fuck."

Alecia laughed. "He really likes to get under your skin."

She was referring to Alden. All widely knew his antics for annoying him.

"I see you won't be getting rid of the witch after all."

"Unfortunately, no. I made a promise to my brother."

Alecia looked at him strangely. He had a sneaking suspicion she might have detected the blood bond. *Fuck.* "Of course you did. Or you may have not heeded my advice and involved yourself with a witch."

"I assure you, it's the former."

"Of course it is." She laughed.

"Thank you for your help with my mother earlier and for your help with the council."

"I know you'd do the same if the situation were reversed, and any council member who thinks to set her free is an imbecile. I'll definitely support you in this. I'll talk to Liam tomorrow, but I can assure you he's already on board to support whatever you need to do."

He knew she was hinting at him taking back the Council, and he still wasn't sure if he was ready to take that step yet.

He simply nodded.

"Well, it was an interesting evening. You should do this again sometime. It's always a good idea to let off a little steam," she said before striding out the door.

Shit. He was going to need a strong drink.

Lucius made his way back to his room. Ignoring her scent and the call of her blood enticing him to follow the pull to her, he made his way to his room, where he took out an old bottle of blood tequila from the bottom of his bureau. Not his favorite alcoholic choice, but it was the only drink that would actually get him intoxicated.

Taking a few swigs from the bottle, he sat in front of the dying embers in the fireplace, waiting for the sunrise so his day could end and he could find solace in hopefully dreamless sleep. He took a few more swigs and let the quiet hum of the house lull him to sleep.

"Lucius, are you paying attention?" Lucius was staring out the window, watching his daughter climb up a tree to get her fur ball of a cat out of the tree.

"I'm sorry, love, but I got quite distracted by our daughter climbing a tree to get Tabitha out again." Mae walked up behind him and put her arms around him. She inhaled his scent. He loved it when she did that. It always made him hard. He grabbed her arm and pulled her to the front of him. He looked into her beautiful golden eyes as she smiled at him.

"Now, you're using me as a distraction." She tried to move out of his arms, but he held on tight.

"What man wouldn't use a beautiful woman for a distraction?" He kissed her, devouring her sweet lips. She tasted like honey. "Someone has been dipping their finger in the honey jar again."

Mae laughed. "Guilty. I couldn't help knowing how much you love it on my lips." He devoured her lips again, but before he could deepen the kiss, she pulled out of his arms.

"No, that's enough distraction. We must finish these party plans before our little gremlin comes in here and spoils the surprise." She glanced out the window to ensure the cat still distracted her daughter and then walked back to the desk. "Now, as I was saying, are we inviting the Holsteins? They have two twin daughters who just turned six, and they invited us to their daughter's birthday party, but we were out of the country, remember?"

Lucius moved over to her and glanced over her shoulder at the list of guests his wife was inviting for their daughter's surprise seventh birthday party. He couldn't believe it had been seven years already. To think that they'd been together forever just made him happy. "Lucius?"

"If we invite the Holsteins, we have to invite the Vances, and after what your nephew did to their daughter at her party, I wouldn't think that's a good idea." Mae burst with laughter, recalling the memory of how her nephew bit their daughter, then cried when he couldn't have more.

"That wouldn't be a good idea." She scratched them off the list. "So now the list is made. I can have the invitations sent out. See now, that wasn't that bad."

Mae folded the list and put it away in the desk drawer. "Now, that's done. I believe I was being a distraction for a handsome gentleman."

She stood up from the desk and walked into his awaiting arms. "How did I get so lucky to have such a beautiful soulmate?"

"That I'm not too sure about. I think you just got lucky." He was very lucky to have found the other half of his soul. She was his entire world, and he would be completely lost without her.

"Yes, I'm a very lucky man." He took her bottom lip into his mouth and suckled it before deepening the kiss to delve deep into all the corners of her mouth, searching for every drop of honey that may be hidden. He was so lost in exploring that he didn't hear the door open.

———◆◇◆———

Patience

"Ew!!! Mommy and Daddy are sucking each other's faces off again. Uncle, cover my eyes before I go blind."

Patience turned to find Ian and his daughter holding her cat, Tabitha, standing in the doorway. "I'm afraid I've gone blind already." Ian joked.

Patience glared at Ian and stepped out of Lucius's arms. She smiled and opened her arms wide so their daughter could run into them, cat and all. "I see you got Tabitha out of the tree."

"Yeah, I did. She was quite stubborn about it. I did the spell you taught me, and she came right to me."

"Aw, I'm so proud of you, honey." Patience smothered her with kisses. "Daddy, help me! Mommy won't stop." She loved her laugh.

"I'm sorry, munchkin, but I'm defenseless against Mommy."

"As always," Ian said, still standing in the doorway watching them.

"So, this is the source of noise that woke up, peanut?" Michael walked up behind Ian, holding their two-year-old son in his arms. "You know he has sensitive hearing."

"Yeah, only when he sleeps. More like he's noisy like his aunt." Ian took his son out of Michael's arms and walked him to the window. "Look, it's snowing." The boy's eyes lit up at the falling snow.

"Uncle Mikey!" Her daughter ran out of her arms into Michael's. "I did the spell Mommy taught me on Tabitha, and it worked!"

"Ah, that's wonderful, sweetie," he said, taking her into his arms. "Now that you've mastered the spell, maybe Mommy can teach you a spell on how to pick up all your toys so your uncle doesn't trip over them and fall to his death down the stairs."

"Now, what would be the fun of that?" Patience said, laughing.

"I'm sorry, Uncle. I'll learn how to pick up after myself. Could you please put me down now?" Michael put her down, and she let go of the cat. She walked over to Lucius, and he lifted her into his arms. She rested her head on his shoulders.

"It looks like someone is ready for her nap." Lucius looked down at his little girl as she rubbed her eyes and fell asleep. He loved his little girl more than anything in the world.

"I'm feeling a little tired myself." Patience gazed at Lucius, knowing exactly what kind of tired she was.

"I'll go put her to bed then, and then I'll come back to put you to bed."

"Now, now, you two. You already have another bun in the oven, so slow it down." Patience and Lucius laughed.

Lucius was about to step out of the room when Maxim appeared.

"I'm sorry to burst in here like this, but I wouldn't have come if it wasn't urgent." Maxim walked over to Patience and fell to his knees. "I need your help."

Patience looked at Lucius, and he nodded his head. "What happened?"

"He's coming, and I don't know what to do. I need to protect my family from him. He has already put her under his spell." Patience touched his shoulder and helped him off the floor.

"Where is she now?"

"I locked her away under a ward spell. I don't know how long it will last."

"Take me to her. I'll help you." Patience walked over to Lucius and kissed their daughter on her forehead.

"You be careful and come back home to me." She smiled at him and kissed him.

"I always do." Patience moved back over to Maxim and grabbed his hand. She closed her eyes and watched his wife disappear before his eyes.

"Is Mommy ever coming back?" He looked down at his daughter and saw she was no longer asleep. Her eyes were wide open. "Of course she is. Why would you think that?"

"He said that Mommy had to go away for a while, but she might not come back."

"Who said this to you, Munchkin?"

"The man with the red eyes in my dream." Lucius looked up and saw that Ian and Michael had heard what she'd said.

Patience woke drenched in sweat, looking around her room. She couldn't shake the feeling that someone was watching her. Red eyes flashed through her mind, and shivers ran down her spine.

She didn't understand; she hadn't been having a nightmare. It was a wonderful dream, one she didn't want to wake up from until the end. The red eyes. They were haunting their daughter. Was this their past or their future? She wished someone would give her the answers.

She hated this feeling—the uneasiness—and it was getting harder and harder to shake. She tried to go back to sleep, but she couldn't. All she could think about was the red eyes and how she could remember her dream. Lucius. He was the key. She wanted to go to him and tell him everything.

Part of her hoped Lucius would come to find her, but he never did, which made her doubt.

She wasn't sure how he would react to her truth. She still wasn't even sure how he would react to last night. Even though she felt a shift within him, she wasn't sure she could trust it.

His changing aura scared her the most. What if he was under a spell? It may explain his aura. So many burning questions ran through her head as she dressed and went to the library to bury her head in a good book. She needed a distraction from her burning questions because, for all she knew, last night meant nothing to him but a good lay. She hoped it wasn't the case because she didn't want to get caught up in thinking otherwise.

Walking into the library, she opened her hand and summoned all the Evictus and Silverlands books. Brushing up on her knowledge about both realms before she started her search for Selene would be helpful. Hopefully, Selene hadn't gone too far.

She lounged in the window seat. She smiled, thinking of how he'd moved inside her last night.

Goddess, she had to concentrate. She grabbed the first book at the top of the pile and read.

Patience became so consumed in her reading that she didn't hear him walk in.

"There you are. I've been looking everywhere for you."

Patience looked up from her book to find Alden standing right in front of her.

Startled, Patience dropped the book. "Alden... what are you doing here?" She straightened. How the hell did he get past the ward in the library?

"I realized we never got to talk yesterday, and I know you have so many questions."

"Yes. Many questions, but are you sure you should be here after last night?" She was afraid of what Lucius would do if he found him here.

"Don't worry about him." He stooped down to meet her eye-to-eye. "Take my hand so we can go somewhere to talk."

Patience gazed at him suspiciously, but she saw he was sincere.

"I need you to trust me and close your eyes for me," he whispered.

She took a deep breath and closed her eyes. The surrounding air swiftly changed.

"You can open your eyes now."

Her eyes slowly opened.

They were on the edge of a forest. She turned and saw the castle in the distance. He hadn't taken her far, which surprised her, but this is the opportunity she'd been waiting for. She had so many questions.

This first being, "How? What are you?"

"That's not the question you want me to answer. At least, not the first one. What you really want me to answer is—"

"How do you know me?"

"Exactly." He stepped to the side, revealing a picnic all laid out. He snapped his fingers, and two candles lit.

"Impressive."

Alden took her hand and helped her sit on the blanket. He then took two wine glasses from a large woven basket and a bottle of red wine. He poured them each a glass.

"Cheers to finding one another again."

Interesting. Who was this man to her? "Cheers." Their glasses clinked, and she took a sip. It was delicious. "So, how much longer will you make me suffer?" She took another sip of her wine, hoping it would calm her anxiety. He could be the key to everything.

"We were friends long ago. You don't remember me?" He put down his wine glass and removed some cubed cheese and grapes from the basket.

"No. I'm sorry, I don't... but you felt vaguely familiar to me." There was something about him that seemed vaguely familiar. She couldn't quite put her finger on it, but something also gave her pause. Possibly the different auras of red and blue that surround him or the ancient power that coursed through him. She could sense its containment. His powers called to her even now, wanting her to reach out and embrace them. It was strange and remarkable, both at the same time.

"When you say long ago, how many years exactly?"

He smiled at her and took a sip of his wine. "Are you sure you want to know?"

That was a good question. After fifty years of searching and failing to unlock her memories and figuring out her past, she needed to know. It was no longer a question of want.

"Yes. Tell me."

"I met you almost two hundred years ago."

She almost choked on her wine. *Bad time to take a sip.* "Two hundred years? At my birthday party? And what age was I celebrating?" And Jafa said he'd met her 150 years ago, so she might have been immortal, or she cast a longevity spell on herself, which was dangerous.

"I know it sounds unbelievable, but it's true. I don't need to lie to you after just finding you again. Yes, it was a grand party, and honestly, I have no clue what age you were celebrating. If I remember correctly, you said it was rude to ask a lady her age."

He had a point. It didn't feel like a lie, and it sounded like her.

"When was the last time you saw me?" Patience finished her wine and held her glass for him to pour more.

"At a ball. I believe you were celebrating the coronation of your sister."

"My sister?" *I had a sister. She had a family.*

"Yes, your sister."

"Is she still alive? Wait, you said coronation. Does that mean—"

One minute, Alden was sitting there, and the next, something... someone slammed into him, sending him flying. Patience stood up, only to find Lucius standing in front of her.

Fury burned within his eyes. "Stay away from him."

"You said he was dangerous, but I need to know about my past." She placed her hand on his chest, trying to calm him down. "Lucius, I'm okay."

His aura changed as he calmed until Alden stepped from within the forest, and it turned dark red again.

"Patience."

"Don't you dare step another foot onto my property!" Lucius roared.

She was curious to know what had caused such hatred between them. "I need to talk with him," she said.

"I know," he spat. "But we have bigger problems right now."

Bigger problems? What the hell does that mean? They needed no more problems than the ones they already had. *Shit.* She never would find out more about her past at this point.

"I don't think the lady wants to go with you." Alden took a step closer to them.

If he moved any closer, Lucius would pounce, and they didn't need that right now. "Alden, I don't want to cause any trouble. Thank you for this."

"I understand. We'll speak again. Just remember." He tapped his chest, her necklace, reminding her she could always reach him. She mouthed "thank you" to him as he disappeared right before her eyes. She still couldn't believe he could do that.

Patience turned back to Lucius to find him looking at her hand on his chest. She was about to remove it when he grabbed it, stopping her.

"What's the problem now?"

"Michael is missing."

"What? He couldn't be."

"Ian woke this evening to find him missing."

Shit. She closed her eyes, reached for Michael, and found him nowhere in the mansion.

"Fuck!" Grabbing his hand, she transported them to the library.

CHAPTER TWENTY-FOUR

PATIENCE

They found Maxim pacing in the library with worry all over his face. She unwillingly let go of Lucius's hand as she approached him to stop him from pacing.

Putting her hand on his shoulder, she asked, "Where is Ian?"

Startled, he stopped and looked at her, concerned. "I had to lock him in the dungeon. He was uncontrollable."

"Take me to him."

Maxim led her to the dungeon with Lucius right on her heels. *If there wasn't one drama after another...* she'd thought she was so close to finding out about herself, but now this. *Will it ever end?*

As soon as they got halfway down the stone steps to the dungeon, a loud banging echoed throughout the hallways. It grew louder as they moved deeper until they stood in front of steel doors.

Pain ripped through her. She fell to her knees, grabbing her chest.

"Patience, are you alright? What's happening?" Maxim said in a panic as he ran over to her, touching her back.

"I can feel it. I can feel his pain." The pain was too much. She needed to make it stop. She placed her hand on the door, stepping through, not having time to use the key.

Ian was trying to punch his way through. Blood was running down his hand, coating the door. He hadn't even noticed she was there. She touched his shoulder, sending energy through him to numb the pain so he could think more clearly.

His pain was replaced with anger until she sent soothing energy through him. She needed him in the right state of mind.

"How do you feel?" she asked.

"Like I need to find him. How long will this calm last? I can still feel it. Though, it isn't overwhelming my thoughts."

"I didn't want to make it go away. I just needed to dull it. It was affecting me."

"How?"

Patience placed her hand on the door. It unlocked. Maxim pulled it open. "Michael and I are connected as well."

Maxim and Lucius stood outside. Relief crossed Lucius's face when he saw her before his expression turned neutral.

"Meet us in the library." She touched Ian's arm and transported them. As soon as they appeared, she went to stand near the fire. The damn dungeon was freezing.

"How long ago did you find him missing?"

"I'm not sure," Ian said with some uncertainty. "He left after I fell asleep. He whispered something about going to see his parents. I thought nothing about it. I thought he wanted to spend more time with them, and I was too caught up in the bloodlust. It wasn't until I woke this evening that I knew he was gone."

"Where are the king and queen?"

"They're gone." Maxim walked into the library with Lucius behind him. "I haven't seen them since they left the ballroom last night."

"Fuck! I thought this drama was over after everything we just went through." Patience knew what she had to do. Michael wasn't dead. She would know. They were bound. She couldn't thoroughly explain it because she didn't entirely understand it. They could feel each other's emotions. It was hard to deal with for the first few years, but they figured out how to manage it. She could find him. She could always find him.

"They had to have taken him," she said. "It's the only thing that makes sense."

"Unless he went willingly?" Lucius questioned.

"Never. I can find him."

"You can?" Ian tried to hold the hope from his voice.

"Yes, I can. This isn't the first time he's disappeared, but I think it'll be faster with your help." She reluctantly turned and looked at Lucius. "And your help as well." She needed his strength to ground her. It was difficult to find someone who disappeared, even with a bond. He could be anywhere.

"Yes, of course, anything. My brother will help, too." Ian stared at Lucius until he finally nodded.

"Okay. Let's make space." They moved the chairs away from the fireplace, giving her plenty of space to make the connection. "All right now. Ian, stand right here."

She pointed toward the center of the room. She sat on one chair and took off her shoes and socks. It made her feel more grounded if her skin touched the floor. She walked into the middle of the room and grabbed Ian's hand. Then she looked back at Lucius. "You need to stand behind me and put your hands on my shoulders. Do not let go of me, no matter what."

He nodded, moving to stand behind her. When he placed his hands on her shoulders, a serene peace went through her, which was odd, but she wouldn't think about it now.

"Maxim, I'm going to need you to leave."

"Okay."

"I mean, leave the building. I don't want to be responsible if you accidentally get sucked into another realm."

"Um... okay." Maxim gazed at them one last time before he left the library and, hopefully, the building.

"Now you both need to close your eyes. Ian, concentrate on Michael, and Lucius, concentrate on... me." Lucius slightly squeezed her shoulder in acknowledgment. "Hold tight, and I mean seriously, hold tight."

Patience closed her eyes and focused. She pictured Michael in her mind and reached out through their connection.

She concentrated on his features first; it was always the easiest: his hazel-blue eyes, nose, lips, hair color, and then the broadness of his shoulders. An electric current pulsed through the room. Then she concentrated on his smile, laugh, smell, and eyes. The current spun. "Hold tight and remember not to let go."

Ian squeezed in acknowledgment. She went deeper. She concentrated on his voice, the sounds it made, his breathing, then the beating of his heart. The current moved faster and faster, spinning around them. Concentrating on the beats, she slowed until each beat brought her to his essence... his soul. Faster and faster, the current moved until she connected with him.

"Get ready. We're about to drop." As soon as she said the words, a portal opened under them, and they dropped.

They landed on their feet. She noticed Lucius's hands go to her waist to keep her from falling.

"About damn time."

Patience turned to see Michael sitting on the bed with a magazine. Ian let go of her hands, then ran over and kissed him.

"Sorry. Wait, what? You're the one who disappeared and made your mate go crazy. Speaking of..." Patience strode over to Ian and lifted her calming spell. "We might want to leave now." She grabbed Lucius's hands, but he didn't budge. "Fine, you can stay, but..." She turned and looked at the clothes coming off. She walked out of the room with Lucius fast on her heels.

As soon as the door closed, Lucius pushed her against the wall and kissed her, shocking her. She got lost in the sweet sensation of his tongue as he parted her lips. This man was driving her crazy. She placed her hand on his chest and pulled away.

"Concentrate. We need to know why Michael was brought here."

He groaned as she stepped away from him to look around. They were standing in a hallway. The walls were made of white marble, and silver candelabras lined the wall. A silver and purple carpet ran down the hallway to the end. From the looks of it, they were in some kind of manor.

"Where the hell are we?"

"My guess is as good as yours, but I know the king and queen are here... somewhere." She began walking down the hall, toward the end. They were here. The king's ancient power rushed through her, attaching to her like a rope and pulling her in one direction. He wanted her to find him.

"Find them so I can kill them. Then we can finish what we started."

"Is that all you think about? Killing people? It's not the solution to everything."

"Trust me, it would help me solve one of my problems."

She suspected he was talking about her. As they walked through the halls, it was eerily quiet, but the farther they walked, the more familiar everything seemed until she knew exactly where she was going.

They walked down a set of stairs and came out into a grand hall similar to the one she'd seen in Ian's mind. They found the king and queen talking in hushed voices with a slender woman with light brown hair.

Lucius cleared his throat. They looked up. "Ah, you're here, finally." Circe walked over to them.

Patience put her arm out in front of Lucius, holding him back. She already knew his chain of thoughts.

"The king will kill you before you even touch her," she whispered under her breath.

"He could try."

"We've been waiting for you." Circe took her hands and led her to Kieran and the other woman. "This is the witch I told you about who helped us."

The woman stood and held out her hand. "Hello, I'm—"

"Estelle." Lucius sounded shocked.

"Estelle, as in Maxim's Estelle?" Patience asked. *No way, it couldn't be. What the hell was going on?*

"Lucius," Estelle said. "Where is Max?"

"Where the hell have you been?" he asked angrily.

"Maxim is home. I'm still waiting for you," Patience answered. There was something familiar about her, but Patience couldn't pinpoint it like Alden.

"He is?" Genuine happiness spread across Estelle's face at hearing the news. "I've been here, trying to protect this realm."

"For almost two centuries?"

"Yes. I know it may be hard to believe, but yes. Please listen, and I'll explain everything."

Lucius still looked pissed, not liking her answer, but he kept quiet.

"As I was saying, maybe she can help us find the half-demon." Circe sat on the king's lap, freeing a chair for Patience. Lucius and the king nodded to each other in acknowledgment.

"You know, you could have just asked instead of kidnapping Michael." Patience sat and nodded to Kieran.

"You're right, but we never planned to kidnap him. He came to our room to talk with us when Estelle called us for help."

"And me, being a dumb ass, offered to go with them." Michael entered the room with Ian by his side, joining their little circle in the enormous room. "I thought with the soul-bond ceremony complete, I could be far from Ian for just a little while, and I was fine for the first few hours until I realized I couldn't feel him, and I became uncontrollable until about thirty minutes ago when a calm spread through me. I knew it was you, Patience, and that you were on your way here. I'm so sorry."

Michael was so lucky she loved him. He would offer to go help without informing the people who cared the most about him. "As long as Ian forgives you, I'm fine. I'll add it to the list of things you owe me."

Michael smiled, knowing she'd forgiven him already.

"So, where exactly is here?" Patience asked.

"The Silverlands," Circe answered.

"The Silverlands?"

"Yes. We're surprised you all could come here," Estelle responded.

"And why wouldn't we just be able to come here?" She knew the answer to that question but needed to be sure since Alden interrupted her before she could finish reading the paragraph.

"Because the path has been blocked to many who have tried," Estelle imparted.

"Which makes sense. This is the realm of the Goddess. But how are Kieran and Michael able to come here? Does that mean the barrier is gone?" Patience tried to stay calm. She couldn't believe she was in the Goddess's realm. The real question was, where was she?

Is Estelle the Goddess?

"No," Estelle said, "I'm not the Goddess. I can see the question in your eyes. The Goddess hasn't been seen in these lands for some time now. I'm not even a Silverlands witch. As for Kieran and Michael..."

Kieran looked over to Circe before he spoke. "A long time ago, the Goddess granted me and my bloodline safe passage through the barrier."

"But why? Why would she let the demon king into the Silverlands? No offense."

"It would make sense if safe passage was granted to protect our child. The Goddess was a forgiving creature, and Michael needed to be protected."

That made sense, but it explained little about where the Goddess was. If she wasn't here, where the hell was she? Her people needed her. "Where is the Goddess? And where are the Silverlands witches? And why are you looking for this half-demon?"

"Honestly, I'm not sure. No one has seen the Goddess in many years, and many witches have left these lands and scattered across different realms. I've been searching for them, but I've only found three so far. One unfortunately died, the other two—well, one wouldn't leave her people, and the other refused to return, so I've been doing the only thing I can do: keeping their wards in place. As for the demon, he's trying to get into the Silverlands."

"Once he frees Lilith, this is the next place he'll come since he couldn't get in alone," Circe interjected. "I also believe the Goddess may have sacrificed herself to protect this place. Therefore, we need to find him."

"Or she could be trapped somewhere just like the both of you were. However, what I don't understand about this half-demon is what's in it for him. I get why Lilith wants in. It's her home, and she thinks she has a claim to the throne, but what about him?"

No one spoke. She guessed her questions were too hard for everyone but Kieran to answer. "From what my spies could gather, he's after this realm's power, but he's also after the Goddess. He may have some sick obsession with her, but no one is sure. He hopes Lilith will get him here, and in return, she'll give him access to the power of the land."

"So where is the Goddess? And where are the Hallows, who are supposed to be guarding?"

"I don't know where she is. I've been keeping the wards in place, hoping she would return, and as for the Hallows, they've all turned to stone. I've been trying different spells, but nothing has worked. We believe they lie dormant, waiting for the Goddess to return."

"Wow. This is a lot to take in." Looking at Estelle, she realized there was something off about her aura and the energy surrounding her, like Alecia.

"I'm sorry. Are you a vampire? How did you get here?" She had a feeling Estelle knew more than she was letting on. What was she hiding?

"Yes. I'm half-vampire, half-witch, and I'm not completely sure. Our family are descendants of one, so I think a Hallow summoned me. When I appeared here, I was trying to get back home to Max, but the wards were falling, and I quickly got them back up. Since then, I've been doing it."

It sounded like a lie, but Patience couldn't pinpoint where the lie was.

"She's like Alecia, her sister," Lucius disclosed.

And the web just keeps getting bigger and bigger.

"I've been trying to keep this place together until the Goddess returns." Estelle said earnestly, "And the Silverlands have been unprotected with the Hallows asleep."

"Well, aren't we in a pickle?" Patience said. "Our priority is finding a Silverlands witch, then getting back into Askaria."

Estelle and Circe glanced at each other. Shaking her head, she tilted back and looked at Lucius, who stood behind her. "You've been quiet. Wish we could go back to the days when you just wanted to kill me."

A ghost of a smirk appeared on his face. She needed a drink. A glass of wine appeared in her hand. Well, that was a first. Usually, it took a little more concentration.

"Be careful what you ask for here. The magic is more potent since you're closer to the source," Estelle warned.

She nodded, taking a sip of wine. It was divine. "So, how do we find him, and how can I help?"

"Come," Estelle said firmly. "I have something we believe is his."

Estelle stood, and Patience gulped down her wine before standing up herself. The cup disappeared from her hand. *Cool.*

She followed Estelle down the hall until they reached double wooden doors. They had the same symbols that were on her vault. *Interesting.*

Estelle touched the symbols in a particular order, and the doors opened. A rush of cold air blew toward them.

"Touch nothing else within. This will be my only warning. Vampire, you're not allowed."

Patience hadn't even realized Lucius had followed them. She turned to glance at him before entering the room.

A dreadful feeling was creeping over her. Maybe she shouldn't do this. Estelle walked over to a small red chest in the middle of the room. She took a key from around her neck and opened the chest. A dark, intense energy flowed from the box, filling the room as she revealed a bloody handkerchief.

"Why do you think this belongs to him?" Patience asked. She went up to the chest, and the dreadful feeling became more intense.

"I don't think you should do this," Lucius called from the doorway.

Neither did she, but if she found this half-demon, they could move on with their lives. "I'll be careful. Thanks for your concern." Her hand hovered over the cloth before she clutched it in her hands. Thankfully, nothing happened.

"Are you sure this is the demon's blood?" The dreadful, tense feeling was still there, but nothing else. It might be different once she started channeling her magic through it.

"No, but it was found in a place where he may have been wounded."

"Okay. Guess we'll find out. You just want me to find the demon's location, correct?"

"Yes. Or find out what his plans are. We want to be prepared. We've been sitting blind for so long."

Patience sat against the wall with her feet planted on the ground. Once she was comfortable, she looked at Lucius.

"If anything goes wrong, get Michael."

He nodded slightly in acknowledgment.

Taking a deep breath, she closed her eyes. Finding someone wasn't always easy because it meant she had to connect with them. If the occupants were weak-minded, they wouldn't know she was there. If they were strong-minded, they would know, and it could drive them mad, knowing there was someone in their space but only feeling them and not being able to see them. She wondered what kind of demon this would be.

Patience clutched the bloody cloth in both of her hands and concentrated. She thought about the cloth and its texture, then about the color. Then the blood on the cloth and its awful smell. She went deeper and deeper until the blood connected her with the creature.

Suddenly, the energy in the room shifted, and his essence was all around her, consuming and caressing her.

"You're looking for me?" a sultry voice asked within her conscious.

"Yes," she whispered back as warmth engulfed her. He caressed her cheek and moved his finger across her lips.

"I've been looking everywhere for you, my love."

"You have?" Patience could only hear his voice and feel his presence all around her. Her senses didn't scream danger; instead, they gently caressed her, telling her he was... home.

"I've always been with you. Open your eyes."

Patience slowly opened her eyes.

Red eyes—the same ones that haunted her dreams—looked at her from across the room. Patience clutched the cloth tighter, not believing what she was seeing. He stepped out from the shadows, revealing himself to her. She screamed.

He wore an alabaster suit that contrasted with his black skin. His forehead had long brown horns protruding out of it, and his teeth were razor sharp.

"PATIENCE!"

She heard Lucius yell over her screams. She forced herself to look away from the demon and at Lucius. He was trying to get into the room, but an invisible barrier blocked him. Estelle was standing right next to him, trying to get in. Lucius stopped banging and yelled something at Estelle. She disappeared.

Patience turned her head back to look at the demon and found him closer.

"Shh... Odessa." His hand caressed her cheek. "I won't hurt you."

Patience stopped screaming. "What d-do y-you want from m-me?"

"I need you to take my hand, love. Come with me." He held out his black hand with long claws.

Lucius continuously banged on the barrier until Estelle appeared with Michael. Lucius stopped and told Michael what was happening. Michael closed his eyes and appeared in the room by Patience's side.

"Patience! Don't!" he yelled, grabbing her to pull her away.

Patience looked down at her hand. She was involuntarily reaching out for the demon. Before her hand touched him, she snatched it away.

"We'll find each other again."

Then the demon was gone, vanishing right before her eyes.

Patience dropped the cloth as Michael bent down beside her. "Are you all right?"

No, she wasn't all right. She was shaken. She'd almost gone with him. So many feelings ran through her, and so many questions. Why did he call her Odessa? Did this demon know her? Was it part of her past? But her most prominent feeling right now was fear.

Patience turned and grabbed Michael, hugging him tightly and burying her head in his shoulder. She didn't like this feeling. She hated it. It made her vulnerable. He was supposed to stay in her dreams and not be real.

"Will she be all right?" Estelle said next to them.

"I don't know. I've never seen her shaken like this. He almost took her."

"Come," Estelle said delicately. "I'll take you somewhere so she can lie down and gather herself."

Michael nodded, and then he helped Patience to stand up. She clung to him as he walked her slowly out of the room. The fear subsided a little once they were away from the dreadful cloth.

She let Michael go and closed her eyes to take a deep breath, but as soon as she did, she saw his red eyes appear. Quickly opening them, she found Lucius staring at her with surprising concern.

Without thinking, she ran to him and threw her arms around him, holding him tightly. Unconsciously, she put up a barrier around them, cocooning them together.

"Are you all right?" he whispered.

"Keep me safe." She buried her head in his neck. His arms wrapped around her made her feel better and safer.

She cautiously closed her eyes. No red eyes appeared. She took a deep breath and let Lucius's scent soothe her.

"Always," he whispered.

"You make me feel safe."

"I do?" Surprise filled his voice.

Patience lifted her head and gazed into his eyes.

"Yes, you do." Then, without thinking, she kissed him.

CHAPTER TWENTY-FIVE

Lucius

The last person who'd told him she felt safe in his arms was his wife. To hear Patience say those words killed him. All he wanted was to take her in his arms and hold her close to him. He didn't care if it was the blood bond. All he knew was he needed her like he needed blood to live.

He swooped her into his arms and walked. He wasn't sure where, but he let his feet guide him.

One moment they were walking down a hall, and the next, they were standing in a bedroom, all without breaking their kiss. When she finally let him up for air, he looked around and realized where they were—in her room in his mansion.

"I need you. I need you to make this feeling go away," she pleaded. "Touch me. Make me forget."

They shouldn't do this again. The blood bond wasn't helping this situation, and the more they had sex, the stronger it would grow, which meant the more complicated it would be to undo.

The way her eyes begged and pleaded with him was his complete undoing. He hated seeing the fear in her, and he wanted to wipe it away.

He pulled her to him and kissed her again as his hands moved down her body, slipping beneath her shirt to stroke the arch of her bare back tenderly. His caress slowly moved its way down to the top of her pants, where he slipped his hands inside to grasp her ass, squeezing tightly. She moaned as he deepened the kiss, eager to explore all the crevices he'd found earlier. He pressed against her, grinding into her, letting her feel how much he wanted her.

There was no turning back. Blood bond be damned. She was his. He would worry about the consequences tomorrow or the next day but not now. Right now, she needed him.

Lifting her into his arms, he put her on the bed then undressed her. He took off her shirt and unbuttoned her pants, pulling them off. Leaving her in her bra and panties, he climbed off the bed and gazed at her. Her beauty mesmerized him as she stared at him with needy eyes begging him to consume every inch of her. He would gladly.

He unbuttoned his shirt, letting her see him for the first time as he took off his pants and removed his briefs. She licked her lips and bit her bottom lip. His cock grew harder.

This time he would taste her. Drawing her to the edge of the bed, he got on his knees, nudging her legs apart. He pulled her up, capturing her mouth in a passionate kiss as her hunger devoured him.

She moaned, falling back onto the bed as he tore her panties, smiling. He really would need to buy her new ones, though it would be better if she didn't wear any at all.

He lifted her legs onto the bed, spreading them wide and displaying her to him. Her pussy lips glistened. His fangs descended, wanting nothing more than to sink into her. He controlled himself, letting his finger slip inside her warmth. She whimpered in pleasure as he moved his fingers in and out of her. It was so good to hear her moan. He never wanted this to end.

Finding her sweet nub, he pressed his mouth to her pussy, sucking her in. She quivered under his touch as his mouth and fingers moved. He kissed and licked her, spreading her thighs wider to sink his tongue deeper into her.

He lapped, sucked, and circled her little sweet nub as she begged and pleaded with him to let her reach her end. "Lucius, please... please." He loved hearing her beg. The more she begged, the more time he took finding what caress made her tick the most.

When he gently bit her nub, then sucked hard, her back arched, and her legs trembled. He continued biting and sucking until her screams filled the air, and she came utterly undone in his arms.

He held her tightly as her body quivered and bucked. The vein on her thigh pulsed in his ears, calling for him to taste. He tried to ignore it as he continued to lick and suck her until she began to crest another climax. As she was close to the edge, his fangs penetrated her, only allowing himself a small taste of her sweet ambrosia.

Joining her on the bed, he gently removed her bra before sucking a nipple into his mouth until it became hardened. She moaned, still coming down from her orgasms. He braced himself above her, gently pressing his lips upon hers, slowly taking his time to devour her mouth. He poured everything he couldn't and wouldn't say to her into his kiss. Letting his tongue dive deeper as his soul poured into wishing he could be everything she desired.

He moved to her neck, kissing its curve and letting his tongue caress her pulse. His fangs wanted a taste of her sweet ambrosia again as they strained against his lips, but he controlled the urge, forcing them to ascend.

Her hands lifted, roaming his body, feeling his every curve and ridge like she was trying to memorize every inch of him.

He lifted his head, gazing into her eyes, searching... searching for what he saw in his dream.

"Take me," she begged him.

He eagerly rose over her as she arched into him, feeling his hardened cock press against her. She opened her legs wider, welcoming his pulsing head into the entrance of her body. He growled as her pussy sucked him in, engulfing him with her warmth. She clenched involuntarily, and he groaned even louder.

As she hungered for him, he saw the untamed fire in her eyes. He pulled out of her and then breached her body with a mind-numbing thrust. He pulled out of her and plunged even deeper. She moaned, then lifted her hips to meet him thrust for thrust until they settled into a steady rhythm until he couldn't take it anymore.

"I need to fuck you... hard," he growled.

"Yes, harder."

Patience grabbed hold of him as his tempo increased. Her orgasm coiled within her belly as he pumped faster and faster into her.

"Oh, God, yes," she cried. "Please. Don't. Stop."

"I don't... think... I can."

Her body trembled as an orgasm ripped through her, and a scream tore from her throat. He captured it, continuing to pump into her until he reached his release. Taking a moment to calm his beating heart, he turned her over and entered her from behind. He was nowhere close to done with her. He planned to make her come again... and again until he had his fill, which may never be.

Patience

Patience quickly sat up in bed as sweat dripped down her cheeks. A shiver went through her as the red eyes faded from her mind—another nightmare.

She turned to reach out to Lucius, hoping to wake him so he could chase away the nightmare with his tongue, but she found his side of the bed cold and empty.

He had left.

The shutters hadn't even closed yet.

She thought after last night, things would be different between them. She'd hoped he had finally accepted her for who she was, but it didn't look like that would happen soon.

It had just been wishful thinking and hope on her part. He'd said nothing to indicate this was anything other than sex, and it was her fault for thinking this was more than it truly was.

She laughed to herself as she remembered this was exactly what she'd asked for—a few tumbles in the hay with him. She got that and more, but why did tears threaten to fall from her eyes?

Part of her had known he would wake and leave her. She just didn't realize she would be so hurt by it. It was foolish of her to want anything more from him.

The sad part was he'd gotten under her skin, not just under but buried deep within her. She let the pain seep down and spread, letting it consume her so she would never forget her foolishness.

CHAPTER TWENTY-SIX

Lucius

Lucius sat in front of the fireplace, lost in his thoughts, trying not to think about her last night or the blood bond when the door opened, and Ian came crashing into the library with an angry scowl on his face. Michael strolled in after him.

"What the hell was that? You both just left us there." Ian was pissed.

Lucius had forgotten entirely about them. He'd been completely wrapped up in the witch, figuratively and physically.

"I'm sorry. We were busy."

Michael smirked knowingly, but Ian still had a scowl on his face.

"How did you get back?" Lucius asked.

"If you must know, the king and queen brought us back... along with Estelle."

He'd forgotten about finding Estelle. He wasn't sure how happy Max would be to see her, especially when she told him why she'd been away all these years.

"Has Max seen her yet?"

"Yes. They're talking right now."

He wished he could go back to two weeks ago. He was sitting in this very library, and his only problem was making sure his alcohol shipment came in. It seemed like that was years ago instead of weeks.

Lucius stood from his chair and rubbed his hand over his face. He was feeling his age, or her feelings were getting to him. They ebbed and flowed like an emotional roller coaster. It was pure torture for him. He'd never known a blood bond to be this strong.

He had to find out if his fate was sealed or if he still could escape this bond. The chances were slim after the number of times they'd had sex last night, but he had to try for his sanity.

"Where are they?"

"In the kitchen. The queen was hungry." Ian took Lucius's seat. "You look miserable for somebody who just got laid. Guess you can't kill her now."

Lucius went over to the table and found the book Patience had dropped the other night on the floor. *Soul Dividas.* Ignoring Ian, he flipped through the pages, searching for signs of a solution to his dilemma.

"You think you can find the solution to your problem in there?" Ian's voice pierced through his concentration.

Without breaking his gaze from the book, Lucius reached for another tome on the table and hurled it at Ian. With lightning reflexes, Ian caught it before it could hit him.

"No, but you might find it in there. I'm trying to break the bond," Lucius replied coolly.

"What bond?" Patience's voice drifted into the library as she entered.

Lucius froze, not having heard or sensed her arrival. The idiots didn't lock the door—as though it would stop her.

"What bond?" she repeated as anger entered her voice.

Michael moved to stand in front of her. "Before your brain goes into overload, it's not our bond."

She visibly calmed. "Then what bond is he talking about?"

Here we go. His brother would spill it all.

"I'm going to let him tell you." He said, surprising Lucius. "I think it'll be better that way." Ian motioned to Michael that they should leave.

"Oh, come on! This is going to be good. Maybe she'll finally kick his ass."

"Michael."

"Fine," Michael grumbled and followed Ian out of the library.

A dreadful feeling washed over Lucius before it disappeared.

The library door closed with a loud thud. He continued to read, trying to ignore the silence and find the solution. At least, that's what he told himself. In reality, he wanted to cross the room and kiss her, then drag her back to his room to screw them both into oblivion.

She went over to him and silently stood next to him. Her smell was driving him crazy. He read slowly through the pages, pretending she wasn't making him solid as a rock.

"Lucius."

He had to admit he loved hearing his name fall from her lips. It sounded even better when her legs were wrapped around him, and she was scream-ing it aloud. "Hmm?"

"Lucius, what bond are you talking about breaking?" She walked her fingers one by one slowly up his shoulders until she reached his neck, then slid her hand down until she came to the small of his back. "What are you hiding from me?"

"Ours," he spat out, unable to keep it from her. Hoping that if he said it out loud, it would change everything.

"Ours?" she repeated, her voice laced with disbelief and hope.

"Yes, ours." He closed the book abruptly and reached for the next one on the shelf, trying to distract himself from the moment's intensity.

"Ours. As in...you and me?" Her words hung in the air as if she couldn't quite believe what he was saying.

He nodded curtly, not trusting his voice to speak the truth again. Instead, he returned his focus to the book before him, until it flew out of his hand and landed gracefully on the floor across the room.

"Explain." Her demand was clear and unwavering.

He sighed heavily, realizing that this conversation required more than words. He needed a drink to steady himself.

"Here." A glass of whiskey appeared in her hand as if by magic. He took it gratefully and gulped it down, feeling its warmth spread through his body.

"Explain," she repeated, her tone softening slightly.

He moved from her to stand near the fireplace to clear his head. "Are you sure you want to know? Ignorance is bliss, they say."

"Lucius," she pleaded with him, taking a step closer.

He exhaled deeply. He could no longer keep this from her, no matter how much he wanted to. This bond was complicating everything.

"In Calidum, I drank from you." The words escaped his lips, heavy with guilt and regret.

"Yes, unfortunately, I remember." Her voice was gentle but held a hint of sadness. "That's not how bonds are created."

She moved closer to him, her gaze piercing and unwavering.

"I know that," he said, unable to meet her eyes as memories flooded back. "You almost died. That witch almost killed you." The memory of her blood pooling beneath her still haunted him. "You wouldn't stop bleeding...so I made a choice. I gave you my blood."

"You what?" Her shock and confusion were evident in her tone.

She stayed silent for a moment before settling into a chair. "I was dying."

"Yes." It wasn't a question. "When we had sex last night, we made the bond stronger between us."

He braced himself for her anger or accusations, but instead, she sat calmly before him. "And now you're trying to break it?"

"Yes," he admitted reluctantly. "Before it becomes unbreakable."

"And you were aware of it the whole time? And let us have sex?"

"Yes." He tensed, waiting for her to scream at him. To even curse him or use her magic on him. She did none of that.

Instead, she held out her hand and let the book from the floor fly into it. "Okay, I'll help then."

She opened the book and read. Her acceptance surprised Lucius. He should be happy she was helping him. Maybe they could solve it together. Why did sadness seep into his heart?

He shook his head and went to read through the other books they had. Soon, this feeling would disappear, and the bond would be broken. He would feel better and like himself again.

So why wasn't he looking forward to it?

⸺⬥◯⬥⸺

Patience

They were bonded.

She couldn't quite believe it. When they slept together last night, she didn't know she would create a stronger blood bond, but... he knew. He knew, and he slept with her, anyway? Why did he save her in the first place? Especially since he hated her... right?

Patience flipped through the pages, knowing they wouldn't find the answers. She knew where they could find them and who would have the answer, but did she want to break the bond?

He had to be the key. Every time he bit her or slept with her, she remembered her dreams. There had to be a way for them to unlock her dreams fully.

There was a connection between them even before they were bonded, and she didn't even want to contemplate what it meant. Right now, she had to find Michael. He would help her figure out whether she should tell Lucius. Maybe he could be there with her when she did.

She stood up and placed the book on the chair. Lucius glanced up at her. He seemed like he was going to say something, but he didn't.

"I don't think we'll find the answers in these books. I've had enough reading today, anyway." She said nothing else and left the library, leaving him to stare after her.

Things were so complicated now. How did she end up getting them into such a mess? She almost wished she could go back, but it wasn't about her anymore. Michael wouldn't have found his soulmate or parents if she'd wanted that. At least one of them was getting the happy ending they deserved. She realized Michael was a freaking prince. *Holy shit.* Her best friend was a prince. *Crazy.*

She found him sitting in the parlor with his mother, father, Ian, and Maxim. They all stared at her as she strode through the door.

"You all were talking about me, weren't you?"

They all had guilty looks on their faces except the king. He was as stone-faced as always.

"How are you feeling?" Maxim came up to her, giving her a much-needed hug.

"I could be better, but I don't feel like discussing it. Last time I checked, we needed to find a Silverlands witch. Any luck with the Council?"

"Silas told me only a few members believed them, but they meet next week, and we'll discuss it there. Also, plans are already underway for the wedding."

"They are?" Ian and Michael said in unison.

"Yes. You didn't think you could have the ritual and not follow through with a wedding, did you?"

The way they looked at each other was so comical that laughter burst from her lips, which shocked her a little. She couldn't remember the last time she laughed. The days had been stressful. She needed a moment. She stared at Michael until he turned to look at her. He smiled, knowing. Turning, he glanced back at Ian. They stared at each other for a moment, and Ian slightly nodded.

"As much as I would love to stay and reminisce about weddings, my dear, I believe I need a moment alone with my best friend," he declared, rising from his seat and taking her hand.

With a shared understanding, she closed her eyes and concentrated on their destination. In an instant, they were standing in his cozy bedroom. The familiar scent of his cologne wafted through the air, providing a sense of comfort.

Sinking onto the edge of the bed together, he turned to her with a serious expression. "I want to talk about anything except for him and what happened in the Silverlands. I need a normal conversation."

A teasing smile tugged at her lips. "When have our conversations ever been considered normal?"

They couldn't help but burst into laughter at the absurdity of it all. "Point taken."

"I'm sorry about the other night," Michael said remorsefully. "I didn't know that was going to happen... especially in front of all those people. I got caught up in the moment. Things just got carried away. And then my idiotic self, following my parents into another realm. Everything just has been hectic."

Patience nestled closer to Michael, laying her head on his shoulder with a contented sigh. "You can say that again," she said, a smile playing on her lips. "Thankful I missed the part where you bit a girl."

He chuckled. "Oh, good! So, you weren't completely traumatized?"

She laughed. "No, not completely. I had my knight in shining armor to rescue me from any discomfort."

Michael's eyes sparkled with humor. "Oh, really? Who do I have to kill?"

"No one, I swear. He was a complete gentleman until he disappeared... literally."

Michael raised an eyebrow skeptically.

"I'm serious!" Patience insisted. "I'm not crazy. He wasn't imaginary. His name was Alden," she joked. "He knows about my past."

"What? Repeat."

She sighed and repeated herself as Michael forced her to look at him. "He knows about—"

"I heard you the first time," Michael interrupted eagerly. "Patience! This is great."

Patience forgot how nice it was to have her best friend all to herself. It had been forever since they'd sat down to talk without any interruptions or distractions. She savored the moment, basking in the comfort and familiarity of their friendship.

"I can't believe you're getting married. How did this all happen?"

"Changing the subject? I'll take it, but I don't want to talk about it yet." She nodded, realizing she wasn't ready to talk about Lucius. Not when her best friend was still going through it. She promised herself she would tell him soon.

"Fine. This is, technically, all your fault. You're the one who wanted to go into a vampire club. Well, this is where it got us."

"I know. You're right. It's all my fault." If only she'd stayed that night, they would probably still be in their apartment, watching a movie or having a good time together. Now, they were no longer a duo, and they were more like... more like... she didn't even know anymore. Things were just a mess. Michael's life was changing, and so was hers. It was as though her happiness was just out of reach. Finding her past didn't seem as important now that it was within her grasp. Honestly, she prayed her dreams were the future and not her past. Because if it was their past, why didn't she remember, and what happened to their children? It had to be their future, so she couldn't think about the other possibilities... or this world would pray to have the Ragana Zidikas back once she was done with it.

The concern and worry etched across Patience's face was palpable to Michael. He could sense the weight of her thoughts and emotions, threatening to pull her into a dark place. With a gentle touch, he reached for her hand.

"Hey, crazy," he said softly, trying to bring some levity to the situation. "No depressive thoughts. You're with me forever. Do you understand?"

Patience forced a smile and nodded, feeling comforted by his words.

"I'm serious, Patience," Michael continued. "Married or not, you're with me."

Her heart swelled with love for him, but she couldn't help feeling guilty for burdening him with her struggles. She quickly changed the subject.

"Enough about me," she said. "How are wedding plans going?"

Michael shifted his body slightly, almost as if uncomfortable with the topic.

"Is this an uncomfortable subject?" Patience asked, sensing his hesitation.

"No...maybe..." Michael trailed off. "I just feel like everything is happening so fast. I wish we had more time to get to know each other before jumping into marriage. And on top of that, I'm still adjusting to my demonic powers. Just yesterday, I woke up on the ceiling. Yes, literally on the ceiling like it was the floor. Ian had to help me down. It was so embarrassing."

Patience put her hands on both sides of his face. "Hey, calm down. You don't have to do this. No one is forcing you to do anything you don't want to."

Michael put his hands over hers and looked her straight in the eye.

"I know, but I love him. It sounds crazy, but I do. My heart, my soul, my mind, and my body—it all belongs to him. All I know is I belong to him, and he belongs to me."

The ridiculous thing was that it didn't sound crazy to her at all. It sounded too familiar to her: to be completely in love with someone, mind, body, and soul. At least Ian felt the same.

"If you know that, silly, you should have no problem walking down the aisle." Patience could see the thought running through his head and knew when he realized she was right when the huge smile appeared on his face. "See? All that worrying for nothing. You just needed me to talk it out with you."

"See, that's why you'll always be with me. Because I need you."

Patience smiled and laid her head back on his shoulder. "By the way, I know I'm late, but what did the king do to you to see if you were his son?"

"If I tell you, I'll have to kill you," he said in a serious tone, then ruined it by laughing.

"I would love to see you try. Seriously, what did he do?"

"He pressed his forehead to mine and spoke these strange words, then the symbol on my arm burned then glowed gold. His did as well. Then I felt it. Our connection. Almost like ours. I think ours may be stronger... possibly."

"Interesting. Can you remember the words?" Patience wondered.

"No. Even if I did, I couldn't even pronounce them."

"Well, I'm glad you found your family and weren't just forgotten."

"Me too. And I've always had my family right here," he said, kissing her forehead. "We're going to find the key to your memories, Patience. I have faith more now than ever before."

"Me too," she whispered. They lay there in their heads for a while. Patience didn't realize she'd drifted off to sleep until Silas walked through the door and woke her.

"Hey, there you both are. I've been looking all over for you."

Patience sat up, nudging Michael. She yawned and paused mid-stretch when she saw the way Silas was looking at her. "Something wrong?"

"You look different," Silas remarked, studying her with a curious expression.

"I do? How?" She asked, suddenly self-conscious.

"I don't know. Did you change something?" He furrowed his brow, trying to pinpoint the change in her appearance.

Michael sat up and stared at Patience as though he was trying to figure out what was wrong with her.

"Holy shit. It's the bond. She and Lucius bonded... unintentionally." Her words rushed out, tinged with panic.

"Michael!"

"What? He was going to find out. He can sense it." Michael defended himself, still trying to process the information.

"Ugh. Long story short. It's just a blood bond. We plan to break it." Patience explained hastily, her thoughts already turning toward finding a solution.

She needed to go to GreyJoy. She needed to find out if there was a way to break the bond. "I've got to go, guys."

Before they could react, she disappeared and reappeared at the bookstore.

"Theá," Jafa said, greeting her. "You look different."

"Fuuuck!!" she screamed. "Is it that noticeable? GreyJoy! Help!"

A note floated down from the ceiling.

Are you certain you want to break it?

Of course, he already knew what she wanted and how to break it. The real question was, did she want to break the bond? Honestly, she didn't know. Things were getting complicated. She was trying to handle everything, but the pressure was getting too much.

Tears flowed from her eyes involuntarily.

"Theá, why are you crying?"

"I don't know." The floodgates were open, and she couldn't get them to stop.

Lucius didn't want her.

Jafa lifted her from the floor. She hadn't even realized she'd dropped to her knees. "Come now, Theá. Please stop crying. You've gone through worse. You'll get through this." He took her to sit on the couch near the fireplace.

She would, but being so close to something, she could almost taste it. He would rather hold on to his hatred than have something good between them. She should hate him for killing her kind, but she couldn't. As her tears subsided, a note floated down into her hands.

You have your answer.

And he was right. She did. She wouldn't break their bond.

Instead, she would focus on unlocking her memories.

"GreyJoy, he is the key. I've seen my dreams. I believe they are of the future."

Another note drifted down,

Of you and Lucius.

"Yes, I dream of us and our future." She wouldn't tell him. At least, not yet. They had bigger problems they had to deal with, and she needed to find out more about her past.

Her sister was a queen. But the queen of what?

She was so close to the answers. She just knew it.

The half-demon, the one who'd been haunting her dreams? Who was this demon? And what did he have to do with her?

She wasn't sure, but she was going to find out. Selene was the one she needed to find.

"GreyJoy, where is Selene? Take me to her, please."

One moment, she was sitting next to Jafa, and then the next, she was surrounded by loud, robust men watching someone on stage.

Patience looked around and realized she was in a club, a strip club.

The someone they were watching was a half-naked silver-haired woman with silver eyes, dancing to a loud, raunchy rock song.

Selene.

CHAPTER TWENTY-SEVEN

ALECIA

"Is it her? The one you've been looking for?" Alecia asked Alden as soon as he walked through the door. She'd been eagerly waiting for his return all day to learn if his plan was working. Though, the grimace on his face was telling enough.

"Yes. It's her."

Alecia helped him remove his coat and handed him a glass of bourbon she'd prepared for him in anticipation.

"She's the one I've been looking for. My Dessa."

Alden took the glass from her hand and made himself comfortable on the couch. She hung his jacket on the coat rack, then joined him.

"Did you feed her the lies about her past?" she cautiously asked. His outward appearance might have looked calm now, but he was angry, and she didn't want to get the brunt of it.

"Unfortunately, we were interrupted, but progress was made. Estelle is now with them. She'll make sure their memories stay locked."

Alecia wasn't surprised to know her sister was now involved, especially when she'd failed to break the connection between Michael and Ian.

"Do you plan to take Odessa? Do you think she'll go with you?"

Alden took a sip from his bourbon before answering her. "Yes. I can't risk her unlocking her memories. Lucius may still hate her, but I would have no chance if his feelings ever changed. This will be better than last time if I can convince her to come with me willingly." Frustration grew in his voice. He drained his glass and placed it on the table. He stood up and paced with worry.

"Their bond is still strong?"

"Yes."

"I told you the spell wouldn't work. A bond like theirs can't be broken." He stopped and glared at her. *Fuck. I should have kept that to myself.*

"I know who has the spell which will finally sever their bond. However, Lucius might do it himself if all goes well. Now, I must prepare. I'll call on you soon. Leave me," Alden ordered.

Alecia was out the door as quickly as her feet would take her. She was relieved she'd left unscathed but needed to contact her sister. She wasn't sure what the hell she'd gotten them into.

GLOSSARY

Anduril – Blade used to kill the Tral'goth demon

Askarian – Capital of Evictus

Aberrants – Witches who were not part of any coven because they chose not to conform. Patience is labeled one unwillingly.

Absergo - a devourer of magic – found in the dark forest by a creature with four arms and no eyes. Realm unknown.

Allure of Souls – Lure charm. Used to attract humans to certain Etherian feeding grounds.

Astral Coins – Will buy a creature three questions from Umber, an Eviathan Troll

Argian – Language of the Silverlands

Astrona - the realm of lightning

Blessing of Ashes - The blessing was a curse. Cursing the bearer to never have children or create other creatures.

Black ankh - vampire emblem found on vampire establishments.

Blades of Flux – Used to kill hokima assassins.

Blade of Valhal – double-edged sword used by hokima assassins

Blood bond – when blood is exchanged with a vampire within 24 hours. Can be broken, if one party is killed. Grows stronger with each sexual encounter or blood exchange.

Calidium – Territory within Evictus ruled by Sucora, a Demon Goddess

Crimson Clutch — a deadly poison meant to hold its victim's death at bay by giving them long slow agonizing death

Daimones – Michael and King Kieran are daimones. Ancient demons were thought to be extinct. Go through two transitions that make them powerful demons. Need a soul gem to complete the second transition.

Demon king – King of the Evictus. Father of Michael and co-creator of vampires.

Drath - half vampires who denounced their witch ancestry. Only a few have magical abilities.

Eviathan – Realm to humans, vampires, witches, and other Etherians. Ruled by vampires and witches.

Etherians - non-humans

Epati - the language of Morian warlocks.

Enoch - dark realm. Birthplace of Lilith.

Evictus – Demon Realm

Euphoria – Prison in Askaria where Lilith is locked away

Fleece of Gilahein - the fleece gifted to Michael by the Queen of the nymphs. Made of Truesilk.

Ganton - a hideous-looking gray creature with three arms

Glopinian – Red velvet pouch used to contain powerful objects like the soul gem

Goddess- Goddess of the witches. Possibly a descendant of a Silverite. Currently, missing.

Glendale weed – erases magic residue

Gutrend spike – a poisonous spike used by the hokima to render a being powerless

Half demon – Unknown Etherian trying to free Lilith. Currently, has taken over Askaria.

Half witch- Alecia and Estelle are half-witches.

Hallows – Guardians of the Silverlands. Currently, laying dormant waiting for the Goddess to return.

Hokima – Guardians of Askaria commanded by the being who sits on the throne.

Igoria – Realm of the lost, where Patience found Michael

Irza – God of Iranti, God of Memory

Kilborn academy – First school of witchery

Kavarian – Nomad Etherians of Calidium

Khedian – a creature with the ability to move undetected and has a photographic memory

King Kieran - King of Evictus. See. Demon King.

Milchan coven – Coven cursed to kill themselves over and over. Patience saved them.

Mastria – Teachers of Magic

Novarians - skilled warrior assassins, part of the nation of Sabia that was lost long ago in the realm of Enoch. The city of light in the realm of darkness. Their kind was destroyed by Lilith.

Orb of Gilean – can control and manipulate people's memories. Lost in the dark realm.

Ragana Zidikas – translation: Witch Hunter. Lucius Cordovan, an infamous witch hunter who slaughtered witches for over a century.

Silverlands - the realm in which the Goddess lived and the source of all magic and the place that connected all the realms.

Seckor – Little ball of light and pathfinder

Sentinel of Light - a Guardian of the Witch's Council

Silverite – first to use magic to create

Soul-bond – exchanging of half their souls. Giving half of one soul to another and verse versa. If one being dies, the other will die too.

Tral'goth - Four thick-horned reptilian demons. Hokima's creature.

Truesilk – used to slow a hokima assassin

Umber - an ancient Eviathan Troll, legend had it he was around before the humans habituated the realm. His Makas kept their ears to the ground and gathered the information for him. If a person had the right currency, he would divulge certain information to the right questions. He covets Astral coins which would buy any creature about three questions.

Vampire Council – made up of ruling members of the vampire clans. Maintain laws.

Witch Council – members of each witch coven are elected to sit on the council to maintain laws.

Whisper of Soul's charm - Used on technology (via website) to lure humans

Also by Charley Black

The Elite Series
Bound
Marked – January 2026
Destined – TBA

Within the Darkness Trilogy
Entwined Within the Darkness
A Dance Within the Darkness
Forever Within the Darkness

Other Books
A Symphony of Shadows – October 2025

ABOUT THE AUTHOR

Hi, I'm Charley Black, and I hope you've enjoyed diving into this series. Writing has been my passion since I was twelve, and crafting stories filled with danger, mystery, and forbidden love is where my heart truly lies. Creating this series has been an incredible journey, blending complex characters, high stakes, and a richly built world I've loved bringing to life.

I live in Rhode Island with my family, where I balance writing, work, and motherhood with the amazing support of my partner and daughters. For me, writing is all about connection—bringing readers into worlds where love, trust, and sacrifice take center stage. I can't wait to share more of this series with you. Thank you for joining me on this adventure, and I hope you're ready for what's to come!

You can connect with me on:
Instagram: @authorcharleyblack
TikTok: @authorcharleyblack
Facebook: @authorcharleyblack
Subscribe to my newsletter:
Website: www.charleyblack.com